The Writer and the Librarian

The Raven Society Book 1

R.L. Geer-Robbins

A friend,

This book was written with a lot of love and even more coffee. I hope you enjoy!

Stay Caffeinated

Dark Rose Publishing Company

Copyright © 2023 by R.L. Geer-Robbins

All rights reserved.

No part of this publication may be reproduced, distributed, or transmitted in any form or by any means, including photocopying, recording, or other electronic or mechanical methods, without the publisher's prior written permission, except as permitted by U.S. copyright law. For permission requests, contact Dark Rose Publishing Company at https://rlgeerrobbins.com.

The story, all names, characters, and incidents portrayed in this production are fictitious. No identification with actual persons, places, buildings, or products is intended or should be inferred.

Book Cover by Getcovers.com

Editor- Latisha Felty

ISBN-13: 979-8-9875639-1-5

Contents

Epigraph	1
Dedication	2
Introduction	3
Prelude- 537 A.D.	4
1. Chapter 1	9
2. Chapter 2	15
3. Chapter 3	22
4. Chapter 4	28
5. Chapter 5	35
6. Chapter 6	42
7. Chapter 7	48
8. Chapter 8	54
9. Chapter 9	58
10. Chapter 10	63
11. Chapter 11	68
12. Chapter 12	75

13.	Chapter 13	82
14.	Chapter 14	89
15.	Chapter 15	97
16.	Chapter 16	102
17.	Chapter 17	111
18.	Chapter 18	119
19.	Chapter 19	126
20.	Chapter 20	131
21.	Chapter 21	139
22.	Chapter 22	148
23.	Chapter 23	155
24.	Chapter 24	160
25.	Chapter 25	165
26.	Chapter 26	172
27.	Chapter 27	179
28.	Chapter 28	186
29.	Chapter 29	192
30.	Chapter 30	200
31.	Chapter 31	207
32.	Chapter 32	214
33.	Chapter 33	220
34.	Chapter 34	225

35.	Chapter 35	228
36.	Chapter 36	235
37.	Chapter 37	241
38.	Chapter 38	245
39.	Chapter 39	253
40.	Chapter 40	260
41.	Chapter 41	266
42.	Chapter 42	272
43.	Chapter 43	276
44.	Chapter 44	281
45.	Chapter 45	285
46.	Chapter 46	292
47.	Chapter 47	298
48.	Chapter 48	302
49.	Chapter 49	308
50.	Chapter 50	312
51.	Chapter 51	319
52.	Chapter 52	326
53.	Chapter 53	333
	About the Author	337
	Acknowledgements	338
	Also By R. L. Geer-Robbins	340

Also By R.L. Geer-Robbins

There is only one thing in the world worse than being talked about, and that is not being talked about.
Oscar Wilde

To those who walk with the shadows- dance with the darkness, and I will dance beside you.

Introduction

'Set The Stage. That Way No One Is Disappointed.' -Book of the Veiled Instructions

No AI was used in the creation of this book.

If I had used AI, I wouldn't have had to spend countless hours fixing all the editing issues and figuring out the difference between 'A' and 'An'.

If you find any editing issues, please let me know. My high school English teacher will be thrilled to have proof that I didn't pay attention in class.

No characters were harmed in the creation of this book. I, on the other hand, am now addicted to TUMS and suffer from migraines if I don't have at least four pots of coffee.

If you stumble across pages with tear stains, ignore them. They were tears of joy. Just kidding, they were tears of frustration because I found another misspelled word.

And finally, friends, I hope you enjoy the story. It was written with a lot of love and even more coffee.

Prelude- 537 A.D.

'It Starts With A Single Moment In Time.' -Book of the Veiled Instructions

In all my years, I never saw so much death. The ground was saturated with blood, sweat, and tears, clinging to my shoes and pants as I trudged through it, looking for her. She had to be here, somewhere in this carnage and misery.

I failed them. Their blood was on my hands. As far as the eye could see, bodies from both sides of the battle were interlocked like tangled in a giant spider's web.

I watched the whole thing unfold from my hillside spot, far from the fighting. My task was to witness the brilliance of our king's victory, capturing the details for future generations to read.

However, from where I stood, no distortion or pretty words would have made this outcome worthwhile.

As I searched through the maze of death, I came upon silent figures of fallen warriors. Frozen in time as if they had asked the gods for a gentle transition to the next world, yet the Fates had not granted them that mercy.

I choked back on bile as the sight of a boy's limp body threatened to overwhelm me. His clothes were charred black, and I could smell his burned flesh and the panic of his last moments. A boy, so young and seemingly on the brink of adulthood, lying still in a pool of his own blood. His arm was tightly clamped around the king's flagpole as if he had wanted to carry it into battle no matter the cost—the pure terror of his last moments frozen on his face.

A face that would haunt my dreams forever.

How had I not seen this coming?

The king had vowed to create a haven where creatures like me could exist side-by-side with mortals. As one of his closest advisors, I believed in his intentions and offered him a blood oath of loyalty. My sister and I would protect him and do whatever was necessary to maintain our place in this world.

A shared belief in our mission fueled the soldiers who fought for us, all fighting for individual causes but with one unified aim- to create a space for the supernatural. The hours before the battle were filled with songs and laughter as the dawn of a new day loomed. My sister and I stood back as they indulged in what could be their last meal, throwing back whiskey like it was water. We all believed we would succeed.

I should have known. It was my job to know.

But I was wrong.

Ultimately, I had no choice but to ask the Fates for help. Their price was high, but I was willing to pay it if it guaranteed our victory.

Unlike me, my sister was engaged in battle. The intensity of her power multiplied since the fighting began. She was the greatest warrior ever to grace the battlefield- her formidable reputation made even the bravest foes quiver in fear. Blood fueled her abilities, battle encouraged her energy, and death's cries strengthened her determination.

Scanning the field, I finally found her and breathed a sigh of relief. Her gold-tinged braided brown hair cascaded under her helmet, and her green eyes sparkled with a golden tone from her heightened enthusiasm for war.

Wielding the famed sword of Caledvwlch, she was a mesmerizing sight as she defeated her adversaries. Her prowess in battle was awe-inspiring; an angel of justice and vengeance rolled into one beautiful figure of courage.

Holding my breath, I watched as she danced across the battlefield. She was as elegant as a swan in flight, fighting her way to the man she loved and cutting down anyone who stood in her way.

"She will not survive," a chilling voice appeared at my side, and I hesitated to look. A tall, dark figure stood there, clothed in a long gray robe that hid his face, flanked by only one of his hellhounds. As if winter had reached its frosty fingers into my soul, the coolness of his voice was only surpassed by the air surrounding him.

I wondered if he would show up.

Standing by my side, he couldn't hide the twinkle in his eyes and his hungry smile as he watched warrior after warrior fall. His eyes darted back and forth, sniffing the air as if he could smell the blood and taste their souls. I recognized that I faced true power as I focused on the unwelcome company—a god disguised as a man. My creator. My friend. And my enemy—Arawn.

"You can't have her," I whispered. "She is mine. That was never part of the deal."

He glanced away from the scene, and his dark eyes fell on me with a warning, letting me know I was skating on thin ice. "You should have ensured her safety was part of your agreement."

"You can't have her," I repeated, growing angry and ready to fight him, whatever the cost.

"Taliesin, you will not win," he said coldly, knowing what I was thinking. "You made your choice; unfortunately, her fate is sealed, which is, honestly, a tragedy. She was meant for so much more than what you doomed her to."

Gazing back onto the battlefield, we watched as my sister made her way to the center of the fighting. Bitterness filled me as I witnessed her last moments. Did she know I loved her? She was the breath that sustained me, the one soul with whom I shared my secrets and fears. She was created at the same time as me, filled with life in the same breath. Our magick was different, but without one, the other weakened.

Everyone knew a twin without its other half was only half a person.

"Please," I begged softly. "Anyone but you."

"The Fates struck a deal with you, not me. I am just as much a pawn in your game as she is," he said dismissively, eyes focused on the battle.

"Her blood will be on your hands, not mine," I growled.

A softness fell over him as he turned to face me. His voice was filled with gentleness as if he were talking to a child. "You asked for power—the power you shared with her through your bond. Your desire required sacrifice," he shrugged as he walked away. "The choice was yours. A soul for a soul. That was the price."

My heart raced as he vanished into the forest. Fury swelled inside me; this was not what I wanted. Power, yes, but not my sister's destruction. If Arawn had her, I would never see her again. I had to find the Fates. This was a mistake. I had made another miscalculation.

Her anguished cries echoed through the clash of swords and armor as I felt my magick hum beneath my skin. I glanced in her direction, watching as she fought ten men determined to kill the brave warrior.

"No!" I shouted, forcing my feet to move quickly and willing my power to ring true. I cursed them, wishing death would pass through them like a plague. The shock of her death pierced my heart like a sharp blade. The pain was too much, and I fell to my knees, gasping for breath. Every muscle and bone in my body felt ice cold as her last words echoed through my mind.

'Taliesin, I know.'

The sun was sinking as I awoke, feeling disoriented and confused. The reality of my sister's death rushed over me; our connection was severed. I had more power than before, but a part of my soul had been removed.

Her magick unbalanced me, but I also knew what to do. I would fix the damage I had caused. For what was death but a concept written in a book?

I just needed to find Lilith. She would understand. She would help.

And once I got my sister back, I would find the Fates and deal the death blow myself.

Chapter 1

'Choose Wisely Before Sending Out Invitations.' - Book of the Veiled Instruction.

I returned from work to find a small calling card with an embossed silver raven taped to my front door. An address was neatly printed on the back, and a simple invitation was handwritten in tiny letters at the bottom: 'Arrive by 7 p.m., Chloe Pairtree.'

This was the moment I had been waiting for. The prestigious literary world had finally extended an invitation for me to join their elite ranks.

With a squeal of excitement, I rushed into the apartment, dropping my bags at the front door with a thud. Pulling out my phone to call my mom, I danced to the kitchen to make a pot of coffee. She would be so proud.

Crap. I hadn't even been officially initiated, and I was already screwing things up. Setting the phone down on the counter, I let out a heavy sigh. It was common knowledge that the first rule of joining a secret society was to keep your invitation a secret. And yet, here I was, already breaking that rule before I even got inducted.

I still couldn't believe I was chosen. I was just a small-time writer, investigating others' lives to make sense of mine. Even though I had a modest following of family and friends, my books were never popular enough to land a spot on Oprah's Book Club or Amazon's best-selling list.

In my teenage years, I discovered a passion for writing and filled entire notebooks with tales of fantastical creatures, fearless protagonists, and mystical lands. But I'd never shared my stories with anyone and often threw the notebooks away once filled.

I didn't want anyone knowing that the characters in my imagination felt more real than reality. A confession that would have landed me on the fourth floor of the local hospital for 'observation.'

Once I completed my college education, I chose to pursue a career in writing. I became an investigative journalist, although others may argue that my natural curiosity and penchant for meticulous note-taking led me to this path.

Obsessed with history, I devoured ancient texts like a ravenous predator. My mind was a maze of connections, linking the past to the present in ways that would shock the world if they only knew. Behind the polished facade of textbooks and lectures lay a treasure trove of scandalous secrets: murder, affairs, rebellions, and lost fortunes.

If you knew where to look.

And I prided myself on knowing where to look. The answers were buried somewhere deep within the chaos of my cluttered desk. The massive cherrywood surface, polished to a high shine, was my pride and joy. But it also served as my greatest enemy, tempting me with endless distractions.

Perched in front of an enormous bay window, it overflowed with pink and yellow Post-It notes scribbled with hasty ideas and timelines. Half-filled notebooks peeked out of broken drawers, hinting at the countless ideas and stories waiting for me to explore. It was a true reflection of my brilliant yet scattered mind.

Beside it stood a floor-to-ceiling bookshelf with all the awards and achievements I'd accumulated over the years. While they celebrated what I'd accomplished, it also reminded me of all I had left to do.

Which was at the moment being inducted into The Raven Society. A society I had only just learned about, but rumor said that it had been established since the creation of the first library.

It was by pure chance that I stumbled upon this information from an unlikely source.

Six months ago, I ran into the Book Shop Book Club while searching for something new to read. Although I'd been invited to their monthly meetings, I'd never gone, primarily because Aelle, the group leader, was a middle-aged woman with strong and often unyielding views on every subject.

We met at the San Francisco Writer's Conference a year ago, both attending as guest speakers. Aelle had recently released her final book in a trilogy on Dutch trade routes and their impact on the economic status of the middle class. I couldn't deny she'd done an excellent job with her research, even if it wasn't the most captivating topic. However, she had a keen eye for details most scholars would overlook.

Unfortunately, she also had a flair for pointing out flaws and mistakes. By the end of day one, three authors left the conference in tears after she used their first chapters as examples of what not to do.

"A reliable source told me I will receive my invite any time now." I overheard Aelle tell the group as they gathered around the electric stone fireplace.

Even sitting, Aelle towered over everyone with her imposing presence. With her sharp features, intense brown eyes, and tightly bound hair, she gave off an air of intensity that was impossible to ignore. And I could only recall a handful of times I'd seen her smile.

"They'd be a fool not to invite you." Another member sat down beside her with a grin. "I told you your book was amazing."

"Yes, it is extraordinary," Aelle agreed with a sly smile. "A fascinating documentary that unlocked the door to The Raven Society. They should consider themselves lucky to have someone like me. Too many writers today focus on fantasy and not intellectual knowledge. It's shameful, really."

My face grew hot with embarrassment, and I quickly turned away. I belonged to the group of writers she despised - the ones who wrote about magic and imaginary worlds.

"What is The Raven Society?" One of the younger women asked as she sat in a lounge chair. She was unmistakably a mother with young kids, sporting socks that didn't match, a wrinkled shirt stained with ketchup, and under-eye bags that seemed like they hadn't slept well in ages.

"My dear, The Raven Society is the most esteemed literary group ever. Each member has made a significant impact on the writing world. It's an honor to receive an invitation to join! Each member must take on the persona of their favorite literary character." She glanced around with wide eyes, thrilled at the prospect. "That is the final test of acceptance. Pick poorly, and the key bearers will ask you to leave. On the other hand, choose correctly, and your career will soar to new heights. I have been narrowing my list for days now and have settled on three: Alice from Alice in Wonderland, Anne Shirley, or Elinor Dashwood."

I listened as the women offered their opinions on the personality Aelle should choose. They were all excellent choices, but I'd never compile such a list. If I had the opportunity, I would prefer someone with refinement, mystery, and dramatic flair.

My opportunity arrived, and I needed to make my decision.

And I had less than 24 hours to do it. No pressure.

The following day, the alarm sounded, waking me up from where I fell asleep on the couch. Was it 4:00 a.m. already? It must have been because I had the same alarm set for the last twenty years. Workday, weekend, or holiday, it didn't matter. The hours between 4 a.m. and 6 a.m. were magickal to me.

That was my writing time.

But today was different—I had somewhere to be, and the nagging feeling of needing to be ready was overwhelming. Despite my anxiety, I forced myself to stay on schedule. As the afternoon wore on, my motivation to do anything productive dwindled. I finally caved in and got ready. I'd already picked an outfit for this important day: jeans, a black T-shirt, a gray cardigan, and black low-heeled boots.

Classy but comfortable.

Trying to curl my hair in my old apartment was always a disaster, thanks to the faulty electric plugs. After fifteen minutes of struggling and getting nowhere, I admitted defeat and opted for my usual messy bun. Despite watching countless makeup tutorials on YouTube, I still lacked confidence in my skills, so I kept my makeup light. My glasses helped conceal the dark circles under my eyes and crow's feet that were starting to show.

I let out a deep sigh, feeling defeated, as I made my way into the living room to wait. Pacing around the room's mess, I glanced at the notecards scattered on the table filled with potential character traits. As I walked back and forth, I tried to weigh the pros and cons of each possibility, but no matter how much I thought about it, I couldn't decide.

It didn't help my mind kept wandering about what walking inside a secret society would be like.

"Do you think they will wear long black robes and Phantom of the Opera masks like on Netflix?" I asked Beacon, a friendly twenty-pound Corgi I rescued from a shady pet store a few years back. "Or will there be a table of members judging me?"

He didn't say anything; he just adjusted his position and gave me a stern stare before closing his eyes to continue napping.

Ignoring his apparent lack of interest, I continued. "Maybe it will be a dark fortress, like Skull and Bones, or a magickally protected castle like in Harry Potter. I can see it now. The candles floating along the ceiling will light up when I walk in, and a seven-course meal waiting for me. Hopefully, there will be a sorting hat who could decide my character for me." I joked half-heartedly.

Lost in my thoughts, I hadn't realized how much time had passed until my phone beeped, reminding me that I needed to leave now if I wanted to be on time. I quickly pulled on my tweed jacket and grabbed my purse before heading towards the front door.

"Wish me luck," I called over my shoulder as I walked out on my next great adventure.

Chapter 2

'To Go Forward, One Must Look Back.' -Book of the Veiled Instructions

I stood before 177 Garden Avenue, admiring the colonial-era white clapboard house. For being the headquarters of a secret society, the exterior had a surprisingly unassuming appearance. It boasted an expansive wrap-around deck with charming white wicker benches and high-top tables. A rustic wooden swing hung from the ceiling, and vibrant flower pots overflowing with red geraniums greeted visitors. A quaint chalkboard sign was propped against one of the Porch's pillars, its message scrawled out in playful handwriting: *Welcome to the Porch.*

What a magickal place, I thought. I could picture myself sitting outside in the morning, basking in the rising sun and sipping coffee while my laptop hummed beside me. At night, I would relax on the porch swing, swaying gently with a glass of rum and a captivating book. This was a home where time slowed and worries disappeared, a true haven for the soul.

As the sun descended, the warm light illuminated the stained-glass windows that flanked the front door. My gaze was immediately drawn to the vibrant colors and detailed designs. Rays of light shone through, creating a kaleidoscope of raven silhouettes, open books with pages fluttering in the wind, and majestic gods from ancient mythology.

The view was breathtaking, but I couldn't help feeling a bit let down. In my mind, I envisioned a grand entrance with a long driveway lined with twisted trees and leading up to a dilapidated mansion guarded by frightening gargoyles. The iron fence I expected to see was nowhere in sight, nor were the warning signs or rusty locks. The atmosphere around the property was far from ominous.

Walking towards the front entrance, I couldn't help but feel a tinge of disappointment that there wasn't an enchanted door knocker to greet me. I lifted my hand and knocked, plastering a broad smile on my face. Time crawled as I waited for someone to answer, anxiously shifting my weight from foot to foot.

Nothing.

Strange. Another heavy thud. It vibrated through the empty home, echoing off the walls and lingering in the air like a ghostly presence.

Still nothing.

Perhaps I was at the wrong house? I looked around, but adjacent to the door, a vibrant display of Spanish tiles featured the number 177. Yup. I was definitely in the right place.

I searched for a doorbell but couldn't find it. My cheeks reddened with embarrassment as anxiety flooded through me. Could it be that no one was answering because they had made a mistake? Did they accidentally put the invitation on the wrong door and were trying to avoid telling me?

The idea of rejection brought a wave of embarrassment over me, and I debated just walking away. Simply turn around and head home to binge-watch a new Netflix series and indulge in a carton of Ben and Jerry's ice cream.

A glance at my watch told me it was 6:58 p.m. There were only two minutes left to make a choice. Was it going to be the comfort of routine?

Or the thrill of the unreal? The Magic of Ordinary Days versus Alice in Wonderland. *How much did I want this?*

I knocked harder, my frustration evident in the echoing sound reverberating down the hallway. My hand throbbed from each heavy blow, but I didn't care. I just wanted someone to come and answer it already.

Nothing but silence.

Not willing to give up, I discreetly tried opening the screen door, but it was locked. *Damn it!*

Disappointment washed over me as I gave up and walked down the steps and onto the sidewalk. Looking back at the house, I frowned at the card in my hand. *177 Garden Avenue.* There was no doubt that this was the right place and time.

Staring at the house, I wondered if anyone alerted the authorities about an unstable woman attempting to break into their neighbor's home. I hoped not. I received the invitation via a calling card taped to my front door, and explaining why I was lingering outside a stranger's home could prove challenging.

My thoughts raced as I searched for a decision when the distinct sound of a cane tapping against the sidewalk reached my ears. I glanced up to find a gray-haired woman with a long braid trailing behind her and an oceanic blue dress billowing around her with each step. Our eyes met, and she gave me a sly grin, her mischievous gaze twinkling with amusement.

My eyes followed her every move as she approached, her body language showing signs of excitement. Despite my 5'5 height, I still somehow towered over her petite frame. However, the confidence in her posture made her seem larger than she was.

"You won't get where you are heading from here. You must go back." She gave a playful wink before strolling past. My mouth dropped, stunned.

"Wait! What does that mean?" I yelled at her retreating form. She didn't acknowledge my question, and I hesitated briefly before rushing after her.

For an old woman, she moved with surprising speed, and it took a second to catch up. "Wait up." I reached out and touched her shoulder to stop her. "Do you know if anyone is home?" I asked, pointing toward the Raven Society.

"Yes," she answered, a small smile tugging at her lips as she eyed me.

Arching an eyebrow, I waited for her to elaborate. "Are you going to tell me?" I asked after an awkward pause, pushing my glasses further up my nose.

"You must find the answer for yourself," she sang. "Following your current path won't lead you where you want to be. To move forward, you must first look back."

"Not helpful." She laughed, and I glared at her. "A phone number would be nice," I mumbled, adjusting my jacket.

"Look back, Chloe; everything is on the card," she declared with finality. The woman glided past me and continued down the sidewalk, leaving me just as bewildered as before. It took a moment for her words to register. She'd addressed me by my name.

But how did she know who I was? And more importantly, who was she?

Completely bewildered, I retraced my steps. Stepping onto the Porch again, I paused to inspect the crumpled invitation in my hand, its once-crisp edges bent from my sweaty grasp. *You need to go back,* the old woman's voice echoed in my mind.

Maybe this was a test? It would make sense for a secret society to put its potential members through a test. Maybe the front door wasn't the actual entrance.

Turning the invitation over, the card now read: *Look back for the entrance.*

Holy shit! How had I missed that?

The invitation hadn't left my sight since I found it. Had I never flipped it over? I knew I had, but it hadn't said anything about a back entrance. I was sure of it. Glancing at my watch again, I hurried around the house and headed to the backyard.

As I rounded the corner, a quaint porch appeared, offering a beautiful overlook of a yard filled with vibrant flowers and fragrant herbs. A small creek flowed through the scene, with a green Japanese bridge reminiscent of Claude Monet's famous house in Giverny, France. For a moment, I was transported to another time and place as I imagined Monet painting his iconic Water Lilies series in this very spot.

With a start, I snapped out of my daydream and focused on my surroundings. My eyes landed on a sturdy, imposing oak door adorned with a sign bearing: "The Back" in bold letters. The address, 177 Garden Avenue, etched neatly beneath it. An air of mystery and secrecy surrounded the entrance, beckoning me to step closer.

I quickly checked my appearance to ensure I still looked presentable, tucking back a stray lock of hair before putting on a friendly smile and heading toward the entrance. A towering older man opened the door and greeted me warmly. He wore a black three-piece suit, shiny black loafers, and warm brown eyes.

"Welcome, Chloe. We've been waiting for your arrival." He gestured for me to enter, pulling the door open wider.

"Hello, thank you for the invitation. I..." I started as I followed him through a mud room and into the main entrance.

"Let me take your things." He interrupted as he turned to retrieve my coat and purse. "Someone will be along to take you to the library." Then, without another word, he was off, leaving me standing in the empty room.

I whistled as I slowly turned to examine my surroundings. The room was a soft butter yellow, emphasizing eight diamond-shaped windows providing a breathtaking night sky view. Rosewood fabric upholstered tulip tete-a-tetes were scattered throughout the room, and bouquets adorned tabletop surfaces. Stained glass vases next to wooden ones filled the room with the soft scent of a garden and mahogany wood.

Dark molding carved with swirls and flowers surrounded manuscript pages on the walls. A total of ten panels, each holding a different page of a classic work with a golden plaque bearing the primary character's name.

My gaze moved across the room, and a framed art piece near a grand staircase caught my interest. It had the words *Dream-Land* by Edgar Allan Poe written in gold lettering and 'Eidolon' beneath it.

Strange and stranger, I thought to myself as I walked closer. *Why would you want to be identified as a shadow?*

I couldn't resist reading the dark and haunting poem, one of my all-time favorites. The words effortlessly drew me in, immersing me in its alluring misery and leaving me lost in beautiful despair. Its vivid imagery painted a harrowing journey through a realm where ghosts and ghouls roamed a desolate, barren landscape.

The idea that there was a possibility of an afterlife comforted me, but the Shadowlands was a concept that I was drawn to more than heaven and hell. It wasn't like I wanted to spend eternity locked in a world of gloom and shadows. But something about the Shadowlands made me feel like I belonged.

Not suitable for heaven, but not evil enough for hell. A wanderer with no place to call home.

"Not many people are drawn to this poem."

I jolted at the sound of a deep voice and glanced around to find a man leaning against the stairs. His ebony hair, deep-set dark indigo eyes, wide mouth, and muscular body enhanced his striking appearance. A pair of well-cut jeans, a coal-black sweater, and a grey suit jacket gave me the impression of an Ivy League academic, while his mannerisms hinted at danger. He was the most stunning man I'd ever seen.

"Welcome to The Raven Society. You must be Chloe?" he asked, raising an eyebrow.

"I apologize for being late." I gave him a half-smile, glancing at my watch in horror, seeing that it said 7:15. "I missed the instructions about going to the back entrance," I confessed as I glanced at my shoes, feeling embarrassed.

"It happens." He shrugged, glancing at the back door with faint amusement before looking at me again. "I'm Eidolon. Won't you join us in the library for drinks?" He pushed himself off the rail and walked towards me, his eyes never leaving mine.

A flush spread across my cheeks as I smiled. "Sounds good."

Eidolon gestured toward an open door and headed in. I hesitated momentarily before taking a deep breath and squaring my shoulders.

Here we go, I thought as I crossed the threshold.

Chapter 3

'The Welcoming Committee Will Be The First Test.' -Book of the Veiled Instructions

The library was breathtaking. As I crossed the threshold, my attention was immediately captured by the high-reaching ceilings and extensive mahogany bookcases lining the walls. Spiral staircases on either side of the room enticed me to climb up and discover hidden reading spots, tempting me to delve further into this literary sanctuary. The warm glow of natural light poured in through the enormous windows, casting a gentle radiance over the rows of books and highlighting the intricate elements of the rich wooden shelves.

A crackling fireplace, stretching from the polished slate floor to the intricately carved ceiling, was expansive enough for three people to sit comfortably inside. The dancing flames radiated warmly over the luxurious room, filled with plush velvet couches and ornate tapestries. Instead of traditional religious depictions, a colossal painting portrayed the Last Supper with famous novelists as guests, their faces immortalized in vibrant colors and elaborate details.

On the lofty ceilings, several frescoes depicted powerful gods peering down at the inhabitants below, their expressions frozen in anticipation for a miracle to occur. An array of elegant writing desks adorned the walls, enticing any passerby to sit down and unleash their creativity.

The wood was smooth and polished, with detailed carvings of lions and lambs adorning each piece.

Determined writers occupied two desks, their pens scratching against the paper in a harmonious rhythm. The floor beneath them was littered with crumpled papers, evidence of previous failed attempts at literary brilliance. But amidst the chaos, the unmistakable scent of freshly brewed coffee, crisp paper, rich ink, and warm applewood permeated the room, creating a cozy and inspiring atmosphere for the writers to work in.

It was the library of dreams, a refuge for authors and readers.

As I stood in the doorway, my eyes drank in every detail. Eidolon noticed my distraction. He cleared his throat and tried to regain my attention, but I couldn't tear my gaze away from the grandeur before me.

A man at the bar leaned towards the woman beside him. "Is that her? The one we don't have to interview. I was suspecting something a little more dramatic." He waved his hand up and down in my direction. "She seems so normal."

"Don't be silly, Watson. Of course, we do the interviews. It's tradition," his companion stated confidently as she took one last sip from her glass and placed it on the countertop. "I have to say, it was one of my best drinks yet," she added with a smirk.

"Isabelle, you've never had a cocktail you didn't enjoy." He chuckled as she drifted towards me, gliding through the room until she reached my side.

"There's something magnificent about it, isn't there? It makes you want to compose, drink, and indulge in sin." She let out a laugh when I gave her a puzzled glance.

Where the hell did she come from?

I introduced myself with a smile and extended my hand towards her. "I'm Chloe," I greeted.

She shook her head, slightly frowning as she glanced down. "I would introduce myself if I could, but it's against the rules until the 'official' introduction," she said before meeting my gaze with a broad grin. "But don't worry, luv. This is just a formality. It'll be over before you know it." She linked her arm through mine and led me toward a sofa alongside a window, her soothing tone easing my tension.

"Unlike you, I had to grovel and plead for an invitation. And even then, I was a bundle of nerves on the event day. I changed my outfit at least seven times before arriving in character. Looking back, it was all unnecessary, but at least I made an impression." She grinned widely and tugged me down to sit beside her.

A smile spread across my face as I observed the intriguing woman. Her hair cascaded down her back like a shimmering golden waterfall, swaying with every gesture. Her eyes shined with a captivating shade of blue, reminiscent of a calm sea on a sunny day. A bold red hue adorned her lips, complementing the light azure dress that hugged her curves and the vibrant scarf draped around her neck.

Her eyes darted up, and I glanced over to see a man walking towards us, dressed in an impeccable three-piece suit and carrying two drinks. "I figured you two could use these. One to settle your nerves," he quipped, handing me a crystal glass. He turned to my new friend with a playful grin. "And one for you to tighten your tongue."

Are you all beautiful? I thought as I eyed him over my drink. He was a Greek god. Light stubble framed the smooth contours of his chin and full lips. His eyes were a striking golden brown that danced like fire beneath his dirty blonde hair. As his eyes roamed over Isabelle, I could see the attachment and feel an undercurrent of sexual attraction. Our handsome companion sat between us, stretching his legs out and relaxing his long arms on the couch back.

"I hope it doesn't take too long tonight. From what I witnessed in the kitchen, I can tell you that those emanating aromas will elevate us to unprecedented heavenly delight." Turning his gaze to me, he regarded me with narrowing eyes. "Please tell me that you have a character in mind. When we summoned the last group, it took three hours," he sighed in mock exasperation.

"Do you remember?" he asked, leaning forward. "What was her name? Wait, don't tell me. Against the rules! Don't worry, she'll be here. She doesn't have anything remotely interesting to do." He scanned the room before settling on a figure lingering in the shadows.

"Ah! There. Standing over by the bookshelf," he whispered. "The one pretending to be ignoring us."

I glanced over, shocked to discover they were talking about Aelle, the fearless leader of the Book Store Book Club. I had last seen her surrounded by a group of timid women, holding her own personal court. However, hiding in the dark intersection of the library was a completely different person. She looked like a scared woman with no friends.

What in the world? I wondered as I watched Aelle stroll among the shelves. She pretended to be searching for something, but I could see her subtly skimming the room from the corner of her eye. Her gaze kept shifting until it landed on Eidolon. A slight smile appeared before she grabbed a random book and started reading it.

The Greek god leaned in closer to me, his voice soft and conspiratorial. "The Welcome Committee nearly rejected her. Her answers were all over the place, as if she didn't know who or what she wanted to be. And when she did choose a character, she couldn't even give a reason. I was sure they would've refused her right then and there. I still can't wrap my head around how they ultimately approved her," he tsk'ed.

I gaped at him in shock. It was like he was preparing me for a death match against giants in Caesar's arena. I turned to stare at Aelle, my stomach churning at the thought. How was I supposed to survive if she had barely made it through?

"What's the Welcome Committee?" I asked, nervously playing with my drink.

"Didn't you get the instruction sheet?" He glanced at me, stunned. When I shook my head, he sighed. "The Welcome Committee will give you details of the entire operation. The do's and don'ts. They are a bit *much* if you ask me. Always following the rules," he explained. "They hold the keys, so you must impress them!"

"What keys?"

He was about to answer my question, but Eidolon strode toward the library's center. My mouth went dry as I watched him turn to address the gathering. He was draped in a cloak, a mix of midnight and dawn swirling within its depths. The intricate designs of ravens were stitched into the fabric and glimmered in the light of the crackling fire. His tall stature emitted a dangerous charm, and his new outfit only added to his rugged appearance.

"Welcome to The Raven Society. We have invited you to join our group as we explore and understand this world through the written word and observations. All you need to do is justify your worth."

A man and woman appeared behind him on a podium, wearing heavy black masks and carrying small wooden stools. As they sat down, gazing regally over the room, their eyes settled on me. Their faces were blank, expressions unreadable as they stared, intensifying my fear. They had obviously been waiting for me, but their lack of emotion was disconcerting.

"That's the Welcome Committee," Watson whispered, and a wave of apprehension washed over me. They didn't seem very welcoming. I glanced around the room, panicking setting in. I hadn't chosen my character yet.

I'd spent hours deliberating, but nothing felt right, and now I'd run out of time. The hooded Master of Ceremonies scrutinized us all with the intensity of a wolf on the hunt. I looked away, noticing two others in the room, their anxiety mirroring my own.

At least I wasn't the only one.

Chapter 4

'Journey Of Legends Begins With A Key.' -Book of the Veiled Instructions

"I am Eidolon," announced the regal figure, gesturing to the two cloaked individuals beside him. "May I present Crichton and Emma, the Bearers of the Keys." The cloaked figures nodded in recognition, their gazes flickering towards me once more.

"Keys symbolize the opening and closing of chapters in our lives. They mean the difference between freedom and symbolic death. To carry a key is to master an indefinite number of possibilities. Those who pass the first test will receive one as unique as the story being shared in these rooms," Eidolon finished, glaring in my direction, his eyes shining as if he dared me to walk away now.

Fat chance, Dumbledore wannabe. I'm not going anywhere until I get one of those keys. Eidolon smirked as he turned back to the group, and I wondered if he had somehow known what I had been thinking.

"The journey of legend will begin tonight." As he spoke, I was overcome with an intense desire, a tingle of excitement and fear running through my body. If anyone needed a way to unlock their future, it was me. "Come forward and tell us your story," Eidolon said, looking at me in a silent challenge.

What was his issue?

"Go on!" Watson urged, and Isabelle smiled encouragingly. "I'll bring you a drink as soon as you're done," he promised with a wink.

"Fat good that will do when I'm escorted out like yesterday's trash," I mumbled as I turned to face Eidolon and his masked friends.

The Welcome Committee, my ass. I felt more welcome at my annual gynecologist appointment. At least there, they played soothing music and had a cute picture of a dog running across a sandy beach on the ceiling.

I sat on the small stool in front of them, and with sweaty hands folded in my lap, I smiled sweetly at the execution squad. Instead of focusing on the Master of Ceremonies, I shifted my attention to Emma, who looked just like Professor McGonagall. I assumed she was the nicer of the three.

"Visitor. Tell us your story."

I glanced back at the man beside her, whose gaze met mine with a startling intensity. In that instant, all my choices drifted away from my mind. It was the moment I had been waiting for, and I still wasn't ready.

It didn't surprise me. My track record in high-pressure situations had always been dismal, and the last thirty-plus years played through my mind, recounting all my embarrassing moments. Memories of lunches at a deserted cafeteria table, not being asked to high school dances, discovering that university students were just as cruel as those in high school, and not getting my dream job flashed through my mind.

This was supposed to be the one area where I would fit in. I was meant to belong to this group. A wave of frustration washed over me, and I embraced the sensation. I was no longer nervous.

I was angry.

"You can call me Chloe. I am the unnamed daughter and successor to a labyrinth of secrets my parents kept. I'm blessed and cursed with a mysterious fate entwined with an inconceivable evil hidden in history's depths. The books I protect link humanity's tragic powers with creatures believed to only exist in mythology. My journeys have proved the stories told in the night's cataclysms are true. But only if you are brave enough to follow the storyline. Generations of historians before me have attempted to break the code to the mysteries, but I alone can explain the myth of reality." Done, I took a deep, steady breath and waited.

Staring at the raven painting behind the Welcoming Committee, I tried to ignore the grandfather clock ticking behind me. The seconds felt like an eternity as I waited for their verdict, beads of sweat dripping down in uncomfortable places. But I refused to let them witness my fear.

If they kicked me out now, I would have time to swing by the coffee shop and ice cream parlor, I told myself as I tugged at the hem of my shirt. I'd buy an extra pint for Beacon. Cookies and Cream. His favorite.

"Welcome. We await your journey."

I stared at Eidolon, doubt and suspicion swirling in my gaze. Was he playing with me? I rose and glanced at Professor McGonagall, who smiled slightly. A wave of relief washed over me.

Oh crap. I'm in!

Suddenly, something materialized in my hand. Slowly opening my fist, I found a lavish ornate bronze skeleton key adorned with stacked filigree layers and a delicate red crystal heart nestled inside the floral center. I glanced at it in disbelief, feeling an odd warmth. I didn't know what the key was intended for, but my two new friends made it seem important.

"You can take your place among your fellow travelers," Eidolon said, dismissing me. With delight, I returned to my two companions, who were jumping up and down in their seats.

"You seem like the kind of person who likes spirits mixed with her coffee. I thought this would help," Watson said, handing me a mug and sliding over so I could sit between them.

I smiled at both and took a sip. It was the perfect blend of coffee and Irish Cream, and I sighed in pleasure.

"Well done. I had almost forgotten about that book! You were referencing *The Historian*, weren't you?" Isabelle asked, and I nodded, pleased that she picked up on my reference.

"Good choice! Eidolon is always searching for people curious about the strange and unusual. If I had to listen to one more person identify with the classics, I would have walked out for a smoke break," Watson declared, rolling his eyes.

Isabelle grasped my free hand and held it in her lap. "I knew that you had it in you, luv. You looked like you were about to hit him when he selected you first. We were placing bets on who would win the fight," she told me, staring at Watson in disgust. "He bet ten dollars on the Master of Ceremonies, but I never doubted you," her eyes danced with amusement.

"Hell has no fury like a woman put on the spot," Watson declared drily, taking a sip from his glass.

I tucked my key away in my pocket, enjoying the lingering heat and shifting focus to the new tribute sitting on the Stool of Agony.

He looked like he belonged. The effortless strength in his posture and demeanor spoke of a man happy to be the center of attention. I couldn't help but envy the ease with which he commanded the room.

"Visitor. Tell us your story," Eidolon demanded.

"You can call me Sydney. You may think I'm lazy, cynical, unable to manage a desk job, and unworthy of praise or recognition. Some might even speculate that I put no value on my existence based on how I dress or my occupation. Despite this, I can see the souls of those the world overlooks. The love I have is deeper than most writers can imagine. The well-being of just one person would be worth sacrificing myself for. I'm certain that this capability will lead me down the road of redemption for my sins."

"I stand corrected. I would not be overly hostile to Sydney Carton. He's one of my favorite characters from the classics," Watson said as he softly clapped for the man.

"Well, knock me over with a gin and tonic! And such a stunner! He will be an enjoyable addition to the team—brains and brawn." Isabelle nodded in approval.

"Welcome, Sydney. We await your journey. You can take your place among your fellow travelers," the Master of Ceremony said in dismissal.

As he returned to his seat, I was curiously excited that he'd been selected also. The lumberjack-looking man sat directly across from me in a high-backed chair and smiled in agreement as he winked.

"Oh! Someone has an admirer," Isabelle purred in my ear. I swatted her away and tried to focus on the final victim sitting in front of the tribunal. Yet, despite my best efforts, I kept looking back at Sydney.

Why had he chosen someone who was both assertive and lonely? Sydney was one of the primary characters in *A Tale of Two Cities*, a man who died never experiencing true love. His story was heartbreaking, and I wondered what happened in Sydney's life to make him decide on that character.

"Welcome, Victor." I turned to concentrate again on the proceedings, overhearing Eidolon saying, "Take your place among your fellow travelers." By everyone's expressions, I could tell it had been a horrific tale.

"I'm intrigued," Watson said as he shook off the last story. "This is the first time all three visitors were invited to stay. I wonder what Eidolon is up to tonight."

The library's double doors opened, and Emma called out, "Dinner will be served in fifteen minutes. Please bring your drinks and join us in the dining room." Once she and Crichton left the room, I finally relaxed. The first test was completed, and I passed.

"Isn't the world always full of pleasant surprises? I would never have thought you'd be invited." Aelle walked over, wearing what she likely assumed was a friendly smile. "I thought the Raven Society took more serious and influential authors, but it seems they're reaching into the juvenile realm. But, of course, there is always a need for fantasy writers to liven up the group."

"Aelle, it's nice to see you again," I said with a hint of sarcasm. I didn't know if she was insulting me or not, but her words made me feel small and unworthy in comparison. I prayed that we wouldn't cross paths, but Isabelle came to my rescue by standing by my side before Aelle could say anything derogatory.

"Aelle, luv! I'm so glad you're here. I was disappointed in how we left things last time," she said as she reached out and squeezed her hand in empathy. "Did you ever find a publisher who would take the time to read your latest book? There *must* be an audience interested in…what was it? Dutch farming techniques during the Industrial Revolution?"

"No, we haven't found one yet, but my agent feels highly encouraged by some recent inquiries," Aelle replied, looking exceedingly uncomfortable.

"Well, we have all had a slight setback with one or two of our books. Keep writing, and I'm confident you'll prove that you are not a one-hit wonder, as that vile man said at our last dinner," Isabelle said with a wave of her hand and then turned to me. "Sometimes writers can be so nasty to one another, always competing even when there is no competition. But, as female authors, we must stick together and support each other. Wouldn't you agree?" Her gaze returned to Aelle, eyes narrowing at the woman.

"Of course!" Aelle replied with a glare that could pierce through steel. "I just wanted to show my support for my old friend and welcome her to the Raven Society."

"How lovely," Isabelle winked. "It's rare that we have two members who know each other from the outside. Let's pretend you don't; otherwise, it won't be as fun." And with that, Isabelle led the two of us into the dining room, chatting merrily.

It was apparent that Aelle was less than thrilled with how the conversation unfolded. But I could tell she was secretly relieved not to walk into the dining room alone.

Chapter 5

'Chose People Who Know What It Is To Walk In The Shadows Of Death.' -Book of the Veiled Instructions

The entryway and library were breathtaking, but the dining room was equally impressive. Deep red bricks encompassed picturesque views of the garden. Massive windows allowed natural light to flood in, illuminating the room and casting a warm glow on the rustic wooden beams above. In the center of the room stood a grand barnyard table, its surface worn and weathered from years of use. It could comfortably seat twenty-five people, with enough space for elaborate dishes and intricate centerpieces.

The warm glow of gently flickering candles and Edison lights enveloped the setting, creating a cozy and intimate atmosphere. The table was adorned with an array of glass jars and elegant mint julep cups, overflowing with a vibrant display of wildflowers and fragrant rosemary topiaries in rustic terracotta pots. The combination of soft candlelight and natural elements brought a sense of whimsy and enchantment to the space, making it feel like a secret garden coming to life.

As I scanned the table for my name card, I wondered how I could already have a place set when I had only been inducted a few moments ago. This entire experience was peculiar, and the idea of the home being haunted crossed my mind. How else could my key appear out of thin air?

Stop questioning and start enjoying; I chastised myself, forcing my doubts away.

I found my seat near the head of the table with Sydney on my right and Eidolon standing at the head of the table on my left. Though I was glad to have my new friends sitting across from me, being in close proximity to Eidolon made me uneasy.

Something about him unsettled me, yet I couldn't help but be drawn to his commanding presence. As the glow from the candlelight danced off his sharp features and guarded eyes, I couldn't shake the feeling that there was more to him than meet the eye.

I hoped to be on the other side of the table, free from the fear of spilling my drink or saying something idiotic. Instead, the rich aroma of cedar and smoke wafted toward me as Eidolon took a seat. My hands trembled with anticipation as our eyes met, his dark gaze pulling me into a mesmerizing spell, rendering me immobile.

"Quite a setup here," Sydney commented as he took his seat, leaning in close. He looked around the room with an approving glance. "A far cry from the McDonald's dollar menu I hit up on my way home from work."

Isabelle beamed at us as Watson courteously held out her chair. "You're in for a real treat," she exclaimed. "The chef is exceptional, and Crichton is a master at choosing the perfect wine to complement each dish."

"I don't drink the stuff much myself. But when in Rome, follow the beautiful lady's advice, as my father always said," Sydney declared merrily, shifting his massive frame in his seat. I scooted to the left to give him more space, feeling a twinge of discomfort as Eidolon sighed and shifted away from me.

"How you doing?" Sydney whispered, glancing at Eidolon with a disapproving frown.

"Not sure." I shrugged, mustering a weary smile as I looked up at him. "Just waiting for the next ball to drop. Like everyone will realize their mistake and send me back to the real world."

He leaned over as Crichton poured us a glass of wine, reassuring me with a slight smile. "You're not the only one."

"What do you have for us today, dear Crichton?" Isabelle asked as she held out her cup for him to fill.

He chuckled, explaining the origins of the wine he had poured us. "It's a Beaumes de Venise. Pliny the Elder mentioned it in his encyclopedia *Naturalis Historia*. It's said that St. Louis enjoyed a glass of it every night during his seventh crusade. If it's fit for a King of France, it's certainly good enough for us."

As he strolled away, Crichton filled glasses for the rest of the group and lightheartedly chatted with them. The sound of their banter was soothing to my ears. It was a welcome change from the usual solitary nights I spent devouring chocolate chip cookie dough ice cream. Slowly, Eidolon's grip on me loosened as Isabelle shared her story.

"I was sixteen when I lost my parents," she began, pausing to swallow the lump that formed in her throat. "I was at my grandparent's estate, enjoying the high life, oblivious to the tragedy about to strike." Her voice shook as she recalled the pain and suffering that followed. "I was utterly crushed. My parents were my whole world, and I was their miracle child."

"The funeral was a grandiose affair, fit for royalty. Every important person in the city was in attendance, their somber faces and black attire creating a sea of mourning. I still remember as my parents were driven to their final resting place, a cacophony of clicking cameras and shouting reporters surrounded the procession like sharks circling their prey," she shuddered.

"In the chaotic scene, I faded into the background, a mere shadow amidst the overwhelming grief and spectacle. My grandparents expected me to greet guests, console them, and provide refreshments. The stress of my loss and the uncertainty of my future ignored as I served others. None of them noticed the young girl barely hanging on. Or they didn't care," she shrugged sadly.

"Feeling overwhelmed, I sought refuge in my grandmother's study. A copy of *Northanger Abbey* sat on her desk, and I grabbed it to distract myself. As I delved into the story, I found Isabelle Thorpe, the quintessential mean girl of the Austen era. She was funny, talented, vindictive, hateful, and loving, all at the same time. Despite her complexity, she was just as lost and unsure as I was."

Watson leaned in and gently held her hand, slightly squeezing it. She looked at him with a soft smile and squeezed his hand in return before continuing.

"That is when I learned that sometimes life makes you play a part you are not prepared for," she explained, her intense gaze pleading with me to understand. "It's not always pretty, sometimes dangerous, but as long as we stay true to ourselves," she pointed to her chest. "We can endure anything."

I remained silent, meeting her gaze, trying to understand what she was telling me. It felt like she was handing me the answers to a test I didn't know I was taking. Before I could ask, her attention shifted to Watson.

"Your turn," she smiled at him pointedly.

"If you insist, my dear Isabelle," Watson grumbled as he fiddled with a small can of mints and popped one in his mouth before speaking.

"My story starts when I was eighteen. I had been accepted into some of the top schools in the country, and my parents were delighted. My father spent weeks trying to determine which would offer me the best chance of becoming president one day. Can you picture me as the leader of the free world?" Watson chuckled as he took a drink.

"Politics never interested me; my goal was to carve out a reputation for myself. Against my mother's wishes, I applied to West Point. It's hard to argue with someone who wants to serve their country," he chuckled again. "So, I traded in my Letterman's jacket for a crisp uniform and an unsharpened sword. Despite the challenges, I stayed focused on graduating and flying under the radar during my four years there.

"Graduation day arrived, along with orders for my first unit. I was overjoyed to find out they were deployed to the front lines. After spending years training, I believed I could conquer the world with a small squad, a skilled craft pen, and a week's worth of rations. My mother wept, my father gave me a pocket watch, and I set off on my new adventure."

Watson's confident and cheerful demeanor dimmed as he fell into a pensive silence. Isabelle, sensing his discomfort, moved closer to offer her support. He took a long, shaky breath before mustering the courage to speak again.

"No one explains that war is personal. No two stories are the same, no matter how many documentaries you see on the History Channel," he sighed, taking a sip.

"I got shot in the ass. Can you believe it?" He gave me a wry smile. "My own Tom Hanks moment, except I didn't get an ice cream cone," he shrugged. "The army showed their gratitude with a medical discharge and a monthly stipend. So, there I was, six years after high school, an educated but disabled war hero."

Watson poured more wine into his glass, then filled Isabelle's with the Crichton's amber-colored vintage. Eidolon reached over and refilled his own, then mine, handing it to me silently. His small kindness caught me off guard, but I was too engrossed in the story to comment.

"Following my therapist's advice, I began journaling. It was an awful experience trying to confront and express my emotions. But what started as an obligatory healing routine became a fixation on observing others' behavior.

"The café I spent most of my time at had a lending library. One day, on my way back from the men's room, I stopped to look at the books. I was drawn to *The Adventure of the Noble Bachelor* by Sir Arthur Conan Doyle. Opening the cover, the pages fell open to a passage that changed my life: 'The Jezail bullet which I had brought back in one of my limbs as a relic of my Afghan campaign throbbed with dull persistence,' he quoted, his eyes closed as if he could see the page in his mind. Opening them slowly, he glanced at me.

"It was like the words had been written for me. I hurried back to my table, eager to devour more of the gripping story. But in my haste, I didn't see the person pushing their seat out, and suddenly, my cane flew out of my hand. I stumbled, unable to catch myself, and fell hard onto the ground. I remember the world going black," he shuddered. "When I came to, I found myself in a hospital room, surrounded by beeping machines and the hushed whispers of nurses.

"Someone left me the complete collection of Sherlock Holmes stories to read while recovering. As I delved into the pages, I realized there was more to Dr. Watson than just being a sidekick. He was organized and intentional and, like me, would carry a dull, persistent pain in the background of existence. But that didn't mean we weren't worthy of a great adventure."

Watson looked at me with the same intensity as Isabelle, as if the story was meant for me alone. I was speechless, not sure how to respond. Sydney let out a small whistle when Crichton entered with trays of coffee and bowls of fresh fruit and cream, and I thanked him gratefully as he sat a bowl in front of me.

Shaking the stories from my head, I glanced at Eidolon, hoping his story was next. But he was too busy making a cup of coffee to notice. Sighing, I returned my attention to my dessert.

"You going to eat that?" Sydney asked as he speared one of my strawberries and popped it in his mouth with a grin.

"Not now." I chuckled, glancing at Eidolon as he rose to his feet. Out of the corner of my eye, I saw Aelle straighten and fix her hair before grabbing a small red notebook.

Teacher's pet, I sneered in my mind, oddly jealous over how she looked at Eidolon. I turned my head and caught him staring at me. A flush of heat tingled across my cheeks as I motioned for him to begin. He blinked slowly, a tiny smile on his lips forming, before shaking his head and glancing around the room.

"We are privileged to welcome our newest members into the Raven Society. Dante Alighieri established the foundation of this organization in the 1300s. It was designed to gather intellectuals and writers who shared knowledge deemed too risky for the public.

"In 1312, the society continued its expedition with the Knights Templar. Followed by the Freemasons between the 1500s and the 1600s and then into the 1700s with the Purgatorio of the Illuminati.

"In 1855, Ralph Waldo Emerson, Samuel Gray Ward, and Horatio Woodman established the Saturday Club, and eventually, the Raven Society emerged in the 1920s. After generations have passed, we have been called on again for support."

I sat up straight, not understanding what was happening, when the dining room doors opened suddenly, and the old woman I met earlier appeared at the threshold.

"What an impressive gathering, Eidolon!" she exclaimed happily. "I told you that the right people would come."

Chapter 6

'A Rewrite Of The Past Is Possible.' -Book of the Veiled Instructions

She glided further into the room, her movements slow and deliberate as if she carried the weight of time on her shoulders. Her ink-stained hand trembled as it gripped a stunning cane, its surface adorned with intricate carvings of ships sailing across rough seas, solemn gravestones, mysterious faces, and books.

As she approached my seat, she reached out and placed a delicate hand on my shoulder, her eyes sparkling with anticipation. "Good to see you found the entrance, young lady," she playfully winked at me. "Sometimes, in order to move forward, we must look back. But I have a feeling you already knew that. Who did you choose as your character?" Genuine curiosity radiated from her expression.

"Me, but a better version of myself," I replied anxiously. I wasn't sure why her opinion mattered so much to me, but it did.

"Excellent decision." She patted my arm and flashed a knowing smile. "In this safe space, let go of your old identity and become what you're meant to be. Life will be easier once you do." She straightened and moved to the front of the table, her gaze sweeping over us with admiration.

"Good evening, travelers. Please call me Moll, a name that has been with me for far longer than I care to remember," she announced with a wry smile, her gaze lingering on the empty bottle of wine. "I fear my tale will be lengthy and require something stronger." Her gaze scanned the room. "Where's Crichton?" Spotting him in the corner, she announced, "I believe we'll be better off in the library, my dear friend."

Without hesitation, Crichton nodded his head in agreement and stepped forward. He extended his arm, offering it as an escort. "I will gladly accompany you. If memory serves me correctly, you prefer a whiskey sour."

"You spoil me, old friend," Moll laughed, taking his arm. "Have you asked Emma to marry you yet?" Crichton groaned as they walked out, chatting away like teenagers.

Following their cue, I rose from my seat, glancing at Isabelle. "Who is she?" I motioned towards Moll as she walked away.

Isabelle's eyes held a question as she replied, "I have a feeling we're about to find out." She leaned closer and whispered, "But she seems to know you. How strange!"

Moll and Eidolon stood side by side, observing as we gathered around the crackling fire in the library. I couldn't help but notice their contrasting personalities: Moll's warm and welcoming nature compared to Eidolon's enigmatic and somber aura. Yet, they appeared at ease in each other's company.

If I'd never believed in witches, seeing Moll would have convinced me otherwise. She radiated power like the summer sun's scorching rays, bright and all-encompassing. It almost hurt to look at her for too long. Despite her commanding presence, her voice was gentle and soothing, instantly drawing the group's focus.

"Let me introduce myself properly. I am Moll Pitcher, not to be confused with Molly Pitcher, the brave Revolutionary War heroine," she smirked good-humoredly, arching an eyebrow in amusement. "Even though we both possess admirable qualities of strength and beauty, we are, in fact, two different people."

I couldn't help but laugh, leaning eagerly towards her as she continued her captivating tale.

"I'm a writer like you all." Her gaze swam across the room with a smile. "Writing, you could say, is in my blood. Because of this gift, I stand before you and offer you a story."

The cadence of her voice was captivating, each word rolling off her tongue with such grace and precision that it sent shivers down my back. As I rubbed my hands together, Moll caught my movement with a slight smile before glancing at Eidolon. He scowled, and she fought back a giggle before returning her attention to us.

"This tale begins with Edward Diamond, a retired sailor known as Wizard Diamond by those close to him. In a time when lighthouses were not well established, Marblehead Bay was notorious for its fierce winds that caused ships to wreck against the dangerous cliffs. According to local legend, Wizard Diamond had the ability to manipulate these gusts and guide ships safely to their destination - or so it was said.

"In those ominous days, when even a hint of magickal abilities could result in dire consequences, Wizard Diamon went to incredible lengths to conceal his powers. It was a heavy burden to bear, but he would do anything to protect his family. He was relieved when his children showed no signs of inheriting his unique abilities, knowing that they would be safe from the persecution and danger that came with such power.

"That is until his granddaughter Margaret was born. Like Wizard Diamond, she held the power of clairvoyance, capable of divining a journey's destiny before a single board of the ship was nailed together. But it soon became evident Margaret's gifts surpassed his own. She could also talk to the dead." Moll's words came to an abrupt halt, a tight smile on her lips as she glanced at Eidolon.

He refused to meet her piercing gaze, instead shifting his weight towards the fireplace. He leaned against the worn mantel, his arms crossed tightly over his chest. The dancing flames cast a warm orange glow across his features, highlighting the lines of worry etched into his furrowed brow. His eyes darted around the room, avoiding any contact with hers as if he could escape the uncomfortable conversation.

With a frown, she turned back to the group. "Just like her predecessors, Margaret's spirit was tormented by memories of the past, unfamiliar voices, and the cries of the dead. A most inconvenient ability at a time when witches and magick were feared," Moll admitted, glancing at Isabelle. She winced, and Watson leaned in closer, patting her hand.

"Is there ever a good time to be a witch?" Sydney interjected, leaning back and stretching his legs in front of him. Moll's gaze narrowed, but Sydney countered with a bright smile. "Sorry, go on," he gestured with a hand encouragingly.

Moll reluctantly nodded in agreement. "You're right," she conceded. "Being accused of witchcraft is never a favorable situation."

"Who were they related to?" I asked with sudden courage. Moll's piercing eyes darted to me, and I shrank back in my chair. "I was just wondering because you said Margaret was tormented like her predecessors," I mumbled. Embarrassment flooded my cheeks, and Aelle couldn't resist a chuckle at my discomfort. I glared at her before Moll cleared her throat to break the tension.

"No, that's a great question. At that time, they could trace their line back to Mother Shipton."

"The English witch?" Sydney asked, sitting up, surprised.

Moll smiled. "The same one. It was rumored Mother Shipton was a product of a liaison between her mother, Agatha, and a deity. Or demon, depending on who is telling the story."

"What do you mean, 'who is telling the story?'" Watson asked, arching an eyebrow.

Moll's shoulders rose and fell in a nonchalant shrug. "Just as I said, it all depends on the storyteller. Some religious leaders branded Mother Shipton as a half-demon. But for those who sought her out to harness her powers of healing and divination, she was seen as a divine being blessed by the gods.

"Mother Shipton was a shrewd woman. She understood she had been cursed twice- first by the devil and then by her powers. Therefore, she made sure to conceal the truth from those who might harm her." Moll beamed with pride as she continued. "She kept a little black notebook with her at all times, writing down every vision she had. No matter if it was good, bad, or life-changing."

"Where's the book now?" Aelle interrupted, pausing in her note taking to glance up.

"Hidden away with the others," Eidolon mumbled into the fireplace. Moll glanced over at her shoulder at him with a frown before turning to Aelle.

"Eidolon's right. Her book is safely tucked away. But that leads me too why I'm here today. Her book is just one among many, a compilation of stories known as the Book of the Veiled.

"These stories, like Mother Shipton's prophecies, are surrounded by secrecy and enigma. They contain predictions of the future, records of past events, and revelations about history," Moll listed off on her fingers. "If these books fell into the wrong hands, I can't imagine the consequences."

"What's this have to do with us?" Aelle pressed.

Moll stood tall, her shoulders squared and her gaze unwavering. As she took a deep breath, the weight of her request hung in the air. "I have come to seek your assistance," she began, her voice strong and determined. "I'm here to ask for your help. I need you to find the Book of the Veiled. It has gone missing, and now a rewrite of the past is possible; the future can be changed."

The gravity of her plea hung heavy in the air as she scrutinized us all.

"Missing?" Sydney arched an eyebrow at her. "Or stolen?"

"Stolen," Eidolon said grimly.

Chapter 7

'There Should Never Be Questions Left Unanswered.' -Book of the Veiled Instructions

As Moll's voice grew weary and she announced her retreat to her room, we followed her lead and stepped out into the backyard. The night air was a refreshing break from the intense events of the story. The calm tranquility of the moment was amplified by the bubbling of the nearby creek and the distant tolling of church bells, marking the end of another day.

Watson flicked open his lighter, lighting the cigarette between his lips. He took a long drag, exhaling billowing clouds of smoke into the air in perfect rings. "Well, that was not what I was expecting."

Sydney's bewilderment was palpable as he ran a hand through his hair, the locks tangling and sticking up in all directions. "And here I thought we'd smoke cigars and discuss Hemingway, Lovecraft, and Voltaire. I didn't realize I was signing up for this," he muttered under his breath, a faint crease forming between his brows.

Isabelle's voice was soft and filled with concern as she hugged herself. "She seemed so sad," she whispered. "Do you think we can help?" The question lingered in the air, and my jaw opened in surprise.

"Wait," I exclaimed. "We're doing this. Trying to find the Book of the Veiled?" Moll's words struck a chord, but I was a writer, not a detective.

Most days, I couldn't remember where I put my keys. If someone needed help finding something, I wasn't the person they should ask.

"Yes, we are." Amid the buzzing of our conversation, Eidolon's footsteps managed to go unnoticed until he was right behind us. We all swiveled our heads to look at him, feeling mortified. A smirk played on his lips as he raised an eyebrow at our visible unease. "As a society dedicated to preserving the impact of the written language, it's our duty to assist Moll in reclaiming what has been stolen."

He looked up at the night sky, clouds floating across the bright moon. He paused to take a deep breath of the crisp air that still held remnants of last night's thunderstorm. "But not tonight. It's getting late. We'll reconvene tomorrow and decide on our next course of action."

"Excellent idea." Watson flicked his cigarette butt to the ground. The fading embers glowed a bright orange before being snuffed out by the cool night air. "Come on, Isabelle. I'll walk you home," he winked, extending his arm for her to take. "You can offer me a nightcap."

Isabelle chuckled, her laughter tinkling like wind chimes. Together, they strolled down the quiet tree-lined path, their arms intertwined and their voices playfully bickering over whose turn it was to provide the cocktail. The full moon cast a soft glow over them, painting their silhouettes against the darkened buildings as they made their way home.

Victor and Aelle nodded in silent agreement before slipping through the inky shadows, their voices hushed as they spoke of ancient manuscripts lost to time. As the darkness swallowed her, Aelle glanced back at Eidolon, silently pleading for acknowledgment of her departure. But he remained still, his gaze fixed elsewhere. Her heart sank slightly before she turned on her heel and strode away, her footsteps barely making a sound on the damp earth beneath her.

Sydney exclaimed with amusement, "Well, this has been more exciting than a carnival performance." He gave me a respectful bow and asked, "May I accompany you home? My father would be livid if I let a lady walk alone at night."

I gave a slight nod knowing I could trust him. "It's a short walk, just a few blocks," I reassured him before turning to Eidolon. "Are you good?" Eidolon's eyes widened in surprise as he took in my concerned expression. "I have some urgent matters to attend to," he said, his voice laced with exhaustion. "I'll see you tomorrow." He pivoted and walked away, his steps resonating off the stone path as he headed towards the Raven Society. Steps in front of the porch, he turned and called out my name, his voice ringing like a faint echo in the quietness of the night.

"Chloe, can you come a bit earlier? There are some matters we need to go over," he said before vanishing into the house without waiting for my response.

As the door clicked shut, I turned to find Sydney studying me. "Strange man," he remarked, shaking his head. "Now, let's get you home. While we walk, you can tell me how you ended up here tonight."

"That's a tale of unfortunate events. How much time do you have?" I laughed, leading him back to my place.

We took our time strolling through the streets as we exchanged stories and got to know each other. Sydney listened intently as I spoke about my passion for writing and my addiction to coffee. In return, he opened up about his career as an engineer and his recent success as a published author.

A genuine smile lit up his face as he recalled the memory. "It all started when I found *The Moonstone* in the public library as a kid. With school on summer break, my mother had enough of me running wild and wreaking havoc in the house. Instead of dealing with my antics, she dropped me off at the library to get me out of her hair. I must have paced up and down the aisles countless times, angry that I wasn't hanging out with my friends.

"The old librarian got tired of my mopping, walked over, handed me a book, and banished me to a corner. She had a no-nonsense face and a stern voice, and I was afraid to argue. Sitting in pure agony, I opened the first page and discovered a new world.

"I stayed up all night to finish the book and begged my mother to take me back the next day, hoping to find something else to read. From then on, my summer was filled with thrilling adventures involving pirates, dragons, and riding through the Wild West. But that one book sparked a realization: I wanted to become a writer.

"As a teenager, I didn't want to lose my street cred by admitting I wrote in a journal," Sydney confessed sheepishly. "I stayed up all night writing terrible short stories with equally horrible plots. Fortunately, writing became a tolerable activity during college. My friends and I spent evenings at the local pub, bouncing ideas off each other.

"It wasn't easy for my work to gain recognition; in fact, most agents dismissed my novels. But I persisted, working tirelessly during the day and staying up all night to write. I was physically and mentally exhausted, yet I couldn't bring myself to stop," he smiled, looking back at his journey with fondness.

"And then, my book was discovered by a stroke of luck. An agent recognized its potential and decided to publish it. For an entire year, I dedicated myself to revising, trimming, rewriting, and revising again until, finally, it was ready for release. It's a cliché but so true - you can't make a living doing what you love," he mused, rubbing the tension out of his neck muscles. "That's why I was ecstatic when I received the invitation to join the Raven Society. I'm hoping that I can quit my day job and focus on doing what I love."

"I get it." I nodded, feeling a sense of camaraderie with him. "I've spent countless hours writing articles, starting novels that never get finished, and diving into endless research. I've tried blogging and social media, hoping for a breakthrough." I held my fingers before me, feeling the wear from all the typing. "And I can't seem to stop either."

Glancing up, I realized we were standing outside my apartment. "Thank you for walking me home," I said with a smile, pointing to my living room window where a curious face with big eyes was peering out at us.

Sydney waved at Beacon before glancing at his watch. "Wow, I had no idea it was already this late," he muttered. He turned to me with a playful grin and wiggled his eyebrows mischievously. "I'll need to catch some shut-eye if I want to be prepared for our hunt tomorrow - after all, we're on the search for a mythic book that supposedly holds the power to bring about the end of the world."

"With so much pressure, I don't know how I will fall asleep," I laughed, waving goodbye as he disappeared into the night. The city lights shimmered and danced like fireflies as I headed toward the front door, knowing I had a long, restless night ahead.

There was a lot to think about.

As I dragged myself up the stairs, the magick of my new world slowly dissipated. I reluctantly opened the door to my mundane home and felt a rush of disappointment wash over me. After discovering only a fraction of the Raven Society's secrets, how could I return to my old life?

But at the same time, I couldn't deny the comfort and familiarity of my previous existence. The conflict within me intensified as I longed for the world of magick yet feared losing touch with reality.

A heavy sigh escaped my lips as I turned the corner into the kitchen, the familiar creaking of the floorboards beneath my feet a comforting sound. The moon's dim light spilled through the window, casting soft shadows across the countertops and cabinets. With a sense of weariness weighing on my mind, I reached for the kettle to make myself a cup of tea before heading to bed.

As I absentmindedly reached for a teabag, my gaze drifted out the window, fixating on the moonlit sky above. How could anyone expect a bunch of writers would be able to find a missing secret manuscript that held untold mysteries of the past and future? Where would we even start looking? It could be anywhere.

On the other hand, it sounded exciting, and my mind raced with endless possibilities of what we could uncover. Answers to mysteries like who killed JFK, the enigma of dark matter, and the confusing concept of calories and how food can magickally become 'calorie-free.' And then there was the ultimate puzzle: what exactly happened to the Roanoke Colony?

Everything that I longed to uncover.

My decision was made, and I headed to the desk to do some research.

Chapter 8

'Be Prepared For The Unexpected.' -Book of the Veiled Instructions

As the morning light filtered through the window, I groggily opened my eyes to find Beacon sitting patiently by my side, his tail thumping against the floor in anticipation. The stiffness in my body from sleeping in the armchair all night was a harsh reminder of how old I was getting.

I entered the kitchen with a heavy shuffle and clicked on the coffee maker before jumping into the shower. As the water warmed up, my eyes drifted to the fogged-up mirror. I couldn't help but notice the deep purplish circles that seemed to have taken permanent residence under my eyes and the faint lines around my mouth and eyes that weren't there before. A sigh escaped my lips as I traced a finger along one of the wrinkles, feeling a twinge of sadness at this obvious reminder of aging.

Time had a way of taking its toll on women, and I was no exception. Soon enough, I would have to pursue Botox treatments and pricey skincare solutions to slow the aging process.

Once upon a time, I could stay up all night, drinking and writing, and still function the next day. Now, I suffered if I didn't get at least six hours of sleep, three cups of coffee, two Advil's, and a multivitamin that promised smooth and luscious skin.

With anticipation bubbling in my chest, I eagerly rummaged through my closet, searching for the soft fabric of my favorite sweatshirt. The faint fragrance of laundry detergent and lingering traces of my perfume filled the air as I pushed past the hangers of clothes I needed to get rid of.

Why did Eidolon want me to come over early?

I didn't want to admit it, but something about him made me feel intimidated and intrigued at the same time. Whenever our eyes met, I couldn't help but shiver, and my mouth would go dry as if I were stranded in the scorching heat of Death Valley. Throughout the night, as I drifted between sleep and wakefulness, his face remained imprinted in my mind, like some infatuation. It wasn't typical, and the feeling irritated me.

I needed to get him out of my head.

"Come on," I called out to Beacon, standing by the front door. "Let's go to the park," I offered as I slipped on his leash. We stepped outside, greeted by the refreshing chill of a new day. The sun had only begun its ascent, bathing the neighborhood in a warm golden light as we made our way to the nearby park. The chirping of birds and the rustle of leaves provided a soothing soundtrack for our walk. As we strolled through the peaceful streets, the scent of dewy grass and blooming flowers filled the air, calming my mind and lifting my spirits.

With our go-to bakery stop complete and our treats in tow, we were thrilled to find our favorite park bench unoccupied and settled in to enjoy an apple fritter together.

I was lost in my thoughts while Beacon happily lay at my feet for his early-morning nap before I realized someone was standing before me, blocking the sun. Startled, I looked up and found Eidolon staring at me, a hint of laughter playing around his eyes.

"Hey," he greeted, and I couldn't help but grin, noting how good looking he was. His toned figure was clad in loose-fitting jeans and a snug black sweatshirt that hugged his muscles in all the right places. A backward baseball cap sat atop his head, adding to his effortless style. With a sly smile and sparkling eyes, he exuded an undeniable charm that drew me in.

"Hey," I greeted him with a relaxed wave, shifting my coffee mug to the side and inviting him to take a seat next to me.

"Looks like he's settled in." With a gentle stroke, Eidolon's hand reached down to scratch behind Beacon's ears. The dog let out a contented sigh and nuzzled closer to him. Sitting back on the wooden bench, Eidolon gave me a quick once over, his piercing eyes narrowing into a concerned frown. "And you look exhausted."

"Thanks," I mumbled, rubbing my neck. "I stayed up late and dozed off in the armchair," I explained with a sheepish smile. "Not the most ideal sleeping arrangement." As I shifted in my seat to find a more comfortable position next to him, I couldn't help but ask, "What are you doing here?"

"There is a coffee shop nearby that I like to visit when I need to clear my head. I was walking back when I noticed you sitting here." He pointed to the bakery across the street. "I hope I'm not disturbing you."

"No, I usually sit here watching him nap." I pointed to Beacon, who was now snoring. "Some company is welcomed."

Stretching his long legs and looking around at the park before us, he smiled. "This is my favorite part of the day. When everything is still asleep, anything is possible."

I nodded in agreement. "That's how I feel, too," I said. "Hoping for the possibility of something extraordinary, but often ending up with routine."

He looked over at me with a quick eye. "Your life seems exciting. You've built a successful writing career and have another book on the verge of publication," he commented, looking down at Beacon, who was happily sipping from the cup he set on the bench next to him. "I've never seen a dog enjoy coffee as much as him."

"Beacon, NO!" I shouted, pushing the twenty-pound beast down. My arms strained against his strong body as he fought against me. "I'm so sorry!" My eyes shot to him in apology.

"No problem," he laughed. "It was getting cold anyway. I'll pick up another on my way home. Gods knows I need the energy."

"Long night?" I asked as I wrestled Beacon from climbing into Eidolon's lap.

"Don't worry," he said, waving his hand dismissively while Beacon settled on top of him. "I've always had trouble sleeping, and I had some research to catch up on." He confessed, running his hand over his tired face.

"Did you find what you were looking for?" I asked, weirdly excited that we'd been doing the same thing. I'd spent the whole night looking up the mystery of calories. It sounded mundane, but once I delved into the depths of medical studies and wartime experiments on service members, it became a dark and intriguing subject.

"Yes and no," Eidolon replied with a hint of mystery, and I felt a little wave of disappointment that he wasn't willing to share what he'd discovered.

"Can I ask you a question?" I squirmed in my chair, uneasy but determined to ask the question nagging at me. He nodded, and I took a deep breath before asking. "You believed Moll's story last night, didn't you? That there is some mythical book that contains the secrets of the past and predictions for the future."

"I have to," Eidolon responded, frowning slightly.

"Why?"

"Because she's my grandmother," he said, gazing at the fountain.

Chapter 9

'Never Accept The First Explanation.' -Book of the Veiled Instructions

"Wow, that's a bombshell," I gasped, unable to look away from the horizon as my mind processed the shocking revelation. "It all makes sense now!"

Surprised, his eyes glimmered as he asked, "What makes sense?"

"I was wondering how Moll knew Crichton and Emma. Or how he knew her favorite drink was a Whiskey Sour. Or why you were so quick to want to help her. It's because she's your family." I narrowed my eyes. "That's the one story I didn't hear last night. Your identity and your reasons for joining the Raven Society."

He chuckled, amused. "You have a lot of questions, and I don't think I have enough caffeine in me to handle them all," he joked. "But here's a deal: you take Beacon back to your house, buy me a fresh cup of coffee, and I'll answer whatever I can."

Beacon wriggled in Eidolon's lap, his keen eyes indicating his agreement. I gave a slight nod and gathered my belongings, an intense curiosity driving me.

Eidolon rose gracefully, his tall frame towering over me as we returned to my apartment. The air was thick with tension and unspoken questions, but I could discern the determination and resolve radiating from him.

As we made our way down the bustling street, weaving between early morning joggers and parents rushing their children to school, I felt a sense of relief wash over me. My previous probing questions didn't seem to scare him away, and for that, I was grateful. However, a nagging unease began to grow within me. Was he going to tell me the truth?

He didn't have an obligation to me, and I hadn't done anything to earn his trust yet. After all, I was just a stranger who had been initiated into his secret society hours ago. If I were in his position, I wouldn't share my story.

At least not yet.

As we rounded a corner, I couldn't resist sneaking a glance at him, and my mouth dried. Eidolon exuded an intriguing mixture of Edgar Allan Poe's mystique, Johnny Depp's allure, and Sean Connery's presence. He was like a work of art in human form, and the fact that I was out in public with this man who resembled my wildest dreams was hard to believe.

My version of a knight in shining armor. Lost in my thoughts, I didn't realize I was walking alone.

"I'll wait here." Eidolon leaned casually against the front of my apartment building; his arms crossed over his broad chest. A small smirk played at the corners of his lips as he looked down at Beacon, sitting obediently at his feet.

How did he know where I lived?

"Beacon stopped," he answered my silent question. "I assumed he was telling me he was home."

My cheeks blazed with humiliation as I made my way back, wishing I could disappear into the pavement. "I hate to admit it, but that's where I live," I muttered shamefully, reaching to take Beacon's leash. "I better get him inside."

His piercing gaze made me falter, and I couldn't help but question the wisdom of agreeing to have coffee with him. Public settings always sent my nerves into overdrive; my heart raced, and my hands shook as I anticipated the many ways things could go wrong - from spilling my drink all over myself to tripping over furniture or mistakenly adding salt instead of sugar to my coffee.

An inner debate raged on within me as I considered my options. I could invite him inside, a safer and more conventional choice. However, the thought of Eidolon seeing the chaotic disarray that had consumed my home over the past few days made my skin crawl.

The inner adventurer stirred within me, urging me to take action. I paused, the question lingering in my mind like a persistent echo. What would the fearless, daring side of me do? With determination and a firm grip on bravery, I pushed aside any doubts and hesitations.

"Would you like to come in for coffee?" I asked, my eyes darting between the tree in the distance and his piercing blue gaze. "I picked up a new blend from the local market yesterday and have been dying to try it out."

"I'd love to," he agreed without hesitation. "Beacon can show me around."

A burst of laughter escaped my lips as Beacon bounded up the front stairs with unbridled excitement. The stub of his tail wagged furiously as he led Eidolon down the hallways, eager to display his favorite toys and cozy napping spot.

"It's a mess," I warned, stopping before my door. "Beacon and I don't have many visitors."

"Who cares?" The nonchalance in his demeanor was palpable as he shrugged, dismissing the concern with ease.

As the key slid into the lock, I couldn't help but feel a twinge of anxiety. Images of unwashed dishes overflowing in the sink and dirty laundry strewn across the bathroom floor flashed through my mind. Did I even remember to water my plants in the past few days? The thought nagged at me as I pushed open the door, realizing that I had forgotten to lock it again, and braced myself.

"Here it is." I placed my purse on the cluttered entry table, filled with books and unpaid bills. "Make yourself comfortable, and I will get the coffee brewing."

"Great!" Eidolon's confident stride carried him straight into the room as if he owned the space. His gaze swept over everything with a sharp eye, taking in every detail with precision and interest.

As I headed into the kitchen, trying to gather my wits, I discreetly monitored through the door as Eidolon sauntered around my home. He appeared to be fascinated by everything Beacon showed him, which I found endearing since most of it was dog toys being tossed in his direction.

I did my best to remain calm as he approached and surveyed the chaotic scene on my desk. Half-finished mugs of coffee and tea cluttered the surface, along with a pile of books and a plate with a half-eaten peanut butter and jelly sandwich.

A sudden jolt ran through me as I remembered the Post-It notes in which I had scribbled his name and tiny hearts during one of my idle moments the night before. Trying to divert his attention from it, I quickly walked in with two cups and handed one to him. I discreetly stepped in front of the desk, blocking his view, and motioned for him to sit in the living room.

"You have a great place," he said as he sat beside Beacon, taking a sip of his coffee. I glanced around the room, trying to decide if he was being polite or was skipping over the mess. I loved my apartment, but it could be too much for most outsiders.

"Thank you. It's not much, but it's home to me." I took a sip of my drink, trying to steady my racing heart. What do regular women typically do in this situation? I was completely clueless about how to act. So, I resorted to what I knew best - asking more questions. "Ready to spill the beans?"

"What do you want to know first?" he asked with an inviting smile, and my heart skipped a beat. His grin widened, and I blushed.

"I'm curious why you selected Eidolon. It's a concept, not living but not dead. A mere reflection of a person."

Eidolon shifted in his seat, his muscular frame sinking into the plush cushions of the couch. His arm, toned and defined, casually draped across the back as he gazed at me with those piercing eyes. My heart began to race, a tingling sensation spreading through my body as I considered moving closer to him.

With deliberate slowness, I brought the warm mug to my lips and took a long sip, never breaking eye contact with him. The air between us was charged with an unspoken tension, making every movement feel significant and intentional.

Eidolon leaned forward, placing his mug on the coffee table before settling back into his seat. "That's a good question," he replied. "It's quite a story."

"I love stories," I replied, settling in.

Chapter 10

'The Dead Are Often Hard To Communicate With.' -Book of the Veiled Instructions

"I was a child when my parents disappeared. It was a typical Friday evening, and they had a standing dinner reservation. The neighbors had kindly offered to babysit, and they dropped me off with the promise of being back by nine.

"We waited anxiously for their return, but as the hours ticked by, it became clear that something was wrong. One of our neighbors grew worried and went to check to see if they were home and had just lost track of time. That's when he found the front door open, and the entire place ransacked.

"The authorities were notified, and a thorough investigation was initiated, but there was little optimism from the start. The car belonging to my parents was in its usual spot in the driveway, and the owner of the restaurant confirmed that they never arrived for their reservation. Despite an ongoing search for six months, the case eventually reached a standstill. They had vanished without leaving any clues behind."

My jaw dropped in disbelief. His story was as tragic as Isabelle and Watson's, and they had shattered my heart. Eidolon exhaled deeply, and I realized there was more to the tale.

"Members from the nearby church took me in until someone could locate my relatives. Sadly, no one came forward to claim me, so I ended up in the foster care system." He winced at the memory. "My basic needs were taken care of. But at school, fitting in was a constant struggle. My peers were harsh and unaccepting towards a kid who had no parents. The teachers made attempts to include me but always treated me with caution as if I were fragile or on the brink of a breakdown." He finished with clenched teeth.

"So, I read. Books became my escape from my ugly reality. I had no one to turn to, so getting lost in stories made me feel less alone." As he reached for his coffee, Beacon hopped onto his lap, halting his movements. "Well, well, look who's here," he chuckled, giving the furry creature a gentle scratch on the neck.

"Sorry about that. We're still working on his manners." I began to stand up, but Eidolon motioned for me to stay seated.

"No bother," he said, looking at his mug, frowning.

"Want some more?" I tilted my head and raised an eyebrow. The coffee was fabulous. And with the direction the morning was taking, we needed all the help we could get.

"Please." With a pleading look, he held his mug out. As I took it from him, he finally noticed the bold letters: *Write Drunk, Edit Sober*. A smile tugged at his lips as he asked, "Is this the secret to your success? You were drunk while writing?"

Shrugging, I walked to the kitchen. With a casual tone, I called out over my shoulder, "Stephen King swears by it. Personally, I tend to consume more coffee than anything else. And now and then, I'll have a nicotine fix."

"You smoke?" Eidolon called out, shaking his head in disapproval. "Never would've guessed."

"Don't judge," I chided as I returned. "According to my doctor, I can do so until I can manage my stress. The original prescription is on my desk. I made sure to send a copy to my mother so she wouldn't yell at me."

"That is funny and a bit sad at the same time."

"It's something I am working on," I smiled as I handed him a new coffee mug that said, *If cigarette taxes were meant to discourage smoking, wouldn't income taxes discourage working?*

"Point taken," he said, chuckling after he read it.

"What happened next?" I questioned as I settled into my favorite chair and pulled my grandmother's blanket around my lap.

With gentle movements, he ran his fingers along the elaborate patterns of a silver bracelet adorning his wrist. I watched as the light danced off its surface, highlighting the intricate symbols of ravens and unknown words etched into the metal - a perfect fusion of masculinity and mystery. I was about to ask him what the inscriptions meant when he started his story again.

"The visions started when I turned sixteen." His eyes narrowed as he tried to figure out how to explain. "It was like stepping into alternate realities every time I closed my eyes. I began keeping a record of them, like Mother Shipton," he said pointedly. "As time passed, I realized the individuals who appeared in my visions were people I knew, and I was getting a glimpse of their future."

"That must have been difficult to deal with," I said cautiously, not wanting him to think I was questioning him.

He cocked his head to the side and blinked slowly as if he couldn't believe how easily I had accepted his secret. A slight frown appeared. "I can still remember the night I knew Mr. Martin would die or that Mrs. Robinson's husband was going to be diagnosed with cancer. At first, their situations didn't impact me personally; they were just unfortunate events in the larger picture of life. And it was easy to cope with when no personal attachment was involved.

"Until I was a senior in high school, that is." He turned to look out the bay window. "A few days before the start of school, I had a vision about the high school's football star and his girlfriend. I'd known them since we were in elementary school. They used to live next door to each other, and their friendship blossomed over the years." A sad smile played on Eidolon's lips, and I knew there wasn't going to be a happily ever after.

"In the vision, they were standing on a cliff's edge, clutching each other. Freezing wind whipped around them as they stared at me with terror. No matter how fast I ran, the gap between us only widened." He paused, swallowing hard. "I couldn't hear their screams for help, but I could sense their desperation. I woke up in the morning to find out they had been in a car wreck. A drunk driver swerved into their lane, and they went over a cliff."

A muscle in his jaw twitched as he stood up and started pacing back and forth in the room. I observed quietly, giving him space to process his feelings.

With a soft, defeated voice, he confessed, "I left. I couldn't face anyone after what happened. It felt like it was my fault. That somehow, I should have been able to stop it from happening. After walking for hours, I stopped at a coffee shop for something to eat. And that's when she found me."

"Who?" I whispered.

"My grandmother," he softly chuckled. "She sat down, and I instantly knew who she was. She had eyes the same color as my mother's. All she said was, 'Let's go home.' We went by the police station first and let the investigating officer know where I was going. And then she took me home to the Raven Society."

He turned to face me. "Along the way, she told me the story of a man who wrote a poem about a place called the Shadowlands. A place where a soul sat on the throne of the dead. She said I had a decision to make. Either try to forget what I could do and live a normal life. Or embrace my gifts and live in two worlds. Obviously, I embraced the darkness," he smiled at me sheepishly.

"Eidolon," I started, but he raised a hand to stop me.

"You don't have to say anything. I've heard it all." He glanced at his watch, exhaustion written on his face. "I didn't realize it was so late. I have to meet Moll for lunch." He glanced up at me. "She wants to talk to you before everyone else shows up."

"Of course," I replied, rising from my seat to escort him out. "I'll be there around four." We walked to the front door, and as he turned to leave, I looked up at him with a smile. It meant a lot to me that he trusted me enough to share his story.

"Thank you," he whispered, his voice laced with emotion. "It's been a while since I've told anyone. I almost forgot how, too." A slight smile lit up his face, and I couldn't help but feel my heart skip a beat at the sight.

"Of course," I said as I opened the door to let him out. Closing it slowly behind him, I stared at the empty living room that had been so cozy and warm a few minutes ago. A hint of sadness and disappointment hit me like a tidal wave, and I knew I was in deep trouble.

I was starting to like him.

Chapter 11

'The Key Choses The Bearer For A Reason.' -Book of Veiled Instructions

As each minute crawled, the clock inched closer to 4:00, and my nerves increasingly frayed. Anxious, I paced back and forth in front of the entrance to the Raven Society. Pausing in front of the stained-glass windows, I fidgeted with the hem of my sweatshirt as I debated whether or not to knock, weighing the potential consequences and benefits in my mind.

On the one hand, Eidolon and Moll were adamant that we needed to find a book said to hold knowledge so dangerous that it had been kept hidden from the world. Its alleged contents contained the power to wreak havoc and devastation if it fell into the wrong hands. Something that sounded like it could end in disaster. Or death.

On the other hand, being a member of the Raven Society was an opportunity to embody everything I had longed to be. It was a chance to bask in the glimmering spotlight and become a revered figure among my peers. I could shed my insecurities and fears and truly shine. To be part of such a prestigious group was like having wings to soar above the mundane world below.

Was I brave enough?

As I stalled, the front door swung open with a soft creak as if anticipating my arrival. The warm glow from within flooded onto the porch, revealing the kind brown eyes of the person standing in the doorway. A sense of familiarity and belonging washed over me, as if this was the place I was meant to call home.

"Hey, Crichton. You got anything brewing?"

"Ms. Chloe." He bowed respectfully and stepped aside to welcome me in. "I just brewed a fresh pot of coffee for you. Moll asked me to show you to the library."

"Great!" I bounced through the door.

Crichton guided me into the room, where streams of golden sunlight poured through the expansive windows. The dance of light and shadows on the floor created a mesmerizing display as if a master painter had brought his canvas to life. The enticing scent of freshly brewed coffee filled my nostrils, instantly calming me.

As I took in the view outside, I couldn't help but be grateful for the serene oasis that greeted me- its lush green lawn and vibrant flowers dancing in the gentle breeze—a welcome change to the chaos of the last few hours.

"Ms. Moll will be down in a few minutes." With a nod, he exited the room, leaving me alone with the tray of drinks and my thoughts.

I filled a coffee mug, grasping it tightly with both hands. Raising the drink to my lips, I took a deep breath and let the warmth of the liquid spread through my body, fortifying me for the unknown journey ahead. This was no ordinary night; it was an expedition into unfamiliar territory, and I needed to be mentally prepared for whatever lay ahead.

"I, too, use coffee to steel my nerves," Moll chuckled as she slowly walked in, the thump of her cane echoing through the library. "Naturally, it's changed over the years. I still remember when the drink was thick like pudding and bitter."

She sank into the plush armchair across from me and reached for a delicate teacup, the steam wafting and tickling her nose. With a contented sigh, she added a splash of rich cream to her drink and stirred it in slowly. "I'm glad you were up to appeasing an old woman's demands," she remarked with a warm smile, bringing the cup to her lips and taking a satisfying sip.

"Of course." A warm, genuine smile spread across my face.

"You're probably wondering why I asked you here." Enthusiasm flickered across her face, and I couldn't help but nod, already intrigued. With a graceful sweep, she gestured towards the empty chairs surrounding us. "There is a tale I want to share with you before the others arrive," she said, her voice tinged with excitement and mystery. A glint of anticipation sparkled in her eyes as she leaned in closer.

"Great!" A sense of excitement and eagerness bubbled inside me as I tucked my legs underneath me, getting comfortable.

"Did you bring your key?"

Her question caught me off guard. I'd completely forgotten about the small key. I had thrown it into my handbag, thinking it was more like a prop than something I had to hang on to.

My hand dove into the depths of my cluttered purse, searching and feeling amidst a jumble of pens, receipts, and loose change until my fingertips finally brushed against the cool metal. I held it out, half expecting her to take it from me, but to my surprise, she shook her head and motioned for me to keep it.

"Keys are fascinating objects," she mused, curiously observing mine. Her gaze flickered up to meet mine. "Everyone possesses one. House keys, car keys, hotel keys, locker keys. Each one serves a purpose. But what makes them truly intriguing is that they safeguard the things we hold dear or fear the most." She tilted her head to the side and posed the question, "Why do we lock away the things that mean the most to us?"

"I'm not sure." I drew out each word, unsure where her line of questioning was heading.

She nodded, a faint smile gracing her lips. "It's because we want to keep our true selves hidden. Keys can shield and preserve the core of who we are and hope to be."

I twirled the key between my fingers, staring down at it, before asking, "Do you think this is hiding who I truly want to be?"

"That's your tale to tell," she shrugged. "Only you know what you're safeguarding from the world." Her gaze was intense, and I squirmed in my chair under its weight.

Moll's hand trembled slightly as she reached for the delicate black ribbon tied around her neck. She carefully retrieved the item from underneath her dress and extended it towards me to see. It was an iron and bronze key, cylindrical, with a thin rectangular tooth attached to one end.

"This key represents my story. A straightforward construction without any shine or glamour. It has stood the test of time and opened many doors for me." A glimmer of pride shined in her eyes as she ran her hand over it. "My grandfather gave it to me the night he passed away."

She drifted into a nostalgic state, her eyes focused on something in the distant past. Abruptly, she returned to the present and turned her gaze towards me. "That night, he revealed our family's 'gifts,'" she used air quotes. "Then he showed me his copy of the Book of the Veiled before he gave me my own copy."

I was stunned, my jaw dropping in surprise as she let out a small laugh at my reaction. "Yes, my dear," she uttered, "I am also burdened with the curse of the Book of the Veiled. It is a family legacy that I swore to uphold on my grandfather's deathbed," she said with a hint of sadness, gazing down at the key in her hand.

"If it's a curse, why not just let it fade into oblivion? And if you really think others shouldn't have access to it, then just don't write it down." I argued, arching an eyebrow at her. It seemed like such an obvious solution, and I couldn't understand why no one had suggested it before.

She snickered, shaking her head. "It's not that simple, my dear. Imagine if you had a story swirling around in your mind, fully formed with characters, scenes, and a classic plot of good versus evil. Would you only think about it? Or would you need to write it down?"

I ran my fingers over the smooth ceramic of the coffee mug, lost in thought. "Probably," I acknowledged with a nod.

"Exactly!" Moll exclaimed, gesturing emphatically with her hands. "Every experience is worth remembering and sharing. We're dealing with real people who have lived or will live in the future. These are not made-up stories or fairy tales." She leaned forward to pour herself another cup of coffee from the pot on the table. "Sometimes, I get curious and look back at what else has been written by others."

I leaned forward and asked, "Have you ever found any mistakes?" A glimmer of hope rose within me as I waited for her response. Maybe things weren't as dire as she and Eidolon had portrayed them. If there had been mistakes, perhaps the Book of the Veiled hadn't been stolen. Maybe someone had just misplaced it.

She shook her head, her eyes conveying exhaustion. "No," she said, and I could tell she was being truthful. "Believe me, I wished I had. Maybe I would still have my family."

"Eidolon told me about your daughter. I'm sorry for your loss." I whispered with sincerity.

As our gazes connected, I could see the sorrow etched onto her face. Her lashes were weighed down by glistening tears, on the brink of spilling over. She nervously clasped her hands together, her trembling fingers revealing her inner turmoil. With a deep breath, she tried to steady herself.

Her voice was soft and somber as she spoke, her eyes downcast. "It's a sad story," she finally said, the weight of it heavy in her voice. "We weren't speaking at the time. And when I finally heard the news, it took me forever to track Eidolon down."

Confused, I tilted my head and asked, "Why weren't you talking?"

"She was mad at me." Her voice held a sharp edge as she spoke through gritted teeth and darted her eyes to the fireplace, flames dancing in the background. A chilling silence hung between us, punctuated only by the crackling of logs and the occasional hiss of an ember. I could feel the tension radiating off her.

"Why?" I pressed.

"Her husband didn't want her to have anything to do with me." Her jaw tightened at the thought. "He thought I was delusional, filling my daughter's mind with talk of magick and ancient texts. And when she became pregnant, he made sure I had no place in my grandson's life."

"I don't understand," I said slowly. "She turned her back on you?"

Moll's head bobbed up and down, her expression solemn. "She wanted nothing to do with the Book of the Veiled or our legacy," she whispered, her voice tinged with sadness and disappointment. "Especially when she started having visions herself."

"Do you know where she is now?" I asked, sitting up. "I mean, if you have the gift of sight, shouldn't you be able to find them?"

She shook her head. "It doesn't work like that. I can't just *will* a vision."

"Why are you sharing all this with me?" I asked, pushing my glasses further up my nose. I could believe in keys that opened secret doors, books that foretold the future, and even the ability to see into the past. But I didn't understand what Moll's missing family had to do with me.

Moll stared at me for a moment. "Because I believe you are the only one who can find her."

My mouth fell open. "I think you have the wrong person," I laughed. "I can't find a pen sitting next to me."

"No, Chloe," she replied, grasping my hand. "My visions are never wrong. You are the one who can go through the doors of history and still return to the present. You are the one who will help Eidolon find his parents and, with them, the Book of the Veiled."

We stared at each other—Moll's determination against my insecurities. But, if I were Moll's lifeline of hope, she was about to be highly disappointed.

The door creaked open, and I glanced up to see Eidolon stepping into the library. The mixture of emotions in his eyes - grief, acceptance, and longing - told me he knew what Moll had asked of me.

A whirlwind of thoughts spun through my mind as I eyed him, a cacophony of doubts and fears clawing at my resolve. This was insane. Stolen books, magickal keys, missing parents. How could anyone believe it all?

But I was a writer—a spinner of tales. I understood the magick of a fairy tale coming to life. The unbelievable could become believable, even if for a moment.

What was to say this story wasn't true?

Chapter 12

'Reality Is Nothing More Than A Concept Created By Man.' -Book of the Veiled Instructions

I remained in my seat, absently twirling my key between my fingers, as Moll retreated upstairs, leaving Eidolon and me in awkward silence. He made a beeline for the bar as our last conversation lingered, heavy with unspoken words and unresolved tension. I couldn't bring myself to break the silence, unsure of how to approach the situation.

"Let's divide and conquer. I say we each go to a different library, sneak into the archives, and find the book," Sydney offered as the rest of the Raven Society walked in. "I volunteer to search the Vatican." He glanced at me with a grin. "I've wanted to pay them a visit since I read the *Davinci Code*."

"That's a ridiculous idea. We have no way of knowing if the book is even in a library. It could be located anywhere." Watson's voice dripped with skepticism as he gestured towards the shelves upon shelves of books looming around us. The scent of old paper and dust filled the air, reminding me of the daunting task ahead.

A book hidden among a million others was like looking for a needle in a haystack.

"It's the most logical place to start," Sydney countered, rolling his eyes. "Books are usually found in a library."

"We *could* be a bit more thoughtful in our approach before we start breaking into cultural icons and resorting to theft," Watson grumbled. "I think we're a little better than that."

"I don't see you coming up with any solutions. What's your brilliant idea?" Syndey leaned forward with a sneer.

"Well, because you asked..." Watson started, stepping towards him before Eidolon jumped in between.

"Gentlemen, let's take this one step at a time. I'm sure we can all come to an agreement. But for now, we should all take a breather and head into the dining room."

Watson and Sydney shared a brief, tense moment of silent communication, their eyes reflecting their frustration. They were eager to continue their argument but ultimately let out a resigned sigh and made their way out of the room. As they strolled through the hallway, their voices drifted as they argued back and forth.

Rolling my eyes, I pushed myself up from my chair to follow, still reeling from what Moll had shared and trying to wrap my head around everything that happened in the last 24 hours. Isabelle slid beside me and looped her arm through mine, "You look like you just saw a ghost, luv. Everything alright?"

"I'm good." I shrugged with a tired smile. "Just another long night of research. I miss the days when I stayed up all night and still function the next day."

"I think I can help. Crichton has a miracle cure. We can ask him to brew you a cup," she suggested, scanning the room. "Emma drinks it every night, and I'm always amazed by how much energy she has afterward."

"That would be wonderful." I flashed a grateful smile at her, knowing any help would be a relief. I was well beyond the point where coffee could make a difference.

"Of course! What are friends for?" With a firm grip on my arm, she guided me towards the door, her face etched with a determined expression. There was a sense of urgency in her every movement, which piqued my curiosity. But a wave of exhaustion settled heavily upon me, and I pushed any thoughts aside as we exited the library.

Walking down the hallway, I was slightly irritated by how effortlessly perfect and well-rested Isabelle looked. She was dressed in loose cotton trousers, a rolled-up men's shirt, an oversized tweed vest, and a stylish green fedora - giving off the impression of being straight out of a contemporary adaptation of an Agatha Christie novel.

On the other hand, I had barely managed to put on a pair of clean jeans, matching shoes, and a clean sweatshirt. Somehow, I'd been able to tame my hair without frying it with a curling iron, so I did have one small victory. But it didn't make me feel any better walking next to the supermodel.

As we settled into the same seats from the night prior, I giggled at Watson's growing irritation with Sydney's incessant rambling about James Bond and his far-fetched schemes to break into the Vatican. His hands gestured wildly, painting a picture of daring heists and gadgets straight out of a spy movie while Watson's eyes rolled in exasperation.

"You have to think outside the box," Sydney grumbled when Watson shot down another one of his ideas.

Isabelle leaned close to Crichton and whispered something in his ear, and a look of concern crossed his face. He excused himself and disappeared into the kitchen before reappearing with a cup of tea. As he handed it to me, a small crease between his eyebrows hinted at the tension brewing beneath the surface.

"Ms. Isabelle told me you may need a little pick-me-up," he said as I took the mug from him. "Be careful, Ms. Chloe, it's strong," he warned.

I wasn't entirely sure what he meant when he said 'strong,' but I was open to anything that would put the pep back in my step. As I held the cup, I appreciated its warmth and the burst of flavors: vanilla and raspberries; with every sip, my mood improved. I sat back in satisfaction as plates loaded with Irish stew, crispy potato cakes, and warm soda bread were placed before me.

As I waited for the others to finish serving themselves, I couldn't resist stealing a glance at Eidolon. His piercing blue eyes roamed the room, taking in every tiny detail calmly as he reclined in his chair like a king on his throne. As he ran a hand through his dark hair, the light glinted off the smooth strands, giving them an almost ethereal shine. The air around him vibrated with energy and refinement, making it hard to turn away from his striking presence.

I attempted to look away, but I couldn't break my gaze from him. He held my eyes with a raised eyebrow as if he could read my thoughts. My face heated up with embarrassment, and I quickly lowered my gaze to the bowl before me. From the corner of my eye, I caught a small smile forming on his lips before he shifted his attention to answering one of Aelle's endless stream of questions.

"So, what do you think? Come up with anything that might be helpful?" Sydney asked between bites, moaning in pleasure as he tore off a piece of bread and popped it into his mouth.

"Nothing, really," I answered. "I was playing around with some theories, but nothing concrete yet." I spun my spoon around in the stew, avoiding eye contact. I didn't want to admit I spent more time daydreaming about Eidolon than actually getting any work done.

"I thought you said you were up all night researching," Isabelle probed, raising an eyebrow with amusement. She glanced at Eidolon with a knowing grin and back at me. "What else would keep you up so late?"

"Looking at questions with no answers." I rolled my eyes in irritation. I wasn't thrilled with what she was insinuating, especially in front of Eidolon. If I was going to have a schoolgirl crush, I wanted to keep it to myself. "Maybe if we understood how mysteries were solved, it might give us an idea of what steps to take next."

The idea dawned on me during the early hours of the morning. Though I wasn't technically "researching," my restlessness gave me ample time to contemplate. And the mystery of the Book of the Veiled served as a welcome diversion from thoughts of Eidolon.

"And....?" Watson asked, pausing mid-bite.

I savored a spoonful of my stew before responding. "Calories are a figment of our imaginations."

Sydney stopped chewing and examined me in bewilderment. "What are you talking about?" He darted a glance across the table at the food like it had offended him somehow.

"Think about it: when it comes to food, we rely heavily on the packaging." I picked up a ketchup bottle and tapped the back. "We make decisions based on what those labels tell us about calories, but in reality, the numbers are just an estimate. The scientists don't know the exact truth about calorie count, but they are the so-called experts, so we trust them."

Sydney grabbed the bottle from my hand. He studied the label, his face scrunching up in discomfort as he read the numbers. "And how does this help us?" he asked, setting it down.

"All I am saying is that reality can be distorted. People can manipulate events to fit their narrative. The key to solving the case of the missing book lies in uncovering its core truth. We must understand the motive behind its disappearance in order to determine its whereabouts." I returned my focus to my dinner, not expecting anyone to take my theory seriously.

Lost in buttering my bread, I didn't hear Eidolon approaching from behind until he coughed loudly. Startled, I knocked over my bowl of stew and gave him an icy glare before grabbing a cloth to clean up the spill. "Warn a person before you decide to give someone a heart attack," I complained.

Eidolon obviously did not care about the mess as he grabbed me by the elbow, and I stared at him in surprise.

"Come with me," he growled as he pulled me out of the room, down the hall, and through a door I had never seen.

He ushered me in and shut the door behind us, and I took a moment to peek around the room in awe. It was a Vogue magazine version of a man's office. Mahogany furniture, a carpet of silver-toned hues, bookcases adorned with novels lining three walls, and an enormous walnut desk dominating the center of the room. A small laptop sat in the middle, surrounded by stacks of papers and five ancient-looking books.

Eidolon stalked to the armchair behind the desk and sat down, pointing at one of the seats across from him.

"You didn't have to manhandle me like that. You could've told me you needed to talk to me in private," I mumbled as I slumped into the chair Eidolon pointed at. My discomfort grew as his unwavering attention bore into me like a spotlight. I shifted uncomfortably in my seat, feeling exposed and vulnerable.

"What's your decision?" The question hung in the air, thick and heavy like a storm cloud. He reclined in the chair, his muscular arms crossed over his chest as he waited for my answer.

"On what?" I replied, trying to reach the same no-nonsense tone and failing.

"Are you going to help us or not?" He sighed, rubbing his tired eyes and raking his fingers through his hair.

"Of course, I'm going to help. But for the record, you and your grandmother got the wrong person," I said calmly, picking at the hem of my sweatshirt.

"Thank you," he started, but I waved off his gratitude. I didn't need it. We needed to see how much I screwed up his and Moll's plans before we began handing out awards.

Eidolon shifted the conversation, "I won't thank you then. But is everything okay? You seem a bit off." There was a hint of concern in his expression, but I ignored it.

"How do I feel?" I echoed, my gaze narrowing on him in bewilderment. "I'm not sure. Okay, I suppose." And I was. I felt amazing. Better than amazing. It was almost unbelievable that just half an hour ago, I felt like I was trudging through thick mud after guzzling cups of coffee like it was the only thing keeping me alive. I glanced up sharply. "What was in the tea?"

Eidolon glanced at me with an innocent expression. "I'm not sure what you mean," he replied, giving a slight shrug. Before I could press him for more information, the office door swung open, and Isabelle, Watson, and Moll walked in, their eyes fixed on me.

Awesome! I thought to myself. This was the moment I found out I had been drugged or was about to be kicked out of the Raven Society.

I knew I should've stayed home and watched Netflix.

Chapter 13

'Inconsistencies Of History Are Reality.' -Book of the Veiled Instructions

Isabelle and Watson pulled chairs around the desk while Moll sat beside me and reached out to take my hand. I tried to snatch it back, ready to bolt at the first sign of rope or a weapon. But to my surprise, Moll's grip was surprisingly strong for an old woman, her fingers firm and determined.

"Chloe, I have one more story to tell you."

My mouth dropped, and I narrowed my eyes. "Another story?" I darted my gaze between her and Eidolon. "No offense, but I've already hit my daily quota." I turned to glare at Isabelle. "You drugged me," I accused.

She laughed and shook her head. "I didn't drug you, luv. Just dusted the cobwebs away."

Watson slid his chair closer to mine, reaching to grasp my hand in his. "Chloe, you need to hear us out."

Something about his tone put my nerves on high alert. "Can someone please explain what the hell is going on?" I glanced at Eidolon, who still refused to make eye contact.

Chicken shit! I thought, staring at him, finding a twisted sense of satisfaction as he shifted in his seat, wincing.

Moll squeezed my hand to get my attention. "Your theory. The one where you need to find loopholes in reality. How did you come up with the idea?"

"I don't know," I confessed slowly, looking her up and down in confusion. "I guess when I was researching diet fads," I shrugged. "That's when I discovered calories weren't a reliable measure of fat intake. It's all just an estimation. But it got me thinking: what else have we accepted as fact without proof?

"And..." Moll pressed.

"Well, it dawned on me that the absence of evidence could be as revealing as the evidence. Our understanding of history is often flawed and incomplete until we delve deeper and unravel why certain information was concealed, unveiling the complete picture."

Moll patted my hand and smiled at Eidolon. "That's where we need to begin."

Eidolon's jaw clenched tightly, his eyes narrowing in disbelief and rage. "Wonderful! According to Chloe's middle-of-the-night investigation on google.com, we'll find the Book of the Veiled in the inconsistencies of history. Why didn't I think of that?" he scoffed, his voice dripping with sarcasm and arrogance.

"Hey. There's no reason to be rude. You..." I had a few choice words to describe what I thought about him, but he held up his hand to stop me mid-sentence.

"Do you know how many inconsistencies we would have to shift through? Thousands! Where would we even begin?" He ran a hand through his hair in frustration.

I couldn't help but feel annoyed and responded, "I do know. After all, I *am* a historian."

Moll observed our interaction with interest before interjecting. "Depends on what book we are looking for."

My brow furrowed in confusion as I posed the question, "What do you mean? It depends on what book." My eyes scanned the group, lingering on each face, noting the tension in their stance and a flicker of guilt in their expressions.

They were keeping something from me.

"The Book of the Veiled is not a single volume but a series of books passed down over generations. Each one contains secrets that intertwine with the others, building upon each other like the plot of a novel," Moll explained. "The books feed off of one another."

"So, it's not one book we are looking for?" I clarified, my mind racing as I processed the information. "We are searching for a series of books?"

Eidolon thought for a moment, his fingers drumming a steady beat on the polished wooden desk. Finally, he spoke, his voice tinged with both hesitation and determination. "In a way, yes. We are searching for the beginning of the series, the source from which all others spawn. And as for the rest... they are safe." His eyes darted around the room as if wary of any potential eavesdroppers.

Before I could get in another question, Crichton barged into the room with a tray in hand. The scent of freshly brewed coffee and delectable sweets immediately enveloped us. He carefully set it down on the desk's edge and filled a cup for me, throwing in a generous amount of Irish Cream for good measure.

"I assumed you would like something to eat since your dinner was so rudely interrupted." His voice held a hint of irritation as his dark eyes narrowed in annoyance at Eidolon.

Eidolon opened his mouth to defend himself, but Crichton silenced him with a dismissive gesture.

"Thank you, Crichton," I said gratefully. He bowed in my direction with a small smile and left the room without another word.

As the door clicked shut behind him, I turned my attention to Eidolon, staring at him over the rim of my mug as I took a sip. "Where are the rest of the books?"

He frowned. "Safe," he sneered, refusing to look at me again.

His condescending attitude pushed me to my limit. They were the ones who had come to me for help, not the other way around. And now I was being treated like a nuisance?

With an exasperated sigh, I set my mug on the corner of the desk. Standing up, I stretched my shoulders. "Alrighty then," I stated, facing the door, "since you seem to have everything handled, there's no reason for me to stick around."

Eidolon's reply was sharp and coated with venom. "Sit down, Chloe. This isn't a game. The books are more than ink on paper. They are intertwined with real lives. One wrong move and the whole world as we know it implodes."

A sharp, incredulous laugh escaped my lips as I couldn't help but find the situation absurd. This was the definition of insanity. And I didn't want anything to do with it. Turning on my heel, I made my way towards the door.

Moll's intense gaze bore into Eidolon, who let out an exasperated sigh in return. "Chloe, please take a seat."

Eidolon's tone bordered on demanding, and I clenched my jaw in frustration. I pivoted to face him. With my arms folded across my chest, I raised an eyebrow expectantly. When he said nothing, I shifted my attention to Isabelle and Watson, who'd been surprisingly quiet.

"What's your part in all this?"

They studied each other before Watson answered. "The Book of the Veiled is protecting our families."

"Protecting your families?" I repeated, pushing my glasses up on my nose. "From what exactly?" I demanded, wanting a clear answer.

Isabelle's pleading eyes met mine. "From mortals, luv," she said, her voice trembling with emotion.

I took a moment to let her words sink in. Protecting their families from mortals could only mean one thing - they were not mortals themselves. The realization hit me like a ton of bricks, and my mind raced with questions.

"What exactly are you?" My voice betrayed both curiosity and a hint of fear as I instinctively pulled my arms tighter around myself.

Isabelle's voice rang out with pride as she gazed at Watson. "A seeress and a revenant," she declared, her eyes sparkling. "Or more commonly known as a witch and a vampire." Her eyes darted back to me, waiting for my response.

I erupted into a fit of laughter, struggling to contain myself. Surely, they couldn't seriously expect me to believe all of this. I chuckled as I wiped away the tears from my eyes.

A quick survey of the group's faces revealed they did not find the situation funny. My heart sank as I turned to face Eidolon, seeing the disapproving look in his eyes. Frustration and anger surged within me. Taking a deep breath, I lifted my chin and held his gaze defiantly.

"What the hell are you then?" I asked with a lot more courage than I felt.

Eidolon hesitated like he didn't want to tell me. "I'm the Librarian," he finally admitted.

I raised a skeptical brow, eyeing him with suspicion. "And pray tell, what does that mean?" I asked, my tone laced with doubt and curiosity.

Watson reached for the decanter of the smooth, amber liquid Crichton had left on the table and poured himself a drink. As he took a sip and settled back into his chair, he explained. "He has to safeguard the Book of the Veiled, ensuring our kind remains hidden from the mortals."

"Our kind?" My eyes widened in disbelief. "You mean like witches and vampires?" My gaze shifted to Isabelle, waiting for confirmation.

"Yes, and others like us. Living all over the world, hidden in plain sight. I'm sure you have met one or two in your lifetime," Isabelle answered with a knowing smile.

"Like the Tooth Fairy?" I asked, arching an eyebrow.

Watson let out a growl in a tone that startled me: menacing and dangerous, almost predatory. "Why is the first question always about the damn Tooth Fairy?" he sneered, darting an exasperated gaze at Eidolon, who shrugged. Looking back at me, he growled. "There is no such thing as a Tooth Fairy."

"She didn't mean anything, Watson; put your fangs away," Isabelle chided, patting his arm. "This is a lot for anyone, and you're not helping the situation. Eidolon, Moll—one of you should start at the beginning."

Eidolon leaned back in his seat, his dark eyes roaming over me from head to toe. It was as if we hadn't spent the entire morning together. His expression had changed, a subtle shift I couldn't quite decipher.

Was he purposely keeping me in the dark? Testing my commitment to aiding him and Moll? The air between us crackled with tension.

"Eidolon?" Moll prompted, waiting for him to say something.

"Fine," Eidolon grumbled, picking up a sizable leather book from his desk, opening it in the middle, and turning it towards me.

I leaned forward and saw a beautiful hand-drawn drawing of the entire world across two pages. An explosion of gold, silver, and blue leaped out at me. I watched in awe as ocean waves crashed against the shorelines and random boats fluttered through the picture. Across all the different countries, an erratic small burst of light would glimmer for half a second and then disappear.

"Two years ago, this book mysteriously appeared on my desk," Eidolon recounted. "The moment I touched it, the entire library of the Raven Society flooded through me." He struggled to find words to describe the overwhelming experience. "It was like being bombarded with a virtual collection of volumes, branded all over my body in an excruciating pain.

"The next thing I knew, Moll was waking me up. And that's when I learned about the two roles in the Raven Society—the Writer and the Librarian. One creates the story, while the other preserves it. My mother was a Librarian before she vanished." His words ended with a tinge of sadness as he gently traced his fingers over the book.

"If she was the Librarian, and then two years ago you became one, wouldn't it mean...." My words slipped out without much thought, and I immediately regretted it when I saw Eidolon's pained expression.

"We had the same thought, but there's a slight chance she could be hiding," Moll responded with a glimmer of optimism. "We're in unknown territory here. The lack of confirmation one way or another leaves room for a different outcome."

"So, what do I have to do with all of this?" I asked hesitantly, unsure if I wanted to know the answer.

"You're my replacement," Moll said, her eyes focused intently on me. "You're the new Writer."

Chapter 14

'A Raven Is The Best Mode Of Communication.' -Book of the Veiled Instructions.

Crichton walked back into the study and informed us that the others in the library were growing restless.

Thank the Fates for small miracles, I thought to myself. Doubts and questions raced through my mind, threatening to tip me over the edge of sanity. Moll's story seemed unbelievable, but there was a small part of me that couldn't ignore its possibility.

"I'm taking a smoke break before we confront the wolves," Watson declared as he stood tall, stretching his tense muscles.

His statement hit me like a ton of bricks. "Wait, Aelle is a wolf?" I couldn't believe it. But it all made sense - her aggression, her ferocity. Her ability to look at people like they were prey.

"No, silly, can you imagine if Aelle was a werewolf? No one would be safe." Isabelle couldn't resist a giggle as she joined Watson, and they both gave me a sly look. "The other two? That has yet to be determined." Their laughter echoed through the air as I stood in shock, watching them walk out onto the porch through the side door.

I glanced at Moll, then Eidolon, and back to Moll, feeling uncomfortable. A throbbing headache began to form, and I rubbed my temples in a futile attempt to alleviate the pain.

One Mississippi, two Mississippi... I started counting in my head.

Someone once told me to count to ten in a stressful situation, but it wasn't helping. What I needed to do was focus on something I could control. *What was in my control? Coffee!* Crichton had left a tray out, so I made use of it and made myself a cup.

At some point, I am going to have to switch to decaf. I chuckled nervously as I poured cream and added two sugar cubes into the cup.

"I don't have visions." I broke the awkward silence as I stirred the mixture, the spoon making a soft clinking sound against the ceramic mug.

Eidolon arched an eyebrow, his mask of cool detachment slipping away momentarily to reveal the man I had spent my morning with. "Don't you?" he asked, a hint of skepticism creeping into his tone.

"No, Eidolon. I don't," I remarked, looking up at him.

He eased into a more comfortable position, shifting his weight and intertwining his fingers behind his head. "You never dream? Never wake up with a new idea for a story?"

"Yes, but..." I started.

Eidolon interrupted with a wave of his hand. "No buts about it. The answer is yes or no."

Moll's eyes followed me as I sat back down next to her. "Predictions and visions don't always happen during the day. For some Writers, they come when they are dreaming. When their minds are free to roam without interruptions. My great-great-grandmother was only able to experience her visions at night. Perhaps you're the same way?"

"I thought this was more like a family business. You know? Born into the role," I countered.

"Usually," Moll admitted, her fingers nervously playing with the handle of her cane. "But there have been instances where Writers, or Librarians, are chosen in times of crisis. I assumed it would have been someone else, but the Fates decided differently. And who am I to argue with them?" Moll shrugged, appearing strangely happy it was me, not somebody else.

Did she know who her replacement was supposed to be? Or was I always the 'chosen' one? I was about to ask when Eidolon cut me off.

"The Fates have never been wrong. You were selected. You received the invitation. You are the next Writer." Eidolon's expression gave nothing away, but I could tell he was withholding information. Again.

"Wait. The Fates sent me the invitation?" I stared at him in disbelief. "Not you?"

With a slight shake of his head, Eidolon redirected his focus to Watson and Isabelle as they walked back towards us. Watson pointed to his watch, and Eidolon nodded, rising from his seat.

I guess the conversation is over, I thought to myself, disappointed. I wanted to know who sent me the invitation.

"Is everything alright?" Isabelle's concerned gaze bounced back and forth between the three of us, a slight frown creasing her forehead as she noticed the tension in the room. I reassured her with a quick nod before turning my attention to Eidolon.

I am not the girl you are looking for. I was on the verge of screaming, but as our gazes met, my voice caught in my throat. His radiant indigo eyes, flickers of silver swirling within them, seared into my heart and kindled a yearning inside me that I couldn't explain.

The intense gaze between us felt like time stopped. I was so caught up in the sensation I didn't realize Isabelle was watching the interaction. But Eidolon did, and his eyes flashed with annoyance before he stormed out of the door, leaving the rest of us to follow in his wake.

"Let the games begin!" I muttered to myself as I headed back to the library, hoping to tuck away my feelings for him in some far-off corner of my mind—a safe place where I wouldn't be tempted to search for it.

Ha! Like that was going to work.

Victor and Sydney were whispering fervently at one of the desks, their eyes locked in conversation. Across from them, Aelle was furiously scribbling something into a red journal. The trio immediately turned towards us as we entered the room.

"Delighted to have you join us at last." Sydney's brow furrowed in concern as his eyes darted towards me to ensure I was still in one piece. I waved and made my way to him.

"The way you all keep disappearing, some would think you are hiding secrets from the group." From her tone, I could tell Aelle was upset she hadn't been included in the impromptu meeting. I would have ignored it, but she was staring right at me like I was the one who didn't invite her. It took everything in me not to stick my tongue out at her, and instead, I shrugged my shoulders and glanced away.

Victor rolled his eyes, a sardonic glint in his eye as he turned to us with a broad smile. "We have some ideas we want to run by you guys," his deep voice rang out. He had been quiet since the Welcoming Committee, but now he came alive with purpose. His words hung in the air, filled with intrigue and excitement for what was to come.

He wasn't conventionally handsome, with a sharp, hawk-like nose, thick waves of hair that fell haphazardly around his face, and piercing baby-blue eyes that appeared to see right through you. Despite his unassuming appearance, there was an air of confidence and intelligence about him.

But I couldn't shake the sensation he belonged in a science lab, surrounded by beakers and documents, rather than in a library filled with dusty tomes and cups of coffee.

"Chloe's theory made me realize the clues could be found in the divergences of language. In other words, in the variations within myths. There are so many missing gray areas and voids in history that I think the Book of the Veiled is concealed inside the facts," Victor explained, looking at me with a knowing smile.

"Books," Eidolon interrupted.

Sydney's eyes narrowed in confusion as he looked at Eidolon. "Books? As in, more than one?" he asked, his tone laced with uncertainty and curiosity.

"Yes. Three," Eidolon said, his mind elsewhere as he stared intently at the scattered papers on his desk. His brow furrowed in concentration, his eyes scanning the documents.

"Just to clarify, three books are missing, not one. So, there is more than one book in the Book of the Veiled?" Victor asked.

Aelle nodded thoughtfully, her hand moving quickly as she scribbled in a worn red book. "Seems reasonable." Her brow creased. "I wondered how that amount of information could be contained in one book. Didn't seem likely."

"Think of it like a cheat sheet that answers all the questions about life and death, magick, and other unexplained phenomena," Moll explained, watching Aelle with interest.

"If it's a record of everything, wouldn't you have known the Book of the Veiled would be stolen?" Aelle looked up suddenly, her eyes narrowing at Moll in accusation.

"Yes and no," Moll shook her head. "Each book holds a distinct essence, molded by the events of its era. Only a Writer from that specific time can truly capture the visions they encounter. This is why writing styles differ between books, almost like each Writer has a unique language. ."Every Writer can see what was recorded, but only so much as the books let them. It's possible a previous Writer may have seen the day when the Book of the Veiled was stolen but not allowed to read it because it could interfere with another Writer's destiny," she concluded.

"That's deep," Sydney commented, crossing his eyes. "I can't even wrap my head around that. So, you're saying that the Book of the Veiled was destined to be stolen?"

"Maybe. It seems like all roads point to the possibility," Moll acknowledged, twirling with her cane.

After a moment of consideration, Victor spoke up confidently. "I believe I may know where one of the books is located," he declared, glancing at Eidolon. When Eidolon raised his eyebrows inquisitively, Victor launched into his theory.

"We've all heard the legend of Avalon, Merlin, and King Arthur countless times. But with each retelling, the story becomes more twisted and distorted. It's no surprise that there are gaps in its plot and many unknowns left unexplained," he exclaimed with a grin in my direction. "Like trying to count calories - you think you have it figured out, but there's always something missing or unaccounted for."

I couldn't believe what Victor was suggesting. "You're saying someone from Avalon stole the Book of the Veiled?" I asked, my eyes darting to Watson and Isabelle, exchanging a tense look behind Eidolon's back. Their expressions raised a red flag for me.

"Eidolon..." Watson said quietly.

"I know!" Eidolon whispered back.

"I am afraid it's not just anyone." Her eyes, wide and searching, darted to me with a hint of worry. "Taking the Book of the Veiled requires immense power to get through the library's formidable defenses." She shifted her gaze back to Watson, dark brows furrowing in consternation. "It seems like our plans may be thwarted, my dear."

Watson nodded grimly. "I hope it's not who I think it is."

I couldn't make sense of their conversation. Aelle and Victor seemed just as bewildered as I was. But not Sydney. He looked like it didn't surprise him at all.

Weird.

Just when I thought things couldn't get any stranger, a raven suddenly flew in through one of the library's open windows, carrying something in its sharp beak. I watched with amazement as it landed on the table where Eidolon stood and dropped an envelope.

The raven then flew to Moll's shoulder and lovingly nuzzled her face before turning to look at me. It observed me with a sense of detachment, tilting its head in curiosity.

Friend or foe?

Imposter or healer?

Worthy or worthless?

As we stood in tense silence, our eyes locked in unspoken understanding, I heard Eidolon's voice cut through the air like a sharp knife. "It's from Esme," he said urgently, his tone laced with concern. "She says the oak tree is glowing, and we should come immediately."

I didn't react.

My world was collapsing, the walls closing in as voices around me dissolved into a deafening silence. The room tilted and swayed, my vision blurring as dizziness overtook me. But amidst the chaos, there was one constant - the raven. Its dark feathers seemed to gleam with an otherworldly sheen, its beady eyes piercing through me with an intense gaze.

As I stumbled forward, reaching out for something to ground me, my hand grasped at thin air, a futile attempt to steady myself.

What the hell did Crichton put into that drink?

I tried calling out to Eidolon for help, but the words were lost in a storm of wind and fog.

Only the raven's eyes could see me.

Then, the world was completely dark.

Chapter 15

'Never Travel Alone.' -Book of the Veiled Instructions

With a slow, conscious effort, my eyes fluttered open, and I found myself standing atop a grassy hill. The panoramic view below was breathtaking, revealing a vast valley stretching as far as the eye could see. In the distance, a small village nestled in the gray landscape, damp from a recent rain storm.

What the hell? I thought as I looked around, feeling like I had been transported into a J.R. Tolkien novel. But seriously, where was I?

A surge of alarm rushed through me as I realized the gravity of the situation. I didn't know where I was. Or how to get ahold of anyone. My cell phone was still in my purse back at the Raven Society.

Don't panic, Chloe. This is just a dream. I tried to convince myself everything was fine, but I was lying. This was anything but fine.

Control the things that you can. I reminded myself as I turned around, hoping to spot any familiar landmarks that might help me orient myself.

Crap! Nothing looked familiar. Anger bloomed through me like an old friend, and I welcomed its familiar touch. Anger was so much easier to regulate than fear. Fear led to irrational decisions; given the already dire circumstances, I did not need to make them worse. With a heavy sigh, I mustered up my courage and began to make my way toward the town in the distance, hoping to find someone who could help me.

I hadn't been walking for long when a solution presented itself. A girl was coming towards me from the next hill, carrying a basket and singing to herself as she gazed into the sky. Her golden hair cascaded around her face, highlighting her bright yellowish-green eyes and sun-kissed skin. Her dress was in tatters and covered in dirt, and her hands and feet were caked with mud. Scratches marred her arms and face as if she had been rummaging through the woods.

"Hello," I called out in greeting as she approached, but she didn't respond.

"Excuse me!" I raised my voice and waved a hand in greeting. But still no reaction. She walked right by me without a second glance. My mouth dropped in surprise.

Well, that's rude. I thought as I watched her walk away. She was ignoring me, or she couldn't see me. Either way, it didn't make me feel any less foolish as I started following her. But what other choice did I have? Something inside me told me that she was why I was here.

Our journey took us down the rolling hill, following a well-trod path that led straight to the village. As we drew nearer, we squeezed through an opening in the tall wooden gate and were enveloped by the sights and sounds of life.

The marketplace hummed with movement, a chaotic scene of merchants shouting their wares and customers haggling for the best deal. The pungent aroma of freshly caught fish wafted through the air, mingling with less savory scents of spoiled food, animal waste, and aging honey. It was a sensory overload, overwhelming yet somehow intriguing in its own way.

I surveyed the village with a keen eye, my gaze lingering on the structures' details and the people's bustling activity. Everything seemed smaller: one-room homes with no windows, signs absent from the buildings, and gray smoke billowing from open doorways. Despite its size, the town exuded a sense of vibrancy and life, with street vendors selling their wares and children running along the narrow roads.

But the townspeople never met my gaze. I didn't exist to them. And that was unnerving. In my mind, I pictured the library of the Raven Society and sensed a connection between this world and my physical body, a wave of relief washing over me. I was still technically alive. But the idea of being in two separate places simultaneously was strange.

I hurried after the mysterious woman as she diverted into a dimly lit alley, struggling to keep my footing on the slick ground covered in mud and grime. My boots were caked in filth up to my ankles, making moving difficult. The scent of damp soil filled my nostrils, mingling with the stench of garbage and decay that lingered in the air. I couldn't help but hunch over, trying to shield myself from the dreary surroundings.

She turned once more, entering a small ransack of a home at the village's end. It was worn-looking, and holes dotted the sagging roof. Its foundation was rotted and ready to collapse. To the left, a wooden fence surrounded a wild and overgrown garden. It was clear that no one had tended to this place in years, allowing nature to reclaim what was once man-made.

To the right stood a dilapidated barn that detained a scrawny cow and an oversized sheep, their enormous brown eyes pleading for relief from their miserable state. Though I wanted to help them, I couldn't resist following the stranger into the murky depths of the house.

"Did you bring it?" a haggard, quavering voice called out from the back corner of the tiny house. I hesitantly stepped inside, my eyes struggling to adjust to the weakly lit space. Beams of sunlight filtered through small holes in the roof, casting intermittent patches of light around the room. The mysterious woman placed her basket on a low table and unpacked its contents.

"I said, did you bring it, girl?" the voice rasped again.

"You know I did," the woman whispered.

"What?" asked the now agitated and sharp, cut through the dimness like a knife. I strained my eyes to see who was being so rude, but the lack of light obscured any features from my view. I couldn't help but feel a sense of unease as I tried to make out the shape in the darkness.

"You know I did," the woman spun around and yelled. "Unless you can get your broken and half-dead body out of bed, you can be quiet and let me finish in peace!"

A deep, guttural sigh filled the room, laced with frustration and anger. The sound of someone shifting in the bed followed, their movements accompanied by rustling blankets.

Anxiously, I inched closer to the table, my curiosity overpowering any sense of fear. The woman's hands moved deftly over the arranged herbs and flowers, muttering under her breath as she gently caressed each cluster. The aroma of rosemary and lavender mingled in the air. Every item had its own place as if it were part of a sacred ritual. Intrigued, I held my breath and continued to monitor the mysterious woman and her intricate preparations.

A small black cast iron pot stood at the end of the room on a worn hearth, simmering over a smoldering fire. The rich, earthy fragrance of herbs and spices wafted through the air, mingling with the warmth from the hearth. I observed with fascination as the woman plucked and chopped each bundle of herbs, murmuring a chant before adding it to the bubbling pot.

What was she doing?

With a gentle hand, she placed the final ingredients into the pot and stirred them with precise movements. The steam rose in wispy tendrils and filled the room. She lifted the pot off the fire and decanted some of its contents into a small bowl. My eyes were drawn with fascination as she approached the bed, pausing just before reaching it.

"And will you uphold your end of the bargain?" she asked, her tone laced with worry. I stepped closer in case the shadowy figure decided to attack.

"Yes," the voice rasped again.

"You will ensure I will never be hungry, cold, or lonely again. You promise that all my dreams will come true?" the woman demanded.

"Yes. All your aspirations will come to pass. Now give me the drink!" the voice yelled.

As she passed the bowl to the mysterious figure in bed, I inched nearer, desperate to see their identity. The person was on death's doorstep, yet somehow, they were still clinging to life.

The powerful magic radiated from whatever lay before me, urging my body to reach out and touch it. As my vision adjusted to the dimness of the back room, I could make out the figure more distinctly. Shock and dismay overwhelmed me, and I stumbled backward, rushing towards the door with my hand covering my mouth. I bumped into a nearby table and winced as my shin collided with a small stool and made my escape.

I didn't reach the barn before my stomach revolted, and I heaved. It took some time before I regained my composure, wiping my mouth with my sleeve and gasping for air. That's when I heard the voice once more, stronger now.

"She is here," it said.

That's not good, I thought as my world grew dark again.

Chapter 16

'Survival Of A Writers First Journey Is Never Guaranteed.' -Book of the Veiled Instructions

I woke up to the weight of a small but hefty dog on my chest and tiny licks against my cheek. Peering through one eye, I saw two gleaming golden orbs staring back at me and heard the friendly sound of Beacon's exuberant barks.

How did I end up here?

Gradually, the memories resurfaced. The scents, sights, and sounds of my vision came rushing back to me: the pungent odor, the vibrant colors, and the harsh tone of a demanding voice. My body reacted instinctively, and I jumped up from my seat and sprinted to the bathroom, where I emptied what was left in my stomach.

After several minutes, I lifted my head from the toilet and leaned against the side of the bathtub to regain my composure. Standing up proved difficult, but I forced myself to reach for the sink faucet and splash some cold water on my face.

After a forty-minute hell-fire shower, I bundled up in a robe and staggered to the kitchen to make fresh coffee and evaluate my life choices.

Obviously, I made some questionable decisions. Starting with finding that damn note on my door three days ago.

"I need a smoke break," I told Beacon, who had been by my side since I woke up. I made my way to the porch, hoping the fresh air would let me gather my thoughts now that I had a warm cup of coffee.

"You know those things can kill you?" a voice called out from the bay window chair.

I screamed, whirling around and throwing my mug at the sound. I grabbed the closest object within reach, which happened to be a copy of *The Art of War*. Holding it in my hands, I couldn't help but laugh at the irony and prepared to defend myself.

"I come in peace." Eidolon stood up, raising his hands in surrender. "Let's put the book down before something else gets thrown at me." A slight grin appeared on his lips, and I thought about throwing it anyway.

Beacon lay sprawled under the dining room table, his tail thumping against the hardwood floor. His eyes were bright and wide as he took in the sights of the show.

Traitor, I thought to myself as I stared down the intruder. What was Eidolon doing standing in the middle of my living room? I didn't remember coming home last night, and I sure in hell didn't recall inviting him in.

"How did you get into my apartment?" I struggled to stay on my feet, holding tightly onto the book. Eidolon moved closer, his smile so gentle that it brought tears to my eyes. It had been a rough couple of days, and everything was hitting me all at once.

Eidolon moved across the room with lightning speed and embraced me, his strong arms supporting my weight. I pressed my face against his shirt, feeling the soothing motion of his hands on my back as he held me close.

"Shhhh, it's okay. First-timers always cry. It's perfectly natural."

It was a while before my sobs subsided. *Deep breaths, Chloe. Deep breaths.*

I attempted to focus on anything other than the rhythmic movement of Eidolon's chest against mine. But I couldn't help but feel the size and strength of his hands as they pressed into my back or the heat of his breath brushing the nape of my neck.

It wasn't working.

Until I remembered that I hadn't wiped away the last of my mascara when I got out of the shower, I was pretty sure I looked like an exhausted raccoon with smudged eyes and a disheveled mop of hair on top of my head.

AND... I was only wearing a robe with nothing underneath.

"This can't be happening." My tears shifted to laughter, and I buried my head back into his chest.

Eidolon's muscles tensed with worry as he leaned in close to me, his breath warm against my ear. "It's going to be okay," he whispered, his voice laced with deep concern. I could feel the heat of his body radiating towards me, a comforting and reassuring presence amidst the chaos.

Despite knowing it would take time to move on from the last few days, having the man of my dreams wrap his arms around me made the past seventy-two hours more tolerable.

I murmured, "Eidolon."

"Yes, Chloe?"

"I need coffee."

He chuckled, a smirk forming as he gazed down at me. "You did toss your cup at me."

"Well, you startled me."

"And then you threatened to clobber me with a book."

I shrugged at that point; he was the one who broke into my home and scared the shit out of me. He should have called before coming over if a misguided coffee cup and the threat of being beaten with a paperback frightened him.

"Eidolon?" I asked softly.

His eyes skimmed over my face as he answered. A look in his eyes I couldn't place but sent shivers down my spine. "Yes, Chloe?"

"I would like to put clothes on now."

Eidolon leaped back, and I quickly grabbed the edge of the robe around my chest before it flew away with him. Taking a hand to his untamed black hair, he turned toward the kitchen, telling me that he would clean up the mess and prepare another pot of coffee. He seemed flustered, which surprised me, and I smiled as I strolled to my room and closed the door.

As I hurried to pull my clothes on, I realized it didn't bother me that he'd seen me like this. Being wrapped in his arms felt comforting, surrounding me in a safe world with his shadows. But that was crazy.

Wasn't it?

After changing into jeans and my favorite sweatshirt, I stepped out of my room, better prepared to face the day. Even though my hair was still piled on top of my head in a wet mess of unruly curls, I'd washed my face and applied some light makeup.

I may have just taken a wild ride through time, humiliated myself in front of an attractive man, and thrown coffee all over my apartment, but it didn't mean I couldn't look a little put together.

I found Eidolon sitting at the kitchen table with two cups before him, a stack of pens, a notebook, and a leather-bound book I had never seen before. He motioned for me to take a seat, and I plopped down next to him.

"What is all this?"

"Homework," Eidolon smirked. "Since you traveled, it's likely your hands are itchy. This will help!"

Looking down at my hands, I realized they were itchy, and I had been rubbing them together for a while. Shaking them out, I reached over, picked up one of the cups of coffee, and held it up to my nose. As I inhaled deeply, the lingering stench of decay and filth from the previous night dissipated.

"What is this?" I reached for the leather-bound book and brought it closer to me, feeling a strong urge to write my truths on its pages. It was as if the book awaited me, and my fingertips tingled with anticipation.

"It's your copy of the Book of the Veiled. It's what you will record your travels in."

My eyes glazed over, and Eidolon yanked the volume away. Looking up, I blinked in surprise at his sudden movement. Like a heavyweight crashing down upon my chest, a wave of disappointment and anger washed over me as if he snatched away my closest confidant without warning.

What the hell? I couldn't explain my anger, but I was ready to defend that book with my life. Taking a sip of coffee, I tried to calm myself down and regain control of my emotions.

"You never did tell me how you ended up in my apartment," I asked again. "What happened last night?"

Eidolon looked at me for a long time, trying to figure out how to tell me. He finally sighed and stated, "There is a stare a Writer gets when they are about to jump. Their eyes grow dim and white; their body stiffens, and then they are mentally gone."

I watched Eidolon rub his eyes, trying to clear his head of the memory and wait while he gathered his thoughts.

"Moll was the first to notice what was happening, and she alerted me. With Isabelle and Watson's assistance, we got you upstairs as Moll created a diversion to distract everyone else. Then all hell broke loose."

"That was quick," Watson commented as they laid Chloe on the bed. "Doesn't a Writer need training and guidance before the curse takes hold?"

"It's not a curse," Eidolon muttered, his eyes never leaving the face of the woman lying in a deep trance.

"That wasn't what he meant," Isabelle reassured him. "But it does seem strange. Not even seventy-two hours, and she's already traveling?"

Eidolon's face twisted in anguish as he ran his hands through his hair, regretting how things turned out. There wasn't enough time to prepare Chloe. Moll hadn't even had an opportunity to explain what it meant to travel.

What if she was stuck, lost in the timeline? What if she encountered something she couldn't handle? What if she couldn't find a way back? Guilt rushed through him as he thought about everything that could go wrong.

For the next two hours, the trio engaged in heated debates over whether or not Chloe could survive her first jump without any training. The odds were not in her favor, and every passing minute only added to their anxiety.

Chloe's sudden scream surprised everyone, followed by her becoming violently ill all over Eidolon's shoes. Isabelle rushed to clean up the mess, but Chloe sat up shakily, her face drained of color and covered in sweat.

Chloe's voice was raspy as she spoke, and she seemed to be searching for something, her eyes shining with intensity. "They're still alive," she said, fear evident in her tone.

"Luv, who's alive?" Isabelle narrowed her eyes.

"I'm so sorry, I didn't know," Chloe apologized as she gazed at Isabelle, her eyes glassed over. Isabelle struggled against the unsettling feeling that overcame her, but resisting was difficult. "We made a deal. I didn't realize it. I'm so sorry."

Watson's voice trembled, "Who is still alive?" He took a step back as the eerie eyes turned to him.

Eidolon swore as Chloe slumped back into bed, falling back asleep.

"I guess we will be getting that answer later," Watson sighed, his hand pulling through his golden hair.

Isabelle contemplated the sleeping form, wiping away the sweat-soaked hair from her face. "I think you should take her home. She should be somewhere comfortable when she wakes up," she directed towards Eidolon.

"Shouldn't you or Moll take her? Wouldn't it be better if a woman was with her when she woke up?"

"No," Isabelle replied firmly. "It needs to be you. Moll has her own things to deal with right now, and you are linked to her for whatever reason."

Isabelle's gaze rested on her friend, her heart heavy at what Chloe would soon face. No one had ever told Chloe about the long line of 'chosen' Writers who came before her. As a Writer, she had the incredible ability to journey through time and explore the past, the future, and even mythical realms.

But most of her predecessors were driven mad by the visions or failed to reappear after their first jump. If Chloe made it through the night, she was one step closer than the last six who were unsuccessful in the selection process.

When Chloe was selected for the position, Isabelle didn't think she'd make a friend in the process. It had been ages since she had a real friend, and she prayed this one wouldn't end up dead.

I stared into the distance, thinking about everything I had just been told about my out-of-body experience from their perspective.

"Still doesn't explain how you got into my apartment," I stated, trying to make light of the situation. Surviving was a stroke of luck, and it was easy to see why some people went mad. My mind felt like mush. Like it had been bombarded with too much information and didn't have enough space to process it all at once.

"*That's* what you're worried about?" Eidolon asked, placing his coffee cup on the table and looking at me in awe. "How did I get into your apartment? It's not that you traveled back in time. Or that someone or something took over your body? Your burning question is how did I get into your apartment?"

My hands were fidgeting again, the tingling urge to move them, to write, growing stronger.

"No," I said thoughtfully, raising an eyebrow at Eidolon and glancing at the items before me. "But you being in my apartment, making coffee, and bringing me a gift comes across as a bit stalkerish."

Eidolon laughed; his eyes filled with delight. "You left your door unlocked." He gestured to the door. "You really should work on your security system if you ask me."

I did have the habit of forgetting to lock the doors behind me. Apart from my books, I didn't have much to steal. And what thief would take those?

"Thank you," I said, wanting him to know I appreciate everything he had done for me. "Thank you for bringing me home, breaking in, scaring me shitless, then making coffee after I threw a cup at you."

"You're welcome," he replied with just a touch of arrogance. "Now, are you ready to work, or do you need another smoke break?"

Chapter 17

'Expanding Your Horizons Makes Room For More Knowledge.'
-Book of the Veiled Instructions

Four hours later, I threw up my hands in defeat and stomped outside for a much-needed smoke break.

Who did he think he was? I knew what he was- he was bossy, overbearing, overly sensitive, and annoying. Taking a long drag, I exhaled my smoke above my head, hoping he'd disappear like the fume. I needed breathing room, time, and distance to process what happened to me.

Eidolon had to leave!

But no, I thought while punching the air, *he wouldn't leave.* As I paced back and forth, I couldn't help but think about all the little jabs and insults he'd thrown my way. 'You can't say that.' 'Why are you so slow?' 'Do you even remember what happened?'

I sneered as I peered through the sliding glass door at Eidolon, who was just as frustrated. Taking out his cell phone, he typed furiously at whoever texted him before shoving it back into his pocket.

Running a hand through his tussled hair, he headed to the kitchen for something to eat. I'd set out stuff for peanut butter and jelly sandwiches, which was all I had. Grocery shopping was not something that I liked to do, so I rarely had real food in the house.

I took another drag, and my anger began to subside. I knew Eidolon was trying to help, but I needed to do this my way. It wasn't like I'd never written anything before; I was a published author, for Pete's sake.

How difficult could it be to write an entry in the Book of the Veiled? According to Eidolon- impossible. I stubbed out my cigarette on the ashtray and made my way back inside just as Eidolon emerged from the kitchen. He glanced at me with a wary expression, his lips forming a half-smile that didn't quite reach his eyes.

"This is not working." He gestured towards the chaotic kitchen table, its surface cluttered with a jumble of half-written pieces of paper, scattered shards of broken pencils, and Post-It notes laid out in a timeline of events.

"You think?" I rolled my eyes. "You know that I can write, right? That I pay my bills by putting words on a piece of paper in a coherent manner that pleases the reader?"

"I do." He shrugged like he didn't believe me. I crossed my arms over my chest and waited.

"What?" He crossed his arms defiantly, bracing himself with a wide stance as if ready for a fight. The tension in the air was palpable as we stood, facing each other like two warriors prepared to engage in battle.

"I am waiting for the apology you desperately want to find the words for." My voice dripped with anger and frustration as I stepped closer, each word punctuating my approach.

He huffed in response and narrowed his gaze at me. "I know you are a writer, but I am sure your editor has a field day with your book. It probably takes four pages to describe how the wind blows across a meadow on a summer's day." Eidolon started stalking towards me, shadows playing darkly behind his eyes.

"Maybe. But does it matter how long the edits take, as long as the finished product is worth the wait?" I snapped back.

"The whole thing matters to me because I have to carry the weight around, for fuck's sake!" Eidolon exploded. "Your words don't just affect you or the book; I am part of the equation, too."

"What the hell are you talking about?" I asked hotly, trying to understand why he meant that he was also part of the equation.

Eidolon went as still as a statue, his eyes dark and his mouth pressed into a firm frown. I noticed a flicker of movement under his skin as if swirling pools of ink were forming and vanishing beneath the surface. I cautiously approached him, unaware that Eidolon was holding his breath.

"Do they hurt?" I reached out to touch his neck, trying to figure out what was crawling around. Despite having plenty of tattoos, mine had never moved before. *Cool.*

"Not always." I watched him with questioning eyes before he continued. "They do tend to become heavy and uncomfortable," he finally admitted.

"What are they?" I held up his hands as the black spots began to form into something I couldn't put my finger on. Like ancient text forming into hazy pictures. Maybe hieroglyphics? Clinging onto his hand, I was fascinated as the blob followed my touch as if we were playing a game of catch.

"Words," he answered with a grimace. I darted a glance up at him, wondering if I'd done anything to hurt him. Eidolon took back his hand and stepped back from me as he rubbed the area I'd been touching. "From the books."

Surprised, I widened my eyes, "The books are inside you?"

"Now they are. Further protection was needed, so here we are," he revealed reluctantly.

"Why? How? When?" I paused after each word, attempting to figure out what to say. "How have you hidden this from everyone? Does Moll know?"

"No! And for her safety, she won't. No one can." He gripped my shoulders and locked his intense gaze with mine. "Swear to me," he commanded.

"I swear," I whispered with a swallow. "But why are you telling me?"

"I didn't tell you." He arched an eyebrow, holding me captive between his grasp and eyes. "They told you. Before you ask, no, I don't know why."

"Is this why you needed me to shorten the story? Because you are carrying the weight of it?" I bit back the urge to yell at him. This was crazy; how could anyone hold that much inside them? And there I was, acting like a spoiled princess. I peered down at the floor in shame, but his hand pushed my head back to meet his gaze.

"Yes and no. I wanted you to hurry so we could get some sleep, and I also knew it would be uncomfortable when you finally decided what to write," he admitted honestly.

"I don't want to hurt you."

"Chloe, you can't physically hurt me. But the thought of you being in a time and place where I couldn't reach you *was* agonizing," he confessed with a strange look, like he didn't want to admit it.

My breath caught in my throat. When was the last time someone showed genuine concern for me? It felt like years ago, maybe even longer. Sure, my family cared about me, but I learned long ago that caring for someone meant putting them in danger.

"It would've been helpful if you started with that tidbit of information. I'll keep it simple," I promised, waving away his worry—no need to open a can of worms that would end in disaster.

We stood in a silent standoff, our eyes locked. Eidolon's gaze drifted downwards, and a flicker of relief played across his face as he met my gaze again.

"Everyone is gathering at 4 o'clock. Get some rest, and I'll see you there," he said, removing his hand from my chin. I nearly lost my balance as he walked past me, grabbed his jacket, and made his way towards the door.

As he reached for the doorknob, he looked back and reassured me, "I can manage a few more books. You focus on what you need to do." He walked out, leaving me staring at the space he'd just occupied.

After he left, the room felt empty and chilly, and I wrapped my arms around myself for warmth. I retreated to the couch and slumped down, feeling as rejected as a teenager not invited to a prom. But what shook me was the emptiness that consumed me once he was gone. I was just as entranced by him as I was by the mysterious Book of the Veiled.

The Book of the Veiled!

I bolted upright and glanced at the dining room table. I rushed towards it, a compelling urge to write washing over me.

I gingerly picked up the book, cradling it in my arms, and made my way over to my desk. I admired the beautiful texture of the book. A delicate red thread was intricately woven through the worn and weathered leather. An imprint of a raven perched on a thorn bush was highlighted with golden flakes. The rich black and green hues popped against the aged exterior, giving off lavender, coffee, and earth scents.

As I held it, tiny gold letters at the bottom formed: *Written by Chloe.*

As I realized I was now the author of this story, a tingle of the adventurer's spirit reverberated through my body. The adventure was mine!

And so, I began.

Three blocks away, Eidolon stopped in his tracks. Something stirred inside him as if his body was expanding to create more space for something coming.

He smiled as he imagined Chloe writing at her desk, chained to pens, post-it notes, and coffee. She was as ready for this as he was, and with that comforting thought, he continued home.

There may be hope after all.

By the time 6 p.m. rolled around, Eidolon and I had long given up on trying to be positive. The Raven Society library was a chaotic war room with conflicting ideas, everyone's voices clashing and overlapping in a frenzy of confusion and anger as they debated our next move.

Victor had become increasingly persistent in his insistence on the whereabouts of the hidden books and the next steps we needed to take. While Aelle scribbled in her tiny red notebook, she frequently interjected with irrelevant historical tidbits, which hindered Victor's thought process.

With the fierce determination of a general preparing for battle, Sydney stood before a whiteboard covered in scattered notes and diagrams. His eyes darted back and forth as he strategized a sneak attack on libraries, his mind racing with tactical maneuvers and potential obstacles.

Sitting next to Eidolon, I observed the unfolding events. His calm facade couldn't hide his tension, and I couldn't help but wonder what was causing it - the energy in the room or something else entirely.

It could have been because I arrived late and encountered a disgruntled Eidolon at the back door. He interrogated me as if I were a teenager breaking curfew, demanding to know where I had been and why I was late. In reality, I'd dozed off, indulging in a steamy dream about the tyrant sitting next to me, and slept through my alarm.

But I didn't want to share that news with him, so I told him Beacon needed a walk, and I lost track of time. His look told me he didn't believe me.

Eidolon's voice cut through the silence, his eyes flicking towards me. "You need to tell me where you are," he mumbled, running a hand through his hair.

I stared at him in disbelief, my mouth dropping. "How does that work? I have to text you every time I leave my apartment. Can I call you if I need to do some grocery shopping? Join me on my early morning runs. I know! You can move into the spare room, and we'll become besties."

"Don't tempt me, Chloe," he replied with an evil grin.

A shiver ran through my body as I imagined what it would be like to live with Eidolon. The thought of him being in my apartment, walking out of my bathroom with just a towel on...

I stopped drifting further into my daydream when I saw Watson smiling knowingly.

Rude!

"It's not like I could call you, but..." I held up my cell phone, rolling my eyes.

"No phone number," Eidolon finished the sentence. Grabbing my phone, he punched in his number and handed it back to me.

"No excuse now," he said with finality. "Call me when you are going to be late."

I had every intention of continuing the argument, but something in his expression told me he wasn't up for it. Shrugging, I turned my attention to the unfolding drama. "I see that we are making progress...." I motioned to the room, cringing when I heard Watson slam down his drink and stood nose to nose with Aelle, arguing over something.

"You can say that." Eidolon nodded towards the center of the room where Sydney was waving us over.

"Get over here, Chloe," he shouted. Despite Victor and Aelle's disapproving reactions, he was set on taking the book back by force. "I know you'll stick with me! Talk some sense into these two."

I got up to walk over when Eidolon grabbed my hand, and a tingle of electricity flowed between us. I gazed up in surprise to see if Eidolon had felt it, too. From the look on his face, he had, but he didn't seem too keen on the idea.

"You don't have to have such an evil eye," I snapped, snatching my hand away. "It's not like I'm about to bite you."

As he looked up at me, I was speechless. The shadows vanished, revealing his pure indigo eyes filled with tired resignation. "We'll talk later." He frowned, and a shadow fell back over him like a closing curtain.

Curious and Curiousier, I thought as I walked away.

Chapter 18

'Remembering Where You Are Is The Only Way Back.' -Book of the Veiled Instructions

As Moll entered the library, I couldn't help but notice how much she had aged in just one day. The lines on her face were deep and etched with a sense of weariness and determination. Once bright and lively, her eyes now held a depth of sadness that weighed heavily on her soul. Without a word, Eidolon pulled out a chair for her beside mine.

"Do you need me to get you anything, Moll?" Eidolon asked kindly, pushing up the sleeves of his black sweater. I hadn't seen Crichton, and I wondered where he was. It was strange that he wasn't hovering in Moll's shadow.

Before I could ask, my eyes fell upon the intricate tattoos adorning Eidolon's arms. They looked like trees were growing from books, and I couldn't tear my eyes away from the fantastic detail of the art. The books gave life to the trees, with their energy radiating outwards and into the foliage that crawled up his biceps.

"Just some tea with a splash of whiskey." Winking, Moll leaned conspiratorially toward me and whispered, "Crichton isn't too happy with me right now. I sent Emma to recover something for me, and he's reluctant to let her out of his sight."

"Why did you ask Emma?" I asked, puzzled. No disrespect to Emma, but she was a bit older and hadn't seemed like the 'adventurer' type. And why would Crichton be upset?

She shrugged and twirled her cane as she answered, "She has the nose of a bloodhound. If something needs to be found, she'll find it." She glanced around the room as she spoke.

We were nestled into the corner of the library that I had come to think of as my own. Three comfortable couches ringed the classic coffee table placed near the fireplace. A Persian rug, its colors mirroring a stormy ocean, spread across the floor, while Tiffany lamps cast their multi-hued glow over the shining oak. Isabelle and Watson sat next to me, and we set to work.

"What's the plan now?" Sydney asked the group. "I vote for flying in, cornering the thief, and stealing the books from under their nose," his eyes lit up with anticipation as he imagined taking on some anonymous adversary.

"If you mean travel by air, then yes, you are correct," Moll said with a smile. "The five of you - Chloe, Eidolon, Isabelle, Watson, and yourself - will be on the 6:00 a.m. flight to Edinburgh and make your way to Peebles. I have arranged for someone to meet you at the airport and escort you into town. Esme will be waiting for you at the hotel."

Aelle and Victor exchanged a glance of dejection as they shifted in their chairs. "You two will remain with me. We still have tasks that require your particular skill set," she assured them.

Aelle's face lit up at the idea, and she smiled at me, far from friendly. I responded with a sweet grin and a thumbs-up, which only made her more irritated. I couldn't help but giggle as she turned away, giving me a scowl in return.

"Why Peebles, Scotland?" I asked, glancing at Moll.

"It's the most logical place to start," Aelle rolled her eyes. "When it comes to Arthurian history, there are a few different claims about where it originated—some say Scotland, some France, and others Marlborough College. But I discovered something promising involving Peebles' local historical society that might prove interesting."

"What did you find?" Eidolon asked.

"They think they found Merlin's grave." Aelle's lips curved into a slight smile as she batted her eyes and ran her fingers through her hair. She was obviously flirting with Eidolon, and my fists clenched in irritation. I wanted nothing more than to wipe that silly grin off her face. "All the evidence I've collected suggests this is the right place to begin our search."

Eidolon leaned forward, propping himself up on his elbows, a grin spreading across his face as he asked, "What did you find out?"

It took all my self-control not to snarl at their interaction, hoping no one had noticed. But when I glanced at Watson, he smirked, his nose flaring.

Oh! Crap. Could he smell my attraction to Eidolon? Embarrassment crept up my cheeks and neck, and I inwardly groaned. Watson's gaze moved over to Eidolon, and a soft growl escaped his lips.

"Historically speaking, I think Aelle is on the right track," Victor interjected, and I gratefully turned my attention to him. "'When Tweed and Pausayl meet at Merlin's grave, England and Scotland shall one monarch have,' Victor quoted. "In 1603, when King James replaced Queen Elizabeth I on the throne, it's said that the River Tweed flooded into the Powell River. Many believe this proves Merlin was in Scotland as late as the 1600s.

"As the old story goes, Merlin was buried beneath a thorn bush near the Tweed River in Drumelzier. Allegedly, he had gone mad while looking for his twin sister in Tweeddale."

My shock was palpable as I blurted out, "He had a twin?"

"Yes, he had a twin. At least, that is what some books claim," Aelle said, arching an eyebrow at me like I should have known. "But she died at the Battle of Arferydd in 573."

"No," Victor corrected. "She was killed in 577 at the Battle of Arderyth."

"Who was she?" interrupted Eidolon, putting an end to the heated discussion about battles and timelines that was brewing. I sighed in relief; Aelle tended to get carried away in arguments like these if no one stopped her.

"That is one of the first inconsistencies," Victor shrugged. "No one is sure—maybe Gwendydd, Morrigan, or Languroreth. The point is that the man the myth of Merlin is built on, regardless of who he was, had a twin sister who died in battle. Merlin was determined to find a way to bring his sister back from the dead. Based on my understanding of the Book of the Veiled, he would need the knowledge contained within those books to succeed. If Peebles is his final resting place, we'll uncover the next piece of the puzzle there."

Sydney furrowed his brow, scanning the group's faces for answers. "I mean, he was buried in Scotland, right? How is it possible that he's still alive?"

Moll twirled her cane in her hand again, looking out into the distance. "The Book of the Veiled holds secrets that can open the bridge between this life and the next. While he goes by Merlin today, that isn't who he used to be," Moll explained. "That is why you are heading to Scotland. You will have the opportunity to collaborate with an esteemed Merlin mythology specialist who just so happens to live in Peebles."

We all stared at her in surprise. I hadn't known that the Book of the Veiled was a portal to the afterlife. Cool. But kind of dangerous.

"That is what I have been doing- remembering," she said wearily, flashing a grin in my direction. "I have a strong inclination that our quest leads us to a man known as Taliesin. He's a recurring figure throughout history, from the 6th century until today. I suspect that the tales and legends are what keep him alive."

"So, Taliesin is the real Merlin?" I asked slowly. Moll nodded her head, and I let out a breath. "Heavy."

"That almost makes sense," Sydney rubbed his face with his hands. "If the gods can stay alive by people remembering them, why couldn't a mythical magickian?"

Sydney made a valid argument. Merlin was a popular individual in entertainment. Plus, it was common knowledge that all witches and warlocks possessed some of Merlin's power within them.

But something was not right.

I believed Moll, but as I listened to the chatter, my mind drifted back to the scene from the night before. Was that Taliesin lying in bed? Was it he who demanded the potion? To come back from his grave.

My mind was running away, and I was lost in my thoughts. The edges of my vision started to blur as if I were watching a plot from the Twilight Show. I struggled to stay calm, but the odor of decay filled my nostrils, and a terrible taste overwhelmed my mouth. Vague images flickered before me as the room grew colder.

I was back on the hill, looking down at the small town below. It felt like an invisible force was pulling me towards that house, my body moving without my control. Suddenly, I was back in the shack.

The raspy voice of the undead pierced through my chest like a jagged knife, demanding that the cure be brought to them. Its gender was impossible to discern, but its putrid breath reeked of sugary raspberries and sickly-sweet vanilla. I was overwhelmed as I watched in horror as a cup was placed on the bedside table. The familiarity of the aroma sent shivers down my spine.

Fighting back a surge of fear, I inched closer to the source, only to freeze in terror as an angelic voice began singing:

But the child sees deep in the Earth.
Two Dragons are spreading their wings.
Two tribes will fight for to claim this land,
Many die, for the folly of Kings....

Who was singing? What about the two dragons? And who died for the folly of the Kings? My mind struggled to make sense of what my eyes were showing me. With significant effort, I forced my gaze back to the bed. *Who was this figure?* I couldn't even confirm if it was human. My curiosity piqued, and I cautiously approached the bed, hoping for some answers.

Only a few steps away, I heard Eidolon's voice calling to me from just outside the house. I spun around and bumped my leg against the table. I held my breath as the creature stirred at the sound, its breath quickening as it searched for the source of the commotion.

Shit! I do NOT want this thing to know I am here; I thought as I shuffled around the table and headed for the opening.

Chloe? Eidolon's voice called again as I pushed aside the oiled cloth hanging from the doorway and glanced around. Where the hell was he?

"Eidolon!" My voice rang out, causing the nearby chickens and sheep to startle. It was clear that I wasn't hidden if the animals sensed my presence. The ailing cow groaned angrily towards me, and I turned to apologize before Eidolon's voice caught me off guard once more.

Chloe, it is time to come back.

I whipped around, panic beginning to set in. I could hear him, but I couldn't find him anywhere.

As I ran towards the hill, I collided with a merchant carrying a handbasket of apples, and we both yelped in surprise. As far as she knew, I wasn't there, but I could see her. Her horrified shriek filled the air as her basket clattered to the ground, fruit spilling out and rolling down the road.

A surge of fear tightened around my throat. Was I becoming real if I could make contact with people? I pushed myself to run faster to the town gate, driven by the terror of being left behind, the chain of my soul losing its hold on me. Time was running out; I was about to be stuck in this period.

Chloe, remember where you are.

I stopped at the foot of the steep incline, bending over, struggling to catch my breath. He wanted me to remember where I was. That didn't make sense. I needed him to give me straightforward instructions for what to do next. I didn't have the luxury of deciphering riddles at the moment.

Remember where you are.

Maybe he meant remembering where my body was. I was sitting in the library at the Raven Society. Eidolon was beside me. That was how I got back? Remembering.

I shut my eyes and let the memories flood in. In my mind's eye, I saw him standing beside me in the library, surrounded by the scent of smoke and cedar. And then I pictured his hands wrapped around me in my living room. The shock of electricity that surged through me when our hands touched was burned into my memory...

Chapter 19

'No One Is Who They Seem to Be.' -Book of the Veiled Instructions

And then I was back in the library. As he leaned closer to my ear, the slight touch of Eidolon's breath on my neck sent shivers down my spine. "You saw something?" he whispered.

I forced a tight nod, suppressing the urge to hyperventilate. I knew I needed to get the hang of this traveling thing soon. As I glanced back at him, I mustered up my most convincing smile and tried to communicate that I was fine.

I wasn't okay, though. I was almost left behind in a vision. What if I got stuck? I didn't even have a coat on, and I was fairly sure my Converse shoes wouldn't have lasted long tramping through mud and muck.

"We will talk later," he promised, his thumb caressing my shoulder as he stood back up. Gods, his touch was a comfort and a distraction at the same time. I turned my attention back to the group, hoping no one had witnessed my near-death experience.

"Why are the books so important to him now?" Sydney frowned, crossing his arms. "After all this time, why would he need to steal them?"

"I'm not sure," Moll replied, shaking her head. "I assume that he needs help, and the books can guide him to where he can find it."

"Are we sure it's Taliesin we are looking for?" I hesitated to ask, but a nagging pull in my stomach told me I should. An unspoken tug within me guided me towards something still unknown.

"Of course not, luv," Isabelle said, looking at me with questioning eyes. "But for the time being, all roads point to him. Taliesin was powerful, and we know he wanted to bring his sister back. Why do you ask?"

"No reason," I mumbled, shrugging my shoulders and looking away. There was no need to bring up the vision that had just flashed before my eyes, especially not in front of Aelle. Her intense stare already felt like daggers aimed at me, as if I had taken something that rightfully belonged to her.

"Do you know what else he would need besides books?" Victor asked.

Watson responded with a tight grin, shifting his eyes to Isabelle. He explained that according to folklore, Merlin always needed more magick. "I assume that it means others like him."

"Where the hell are we going to find mythical creatures?" Victor asked. "Last time I checked, they only existed in fairy tales."

I held my breath, waiting to hear what Isabelle and Watson would say next. Were they willing to tell the rest of the group their secrets? I cast a quick glance at Aelle, still unsure if I could trust her. The way she was staring at them only heightened my suspicion. It seemed like she was searching for something, as if they held a mystery that she was determined to solve.

"Well, Bibbidi-Bobbidi-Boo," Watson said with a smirk after a pause. "All your wishes come true today!"

Aelle and Victor were visibly stunned, and I couldn't help but find their reaction amusing. It made me wonder what my face looked like when I first heard the news.

"And before you ask," Watson added before they questioned him further. "No! The Tooth Fairy does not exist."

"Well, thank the gods for small miracles," Victor muttered. "She always scared the living shit out of me. Imagine! A dragonfly-sized woman flying around with a bag full of teeth." He trembled at the thought, and Sydney laughed. "You're a witch, aren't you?" Victor asked, looking at Isabelle with a newfound appreciation, and she nodded in agreement. "Like dancing in the moonlight witch,' or 'I will turn you into a frog with a look' witch?"

"That is for me to know and you to find out. But I will warn you, I've been known to travel with someone who bites," she said sweetly.

Watson grinned at Victor, displaying his teeth, which weren't quite what the movies had depicted vampire teeth as being. However, I had to admit that Watson did appear paler, and his lips were an odd shade of red.

Perhaps the filmmakers weren't entirely off the mark?

"Let's not get too hung up on the unimportant details right now." Eidolon's hand rested reassuringly on my shoulder, momentarily distracting me. I blushed and quickly refocused on his words. "We'll have plenty of time to question Isabelle and Watson about all the misconceptions and realities of mythical creatures later. I think we should all head home and get some rest."

We all shared a silent nod of understanding; my exhaustion mirrored in each of their faces. As we stood up to depart, Eidolon leaned in close and said, "Follow me."

He led me through the winding corridors of the house until we arrived at the kitchen. The room was warm and inviting, with a massive butcher block island taking center stage. I leaned against it, gazing up at him as he turned to face me, his features bathed in soft light from the windows. The aroma of freshly baked bread and simmering soup filled the air, making my stomach growl with hunger.

"Is everything okay?" I feigned innocence, though I knew we'd agreed to discuss my vision. But now that I was alone with Eidolon, my tongue had a mind of its own. As he leaned against the kitchen sink, his arms crossed and his full attention on me, my toes curled in response.

"I have the same question. You seemed distracted there- like your thoughts are moving in a thousand different directions," he asked, arching an eyebrow.

"Nope, I'm good to go!" I lied. I didn't want to tell him I doubted that Taliesin was the person we sought. Something wasn't making sense. There was more to the puzzle than I had been told.

"You sure?" he asked again, taking a small step towards me, the blackness of his eyes swirling like smoke. "What *did* you see in your vision? Was someone there? Did they say anything to you?" The questions came barreling out, with a seductive undertone but questions, nevertheless.

As the room heated, each step he took brought us closer together. I struggled to resist the urge to run towards him, but it became increasingly difficult. My body was giving in to my desires and moved towards him without my consent. I could feel the anticipation building in my fingertips, eager for what might happen between us.

"Chloe, what are you feeling?" Eidolon asked, his eyes bored into mine.

"Excuse me, Eidolon. I hate to interrupt," Crichton called from the kitchen doorway, looking guilty. "Moll is asking if you would please meet her in the library for a few minutes."

The moment was gone, and the weight of what I was about to do sank in. He wanted me to share my vision, not make a move on him. I sighed in frustration and stepped back, trying to hide any signs of turmoil in my mind.

Eidolon's eyes sharpened as he glanced at Crichton like he was about to dismiss him but thought better of it. He turned back to me, standing rigidly and emotionlessly, his gaze giving away nothing. "I guess I must have been wrong," he said, the darkness growing across his face. "I'll see you tomorrow morning, Chloe."

He turned and trailed behind Crichton as they returned to the library, leaving me to my thoughts in the now desolate room. As I walked home that night, I wallowed in self-pity and pondered how I would survive traveling with him for the next couple of weeks without making a complete ass of myself.

Chapter 20

'Time Is Nothing But A Number.' -Book of the Veiled Instructions

Dragging myself through the security checkpoint the following day, all I had on my mind was a decent cup of coffee.

Who the hell takes the 6 a.m. flight? I thought as I pulled my bag further up on my shoulder. I spent the entire night going through my closet, realizing that I didn't own any suitable clothes for traveling and trying to come up with what I would say to Eidolon. Hopefully, on our six-and-a-half-hour flight, he would answer some of my questions—and, if I were brave enough, I would answer his too.

As I got closer to our assigned gate, I worked to maintain a leisurely gait, wanting to look like I was a world-roving wanderer, though I hadn't been abroad in over six years. Honestly, I wouldn't say I liked flying. Not only were the planes noisy and filled with people, but I also didn't know if I should start a conversation with the stranger sitting beside me.

The last time I flew, I was seated between two siblings who were not getting along in the dreaded middle seat. One sister continuously made snide remarks as she shifted restlessly in her seat, while the other intentionally went to the restroom every thirty minutes. Stuck between them, I had to constantly stand up to let her pass, unable to lose myself in my book and escape the tension.

I was too polite to say anything, but every time a flight attendant walked by, I tried to flag her down with my eyes. I hoped she could sense my frustration and offer me a new seat. But no such luck.

Five hours later, I escaped with minor bruising and a migraine.

When I arrived at Gate Twenty-Three, Eidolon was already settled in his seat with headphones on and his bags occupying the chairs beside him. His eyes were closed as if he was trying to steal a few more minutes of sleep. Despite his relaxed attire - sweat pants, a plain shirt, and a backward baseball cap - he still managed to look effortlessly attractive.

I brought my mug of coffee to my lips before wiping my mouth as I realized I missed the hole in the lid. Coffee went everywhere, and I watched in dismay as it slid down my brand-new sweatshirt.

Perfect. What an excellent beginning to my journey.

Feeling self-conscious about my lack of swagger, I sat in one of the chairs behind Eidolon and spent my time people-watching. The flight was a popular choice for newlyweds and those celebrating an anniversary. Couples in love were everywhere I looked.

Rude.

I slid further down my seat and opened the novel I picked up at the bookstore last week. I prayed that the newest Sarah J. Maas release would keep my mind off Eidolon and the Book of the Veiled.

Almost forty minutes later, as I was rooting for Rowan and Celaena to realize they were meant to be together, they announced it was time to board. I closed my book and joined the queue for Group C. I searched the area for Eidolon and spotted him engaged in a spirited discussion with Sydney, oblivious to my presence.

I was torn between joining them or standing back when a whirlwind of activity blew across the terminal, and my two new friends appeared before me.

"Moll told me that we are sitting together." Isabelle slipped her arm through mine. "We'll have so much fun gossiping and reading trashy magazines."

Watson grinned mischievously. "I made sure to bring plenty of drinks for our entire trip," he boasted. He pointed to where Eidolon and Sydney stood, chatting animatedly by the window. "Looks like they're getting along," he commented. "Maybe Eidolon can convince Sydney not to storm Buckingham Palace." Watson chuckled and shook his head in amusement.

I put on a facade of a smile, but beneath the forced politeness, I couldn't hide my disappointment. "Maybe," I shrugged. "His loss. I can't think of anyone better to sit next to for six and a half hours in shitty seats!" I tried to sound enthusiastic as we walked down the hallway and boarded the plane.

I tried to pay attention to Isabelle's childhood stories and fashion tips for the first two hours of the flight, but my mind kept wondering why Eidolon was acting so coldly. He quickly nodded to everyone on the plane, but his gaze skipped over me. Had I failed by not spilling my secrets to him in the kitchen? Did he feel slighted by my silence?

"You'll have permanent wrinkles if you keep scowling like that," Isabelle joked when I'd been staring over the top of the seats and at the back of his head for a while. "Wouldn't it be better if you told us what's going on? Talking might help."

I rolled my eyes to the plane's roof, "It's dumb. I thought Eidolon and I had a moment a couple of times, but I must have imagined it." I peeked over at Isabelle and frowned, feeling foolish.

"The connection is there," Watson offered, putting down his book and taking out an air pod. "I can't say whether it's sexual or not, but I can smell a bond between you."

"You can what?" My eyes widened in horror. What the hell did a connection even smell like?

Watson stopped to think about how best to explain his point. "Every person has a unique scent; when two people connect, their scents blend. Think of it this way- you have two candles, one apple, and one cinnamon. Both are strong on their own, right?" he asked, and I nodded. "But when mixed, they create a new fragrance. The individual aromas haven't been weakened, but now it only takes one to enjoy them both."

"How poetic." Isabelle teased, taking a sip of her drinking.

Watson grinned and gave her a playful wink before he plugged his earbuds back in and returned to his book. Isabelle's cheeks flushed pink.

Ahhhhhh! I thought. *There is something between them.*

"She wishes," Watson muttered into his book, not looking up. I glanced at him in surprise, realizing he heard me somehow.

"Are you some kind of psychic?" I joked halfheartedly, afraid that he was about to confirm what I'd suspected.

Watson sighed, not looking up from his page. "Yes, we are, and yes, we can. You must learn to control your thoughts so they're not broadcasted for everyone to hear."

"You *can* read my mind?" I felt my cheeks heat in embarrassment. I was sure I'd had a ton of inappropriate thoughts while they were around, more than I could count.

"After the first naughty thought about Eidolon, I shut you out. But it doesn't help with the heightened sense of smell," Watson laughed, glancing at me, winking. "But I appreciated that you thought I looked like a Greek god."

I blushed as I remembered my initial thoughts about them. "In my defense, I thought she resembled a fairy," I countered, nodding at Isabelle, who was grinning ear from ear.

"You were close. Just wrong about her award-winning personality. She's a nuisance if you ask me."

A slight frown spread across Isabelle's face as she playfully hit Watson on the shoulder, "Stop talking and get back to reading. You're embarrassing her." She came to my defense. "It takes some getting used to, but you learn how to manage the bond."

"Does Eidolon know? Could he hear my thoughts, too?" I asked as I lowered myself further into my tiny seat, praying I could escape this nightmare somehow.

Neither of them responded, which spoke volumes. Eidolon knew! The humiliation nearly brought me to tears.

No wonder he ignored me this morning.

"Give him some time. Men are always dim-witted; it takes ages for them to see what is standing in front of them," Isabelle reassured me.

"Maybe," I said weakly as I fought to control the tears threatening to fall.

"No, really! When Watson and I first met, it was a mess," Isabelle chuckled. "It took us years to figure out how to work together."

"But you both are so relaxed together." While embarrassment was still flooding through me, I sat up in my seat. I'd been questioning their relationship and would finally get the whole story.

"Took almost a hundred years," Watson confirmed, still not looking up from his book. "I found her cocky, untrainable, obsessed with her appearance."

"I forgot that we were talking about you." Isabelle rolled her eyes. "But he's right; it took us nearly a hundred years to find a good place. Mostly because of our families."

"You have families? I thought vampires were solitary creatures. How does that work? A witch and a vampire, I mean." I stumbled over my words, hoping I wasn't putting a foot in my mouth.

"I promise you I don't sparkle, and Isabelle doesn't need the eye of wort for her cauldron spells. Stop watching those awful television shows," Watson grumbled.

"As someone who doesn't want people to recognize what you are, I am impressed that you care so much about misconceptions," I shot back.

"It's always been a sore spot for me," Watson agreed, taking a drink from his flask. "But, yes, I have a family. They're not always pleasant, and it's been years since I have spoken to them- but they belong to us."

"Us?" I asked, needing more details. "Like to the Raven Society?"

Keeping his gaze fixed on the book, Watson shook his head, "No, not to the Raven Society. Isabelle is my wife."

Now, my mind was racing a million miles an hour! Were they married? Like married, married?

Isabelle squeezed his leg and corrected him, "Technically, I am his mate. He is my husband."

"What's the difference?" I asked, confused.

"Packs have mates. Clans have spouses," Isabelle explained. "Vampires live in packs like werewolves, naguals, or demons. Witches live in clans like fairies, merpeople, or banshees. It is rare to find two different species mating with each other, though there are a few. But not too many are willing to take on the challenges."

"How does that work? Aren't vampires immortal?" I questioned, thinking of the stories I'd devoured and the movies I watched in guilty pleasure.

"Gods, I hope not! Or this world would be filled with them!" Isabelle burst into laughter, prompting the other passengers to glance our way. Her smile widened as she waved to them before they all returned to their conversations. When they were no longer paying attention, her eyes focused on me.

"Nosey humans!" She nodded in their direction. "But, no, vampires just age differently- slower."

"How?" My eyes widened in surprise.

Watson blinked, bringing himself back into the conversation. He gently slid a bookmark between the pages of his book and closed it with precision. Sitting up straight, he began to speak with the same level of attention as an academic discussing the origins of life.

"Tell me how long people lived in the Christian Bible."

"I don't know," I hesitated. "I think it was a long time, though," I confessed, unsure where this conversation was taking us.

"Mahalalel was 895 years old, Enos was 905, Seth survived to see 912, and he was the son of Adam and Eve. Living for hundreds of years is not unheard of- just forgotten."

"Are you saying that the people in the Bible were vampires?" I asked, astonished. "How old *are* you?"

"No," he chuckled. "They weren't vampires; they simply had a long lifespan. It's impolite to ask someone their age, but I have been on this earth for quite some time. Isabelle isn't far behind, though," Watson teased, tugging playfully on her braid.

"How?" I asked Isabelle. She needed to share her secrets with me- she didn't look a day over thirty.

"Witches can extend their lifespans if they choose," Isabelle explained. "There needs to be a reason or an extreme need for it to be worthwhile, but it has been known to happen."

Watson poked Isabelle, "Go ahead and share what your need is..." his eyebrows lifted high into his hairline.

Isabelle gave him a look of contempt and rolled her eyes. "I possess healing abilities, and by some fortunate or unfortunate twist of fate, I have the power to heal. I don't know how it works." She shrugged. "And just to clarify, it has nothing to do with magic spells or charms - I've just lived a long life."

"And..." Watson prodded Isabelle.

With a wry grin, she continued. "I can also control the effect of emotions, which is helpful for aging. Without the pressure of stress or fear, I can slow down the aging process."

"We are stuck together for at least another 700 years, by my calculations," Watson declared, pretending to count on his fingers. "That's like forever!"

"And it will still not be enough, my luv." Isabelle leaned over and kissed him on the nose.

Chuckling, Watson reopened his book and resumed reading, yet I heard him murmur, "It won't be nearly enough, sweetheart, even with 700 plus another 700."

Isabelle stifled a giggle before returning her focus to the movie playing on the headrest in front of her. Watson moved closer and laid his hand on hers, entwining their fingers in an inseparable embrace.

The conversation was over, which was fine; I needed to process this latest information anyway. Leaning back against the seat, I stared out the window.

Would I ever find that kind of love? The kind where 700 years plus 700 years were not enough?

Chapter 21

'Walking Will Brush The Cobwebs Of Travel Away.' -Book of the Veiled Instructions

As Moll promised, a car awaited us in the parking garage- a large SUV with three rows. Being the shortest person, I crammed myself into the back with all the baggage, which was fine, as I was still mortified by what I learned on the plane.

I spent the duration of the flight attempting to create an invisible barrier in my mind to block out the never-ending barrage of thoughts that kept resurfacing.

It went as well as trying to teach a turtle to ride a bike.

It was a quick forty-five-minute drive to the hotel in Peebles, and my embarrassment over Eidolon diminished while I took in the breathtaking Scottish landscape.

As I sat staring out the window, I played with a spring of white heather, which a kind old man handed me at the baggage claim. He told me it was a good luck charm to help me in the coming days. I wasn't sure what he was talking about, but I was willing to take any assistance I could get, even if it was from a stranger.

Before I could express my gratitude, he vanished into the bustling crowd. Something about him seemed oddly familiar, but I couldn't put my finger on it. His eyes held a resemblance to someone I knew, but who? Watson quickly took over as our impromptu tour guide, and I pushed all thoughts of the mysterious man out of my mind.

"I devoted my formative years traveling through this part of the country," Watson told us as we headed down the motorway. "The history of the Tweed Valley is fascinating. In the twelfth century, the River Tweed became the boundary between England and Scotland. One of my favorite places is Neidpath Castle." Watson's eyes glazed over with nostalgia. "I spent many wonderful days on the grounds, running around with my cousins, fighting off invaders from the southern borders."

My thoughts whirled, thinking about the wars he must have seen and the battles he'd faced. How many leaders, countries, and dictators had risen and vanished during his lifetime? He and Isabelle had lived through it all.

Watson continued his story, a twinkle in his eye. "The castle was built in 1190 by Sir Gilbert Fraser, who passed it down to his descendants until 1306. One notable descendant was Sir Simon Fraser, known for his bravery as a soldier during the Scottish Wars of Independence.

"Despite being outnumbered three to one by the English, his army emerged victorious. In recognition of his bravery and loyalty, Robert the Bruce granted him the honor of bearing three crowns on his family crest, representing the three times he had saved the king's life."

"If the Fraser family was such an influential part of Scottish history, why is the castle in ruins?" I asked, peering out the window, hoping to see the castle.

"Ahhhhh, great question. As with any intriguing story that seems too good to be true, Fraser's streak of luck ran out in 1306. Simon's fate was sealed when the English took him prisoner. He was deemed a traitor and sentenced to death. His execution was brutal and inhumane: Simon was hung, cut down while still alive, disemboweled, beheaded, his limbs removed, and his head put on a spike on London Bridge right next to William Wallace's. The final insult came when the English burned Neidpath Castle to the ground."

Running a hand through his hair, Watson glanced over in the direction where the castle had once stood. "It never returned to its former glory," he finished sadly.

"That was a disturbing story," Sydney shouldered.

"No, what is disturbing is what happened next. In the late seventeenth century, Neidpath Castle belonged to Sir William Douglas, who had three daughters. The youngest, Jean, had fallen in love with the Laird of Tushielaw, but her family disapproved of him as a suitable match. Despite the Laird's pleas, Douglas stood firm and refused to give his daughter's hand in marriage.

"Jean remained hopeful, convinced that Douglas would never leave her behind. However, as months passed without any sign of his return. The poor girl wasted away as she sat by the window watching the road."

"He never came back?" I asked.

"He did, but by that time, Jean was so emaciated and weak he didn't recognize her and rode right past the castle. Jean died soon after from a broken heart. Rumor has it that a figure of a woman wearing a long dress still walks the castle lands, waiting for the Laird to return," Watson turned in his seat to look at me. "Sir Walter Scott wrote his famous ballad after the tale, *The Maid of Neidpath*."

Such a sad story, I thought. The love between Watson and Isabelle was the type found in fairytales, but there were also tales like this one. A woman who loved a man so deeply that she was willing to wait for him to return her affections, even beyond her death.

Was I capable of loving anyone that much?

I thought about the ghost of Neidpath Castle until we reached our destination. A kind woman with a bright smile was waiting to greet us on the hotel's steps.

"Thank you, Mac, for picking them up!" she called out, waving to the driver as he dropped us off. "Come in and get warm! I have tea or coffee, whichever suits your fancy." She turned to usher everyone inside and joked, "Rain jackets are in the front lobby on the coat rack; you will need them while you're here; the land knows when a newcomer has arrived and always shows out with the rain." We followed her up the steps. She pivoted before opening the door, and we stopped short.

"Moll called and demanded you all receive the royal treatment, which means I've put fancy soap in your room." She laughed with a sound that could bring a smile to the devil. "For this week, I am the owner, caretaker, housekeeper, and chef. My husband is so sorry he can't be here to greet you. I've set out dinner in the kitchen so you can enjoy it whenever you're ready."

"Thank you!" Smiling, I asked, "Not to be rude, but who are you?"

"Oh my gosh, of course! I'm Esme. You must be Chloe?" Her sparkling eyes were filled with warmth and genuine friendship. The gentle lilt of her Scottish accent wrapped around me like a comforting embrace, calming my nervousness.

I smiled at her enthusiasm. "Yup!"

"Deary, you look exhausted. I'll show you and Isabelle your rooms. The boys can bring in the luggage," she said with a smile as she grabbed our arms and guided us through the front door.

Watson let out a groan as he surveyed the pile. Isabelle had packed as if she were moving in, and Watson was guilty of the same. Between the two of them, they brought six bulky suitcases and three small carry-ons.

On the other hand, I had only packed a duffle bag, hoping this trip wouldn't drag on. I had a manuscript deadline looming in two weeks and couldn't afford to be away for too long.

"We're thrilled you've arrived! Imagine searching for a long-lost book in our humble village," Esme gushed. "Moll said it might change history!

"Now Maxwell will be here tomorrow to take you on the Magus Trail and to give you a brief account of Taliesin's life. Not that you all need it," Esme giggled. "Just tell him to keep quiet if he gets too excited. That boy will talk the paint off the ceiling if you let him." Esme turned to the left at the top of the stairs and opened the first door, ushering us inside.

It was a spacious room with an enormous walnut four-poster bed dripping with thick draperies of subtle blues and greens. A heavy cherry wood desk was pushed against one of the walls, and a stone fireplace was tucked into the other. I was thrilled to find a massive bathroom with a clawfoot bathtub and gold fixtures suited for relaxing.

But the marshmallow fluff to the peanut butter sandwich was the immense picture-framed window overlooking the mesmerizing Scottish landscape.

It was perfect, and I pivoted to Esme to tell her.

"It's my favorite room, and the view is exceptional," she agreed with a blush before turning to Isabelle. "Your room across the hall has a bathtub for two." She winked with a sassy smile.

Isabelle smiled gratefully. "You have always made Watson and I feel welcomed here like it's our home away from home."

Esme's cheeks turned pink with delight, and we all started towards the hall when the muffled noise of the boys coming up the stairs reached us. Eidolon and Watson seemed to struggle with the heaviness of Isabelle's bags while Sydney carried five suitcases effortlessly.

As Sydney climbed the last step, a wide grin spread across his face when he saw Esme. I couldn't help but notice he had been livelier since we arrived in Scotland. It was as if this place was where he belonged.

Esme scanned him over; her expression was both curious and conspiratorial. A knowing smile danced on her lips.

"You look like a real Scotsman!" Esme exclaimed as she placed her arm through his and led him towards his room. "Once you're all settled in, we will have to introduce you to a wonderful young lady." She continued as they walked.

"Poor guy. He'll be engaged by the end of the week." Watson shook his head with a hint of feigned disappointment. Looking at his partner, he said in a seductive tone, "Shall we retire? I could use a bath." Isabelle let out a girlish giggle as they disappeared into their room, closing the door behind them.

Don't bother us until morning; I heard him calling through the bond.

So, it works both ways. Interesting. I chuckled a bit before realizing Eidolon stood beside me, and my smile faded.

We remained frozen in place, Eidolon's eyes never leaving mine. Glancing downward, I noticed black words scrawled across his arms, moving around like they wanted to tell me something. Eidolon coughed quietly, and I shifted my gaze back up at him.

Now, this is awkward!

"A shower sounds perfect right about now. Thanks for bringing up my stuff." I snatched my bags and fled into my room before doing something embarrassing.

Gods, his eyes were beautiful. With a sigh, I tossed my duffle bag onto the bed and rummaged through it until I found my hygiene kit, trying to distract myself.

A knocking at the door scared the gray right into my hair.

Oh shit! Did I say that aloud or in my head? I tried to compose myself before reaching for the door handle. "Can I help you?" I asked with the same disinterested tone he had been using towards me all morning.

Two could play this game.

"Want to walk off the jet lag with me later?" Eidolon asked pleasantly.

"A walk?" I gawked at him in surprise. "You want to go on a walk with me?"

"I was thinking after your shower, we could. There's a coffee shop up the road with the best pastries." He pointed toward the town center. "It might help," he shrugged.

"Oh." My heart skipped a beat, and I just stared. *Good call, Chloe. Keep him intrigued with your extensive vocabulary. That's the way to win him over.*

"I was considering inviting Sydney as well," he said, glancing towards Sydney's room. "That is if he isn't already occupied." He chuckled, turning back to look at me.

And there it was! My heart dropped a notch. Of course, it was just a friendly invitation. Why would he want to spend time alone with me after all the mental daydreams I threw down the connection pipeline? It was damn near soft porn.

I forced a smile onto my face despite feeling a wave of embarrassment wash over me. "Sure. Sounds good. Give me thirty minutes, and I will be ready," I answered before he could say anything else, closing the door.

You are really winning cool points today! I leaned against the doorframe and took off my glasses, rubbing my eyes. My head was starting to ache from the lack of caffeine, and I was beyond exhausted.

Another knock. *Now what? Do we need to invite Esme also?* Sighing, I opened the door, peering through the narrow crack. "Yes?"

"Or just us," he said with a slight grin. "We'll be working together, so we should get to know one another."

"Working together?" I arched an eyebrow at him. Eidolon nodded. Okay, so we are 'working together.' Duly noted. "Yeah, that's fine. See you in thirty minutes." I was shutting the door when Eidolon placed his hand against it.

"I would like to get to know you better," he said, a smirk playing across his outrageously kissable lips.

My breath hitched, and I cleared my throat, trying to sound calm. "Okay, but can you wait until I close the door before starting the timer?" I laughed, hoping he couldn't see the blush creeping up my cheeks.

He nodded and headed to his room. I rushed to grab my things and walked into the bathroom for a scorching shower. As the water heated, I caught a glimpse of myself in the mirror. The reflection made me frown. My smudged glasses hid dark circles under my eyes; my hair was unruly and overdue for a cut, and faint lines around my mouth appeared overnight.

I looked like an exhausted middle-aged woman in desperate need of a makeover.

Chloe? I caught wind of the distant voice before I managed to step into the tub. I paused mid-step, wondering if Eidolon had snuck into my room.

Yes, I answered cautiously as my hand hovered over the door handle, realizing he was talking to me through our connection.

In less than 72 hours, you have vomited on me, tried to take me out with a coffee mug, thought about punching me, and disappeared without a trace. I wouldn't have asked if I didn't want to be around you.

Really? The way he was putting it, I wouldn't want to be around me either.

Really.

You would think differently if you knew what I called you when you insulted my writing style.

I heard. He laughed. I grimaced.

Eidolon?

Yea?

The thirty minutes don't start until you get out of my head.

I overheard him laughing through the wall.

Chapter 22

'There Must Always Be Two.' -Book of the Veiled Instructions

N aturally, I was running behind schedule. It was hard enough getting ready under normal circumstances, but factor in the effects of jet lag and a lost hairbrush - it all became a chaotic mess. To top it off, I was meeting my dream guy for coffee, adding even more pressure and setting the stage for disaster.

When I walked down the stairs 45 minutes later, I was barely coherent but managed to put on some presentable clothes.

Eidolon stood beside the roaring fireplace, his rugged features highlighted by the flickering flames. He wore a pair of fitted jeans, a black hooded sweatshirt hugging his broad chest, and a backward ball cap, enhancing the casual charm of his overall presence. Despite his relaxed attire, he exuded an undeniable air of danger and allure.

I stopped mid-step and stared. The bond stirred, and a tingling sensation sparked in my fingertips. He must have sensed it, too, because he turned to look at me, his gaze guarded but friendly.

"Ready?" I asked, my nerves fluttering like a trapped bird in my chest. I fidgeted with my hands, unsure of where to place them. In my pockets? Folded behind me? Remembering that I left my purse at home, I settled for stuffing them into the warm confines of my sweatshirt pocket.

"Coffee awaits!" He smiled, gesturing towards the exit.

We stepped onto the street, grabbing the raincoats Esme left for us on the way out. It was a quiet neighborhood, and we strolled down the road together. He mentioned that he bumped into Sydney on his way down. He'd been invited to Esme's house for a family gathering. She insisted he join them for dinner and wouldn't let him go to his room until he agreed.

"Poor guy." I laughed. "Maybe Watson was right. We'll be celebrating an engagement before heading home."

"I think he was looking forward to it." Eidolon shrugged with a smirk. "He likes large gatherings and noise."

"And you don't?" I glanced at him as he opened the door for me at the coffee house. The cozy room was packed with small tables, each adorned with a crisp white cloth and a flickering candle. The rich aroma of freshly brewed coffee wafted through the air, mingling with the mouth-watering scents of whatever the talented cook had whipped up in the kitchen.

The hostess led to a secluded table in the corner, surrounded by vibrant paintings of the lush Highlands and framed photos of the cafe's beloved soccer team. Every inch of the space was filled with warmth and character, making it impossible not to feel at home in this charming little cafe.

"Not really. I don't fit in. I would rather be at the Raven Society with my books and work," he admitted, pulling the chair out for me and then walking around to his seat.

"Don't you get lonely?" I scanned the menu, trying to distract myself from the growing awareness of his presence next to me. Despite my best efforts, I couldn't help but notice how close his leg was to mine, sending a tingling sensation through my body.

"Do you?" he retorted, his eyebrows raised.

As I reached for my water, my hand hesitated mid-air as I saw the waitress approaching. Her fiery red curls bounced with each step, and her sparkling emerald eyes danced with laughter. Her skin had a moonlit glow, smooth and flawless like a precious gem. And there was no denying her slim figure, highlighted by the form-fitting uniform she wore. She was a bombshell, and I couldn't help but appreciate her beauty.

Gods, I hated her.

As she listed the daily specials, her eyes remained fixed on Eidolon, emphasizing the cherry-topped ice cream sundae for dessert tonight.

Gag me.

"What can I get you?" she asked seductively, her gaze roaming over Eidolon's physique as if it were hers to claim.

"Two coffees, please. One with cream and sugar for my date. Black for me." He winked in my direction as my head shot up.

Date?

The waitress glanced at me for the first time, clearly unhappy about being forced to acknowledge my presence.

"Oh, and we will share a slice of your chocolate cake. Just one fork needed," Eidolon said casually. The poor woman looked me up and down again and returned to the counter with a slight frown and confusion.

"You didn't need to do that," I chastised. "It doesn't bother me. Once, I stood in line for twenty minutes *in front* of the grocery checkout attendant. He never knew I was there until some cute college student got in line behind me. You should've seen the look on his face when he turned around, and I was nose to nose with him," I shared, laughing at the memory. "I'm used to not being seen."

"I see you," Eidolon shrugged as another waitress set the coffee before us. The original one was obviously unwilling to return since Eidolon brushed her off for me.

A tiny bit insulting, but who am I to judge? The thought brought a slight sense of satisfaction.

I was at a loss for words, so I took a sip, hoping to steer the conversation in a different direction.

Dear gods, the coffee was delicious. Thick with heavy cream and enough sugar to take the bite away. I happily took another sip and wondered if I could order another one now.

"So, tell me about yourself." Eidolon placed his mug on the table and reclined in his chair, his muscles rippling beneath his toned arms as he crossed them over his chest. The flickering candlelight cast shadows across his chiseled features, highlighting the intensity in his gaze as he surveyed me.

"Nothing to tell," I said, shrugging my shoulders. "I write. I spent the last three years trying to become a runner, and then I realized it was a horrible hobby, so I quit. I read. I drink too much coffee and never finish an art project I start."

"Are you close to your family?"

"Yup, we have dinner every other week."

"Do you have hobbies?" he pressed.

"Not really. I've tried a lot of different things, but none can be considered hobbies."

"Do you have a boyfriend?"

The question caught me off guard, and I almost spit out my drink. It was a bit too personal for comfort. But then again, I was dying to know if he was in a relationship.

"Do you have a girlfriend?" I countered.

"I haven't found somebody willing to put up with me yet," he said, arching an eyebrow.

"No. I had a couple longer relationships in the past, but it's become harder to find someone compatible as I get older." I felt the need to justify my statement, but admitting that I enjoyed being alone was uncomfortable. It was familiar and uncomplicated. "Why do you ask?"

"I'm curious to know if anyone else is vying for your attention," he said, glancing at a photo.

"Kinda personal, don't you think?" I looked up as the waitress placed a slice of rich chocolate cake in front of me and handed me a fork. I thanked her and then turned my attention back to Eidolon, trying to keep my composure.

Eidolon shrugged, "Because Moll thinks you are my mate."

"Excuse me?" I spat out along with some of the cake I'd just taken a bite of.

"Moll thinks you are my mate," he repeated slowly.

"I caught that part," I said, putting down the fork. "Why?"

Eidolon reached over, picked it up, and took a bite. Surprised, he glanced at me, "Now that is an excellent cake!" He took one more taste before setting it down and leaned back in his chair. "Librarians and Writers work together, as you know. However, they rarely have a bond that manifests as quickly as ours." He glanced up and waved at the waitress for another coffee before continuing.

"A solid foundation is essential for a successful relationship, which is why family connections are usually involved. In our case, you assumed the role. Moll believes that when the books were stolen, someone determined that a new line of Writers and Librarians was needed. It's not unheard of, but it hasn't happened in decades."

"Who decided?" I asked, confused. "And what do you mean by a new line?"

"I don't know. Maybe the gods? Perhaps the Fates?" He waved his hand as if encompassing the world in his words. "Moll's line dies with me. She thinks this is how the book chose to keep it in the family."

"So, you are telling me," I said carefully after a few minutes of staring at him. "That a book decided your family needed a new line to take over the family business. And for some mythical reason, I was the lucky candidate?" My anger was beginning to boil to an unnatural level. This was not what I expected, and a tad more than I could take in after the last few days.

Was this what our connection was all about? Building another dynasty of Writers and Librarians?

Not on my watch.

We could make a good match and co-exist comfortably. Wasn't that what every woman wanted? Why is she mad? I heard him think to himself.

I guess he forgot to build that wall around his mind as well.

"Comfortably?" I sneered. "You think I'm willing to settle for *comfortable*? Because you, Moll, and some unknown deity decided I'm the most suitable candidate to carry on the family tradition, I would jump on board all willy-nilly?"

"That is not what I meant, Chloe." He held his hands before him as if to ward off an attack.

"Thank you for the coffee," I said, getting up from the table and throwing my napkin down. "I think our *date* is over. Don't worry about walking me back." I turned and stormed out, leaving Eidolon alone.

As I walked out the door and down the street, the strange attachment between us was tugging as if it wanted me to return.

Fuck that.

I was not interested in a relationship or friendship with anyone who saw me as a means to an end. I had no idea where I was heading; I just knew I needed to walk to clear my head of the man I started to become attached to.

After spending a couple of hours aimlessly wandering around the hotel grounds, jet lag hit me hard. I trudged up the stairs to my room, resisting the urge to collapse onto the inviting four-poster bed. Instead,

I pulled out my copy of the Book of the Veiled, settled at the desk, and flipped through its pages.

Was it like a magick eight-ball? Could I ask it questions, and it tells me my heart's desires?

Hey, I said in a silent greeting. *I'm not sure why I'm here, talking to a book. But Moll said that sometimes the book will show Writers what they need. Is there anything you can show me to help a middle-aged woman on the brink of a mental breakdown? Like an instruction manual? Or a cheat sheet on what I'm supposed to be doing?*

I waited for an answer, my eyes darting around the room just in case. Nothing.

Sighing in disappointment, I got up and carried the book to bed. I didn't have the energy to put on my pajamas, so I crawled underneath the covers, fully dressed, and held it to my chest.

I tossed and turned the rest of the night, my dreams filled with gray landscapes and misty figures roaming in and out. A towering figure loomed in the distance, his gaze fixed on me as I stood at a crossroads. I could feel his eyes penetrating deep into my being. A dim light flickered behind him like a dying flame.

Even from a distance, I could feel his commanding presence emanating like sweet syrup. It seemed to seep into the very earth beneath our feet.

Who was he?

And why was I not afraid?

Chapter 23

'Guides Will Be Needed In Your Travels.' -Book of the Veiled Instructions

I dragged myself out of bed early the following day, taking extra care to disguise any signs of sleep deprivation. It wasn't much more than a halfhearted attempt to cover the circles under my eyes with concealer and foundation that I was sure was two shades too light.

I mentally braced myself for the day ahead as I put on my Xtratuf boots and a rain jacket. After the past week's events, I didn't think anything could top how awkward and bizarre things had already been. Before heading out, I took two Advil and my daily multivitamins to ease the tightness in my neck muscles.

I squared my shoulders, my resolved set, ready to head down to the group. Eidolon shouldn't feel obligated to pursue a relationship with me simply because of his grandmother's intuition. It wouldn't be fair to either of us. We could address it and move on as if nothing had happened.

Co-workers. That was it. Just two people hunting down a magickal book that was stolen by a mythical creature. And any hopes, dreams, or fantasies I may have harbored about Eidolon falling in love with my award-winning personality and unmatched expertise in all things related to coffee? Well, that would be put in a box, wrapped up tight, and stuck on the top shelf of my mental closet.

Easy peasy.

That was until I found Eidolon with a shy smile, waiting in the lobby with a cup of coffee in his hand.

Shit! This was going to be more challenging than I'd hoped, I thought as I walked down the last few stairs to where he was standing.

With a grin, he extended the mug. "Truce," he declared as I snatched it from him.

"Truce," I confirmed, nodding. His eyes sparkled as he gazed at me, and I found it difficult to look away from him.

Gods, he was gorgeous.

For a moment, it seemed like he wanted to say something to me, and I held my breath, hoping it would alleviate the tightness in my chest.

I needed him to say something, anything, about our date. That he liked me for who I was, not because of some comment from his grandmother.

Instead, he nodded, pivoted on his heel, and sat on the couch in the lobby next to Watson. I squeezed my eyes shut, trying to hide my disappointment, and willed my face to remain expressionless.

Co-workers. Nothing more, I reminded myself.

Yea, co-workers. That's believable! Watson laughed, glancing between us.

I let out a fierce growl as I turned to face him, my eyes burning with determination. *Get out of my head!*

If you stop thinking so loudly, I wouldn't have to listen, Watson responded nonchalantly. My attention shifted back to Eidolon, observing the exchange with curiosity.

Rude.

Isabelle linked arms with me in a display of solidarity. Their faces flushed with embarrassment, their guilt oozing like melted ice cream as we scowled at them.

Sydney, perched on the couch with a newspaper in hand, glanced up in bewilderment as he observed our wordless confrontation. He set the paper aside and leaned back, intrigued by our silent battle. I could tell from his posture that he knew what was going on.

That's awesome, I thought. *Him too?*

A man's voice called out from the dining room doorway, interrupting my thoughts. "Good morning! I'm Maxwell, but you can call me Max. It's an honor to have you here in Scotland, where Merlin was born and laid to rest," he greeted enthusiastically.

I glanced over and saw a man in his thirties with youthful features and a wide grin. His wet glasses and tousled hair gave him an older Harry Potter vibe, while his oversized, tattered jacket, faded jeans, and scuffed Brandecosse boots made him appear more like a farmer than a historian.

Eidolon rose from his seat to offer a handshake. "Max, we appreciate you letting us intrude on such short notice. Esme mentioned that you are the foremost authority on all things related to Merlin," he greeted with a tone of professionalism and detachment.

My sympathies flowed out to Max as he shuddered under Eidolon's gaze. A man like Eidolon was intimidating regardless of mood, but when focused, he was deadly.

Max instinctively stepped back as he faced the intense stare, only to bump into Sydney. He turned and looked up at the towering giant, taking in his immense height and size. To his surprise, Sydney smiled at him and even gave him a friendly pat on the shoulder as if they were old friends.

"I thought you would be in a kilt," Sydney commented, looking him up and down in disappointment.

"Yes, well..." Max mumbled, adjusting his glasses and pushing back his shoulders. "Kilts are usually worn for special occasions. And to lure rich unsuspecting tourists into buying cheap souvenirs."

Sydney laughed and patted his shoulder again, "Good call! I have questions for you about them, though. Is it true that you don't wear anything...?"

"Hello, Max. Thank you so much for meeting us." Max's focus shifted to Isabelle as she greeted him with a charming Southern accent. I let out a breath of relief, glad the conversation wouldn't steer towards an uncomfortable topic such as what may or may not be hidden under a kilt.

With Isabelle's beauty and ability to control emotions, it was no wonder that Max's smile became brighter, and I wasn't surprised. She could easily grace the cover of L.L. Bean with her long, blonde hair in a casual braid, a cozy plaid scarf around her neck, and dressed in stylish jeans and an oversized sweater. She looked like a runway model, not a woman about to hike through the rugged Scottish terrain.

Max took in the whole view, appreciation evident on his face.

Watson's voice dripped with warning. "Watch out! She's got a ferocious companion who loves to sink their teeth into unsuspecting prey."

Max paled, frantically scanning the room for an escape route. I rolled my eyes at the exchange. The way things were progressing, we wouldn't have a guide for long.

"Watson!" Isabelle slapped him on the arm before sending a heartbreaking smile to Max. "Now that you've met Watson, I recommend staying as far away as possible. Obviously, he is lacking in manners." Turning to introduce me before Watson could say anything else, Max cut her off.

"You must be Chloe! I recognize you from your book cover. It was a fascinating new glimpse into history." He stepped forward to shake my hand.

"Well, thank you," I laughed, enjoying the praise. "I've read your articles, too. They are well-researched and beautifully penned. I was intrigued by your argument about the difference between magick and miracles. I would love to know how you arrived at your conclusions," I complimented him.

The night before we left, I searched the internet for information about Merlin's myth. Max had composed several articles on the subject, and I spent some time on the flight reviewing them all. Unlike scholarly reports that discuss Merlin's impact on pop culture, Max recreated Merlin's life before Disney's influence.

"Of course! We're going need our energy today, so let's get something to eat, and I'll tell you the story." Offering his arm and smiling, he guided me out of the room towards the breakfast table.

I let Max lead the way, his warmth and generosity already rubbing off on me. I could envision us becoming close friends in no time. Eidolon hissed behind me, and I smiled even wider.

Chapter 24

'Books That Are Wiped From Existence Usually Have The Answer.'
-Book of the Veiled Instructions

The rest of the group followed us into the grand dining room, with its high vaulted ceilings and opulent chandeliers. The massive table was laden with an array of delectable treats that made my mouth water in anticipation. I was starving after my laps around the hotel grounds last night.

A pot of glorious, thick coffee sat in the middle of the table, and I made myself a cup. I would have to remember to bring some home when we returned to the States. The coffee was terrific here.

Max settled into the seat next to me, scooting his chair closer. I suddenly felt an intense energy beside me, and when I glanced over, I saw Eidolon sitting on my other side. He glared at our host, emanating a mix of darkness and intense emotions that I couldn't quite decipher.

Max leaned back, clearly untrusting that Eidolon wouldn't eat him for breakfast.

Stop glaring, I said to Eidolon through the bond. *You're going to scare him off before breakfast.*

I don't like how he looks at you, Eidolon responded curtly.

He doesn't look at me in any kind of way. I rolled my eyes at the suggestion. *He's just enthusiastic about helping.*

That is not what I see. He casually draped his arm across the back of my chair, exuding an air of ownership and possession. It was a subtle gesture but spoke volumes about his intentions. As his piercing gaze met mine, I couldn't help but feel both nervous and excited simultaneously.

I turned my attention back to Max, wanting to ask him about one of his articles. However, seeing the furrow in his brow, I reconsidered. Fortunately, Isabelle jumped in and asked him what sparked his interest in the legend of Merlin.

"Ah, I'm glad you asked." Max leaned forward to grab a pastry, ignoring Eidolon's pointed stare.

What are you doing? With a grumble, I delivered a swift kick to Eidolon's shin as Max began to tell his story. Eidolon winced in pain and sipped his drink to hide his groan.

I feel bad about last night. If you let me explain...

Watson cleared his throat, directing our attention to our guide. Glancing over, I saw Max watching our silent interaction. I smiled encouragingly, hoping that he didn't think I was being rude on purpose.

We'll talk later. Eidolon promised as he moved closer to me, his leg grazing mine under the table. My heart pounded, and heat flooded my cheeks as I became aware of his proximity. The urge to grab his hand was strong, but I resisted when I caught Watson's smug expression out of the corner of my eye. I stuck my tongue out at him and focused back on our host.

As I enjoyed my breakfast of hearty sausage, fried eggs, flavorful baked beans, tender sautéed tomatoes, and crispy toast, Max posed a question to the group: how much did we know about Merlin? Sydney shrugged his shoulders and loaded his plate with food like he hadn't eaten in days. I couldn't help but wonder where he put it all - the man didn't have an ounce of fat on him, yet he devoured every meal as if it were his final one.

"Pretend we have no idea," Eidolon instructed.

Max rolled his eyes as he cleared his throat. "My fascination with King Arthur began when I stumbled upon Geoffrey of Monmouth's History of the Kings of Britain. Merlin was renowned as one of the greatest sorcerers and prophets in this legendary tale. What captured my attention, however, was Geoffrey's claim that Merlin was the offspring of a nun and a demon."

"A nun?" I asked, my ears perking up, remembering an article mentioning that the Abbot of Beverly sent Agatha to a nunnery. Was there a connection? The idea of some affiliation crossed my mind, and I made a mental note to ask Victor and Aelle about it later.

"Yes, a nun," Max answered. "Despite never having been in a romantic relationship with a man, she could recall a dream where a mysterious stranger kissed her. The intensity of the kiss was so strong that it resulted in her becoming pregnant. Nine months later, she gave birth to a baby boy.

Watson glanced at Max with a frown. "Do you have any idea what kind of demon got her pregnant?" Isabelle's expression turned sour as she squeezed Watson's hand.

"No one knows," Max shrugged. "Geoffrey believes one of the demons cast out with Lucifer was the culprit."

Sydney paused mid-bite. "I never knew demons were also kicked out of heaven."

Max leaned forward in his chair, shifting his gaze toward everyone in the room. "Legend has it that a third of the angels from Heaven joined Lucifer in his exile, along with the demons. This belief is not limited to just Christianity but is also accepted in other religions such as Judaism, Hinduism, Buddhism, and even ancient Egyptian texts."

"So, where are they now?" Eidolon asked. "Did they just disappear?"

"I think some survived and are still here," Max confirmed grimly. "And I think Taliesin was a creation of theirs."

"Creation?" Isabelle asked, unnerved by the word. I couldn't blame her. He made it sound like Dr. Frankenstein whipped up some body parts and created demons on a rainy night.

"Yes, created. Formed in Lucifer's likeness, just as humans were made in the image of God. A brief mention of demon sex appears in the Jewish and Christian texts. They reference fallen angels who mated with mortals and created the race of giants. Generally speaking, the theory is overlooked. Yet, the past always finds a way to reveal itself. In the 1940s, an unearthed Dead Sea Scroll, written in Greek, was so controversial that it wasn't permitted to be part of any religious text."

"The Book of Enoch," Eidolon whispered. "A man so worthy that God allowed him into Heaven before he died."

"Yes!" Max regarded him with more respect. "Interestingly, the man who was so pleasing to God that he was invited to Heaven ended up writing a book that most believe is full of lies." Max laughed at the thought. "According to the text, fallen angels taught humans magick, astrology, and other mythical qualities, resulting in the supernatural races."

Isabelle and Watson's faces paled as they glanced at each other.

"So, you think Taliesin had magickal powers because a demon mated with a human, and he was born from the union?" I asked.

Max thought about this question as if searching for the right words.

"Merlin was the last time we saw authors attempt to illustrate the coexistence of magick and mythical creatures with humans. He was designed to explain the existence of genuine people with natural magickal abilities. Because he repeatedly appears in literature up to the present, I believe Merlin and Taliesin are the same. Whenever he emerges, he does something to establish himself as a historical figure. It's as if he wants to keep people from forgetting about him."

Seeing everyone in deep thought at the table, I took a moment to process Max's words. A supernatural creature who uses books to stay alive? It couldn't be a coincidence.

Could it?

Chapter 25

'The Answers Are Always Found In The Library.' -Book of the Veiled Instructions

Sydney broke the silence first. "I heard that there is a trail. When do we get a chance to explore it?"

"I'm ready when you are," Max replied, looking excited.

After finishing breakfast, we headed out into the brilliant green of a rare sunny morning. After the last few days of excitement, I needed fresh air and exercise to help me collect my thoughts. And Scotland was the best place to do it. Turning around a bend in the path, we were greeted by a sprawling meadow that stretched out as far as the eye could see. The ground was blanketed with a sea of bright yellow and white flowers, their delicate petals swaying in the cool breeze. It was as if nature itself was putting on a grand performance even though the distant clouds promised an afternoon of rain.

Leaving the group behind, I let my feet lead me toward the winding river, drawn in by the haunting whispers of the river. The melody was enchanting, pulling at my heartstrings like a siren's call. I glanced back at Eidolon, but he seemed oblivious to the alluring song that beckoned me forward. I couldn't resist the pull and stepped closer to the water's edge, eager to discover the source.

Something lurked in the murky depths below. I couldn't see it, but I could feel its weight pulling me closer. My instincts screamed for me to turn away, but my curiosity drew me in deeper towards the ominous darkness. What secrets lay hidden within its grasp? Only one way to find out...

"Lovely here, isn't it?" Max's voice jolted me back to reality, his perceptive eyes locking with mine as if the melody had once entranced him. I managed to nod in response, tearing my gaze back to the river.

"My grandmother used to warn me about coming here," Max offered as he took my arm and led me back to the path. "Legend has it that the river is filled with the spirits of those who were drawn in by the alluring song of the Sirens, forever trapped and unable to find their way back to the shore."

As much as it pained me to admit, I found myself nodding in agreement with Max. The alluring waters were beckoning me forward, their gentle ripples whispering my name. If Max hadn't stopped me, I might have leaped in to join them.

"What made you study Taliesin when he is considered a myth?" I asked, needing something else to think about. "Not many people take the legend of Merlin seriously."

Max took a breath and gave me a side look. "While that may hold true in other parts of the world, it is not the case here in Scotland. We cherish our myths and see them as a connection to our heritage. We are raised with the belief that every myth and tale holds a piece of reality. Taliesin, Merlin, or whatever you want to call him, is both myth and reality. A link to magick, I believe, existed and still does today," he explained, looking over to the forest's edge as if waiting for something to appear. "But I also believe it's fading away, and I want to understand why."

I nodded in understanding. I had long hoped magick still existed, even in its simplest form, and I desperately wanted it all to be true.

"And you think he is still alive?" Eidolon asked, appearing next to me. I hadn't heard him sneaking up, and I glanced at him in surprise.

"Yes and no. His physical body is buried, but I believe that his essence, who he was as a person, still lives on. A soul never truly dies." He glanced towards the trees with a slight frown. "Taliesin was a powerful Druid; he may have been able to discover the Elixir of Life."

"So, Taliesin *was* a Druid?" I asked, and Max nodded.

"Let's say he was. What would his training have been like?" Eidolon asked.

"Contrary to popular belief, Druids were not just mystical figures. In reality, they were highly educated individuals who specialized in various fields such as law, history, philosophy, astronomy, prophetic work, healing, and teaching. Their vast knowledge earned them the respect of clans and thrones, making them influential political and religious leaders.

"However, their power extended beyond mere political sway. They possessed a profound connection to the world that was not widely understood at the time. The Druids were well-versed in historical events, able to make sense of current affairs, and even foresee future events. I suspect that only a select few were true Druids, all coming from either the Taliesin or his sister's lineage."

Sydney, Isabelle, and Watson strolled over, overhearing our conversation.

"Are there any records of his writings left?" Sydney asked.

"From Taliesin? No," Max laughed. "Most of the tales are passed down through oral tradition, but there is one writer whose work was said to be influenced by him. His collection of stories can still be found in his personal library.

"Do you believe that it was?" Eidolon pressed. My heart skipped a beat as we waited for his answer. I

"Yes, I do." Max looked him in the eye confidently. "My informant claimed that he had encountered Taliesin in a pub. They struck a deal - Taliesin would divulge the secrets of magick and the supernatural, and he would assist in writing Taliesin's tale."

Sydney's eyes narrowed. "Are you *absolutely* certain about this?"

It was a difficult tale to accept. A legendary being appearing out of thin air and sharing his story? Even I had my doubts.

"Yes."

"How?" Eidolon asked.

"Because they are in my family's library." Max's head swung to meet Eidolon's stare. "I don't think my great-great-grandfather would lie about something like that."

My jaw fell open, shock and awe washing over me. Max's great-grandfather had met Taliesin? The elusive figure from ancient lore that I had only read about in books. A thousand questions exploded in my mind, eager to learn the details of this extraordinary encounter. How did it happen? When? Why was Taliesin there with Max's ancestor?

"You have the journals? And they mention Taliesin?" Sydney asked septically, "That he saw Taliesin in person? And it wasn't just a dream?"

"No, it wasn't a dream," Max shot back, his voice holding a note of defiance as he stood tall and proud. Something stirred in my chest, a warm connection to Max's story, as a flash of a memory flew through my head like a shooting star. It was brief but vivid, a moment frozen in time that filled me with an inexplicable sense of familiarity. I could almost see the scene unfolding before me, like a movie playing out behind my eyes.

A wrinkled, weathered man sat hunched over a massive oak desk, the scratching of his quill against parchment the only sound in the dimly lit room. Across from him stood a figure cloaked in shadows, their face obscured by the flickering light of the nearby fireplace. The old man glanced up at the figure with a mix of surprise and curiosity before returning to his task at hand.

Shivers of electricity ran down my spine as my vision faded.

Max was telling the truth.

"How do you know they weren't dreams?" Eidolon asked.

"Because I've seen him too." A hush fell over the group as Max's words drifted through the air like a fragile whisper. The tension in the clearing was palpable, and even the rustling leaves held their breath. My companions all gasped in unison, their eyes wide with surprise. Max's words had struck a chord. Eidolon's face hardened, his piercing gaze narrowing and his muscles tensing.

"What do you mean you have seen him?" Eidolon demanded, taking a menacing step forward. Max squared his shoulders and advanced as well, their confrontation resembling two vicious wolves ready to tear each other apart.

Isabelle's gentle hand came to rest on Max's tense shoulder, a soothing touch that calmed him down instantly. Sydney, with calculated movements, positioned himself between Max and me, creating a physical barrier between us. I didn't know why, but Eidolon silently acknowledged him with a nod of gratitude before narrowing his eyes back onto Max.

"I only have one question," Sydney said with a huge smile, breaking the tension. "What does a guy who has been dead for over 1,400 years look like?"

As they walked along the winding path, Sydney, Isabelle, and Watson were immersed in a passionate debate about the existence of souls after death. Max trailed behind them, occasionally chiming in with his thoughts.

As we trailed behind them, Eidolon leaned in close to me, "Do you believe him?"

"I do," I said, watching Max. "Something tells me to trust him."

"Same here," Eidolon sighed, gazing out at the countryside. The rain had returned, giving the Scottish landscape an otherworldly feel with its dark skies and light drizzle. A thick fog engulfed the forest, silencing even the birds in its grasp. The only sign of movement was the river to our left, rushing over rocks. But its once inviting melody had turned into a haunting plea to stay away, and I couldn't help but agree.

"The question is how and why?" he asked after a pause. I had been wondering the same thing. Why go through all the trouble of stealing the Book of the Veiled to bring his sister back only to hide them? Something wasn't adding up.

"I don't know," I answered honestly. "But I know what it is like to be willing to do anything if it means bringing someone back. The real question is, why does he need the Book of the Veiled if he found the Elixir of Life?"

Eidolon shrugged. "The Book of the Veiled contains all the hidden truths and forbidden secrets that people refuse to acknowledge. It delves into the dark deeds of both humans and supernatural beings, offers glimpses into possible futures, and exposes the true history that has been concealed. If in the wrong hands, one can manipulate and distort the past however they please." Eidolon's eyes narrowed with determination. "We can't let that happen. No matter how 'noble' the reason."

"What if the book was not stolen to bring back one person- but to bring back all of them?" I asked, glancing at him. The question had been plaguing me for a while.

"All of whom? The supernatural?" He glanced down at me, and I nodded.

It weirdly made sense. In recent years, magick and myths have enjoyed a comeback. Old religions were being reexamined, practices once banned were now accepted, and everyone wanted a piece of the magickal pie. I wasn't immune to it myself—trips to Orlando to visit Harry Potter Land, magickal wands, and dragon incense holders. I even had a book on how to read Tarot cards on my bookshelf.

"The Book of the Veiled did more than hide the supernatural from humans. What if the person who stole the books was not only interested in bringing back the dead? What if it was more than that?"

"So, you are saying this Easter egg hunt is not about Taliesin's sister?"

"Think about it. Max said Taliesin was constantly reappearing, rewriting his history. What if he was trying to bring the supernatural back?" My vision was still a blur, and I struggled to make sense of what I had seen - or hadn't seen. But one thing was clear, the figure lying in that bed was not Taliesin. It was something else. Fidgeting with my hands, the urge to write intensified, and the key around my neck hummed as if it were trying to guide me toward the truth.

Eidolon glanced back at the rest of the group, his eyes falling on Max as he considered the situation. "I don't know Chloe. Let's hope Max has some answers."

Chapter 26

'Don't Touch Magickal Things You Don't Understand.' -Book of the Veiled Instructions

Max led us down a narrow, twisting trail enclosed by towering trees, their branches reaching out like gnarled fingers. The fog lingered around our feet, dampening the earth and coating everything in a ghostly haze.

The eerie stillness of the forest sent shivers down my spine as if it had been plucked straight from the set of a horror movie. Even the rustle of leaves and creaking of branches seemed to hold an ominous tone.

Watson reached for Isabelle and readied himself to shield her from danger. His actions did little to ease my nerves as I looked at the eerie and threatening trees closing in on us. I inched closer to Eidolon. I was aware that my survival depended on recognizing my limitations, and my biggest weakness was definitely my lack of speed.

But I could fight. I loved the adrenaline rush of a controlled fight or a barroom scuffle. After a few swift punches, maybe one or two insults for good measure, everyone meeting up for a beer afterward. Nothing serious.

But in the world of the supernatural?

I couldn't do anything but rely on my quick wit of sarcasm. And I didn't think that that skill would get me far.

Only Sydney seemed content in the woods, his eyes shifting through the obscurity like a moth drawn to light. He quickly established himself as the group's warrior by bouncing around, scrutinizing everything before allowing us to move forward.

Show off.

"Like everything else surrounding Taliesin, there are many different narratives about his fall from glory, his death, and where he was buried," Max told us as we walked further into the darkness. "The most heartbreaking part of the legend is when he was betrayed by the woman he loved. She tried to kill him." He looked back at me over his shoulder.

"Who's Vivian?" I asked.

"Before King Arthur ever married, he was introduced to a woman named Vivian. It's said she was breathtakingly beautiful—jet black hair, sapphire eyes, and skin that blended in with the snowfall. Her voice was like the melodic trill of birdsong in the springtime air, and her laughter had an enchanting power that could rattle even the mightiest warriors."

"She sounds perfect," Sydney called out as he swung from a low tree branch. Max nodded.

"She was. While initially intended for the king, she and Taliesin fell in love. They say Taliesin was so enamored with her that he shrank from his duties, instead spending all his time with her. As with any fairytale gone wrong, Vivian's intentions soon became apparent. She demanded Taliesin teach her magick.

"Blinded by lust and love, Taliesin promised to share everything he knew with her. The king warned him that Vivian was using him and that he didn't trust her. But Taliesin was in love and brushed his concerns off. The king's worries were justified. If Taliesin hadn't been distracted, he would have seen that Vivian was more than just a beautiful woman. She was a demon, created in the image of Lilith to snare Taliesin and his magick for the demon's own."

"That's an unfortunate twist," Watson commented softly, and I nodded in agreement as Max continued.

"A task that Vivian craved above all else was the ability to cross the gates between the mortal world and the Otherworld. It was a gift Taliesin refused to share, regardless of how much Vivian begged or pleaded. Eventually, he began to suspect that Vivian wasn't who he thought she was, so he ended the relationship.

"As retribution for his 'mistreatment,'" Max air quoted the word, "Vivian used the magick she had learned to try to kill him. But she didn't realize that Taliesin had created a link between his soul and this world. A connection would stay as long as his name was spoken. The king was devasted when Taliesin died."

"How did the king know?" Sydney asked, pausing in his mock battle with a tree stump.

Max paused, taking a few moments to get his bearings before he set off walking once more. "The Fates visited the king in a dream and told him. They showed him where Taliesin had been buried and what Vivian's true form was. The king was beside himself with grief. He searched for Taliesin for years, finally finding his body completely intact, hidden by the River Tweed."

He stopped again, glanced around, and then turned off the narrow trail, heading deeper into the forest. "The king planted a white oak over Taliesin's grave partly as a marker and to link his body to the mortal realm. He believed that Taliesin would be able to return from the dead."

"Is that why the Druids are known as the Knowers of the Oak Tree? Because Taliesin was entombed under one?" Isabelle asked.

But Max didn't answer as we approached a small open area. A pale blueish light glowed dimly from the darkness, and I felt a power shift in my core as if the earth were coming alive. Gradually, warmth spread through us, whisking away the moisture that had soaked our clothes and shoes.

"What the hell," Watson exclaimed softly as he looked down, watching the fabric of his shirt dry. Isabelle inspected her clothes with glee and seemed to take note of the difference between the air and the ground under us.

"I can sense something," she muttered. "Strong magick, nothing I have experienced before. Almost like a protective charm but with something a bit darker mixed in," she commented, looking around the area as if trying to figure out the workings of the enchantment.

"It's the spell that protects Taliesin," Max explained as he walked further into the clearing, his steps slow and measured. "A shield surrounds the place." Pride in his eyes shined brightly as if he were the one who had cast the enchantment. "The king realized Taliesin needed to be hidden in a safe spot where no one could find him. He told everyone that the River Tweed had buried Taliesin and instead brought him here."

"What's so significant about this location?" Eidolon asked cautiously, looking around wearily.

"It is where Taliesin taught him how to be a king," Max answered as he gazed up at a tree with longing.

Before us stood a single, massive tree in the middle of the clearing; it was at least a hundred feet tall, and I whistled softly as we all tilted our heads up to take it in. Its branches were draped in silver, its trunk shining with a bluish tinge, and warm energy emanated from its base.

"Why is the tree all glittery?" Sydney asked in amazement.

"This is why I am glad Moll called and said you were all coming. The glowing started about a week ago with no rhyme or reason. One moment, I was sitting at home, and the next, I felt a strange urge to come here. When I arrived, what you now see was waiting for me."

Eidolon's eyes flew over to Max as he took in what he had just said, "Did you say a week ago?"

Isabelle gasped, and Eidolon stepped slightly in front of me protectively.

"Eidolon," I whispered, and he squeezed my hand in reassurance. A week ago, I made it through initiation and became a member of the Raven Society, and we were tasked with finding the missing books of the Book of the Veiled.

I couldn't tear my eyes away. It felt as if the essence of its life was calling to me. The tree was familiar and lonely, and I reached for it when Eidolon pulled me closer to him.

"No touching magickal trees until we know what's causing it," he whispered. I wanted to pull away, but he held on tightly to my hand.

Watson and Sydney moved to stand on either side of us, and Isabelle walked around the tree, mumbling to herself. I sensed a connection as if the white oak was interested in what she was saying, almost gleeful that someone had taken the time to talk to it.

"What's wrong?" Max asked, looking over at Eidolon's hand holding onto mine, a look of concern flashing across his eyes. "Am I missing something?"

"No," Eidolon replied dismissively. "What do you think this means?"

"I know what it means," Max paused and took a deep breath. "When my family found my great-grandfather's hidden journals, a whole section was devoted to his interactions with Taliesin and his trips to this spot." His eyes grew sad.

"You have to understand my grandfather was in a desperate situation. Money was running short; his writing was not getting the same notice as before. The creditors were knocking. Then, one day, a stranger appeared, promising my grandfather that if he helped with a small task, he would never have to worry about money again."

"Eidolon," I whispered again, needing his attention. The tree sent a jolt through me again, but this one was different. This one asked me something I couldn't put my finger on.

Oh crap, here we go again, I was pretty sure that I was about to travel. The world was getting darker, and I could hear a voice calling. I just needed Eidolon to pay attention.

"What did your grandfather have to do for that promise?" Watson asked. The fact that no one noticed as my body started to fade away was unsettling. I attempted to bring one of my hands up to my face, but it seemed like it had a mind of its own.

That's unnerving.

Max seemed uncomfortable as he faced us. "All I know is that he helped Taliesin find a person who knew where some book was located. Once he found them, my grandfather's luck turned around. Taliesin never materialized again."

"Who was he looking for?" The darkness around Eidolon started to move and swirl, forming letters that morphed into words. I tried to grab his attention, anticipating that whatever was about to transpire would not be pleasant. But he stayed focused on Max.

"A woman. Someone who could see into the future. There are paintings of her in his office. I tried to take them down, but they seem permanently attached to the wall."

"What is the woman doing in the paintings?" Eidolon asked slowly.

"Running. Every single one of them is of her running, clutching a book in her arms, and looking over her shoulder," Max said, watching Eidolon with growing concern.

Isabelle walked over to place her hands on Eidolon, forcing him to face her. "Before we jump to conclusions, we need to see the pictures." Eidolon's face contorted with grief and hope as he looked down at her.

"What was the woman's name?" Isabelle turned to ask Max.

"Diana."

That was all I heard before I passed out behind them.

Chapter 27

'There Is No Punishment Worse Than Being Bound to Reality.'
-Book of the Veiled Instructions

"The first couple of times are always the hardest." A gentle voice pierced through the darkness, and I slowly woke up.

Gods! My head hurts. I raised my hand to massage my temples. The trip felt nothing like my first experience traveling. It was as if someone else had been in control, pulling me through a haze of unfamiliar memories.

One eye fluttered open, and I eyed the bustling room before me. The kitchen was a hive of lively activity, with trays of food transported by men and women through a side door. On one side of the room, two women were putting the final additions on a tray of desserts. And on the other, two young boys sat on tiny wooden stools peeling potatoes.

Above, aromatic herbs hung from the ceiling, blending with the savory scents of cooking dishes. To the back, an extensive storage area held shelves filled with neatly labeled jars of jams, canned fruits, and other mysterious ingredients that added to the room's charm.

I sniffed, breathing in the intoxicating aroma of sizzling meats and exotic spices. On the back wall was an extensive fireplace where various cuts of beef were slowly spinning on spits over an open flame. The fire crackled and flickered, casting a warm glow over the room. Nearby, pots bubbled and steamed, their contents releasing mouth-watering scents that made my stomach grumble.

Did I get to eat on this journey? I hoped so.

It seemed like eons had passed since breakfast, and I desperately needed coffee. I collided with someone just as I was about to sneak over to the drink cart. Quickly stepping back, I braced myself to flee.

For pete's sake, can people stop trying to give me a heart attack? I thought as I clutched my hand to my chest.

My eyes were drawn to the woman's commanding presence. She wore a midnight blue dress, the bell sleeves decorated with silver ravens at the cuffs, adding a touch of elegance to her already stunning appearance. Her raven-black hair was styled in soft curls that cascaded down her back, completing her ageless beauty. As my gaze traveled down, I noticed the pewter belt loosely tied around her waist, highlighting a chain with a raven pendant and gray leather boots peeking out from under the hem of her skirt.

Dazed and disoriented, I gazed at my surroundings. Just minutes ago, I was deep in the heart of a forest, gawking at a glowing tree. But now, standing next to me was a woman I didn't recognize, and in a home I'd never been in before. "Are we...inside the tree?" I stammered, having a hard time taking in everything.

"Technically, we're in a kitchen," the woman chuckled.

"Why, and how?" Turning to glance at the woman, I saw Eidolon's eyes watching me. Deep blue, almost purple. Her face held the same strong chin, soft lips, and that uncomfortable ripple of stillness.

Holy shit, Eidolon's mom. She was alive! But if she was alive, why was I here and not Eidolon? I started to ask, but a wave of her hand stopped me.

"I need a favor, and I figured it would be best to ask in person." She motioned for me to sit with her at a nearby table, and I approached cautiously, studying her features more closely. She wore a blend of ethereal grace and deviousness, much like Eidolon. I couldn't help but stare, my mouth open in disbelief.

She tilted her head, examining me. "Coffee?"

Blinking once, I found my voice. "Yes, please."

She poured us a mug, the rich aroma wafting through the air. "How is he doing?" Her concerned gaze met mine as she waited for my response.

Guess we are skipping the small talk; I grimaced as she handed me one of the mugs. "I assume you are talking about Eidolon?"

"Eidolon?" She raised her eyebrows in surprise. "Is that the name he goes by? Interesting." She twirled the handle of her mug absentmindedly, lost in thought.

"I think it's more of a joint decision," I said dismissively. "He and Moll came up with it." Her expression turned into a frown at the mention of her mother, her dark eyes swirling with irritation. "You know he's looking for you, right?" I questioned, reaching over for a sugar cube.

The flicker of pain in her eyes made me want to reach over and console her. But I resisted the urge. After all, she was still alive and hadn't tried to reconcile with her son. She was the one at fault here, not the victim.

As she sensed my growing annoyance, she squared her shoulders and looked me straight in the eye. "I want my son to give up searching for me," she said firmly.

I sat with my mug halfway to my lips, frozen in shock as I tried to process her words. My cup trembled slightly as I slowly lowered it back to the saucer, the sound of porcelain against porcelain breaking the tense silence. My hands shook as I folded them tightly in front of me, trying to contain my anger. With a deep breath, I raised my head and locked eyes with Diana, determined to match her steely gaze with my own fiery determination.

"Tell him yourself, Diana," I said sweetly, my voice laced with thinly veiled sarcasm. "I'm sure he would be thrilled to hear from you."

"Impossible." She waved my recommendation away. "Which is why I invited you here, Chloe."

"I was invited?" I raised an eyebrow in disbelief. "I don't recall receiving an invitation," I added with a hint of sarcasm. "Where am I?" I gestured around the unfamiliar surroundings. "And why have you brought me here?"

The words escaped her lips with a solemn sigh, like the weight of a thousand burdens. "This is my home," she murmured, her voice laced with bitterness and resignation. "Or my prison. It all depends on how you choose to see it." She paused, gazing around at the walls that held her captive. "But here I am, unable to change my fate." The air hung heavy with defeat and acceptance.

"What do you mean by *fate*?" I asked, wanting clarification.

"That's a long story," she sighed, taking a sip.

Wasn't it always? I was exhausted from all the stories, each one creating another gap in my sense of reality. But this one seemed important. "Well, I'm here now," I grumbled, rubbing my temples, "and have some free time. So why don't you tell me?"

She reclined in her seat, intertwining her fingers in a manner reminiscent of Eidolon's natural poise. As she did so, any lingering uncertainty about her identity as his mother dissipated. "I love my son. It pains me to be apart, but it was necessary for his safety."

"How did leaving Eidolon to be raised by strangers keep him safe?" I challenged. "Seems to me that is the opposite of keeping a child safe."

"I don't expect you to understand my reasoning, but I ask you to at least listen to what I have to say," she shot back with a scowl. The same scowl I'd seen Eidolon give me hundreds of times. I nodded in reluctant agreement. It was the least I could do.

"From the first moment I laid eyes on Eidolon's father, I knew he was the one I wanted to spend the rest of my life with. We graduated from college and embarked on a journey to explore the world's wonders together. With stars in our eyes and love in our hearts, we exchanged vows and started a family soon after. Despite my family's expectations and obligations, we forged our path and built a beautiful life."

"So, your husband knew about your and Moll's abilities?" I interrupted. Moll had mentioned he did, but I wasn't sure I'd believed her story. But I was beginning to.

"I think he knew more about my abilities than I did," Diana laughed. "Comparing my family's magick abilities to James is like comparing a single finger to an entire hand. Eidolon, who inherited his father's power, displayed extraordinary qualities from birth. Even as a child, it was clear that he was a gifted Caul Bearer."

"Isn't a Caul Bearer just some superstition that sailors believe in? Like, if they were born with a caul, they would be protected from drowning?" I took one of the scones that Diana offered. Taking a bite, I couldn't help but moan in pleasure.

"Yes and No. During birth, the caul is formed when a part of the amniotic sac breaks away and adheres to the child's face, creating a veil around the child. It's a sign of someone exceptional and extremely powerful. It's believed those born with it can navigate between the living and the dead," she explained.

"Tibetan Buddhists considered them to be reincarnations of spiritual leaders. Other cultures treated them like royalty or even used the caul to ward off evil spirits. To these folks, a Caul Bearer has undeniable power."

Between bites, I asked, "How does this tie in with Eidolon?" It was intriguing that he'd been born with a caul, but what did it have to do with Diana's need to protect him?

Diana took a deep breath, and I eyed her wearily. "Sorry, please continue."

She nodded. "I still remember the day I came face to face with Eidolon's abilities. I was cooking dinner, and he was playing outside. I looked away for one second, and 'poof,'" she motioned with her hands, "he disappeared. After twenty long minutes, he reappeared with a stranger by his side. Calmly, he explained that he needed to escort the man to the afterlife and would return shortly.

Diana sank back into her seat, a hand pressed firmly against her chest as she relived the day's events. I couldn't fathom the agony of not knowing where your child was, especially if they could travel between worlds.

"Fear consumed me as I waited for his return. Eventually, he came home, visibly exhausted from his journey. Over dinner, he revealed his newfound understanding of portals that linked the various afterlife realms. Each religion had two gates carved to be recognized by the deceased as their own. He saw it as his duty to guide lost souls through these entrances." She shook her head like she still couldn't believe what Eidolon could do.

"James and I had a serious discussion about what to do. Having a child with such immense power was a risk we couldn't ignore. So, James crafted a bracelet that would bind his soul to reality. We put it on him when it was completed, linking his body to the mortal world. He was furious, convinced that the act would disrupt the balance of life and death. But we refused to entertain such thoughts or discuss the topic again afterward.

Her words trailed off into a heavy silence, and I lost myself in the weight of what Diana shared. It was a lot to process, but it validated Eidolon's narrative about his visions. The realization of his truth sent tingles down my spine and filled me with awe and fear. How incredible and terrifying it must be to have such a gift.

I leaned back in my chair, the wood creaking beneath me as I adjusted my glasses on the bridge of my nose. With a curious tilt of my head, I asked, "What happened then?"

A quick glint of anger flashed in her eyes, reflecting the flames burning in the fireplace. "Even with all our careful planning and precautions," she began, her voice laced with frustration and regret, "whispers and rumors started to spread about his abilities a few years later. We knew that he would never be safe." She laughed harshly before continuing, "So we ran, abandoning our old lives and identities in a desperate effort to stay one step ahead." She paused, her fingers anxiously tapping against her thigh, as she added, "But it wasn't enough. She found us anyways."

"Who?"

"Vivian." She spat the name with disgust.

"Vivian? Taliesin's lover?" I questioned. "Isn't she dead?"

Diana's laughter was strained, a weak endeavor to hide her true feelings. "No, she's very much alive," she insisted with a fake smile. She tossed her napkin onto her plate and turned to me, her eyes filled with anticipation. "I want you to meet someone."

"Who?" I asked, unsure if I was ready for whatever she had in store.

"James, Eidolon's father," she replied as she got up. "He can explain all this better than I can."

Chapter 28

'People Believed Before There Was Faith.' -Book of the Veiled Instructions

As we entered the room, the warm glow of a blazing fire in the stone fireplace welcomed us. Above the flames hung a considerable, black iron kettle, bubbling and hissing. I whistled as I glanced up where a fresco painting adorned the lofty ceiling, depicting fierce lions, slithering snakes, and watchful ravens. The vibrant colors glowed in the natural light streaming through the immense windows.

Glancing down, I noticed rows of books stacked neatly against the walls. High-backed chairs stood scattered around the room, each holding a stack of scrolls that looked like a reader had hastily put them aside in a hurry. An assortment of ink pots, pens, and paper sheets adorned a redwood desk in front of the western-facing window.

A set of spiral stairs at the far end of the room, leading up to a second-story library, caught my attention. A charcoal gray feline sat on the steps, idly swatting its tail and gazing at me with piercing yellow-green eyes flashing with flecks of silver. I froze in place as it sized me up.

Cats had never been my favorite animal; this one was no exception. There wasn't anything inherently wrong with them, but their attitude towards humans always seemed off-putting. They acted like humans were at the bottom of the food chain and were only here to serve them.

And this cat was no different as it started pacing back and forth, resembling a predator lurking for its next prey.

Reminder- don't pet the magickal attack kitty. I kept a watchful eye on the cat, just in case, as Diana made her way over to a figure with his back turned towards us. He sat at one of the desks by the east window, scribbling furiously and muttering.

"Sweetheart." Diana placed a hand gently on his shoulder. "Someone is here I would like you to meet."

"Who?" A middle-aged man whirled around to examine me with confusion, obviously not expecting a guest.

He wore glasses with silver frames and long reddish-brown hair pulled back by a strip of leather. His face was like something carved from granite, with a sturdy frame. He wasn't necessarily the most good-looking person I had ever seen, but his eyes were mesmerizing. They were a vibrant emerald green filled with shimmery sparks that moved like lightning through a stormy sky.

Without being warned, I knew I was facing a formidable sorcerer, and only one individual fit the description.

"Taliesin," I spoke the name to myself in a hushed tone, hoping I was mistaken. Diana mentioned her husband's influence and power, but it never crossed my mind she was married to a legendary figure. Neither had Eidolon nor Moll.

But Diana referred to him as James. Could I have been mistaken? I kept my face neutral, not wanting to bring it up in case I was wrong. However, the longer I stared, the more convinced I became I was right.

He called out my name as he made his way towards me. With a warm smile, he reached out and hugged me tightly. "It's wonderful to meet you finally," he exclaimed, pulling back to gaze down at me. "I'm sure you have questions. But before we get into it, let's have some refreshments. I find that tea and pastries make for excellent conversation starters."

"Thank you," I muttered, trying to breathe against the cement wall of his chest.

"James, you're smothering her," Diana chuckled, leaning back in her chair at a cozy wooden table tucked in the corner of the room. I hadn't realized how hungry I still was until I spied the scones and jams set out and quickly walked over to sit next to Eidolon's mother.

"Eat," Diana demanded with a wave of her hand. "I remember how exhausting traveling can be."

"When was the last time you traveled?" I inquired, helping myself to the spread of food before me. Diana made me a large cup of steaming tea, mixed with the right amount of cream and sugar. As I took a sip, the familiar flavors of ripe raspberries and sweet vanilla danced on my tongue.

"I haven't in years," she said, toying with the fabric of her gown. "My ability vanished as soon as we arrived. James spent twenty-five years searching for a way to bring you here." Pride filled her as she glanced at her husband, and he returned the gaze with a tender smile.

"Why me? Why not Eidolon or Moll?" I asked in disbelief. "They're your family."

A somber expression crossed James' face as he shifted his weight and cleared his throat before speaking. "Chloe," he began, "how much have you been told about your ancestral tree?"

I shrugged. "Not much. Just what Ancestory.com was able to share. There wasn't a lot of information," I answered honestly. "As far as I can tell, we are one of the few families who can't claim a link to some monarch or famous person. My ancestors are the textbook example of hard-working people lost to history."

"Somewhat true," James confirmed. "However, it's not for the reason you might assume. Your family wasn't forgotten because they were average. They deliberately avoided the spotlight and chose to remain unnoticed in history."

"Why?"

"That's the question of the day, isn't it," he laughed. "Have you heard of the Witch of Endor?"

"No," I said slowly. "Should I have?"

He shrugged. "Not many people know about her. She was a highly skilled witch, living during the reign of King Saul. Unfortunately, society at the time did not appreciate individuals with unique abilities. However, she managed to escape persecution and passed down her extraordinary talents. My sister Morrigan is one of her descendants. So are you."

"I thought your sister was dead," I said, confused. "At the Battle of Camlann."

"That is what is written. But we both know what is recorded can be different from reality. The confusion around her death kept her safe," he chuckled, "but very much alive. I believe she has been tasked with protecting the supernatural."

"Like witches, vampires, and werewolves?" I grimaced. "I just found out they exist."

"That's a fraction of the vast collection of existing myths. Consider the bigger picture: countless tales involving gods, dragons, mermaids, fairies, griffins, and centaurs. Do you honestly believe these creatures materialized by chance?" James leaned forward, his piercing gaze fixed on me.

"I have a question for you. Do you believe in the existence of supernaturals, or are they all made up by people with overactive imaginations?"

"I'm not sure," I struggled to find the right words. "I used to think they were just myths and legends." I absentmindedly ran my fingers through my hair. "But after becoming a member of the Raven Society, I can no longer deny their existence."

"Good." He nodded. "It's interesting to note that before religion, people believed in the existence of supernatural beings simply because they believed in them. But as religion gained power, faith in such things diminished."

A pained expression contorted his features as he reached across the table to grab his mug. "My sister understood better than anyone else that the supernatural would never be safe, regardless of any promises made to them. I believe Morrigan created a new realm specifically for their protection."

I peeked over at Diana, hoping for some clarification. This discussion was interesting but didn't answer my burning question: What did they want from me?

Diana's warm hand reached over and clasped mine in a comforting understanding. Her gentle touch reminded me of a mother soothing her child. "James is trying to convey that your ancestry can be traced back to Morrigan. And because of this ancient bloodline, you inherited her abilities."

The weight of Diana's words settled on me like an invisible cloak, tingling with energy and potential. My mind swirled with thoughts and questions about my newfound heritage as I gazed at the woman who revealed my identity.

"I'm a witch?" I couldn't believe the words that tumbled out of my mouth. The hope had always lingered in the back of my mind, but now it was out in the open; I was excited. I looked down at my fingers, hoping to see some sign, some manifestation of power. But they stayed ordinary, with chipped nail polish and rough skin from years of demanding work.

Disappointing!

"Not the Hallmark Channel version of a witch," Diana explained. "More in the researcher way. You can find loopholes and inconsistencies in history."

"Oh," I said, looking up at her sadly. I had been hoping I would never have to do laundry again. "Why are you telling me all this?"

"Lilith is back and searching for Eidolon and Moll. That's why we had to contact you, Chloe. If we sent a message to either of them, she would be able to find them. And that is the last thing we want."

Chapter 29

'Imprisonment Is A State Of Mind.' -Book of the Veiled Instructions

Diana narrowed her eyes at me, "Moll told you about my abilities, I assume." I nodded. She leaned in closer, "But did she tell you the whole story of what happened between us?"

I shook my head, my eyes darting between her and James, not wanting to repeat what Moll said.

"Diana, you don't need to do this." James leaned over and grabbed her hand. "There's no reason to bring up the past."

She shot a piercing glare at her husband, her lips pressing into a thin, tense line. "No, she needs to know the truth," she stated, her voice laced with determination. Diana shook her head, a stray lock of hair falling across her face. James reached over and tucked it behind her ear before gently kissing her forehead. A small smile crept onto her face as she leaned into his touch.

He hesitated for a moment before sinking back into his chair. "If that's what you want," he mumbled, unconvinced.

Diana's voice trembled as she began her story, her fingers drumming against the wooden table. "My visions started when I was in my early twenties," she started, her gaze fixed on the windows behind me. "Always the same. Someone was chasing me down an endless hallway lined with countless doors." She glanced in my direction before continuing, "I had the Book of the Veiled. Whoever it was was trying to take it from me."

I gave a subtle nod, trying to follow where she was going with the story.

Diana's frown deepened as her gaze shifted to James. She quickly clarified, "Moll was convinced it was him. She forbade me from ever seeing him again."

Well, that explained why Moll and Diana don't talk, I thought, mulling over the story. Moll and Eidolon were convinced Taliesin was responsible for stealing the Book of the Veiled. I wasn't sure if the man was even Taliesin. It was just a hunch.

"Was it you?" My eyes flicked towards the man sitting beside me.

"No," he chuckled, shaking his head.

"Then who was it?" I shifted my gaze to Diana.

"Lilith," she answered.

"Lilith?" I laughed. "Bible Lilith? She's a myth."

"Not a myth," James interjected, his voice carrying a weight of conviction. "A person, just like you and me," he added, emphasizing the word 'person' with a firm nod. "But fundamentally different. Older than the gods themselves and infinitely more powerful." He paused for dramatic effect, his eyes scanning the room before continuing. "And perhaps, just as dangerous." His words hung in the air, heavy with foreboding.

"You talk about her like you know her." I reached for the teapot to pour another cup, needing a distraction.

His brow furrowed as he thought about what to say. "I am familiar with her," he said, casting a quick glance at Diana, who tilted her head towards him in acknowledgment.

I couldn't believe what I was hearing. My jaw dropped open as I stared at him. "How old are you?" I asked, cutting right to the chase.

I nervously crossed my fingers under the table, desperately hoping my intuition was incorrect.

Please don't let this man be Taliesin! I thought to myself. Please, please, please.

"It's considered rude to ask someone their age." He looked down his nose at me. "But since you asked, old enough to have been around since before Rome fell."

Shit, he is Taliesin. I braced myself, unable to resist the urge to glance at Eidolon's mother. Did she have any clue her son saw Taliesin as a monster? And did Eidolon even know the truth about his own father?

James looked at me with kind eyes as he watched me struggling with the information. "The person I once was, is not who I am anymore. But I have lived through many different iterations of my existence," he acknowledged.

"How?" My voice was barely a whisper as I nervously fiddled with the spoon on the table. My eyes remained glued to it, refusing to look up at either of them. The silence between us hung heavy, filled with unspoken questions and a tension that could be cut with a knife.

With a thoughtful expression, James leaned forward onto the table, his eyes focused on me. "Plato asked the same question back in the 300s." His voice was smooth and steady, carrying a hint of wisdom that only came with age and experience. "There are multiple ways to approach it - a comprehensive explanation or an easy one."

"Easy," I responded firmly, looking up at him with anticipation, eager to keep the momentum going. My hands were itching to put words down on paper, and the key hanging around my neck was getting warmer. I could sense Eidolon's growing anxiety through our bond and didn't know how to reach out to him to reassure him I was still alive.

He leaned back in his seat, crossing his arms once more. "The easiest explanation would be reincarnation. Did you know that the average cells in an adult body are no more than ten years old?"

I shook my head, wondering where in the hell he was going with the science lesson.

"Not many people do," he said, a gentle smile forming. "But the fact is significant because it shows that our bodies constantly change, yet our true selves remain unchanged.

"1,485 years ago, my consciousness and soul were in the body of Taliesin. His actions were my actions. However, as the world has changed over time, so have I. The man sitting across from you is who I have evolved into. A husband to Diana and a father to Eidolon. The son of a mortal and a deity. Brother to a powerful witch. And, by extension, a distant uncle to you, Chloe."

"How old are you now? If you were to add all your lives up. Even the ones before you were Taliesin." I attempted to do the calculations in my mind, but it was impossible even to come close to his actual age.

"Old enough that I know Lilith," he admitted.

I offered a small smile. "That's rather ancient." I hesitated before asking, "So, the first time I went back in time, it was Lilith that I saw? It wasn't you coming back to life. It was Lilith?"

Diana and James nodded, and my heart sank.

"And who was the other lady in the room? The nice one who was helping Lilith out?"

"Oh, that would have been Vivian," Diana sneered. "She is Lilith's longest-serving acolyte and a nuisance to the world."

Well, let me know how you really feel. Apparently, Diana must still harbor ill feelings towards her husband's first girlfriend.

"Now, Diana, let's give credit where credit is due," James scolded and then looked at me. "Vivian is no beginner. Lilith has helped her understand and use my magick. She is no one to be trifled with, and if she is helping Lilith - you will need to worry about more than just finding three books."

"Why do they need the Book of the Veiled?" I asked, realizing this conversation was taking a different turn than anticipated. My mission to retrieve missing magickal books seemed not as simple as I had initially thought; instead, it was a treacherous and challenging battle against formidable supernatural entities.

This was not written in fine print on the invitation, I thought grimly while waiting for the answer.

"Lilith is the mother of all supernatural," James explained. "The first mortal to gain access to the magick of the gods. Her alliance with the fallen angels gave her the power of the gods without the damnation they faced. Initially, she was not the terrible woman many believed her to be. She was a lover, a caretaker, a mother, and a fair practitioner of magick.

"As with most, the lure of her power drew her farther and farther down a road of no return. As religion grew and faith was lost in the old ways, Lilith watched as her children were burned at the stake, murdered in their homes, tortured into confessions of devil worship, and then cast out. The blood-soaked land called to her, begging her to right the wrong committed against the innocent. So together, she and Vivian devised a plan to rid the world of mortals, and they almost succeeded."

"What did she do?"

"Her plan stretched across the entire planet and led to the death of millions over four years," James confessed sadly.

Four years and the death of millions? I racked my brain for a historical moment that fit the criteria.

You got to be kidding me!

"Lilith and Vivian are responsible for the Black Plague?" I asked, my voice laced with doubt as I stared into the distance.

"Yes," James said sadly. "A cleverly devised plan that we were almost unable to stop. She called it the 'Katharízo' or the cleanse. Finding her and Vivian and then confining them to the Otherworld took years.

"We hoped that by containing them there, they would fade into obscurity over time. But as history often does, it repeats itself. The old ways were revived, people devoted their energy to the ancient gods, and a belief in the Otherworld resurfaced. It was inevitable that souls would once again arrive at the gates."

I finally grasped the situation and turned to Diana. "You mentioned that Eidolon went to those gates as a child. One soul enters as another one leaves," I trailed off, realizing what it meant. My heart stopped beating. "She needs him to go through so she can be freed."

"Yes. Lilith needs Eidolon and the rest of the Book of the Veiled to return to the mortal realm. If that occurs, I cannot even fathom the extent of the destruction it would cause."

"So, this is a save the world mission, then?"

"Yes." Diana's gaze met James'; sorrow reflected in her eyes. Something was troubling her, but she said nothing. I waited for them to speak, but the silence persisted.

"What am I supposed to do? I am a witch with no witchy abilities, remember?" I dangled my unimpressive hands in front of them.

"The longer Eidolon carries around the books, the more he will be attracted to the Otherworld. If he gets pulled into their realm, there's a risk that Lilith will steal his powers and trap him in exchange for her freedom. James' complexion turned pale as he let out a heavy sigh. "That's where you come in. Before Vivian trapped us here, she struck a deal with the Fates regarding the Book of the Veiled. We're not sure what this deal entails, but we were hoping you could locate and intervene on our behalf.

"Vivian imprisoned you here. How?" My eyes darted between the two of them.

Diana's voice was tinged with sadness as she spoke, her eyes avoiding mine. "Another story for another day. Our time is almost up." I watched as she pointed to the hourglass perched on the fireplace mantel, its slender frame adorned with intricate gold designs. The remaining grains of dark gray sand quickly slipped through the narrow opening at the bottom. With a heavy heart, I knew I had to leave before the last granule fell through.

James grabbed my hand as his eyes pleaded with mine. "There is only one other person I know who can walk through the Otherworld without being affected. Once, long ago, I would have been able to reach out to him- but I am afraid that that relationship has been tarnished over the years."

My body tensed as I listened to his words, my mind racing with determination. "Sure, of course," I replied, trying to keep the excitement and urgency out of my voice. But inside, I knew I would do anything - absolutely anything - to save Eidolon.

"Arawn - the original God of Death and the Otherworld."

My eyebrows shot up in disbelief. He couldn't be serious. "That's all? I just need to contact the God of Death?" I asked incredulously, nodding my head slowly. "Well, that sounds simple enough! Do you, by any chance, have a phone number or address for him? I can catch an Uber and meet him for dinner."

As my frustration grew, a dark shadow began to fall over the room. The foggy mist from the nearby forest seeped through the windows, bringing a chilly breeze that sent shivers down my spine. This was not a welcoming presence; it felt like something sinister was approaching and did not want me here. Every hair on my arms stood on end as I braced myself for whatever was about to happen.

Diana's eyes pleaded with me as she spoke, "I need you to keep him safe, Chloe. But he can never know where we are." She quickly reached into her pocket and tossed something at me before the fog engulfed us. And just like that, I was falling through the darkness, visions shifting outside my view, logic barely within my grasp.

Gods, I hope the landing didn't hurt this time.

Chapter 30

'Trees Are The Most Effective Means Of Communication.' -Book of the Veiled Instructions

"Is she alive?" Sydney peered over Eidolon's shoulder, looking down at me.

Eidolon's voice dripped with frustration as he growled, "Of course, she's alive."

As his voice pierced through the hazy vision, I shook myself awake. My head sat cushioned in Eidolon's lap, his strong hands tenderly caressing my hair away from my face. His body was taut with contained energy, a protective stance assumed as he leaned over me.

I knew I needed to speak up and let them know I was safely back in my own body. But the comforting scent of smoke and cedar, paired with Eidolon's embrace, surrounded me in a warm cocoon that I didn't want to leave just yet.

"She smells different," Sydney commented as he leaned forward to sniff me, pulling back with a disgusted glance. "Old. Like mothballs and seawater."

I cringed at his unkind words, praying he was making it sound worse than it actually was. I took a small inhale and didn't detect any odor. *Thank the gods,* I mentally rolled my eyes.

Watson leaned in closer, his eyebrows raised in intrigue. "How do you know what she smells like?" he asked, his curiosity piqued.

"I don't know, she just does." Sydney shrugged as he stood up, meeting Eidolon's gaze. "Want to tell us what just happened?"

Isabelle glanced at him with a reassuring smile. "We'll give you all the details once we return to the hotel," she promised. "For now, let's wait for her to return."

Max's voice was full of worry as he moved to stand next to me. "Where is she coming back from?"

I was beginning to tire of being the focal point, and the tingling in my extremities intensified, becoming quite uncomfortable. Slowly, I opened one eye and gave Eidolon a half smile. The relief on his face was palpable, but it quickly faded into a look of concern once again.

"She's waking up," Eidolon exclaimed as I shifted under him.

"Oh, thank the gods." Watson ran a hand over his face in relief. "I was *not* looking forward to calling Moll and explaining why Chloe went missing."

Max's perplexed gaze darted back and forth between me and Watson. "But she didn't go missing." His puzzled frown deepened. "She was right here, with us, the entire time."

Isabelle's firm voice cut through the chatter. "Let's get her up before we play twenty questions," she commanded. Her eyes returned to me, filled with concern as she scanned my appearance. "You must be freezing."

I nodded. My body was trembling, but not from the icy ground beneath me. As I shifted to look at Eidolon, a mix of fear and guilt overtook me. I knew where his parents were and why they hid it from him.

And then there was the pesky little issue of who his father was.

I didn't relish the thought of being the one to break the news that his father was someone he loathed. It was definitely an awkward and uncomfortable situation, one that I wasn't looking forward to. But I knew it was something he needed to find out sooner rather than later. The big question was whether I should be the one to tell him or if someone else would beat me to it.

I needed to come up with a solution, and fast. But that would have to wait until I had a moment to process everything, preferably over a cup of coffee.

"Hi," I whispered.

"Hey, you!" he replied with a devilish smile, making my heart skip a beat. "How was the trip?"

"Very informative, to say the least. Can you help me? There's a rock under my ass, and it's a bit uncomfortable," I shifted painfully.

Sydney and Watson stood on either side of me, lifting me up from the ground. My legs were weak and unable to hold me upright. I stumbled forward, and Eidolon quickly reached out to wrap his strong arms around my waist, helping me regain my balance. The world swirled around me, but I concentrated on the comforting scent of Eidolon.

"You do find the most inconvenient times to travel," Watson whispered into my ear. I wanted to tell him he didn't know the half of it, but I restrained myself and gave him a crooked smile.

As I regained my balance, my eyes locked onto the White Oak tree. Its ethereal glow had vanished, and it looked to be just a regular tree once more. Puzzled, I cautiously moved closer and reached out to touch it.

Max suggested Taliesin cast a spell to keep himself connected to reality; it could be how he communicated with the world outside. I remembered from my high school science class that trees were interconnected through their roots and could send messages to one another.

Had Taliesin been responsible for the glow? Did he use the tree to guide us to this spot?

"Well, that's strange," Max commented as he followed my eyes to the tree. "When did it stop glowing?"

Isabelle's voice broke the eerie silence, pulling me out of my thoughts. I released my grip on the tree and turned towards her, noticing the concern in her eyes as she stared up at the towering trunk. "Can you walk?" She looked back at me before glancing around. "Something feels off. The atmosphere has shifted. We should probably keep moving before we find out what it is."

I nodded, sensing the same ominous presence as her. Faint laughter echoed through the thick air, growing louder and closer to where we stood. A tiny tendril of fog slinked across the forest floor and wounded itself around Eidolon's feet.

That's not good, I thought as my eyes darted around with apprehension. Another giggle and my eyes shot to the tree line where a young woman was walking towards us. Her hair billowed out behind her, her eyes dancing with mischief and a hint of insanity, dark clouds swarming over her feet as she glided across the ground.

Vivian.

"We need to leave now." I grabbed Eidolon's arm, my fingers digging into his skin as I tried to drag him along with me. But he remained frozen, like a statue carved from unyielding stone. I turned to look at him and let out a sharp gasp. The usual sharpness in his eyes was obscured by a murky layer, spreading like a malevolent cloak over his body.

"Eidolon?" I shook him.

His clouded eyes glanced down at me. "They want me to go with her," he muttered, trying to break free from my grasp.

I scrambled in front of him, trying to push him back, but my efforts were futile against his larger frame. He continued to advance. With a sharp inhale of breath, I let out a gut-wrenching cry of agony as my feet sank into the soft and unforgiving earth beneath me. Every muscle in my body screamed in protest as I struggled to stay on my feet.

"Watson," I screamed.

As soon as my voice pierced the air, Sydney and Watson appeared, their figures breaking through the darkness. They reached out and grabbed his shoulders, struggling to pull him back. Despite our combined efforts- me pushing and them pulling- it was a struggle to turn him around.

"We don't play with magickal things we don't recognize," Sydney grunted, his fingers tightening on Eidolon's jacket collar as he pulled him away from the clearing. The sinister black fog trailed behind us, its tendrils reaching out like beckoning fingers, but Sydney swatted it away with his enormous hands.

"Run. Fast!" Sydney growled as we burst out of the forest and into the open field, pulling Eidolon behind him.

We ran.

Exhausted and trembling with fear, we collapsed in a heap on the ground when we reached the trailhead. It took some time for us to regain our breath, and during those moments, none of us uttered a word—the recent event too strange to put into words.

"I think we should take this spot off our list as a potential picnic area," Sydney said as he looked back over his shoulder.

"I would have to agree," Max muttered, looking at the forest like he lost a dear friend. "Whatever that was, it is not something I want to meet again."

"You okay?" I watched Eidolon struggle to shake off whatever had taken control of him.

"I'm good." He glanced over at me, running a hand through his tousled hair. Standing up slowly, he reached out to help me up. "I think we are done here for now." He glanced over at the forest with a shudder.

Understatement of the year.

"I agree." Sydney looked at us with a wide grin. "Anyone else starving?"

The walk back to the hotel was quiet, with each of us absorbed in our own thoughts. Eidolon stayed close by my side, only a few inches away at all times. I snuck a quick look at him, but he seemed lost in contemplation. I didn't interrupt the silence, instead keeping my eyes on the path ahead. It was best to give him some space and time to sort through his thoughts. I knew he would share with me when he was ready.

Besides, I had my own worries.

How did Vivian even know Eidolon was in the area? Did she and Lilith realize we were in Scotland looking for the Book of the Veiled? And how were they able to imprison Taliesin and Diana in a tree?

Diana claimed she didn't want to be found, insisting it was better for Eidolon's safety. But I didn't understand why. She knew Eidolon held the Book of the Veiled within him and that Lilith and Vivian needed both him and the book to escape their prison in the Otherworld. So why weren't they helping him?

I quickly scanned the rest of the group; their expressions mirrored my own, a mix of solemnity and nervousness. The gravity of our predicament had finally sunk in for all of us. The only thing I knew for sure was this group of people was now my tribe, and I was going to protect them all with everything I had.

Even Aelle.

The boys headed straight to the bar to grab a drink when we walked through the hotel doors.

Isabelle and I said our farewells to them and headed toward the stairs to wash off the mud. She linked her arm through mine, and we made our way up. As we ascended, I could feel my tension dissipating and my headache easing.

I shot Isabelle a grateful smile.

"I'm sure you have a million questions, luv, but this is not the time for them," she said firmly as we arrived at my room. Raising a finger to silence me before I could object, she continued, "Your first task is to go into that beautiful bathroom and take a relaxing bath. No worrying about the forest, glowing trees, or anything else until we are clean and fed. Understand?"

I nodded weakly, thankful for the reprieve. I wanted to tell her about my meet and greet with Eidolon's parents and my vision of Vivian, but her face quickly changed my mind.

Isabelle's gentle yet firm push propelled me through the door. "No thinking," she scolded.

"Thank you, Isabelle," I said, looking over my shoulder. "For everything."

"Of course, luv. It is what friends do," she answered with a wave of her hand as she walked into her room. Her voice was casual, but I caught a tiny hiccup of fear. She was keeping something from me, but I didn't have the energy to ask what. Isabelle would tell me when she was ready.

I turned the faucets and waited for the bathtub to fill. The key hanging around my neck, usually just a comforting weight, began to emit a soft warmth that quickly became a beautiful melody.

Removing it, I held it in front of me, hoping for some kind of miraculous event to occur. When nothing happened, and no portals to other dimensions or answers were revealed, I sighed, disappointed, and placed it on the counter.

I was beginning to realize I'd gotten the raw end of the magick stick.

Chapter 31

'Travel Where You Are Needed Most.' -Book of the Veiled Instructions

The group of boys were huddled around the crackling fireplace, surrounded by stacks of papers, books, and laptops on the coffee table in front of them. My eyes couldn't help but wander over to the side table nearby, which was adorned with an array of tempting treats - scones, coffee, tea, and fresh fruit. I made my way towards it.

As I nibbled on the scones, I halfheartedly listened to the boys debating whether Eidolon should contact his grandmother and have the rest of the Raven Society flown over. From the look on their faces, they had been discussing it for a while.

Eidolon let out a frustrated sigh and rubbed his temples. "All the resources they need are at the Raven Societies library. They stay."

Max let out a groan. "You're making a mistake, Eidolon. Your library is good, but you don't have all the necessary information. Taliesin and my grandfather were working together on something. Here in Scotland. Moll needs to be here and help me go through my collection."

Eidolon shook his head. "It's too dangerous. I can't keep her safe here."

"In case you failed to notice," Sydney chimed in, his voice soft as he rose from his seat and headed to the side table. "There's a clan of shapeshifters here that I'm sure would be willing to help protect her." He loaded his plate, inspecting an apple before setting it back down and choosing a scone instead.

A clan of what?

I whipped my head up from my plate, narrowing my eyes as I studied his imposing figure. He avoided my gaze, but his guilty expression gave it all away. Our eyes met briefly before he glanced away in shame.

Ah Ha! I studied him with new appreciation. With broad, muscular shoulders and a size that towered over most, Sydney was a protective male. His fierce loyalty knew no bounds, and he would willingly give his life to protect those he loved. And when it came to food, he devoured it as if there were not enough to satisfy his voracious appetite.

"That explains why you are always hungry," I cried. "You're a werewolf."

"Hardly," he huffed in horror. "My family is descendants of King Arcas, ruler of Arcadia. He was a shapeshifter," he finished proudly, turning his attention back to the table of food.

"What's the difference?" I asked as I fought the urge to reach out and touch him.

"We're all offsprings from the original werewolf, but unlike the traditional packs, my line can shapeshift when we want. We also have better control of our emotions and hunger." Sydney returned to his seat and sat, theatrically popping a grape into his mouth.

Curious, I asked, "What form do you take on?" I expected him to say something like a lion or a panther: assertive, sleek, and independent.

"I happen to be a Black Ram." His chest puffed out in pride.

A Black Ram? I wasn't expecting that. But the more I thought about it, the more I realized Sydney was the embodiment of the animal. They were influential animals worshiped by cultures across the world. Known for their strength, wisdom, and fertility.

Max tried to hold back a laugh but failed miserably.

Eidolon's dark eyebrows shot up in a questioning arch. "Do you have something to add?" he asked, his deep voice filling the space with a commanding tone. The tension crackled like electricity between the three men.

"It has nothing to do with what his animal is, I swear." Max held his hands up in surrender. "But he is skipping the family drama leading to the two bloodlines."

He turned towards me, and I smiled gratefully. Obviously, he was the only one who would give me a straight answer.

"One of the first kings of Arcadia, King Lycaon, was the son of Zeus and, according to Greek mythology, he was the first mortal to walk on earth. It's up in the air if he was a good king, but the people liked him for the most part.

"He established the city of Lycosura, named Mount Lykaion after himself, instigated the Lycaena Games, and even built a temple dedicated to his daddy," he explained. I arched an eyebrow, unsure where the history lesson was going.

"It was rumored that King Lycaon, and his many sons were arrogant and vain, even going so far as to sacrifice small children. Naturally, this did not sit well with Zeus. Outraged, he decided to visit the city disguised as a commoner to test his son." Max shook his head. "How exactly a god can disguise himself is unknown, but it didn't take long for his identity to be revealed. King Lycaon, angry, decided to sacrifice a child and present it to Zeus on a platter.

"Yuck," I let out a gasp, shuddering.

Max nodded. "It gets worse. The child was Zeus's grandson. Furious, Zeus got his revenge." Max frowned. "Either he killed King Lycaon and his sons with lightning bolts, or he wiped out the family in the Great Flood. Either way, King Lycaon's family was destroyed."

"That's a horrible story," I sputtered, looking at Sydney wide-eyed. He shrugged with a mischievous grin.

"All's well that ends well. Zeus brings his grandson back to life and crowns him king of Arcadia. He was well-known for his love of hunting. His favorite prey was wolves." He wiggled his eyebrows in delight.

"Oh." I nodded my head up and down slowly.

His smile widened as he reassured me, "Typical family drama. But we've moved on." He chuckled and added, "We even invite the wolves to our holiday gatherings now. Of course, we don't ask them to bring any food. Just in case." His expression turned earnest. "I wanted to tell you, but Emma asked me not to."

"Why would Emma ...." I started again before another piece of the puzzle fell into place. Moll mentioned that she had tasked Emma with finding something, as she was the most skilled tracker she knew. "Emma's your grandmother, isn't she?"

His eyes pleaded with me to understand before he glanced at Eidolon and back at me.

"Why didn't you?" I asked, not taking my eyes off Sydney.

Eidolon began, "We wanted to ensure you had enough time to..." I held up my hand, waiting for the shapeshifter to tell me. Sydney gave Eidolon a sharp look before turning back to me with a grave expression.

"We thought you should have time to get used to your new abilities. I was against it initially, but then you traveled so quickly that I worried you would've gotten lost if we told you too much." He paused. "My family's job is to protect the Writer and the Librarian. But I was planning to tell you soon if he," Sydney nodded back at Eidolon, "didn't get up the nerve to do it himself."

I stood staring at him, trying to decide what to do. I was a grown woman who had somehow miraculously been able to live on my own for years. I did not need some haughty, over-educated, egotistical man dictating what I was *ready* to know.

I turned to face Eidolon, my blood boiling with rage as I prepared for a fight. Isabelle's hand on my arm and her whispered words kept me from unleashing my rage.

"He didn't mean anything by it. Eidolon was scared. He won't admit it, but he was afraid of losing you."

My anger was quickly doused by reality, and I let out a sigh knowing my frustration would have to take a backseat for now. But I promised myself that once this mission was over, Eidolon and I would have a serious conversation about what I did and did not have a right to know.

Eidolon flinched as I sent the thought through our bond, making sure everyone heard it. Isabelle and Watson both laughed while Sydney gave Eidolon a sympathetic look.

"It's all good," I said, refusing to meet Eidolon's stare, focusing on Sydney instead. "But don't ask me to carry your clothes for you!"

I moved to the couch, sitting beside Watson and Isabelle as Sydney's laughter filled the room. Max eyed Sydney with concern.

"Don't worry, young man. You won't be eaten. I already told the family that you're off limits," Sydney reassured him as he popped a scone into his mouth. Relief filled Max's eyes, and it took everything that I had to hold back a laugh.

"Can we please go back to the task at hand and not Sydney's family's barbaric eating habits?" Watson asked, exasperated, adjusting his sweater. "I would love to know where Chloe traveled and why she returned smelling *old*. Then we can debate whether we need to bring Moll and the rest of the crew here."

Everyone in the room nodded in agreement. I got comfortable, tucking my legs under me, and inhaled deeply. A pleasant sea salt and coffee aroma filled the room, and I immediately knew where it was coming from.

With a smirk directed at Eidolon, I eagerly prepared to watch the show unfold. His gaze held a hint of curiosity before it quickly shifted towards the doorway in a sudden expression of surprise.

"I assure you, Watson, no discussion needed. I decided for you," Moll declared as she moved beside the fireplace, warming her hands.

I grinned as Moll peeked over at me. "My dear unfortunate successor," she hurried over to hug me. "Thank you for sharing her with me," she whispered.

I winked. While trying to throw messages down the bond to Eidolon during my time with Diana and Taliesin, I found a bright blue link tied to Moll's consciousness.

Hopeful she could hear me, I sent her snippets of our conversation and visions of her daughter. It wasn't much, but I thought it might mean something to her. I was fairly sure that neither Diana nor Taliesin suspected and was relieved that Moll had gotten the news.

Her gratitude did not last long as she turned with the energy of a tornado and faced Eidolon head-on. "I heard you were trying to keep me away?"

Eidolon quickly tried to explain his position before Moll cut him off. "No need to argue about it now! I'm here and safe. Crichton, Emma, Aelle, and Victor will join us soon." She glanced at Isabelle and me with a knowing smile. "Their flight was a bit longer than mine."

I made a mental note to ask Moll if I could also travel like that. It would make grocery shopping much more pleasant if I could zip in and out.

"It seems like I have no choice in the matter," Eidolon said as he got up to hug his grandmother. "You were never one to listen to reason."

"Young man," Moll started as she patted his cheek. "You have no idea what I'm capable of. Or her," she added as she pointed to me. "Now, Chloe, tell everyone who Taliesin asked you to find."

The room erupted in gasps, and I knew Eidolon was trying to catch my eye. A twinge of guilt shot through me - I should've talked to him beforehand, but I hadn't the opportunity.

I don't think it's the right time to tell him who his father is, I heard through the bond with Moll.

Shouldn't he know his mother and father are alive, at least? I asked, glancing at her in surprise.

Yes. But not yet. We need to find the Book of the Veiled first.

Okay, I agreed unwillingly, knowing the decision would bite me in the ass eventually.

Chapter 32

'The Afterlife Was Not Always What It Seems.' -Book of the Veiled Instructions

During the next thirty minutes, I told them everything I knew about Lilith and Vivian. I took special care to be as informative as possible, ignoring the parts that would expose Taliesin and Diana.

Now for the best part.

I took a deep breath and counted to four before exhaling slowly for six seconds. The brief moment allowed me to focus on calming my thoughts and preparing for whatever was to come next.

"We need to find Arawn and convince him to help us find the Book of the Veiled," I paused. "In the Otherworld."

I studied Eidolon closely after I finished, trying to gauge his reaction. His hands clenched into tight fists when I mentioned the Otherworld.

"How do we reach Arawn?" Isabelle was the first to find her voice after I stopped talking and got up to get another cup of tea. "There hasn't been a whisper of him in centuries." She looked between Watson and Moll, who both shook their heads.

"My grandfather talked about him," Max recalled, scratching his chin. "When he was writing his book *Letters on Demonology and Witchcraft*. My father used to tell me stories about Arawn; he was one of his favorite gods. It always bothered him that Arawn was portrayed as more demonic than he was."

"What do you mean?" I looked at him in disbelief. "He is the God of Death and the Otherworld. I believe demonic would be an accurate way to describe him."

Max's expression contorted into a mixture of disgust and pity as he turned his gaze towards me. "In our culture, Arawn is highly regarded," he explained. "He represented honor, duty, war, death, tradition, terror, and hunting. And contrary to the depiction in Dante's Peak, Arawn's realm was not a place of eternal punishment. It was seen as a peaceful afterlife." He crossed his arms and sat back.

"What happened to him?" I inquired, sensing that there was much more to learn about the deity I was supposed to locate.

"He was rewritten," Max explained sadly. "Instead of the beloved ruler, he became a terror of evil, and his home became a sanctuary for evil. In some Arthurian legends, Merlin is equated with Arawn, and the two began to have a troubling relationship in mythology. In one respect, they were both virtuous and divine. But in another, they are the commanders of corruption and doom."

"Why were there such contrasting stories?" Sydney walked over to get more food, his eyes scanning the options before finally settling on a cranberry-orange scone.

Max looked over his shoulder at him. "Easy, because religious leaders changed the stories in the Middle Ages. Everyone knows that whoever holds the pen is the author of history."

"So, how do we find him? Does he still exist after all this time?" I glanced at Moll, hoping for reassurance. However, she was fixated on Eidolon, who sat stoically in his chair, his face betraying no emotion. When she turned to face me, I could see the worry in her gaze.

"Let's wait until Samhain. It's still thought to be when the veil between the two worlds is thinnest. We can attempt to summon him then," she proposed, glancing at Eidolon again.

I had a mental picture of the eight of us putting a cell phone on speaker and dialing the God of Death. I wondered what his number would be.

1-800-YOU-DEAD?

Isabelle squared her shoulders and cleared her throat. "Samhain is only three days away," she stated, sounding like she was preparing to face a firing squad. "Perhaps my family could provide us with some helpful information."

"We'll need to bring a gift for his hellhounds," someone called out from the doorway. "I don't know about you, but I would rather not be eaten by a pack of ghostly hounds. It is as unsettling as the Tooth Fairy." The voice shuddered.

We all turned our heads in unison, startled by wet footsteps in the front hall. Aelle, Victor, Crichton, and Emma stood before us, their clothes drenched and hair plastered to their faces. The lingering scent of rain filled the air as they dripped onto the polished hardwood floor. Their expressions were a mix of exhaustion and determination, hinting at their adventure getting to Scotland.

Victor grumbled as he shook the rain from his jacket and wiped droplets from his face. "You should have told us an umbrella wouldn't be enough to keep us dry," he complained, shivering from the cold. "I don't think I'll ever feel warm again."

Esme appeared suddenly, strolling out of the kitchen with a tray of hot drinks and more food. "When I got a call about a group of angry Americans wandering aimlessly in the pouring rain with only one umbrella and not a head covering in sight, I knew your friends had arrived."

She placed the tray on the table and walked right over to Emma. "Welcome home, cousin! It has been too long since you visited."

"Esme! You look wonderful! Not a day over twenty-three," Emma cried as she hugged her back. "How was my grandson? Did he eat you out of house and home?"

"No, he was fine. I did introduce him to Charlie's daughter." Esme winked. "She is as cute as a button-nosed puppy and a fabulous cook!"

"Esme! I'm sitting right here," Sydney laughed as he got up to hug his grandmother. "Stop trying to marry me off!"

"Excuse me!" a female voice called from behind them, sharp and loud. Aelle stood with her hands on her hips and a scowl on her face. "I thought we got summoned here to work." She looked across the room, barely concealing her contempt for me.

She stopped glaring when she saw Max, giving him a curious look. I wanted to stand up and shield him from any potential emotional pain she might inflict, but something held me back. She wasn't giving off a hostile vibe anymore.

What in the world?

"You must be Max. I heard you have a library the public hasn't accessed in generations."

"Yes," Max stammered under her intense gaze. I felt sorry for the man but saw a tiny shimmer of interest in his eyes. "My great-grandfather's library."

"It doesn't matter who owned it. I just need to see it," Aelle said as she turned to pick up her suitcase. "I assume my bedroom is upstairs?" She arched an eyebrow at Esme in question.

So much for introductions and small talk.

"Third door on the right," Esme directed, not even batting an eye at the rudeness. She had undoubtedly encountered her fair share of angry Americans throughout her career. But Aelle was going to present a whole new challenge.

"I am going to shower, change, eat, and then you, Max, will accompany me to your family's library, and we'll get to work." she stated as she headed up the stairs without another word.

As she stood at the top of the staircase, I could see that she was hesitant. In a fleeting moment, her gaze flickered towards Eidolon, and a hint of sadness flashed across her face before she shook it off and continued on her way.

What was that about? I thought as I watched her retreat, glancing at Eidolon, who looked as confused as me.

"She has been the picture of decorum and pleasantry since Moll told her we were heading here." Victor rolled his eyes. "We were upgraded to first class within ten minutes of boarding because the flight attendant was terrified of her." Victor laughed as he came over to hug me.

"Glad you made it," Sydney got up and slapped him on the back. "Esme prepared a room for you next to mine. I'll show you to your room first, and then we can grab a drink at the pub. I can fill you in on all that's happened."

They walked upstairs while Crichton carried luggage to the first floor's back rooms. "I assume we are in our normal chambers?" he called over his shoulder. Esme nodded.

He stopped as he passed me. "Hello, Ms. Chloe. I am glad to see you are doing well. How was the journey?"

"Eventful," I admitted.

"I can't wait for you to fill us in," he declared, looking around the room. "Dinner will be at 7:30 sharp. We will start preparing then." He turned to Moll. "Let's get you settled. We can talk shop after you rest some."

She nodded, squeezed Eidolon's hand, and trailed after Crichton, Esme, and Emma, already gossiping about family drama.

"Well, my head hurts," Watson joked. "Guess we will all be meeting up for dinner?"

I nodded in agreement. I was beyond worn out, and I only wanted a nap.

Let the games begin.

Chapter 33

'Keys Do More Than Just Protect Valuables.' -Book of the Veiled Instructions

My nap was shattered by troubling dreams of the Otherworld, a desolate and colorless land that seemed to exist only in shades of gray. The landscape resembled a watercolor painting washed out and drained of all vibrancy. As I walked through the haunting realm, the whispers of lost souls filled my ears, and their stories played out in my mind like vivid scenes from a forgotten history.

Tales of love, betrayal, homicide, and thievery echoed throughout the land. Every one of them imprisoned for their wrongdoings during their lifetime, serving their sentences in this desolate place. I wondered how many souls were trapped here; it was impossible to know for sure because they weren't corporeal beings, only remnants left behind in the form of memories and thoughts.

The landscape felt strangely familiar, like a distorted version of the countryside we'd explored earlier. Without the vibrancy and life. A heavy, suffocating feeling settled in my chest. I scanned my surroundings, turning in a circle to take in my surroundings. The only word that came to mind was "dull." The world lacked color or life.

This was where Lilith and Vivian lived? In limbo between reality and thought?

I ventured towards the entrance of the dark forest, a faint light beckoning me in. Standing in the tree line was an enormous figure cloaked in a long gray robe with a heavy hood concealing half its face, and on either side of it stood three tremendously large white wolves as large as a small bull with paws almost as wide as my hand.

The animals eyed me intently, their red eyes glowing and tails wagging as I approached.

The air filled with the sweet aroma of white heather, and I could feel the god's strength radiating from him. He wasn't as intimidating as I'd imagined; in fact, the guardian of the dead seemed almost reluctant.

His familiar eyes drew me in, yet I couldn't place him. I'd met him before. I knew that I had.

"Good to see you again, Chloe." He handed me a spring of heather, and I eyed it curiously.

"Is this hell?" I asked boldly. My penchant for being overly curious had gotten me into trouble many times, and my mother often warned me that I was running out of chances. But I felt at ease with the god. Comfortable enough that I reached out and petted one of the oversized wolves behind its ears. The shaggy fur felt like silk threads through my fingers, and I chuckled as it turned to nuzzle my arm.

"That's what some call it," the figure in the hood remarked, his eyes fixed on the river. "But it wasn't always this way. It used to be a place of tranquility and natural beauty." I turned my head to see what he was staring at as he spoke.

With a narrow gaze, I could barely distinguish the frantic figures of people clambering onto the slick stones, their desperate grip fighting against the relentless crashing waves. Each surge threatened to swallow them whole as they struggled to stay afloat. Their hands shook and slipped, grasping at anything to keep them from being swept away by the river's force.

"What happened?" I asked, fighting back the need to save them. Their punishment was so dreadful that it must have been for something heinous in their past life. I didn't even want to imagine what actions led to such an awful fate.

"Someone rewrote it." He shifted his gaze to a woman screaming as she was washed away, only to appear in the same spot. I watched the torment wash over him like he was battling the urge to rescue her. Defeat finally rested on his shoulders as he averted his eyes.

"How?"

"Taliesin."

I woke up suddenly, struggling for air as I untangled myself from the sheets. I'd somehow managed to kick off the heavy comforter, and most of the pillows were scattered around the room. The curtains were still drawn open, and I gasped for breath while staring out at the expansive view before me. A loud and insistent knocking at my door jolted me out of my thoughts, and I hurried to open it.

"Are you alright," Eidolon asked as he let himself in, his eyes darting around as if he were prepared to find an intruder.

"I'm fine," I answered, scrambling to put on a baggy hoodie. The room had been cozy when I fell asleep, but now it was freezing. My breath turned into wispy clouds as I hurried to the heater and cranked up the temperature.

Strange, I thought as I looked around in worry.

With a furrowed brow, Eidolon settled onto the small couch next to the elegant writing desk. His intense gaze followed my every movement. "Who were you talking to?" He demanded, his voice laced with suspicion and concern.

"I think I had a dream about Arawn," I said as I wrapped my arms around me, wishing I had a cup of coffee. "Somehow, I ended up in the Otherworld, which, by the way, looks a lot like Scotland."

"You saw Arawn and the Otherworld?" His voice trembled with fear, matching the wild regard in his eyes as his body tensed and his hands clenched into fists.

Without a word, I sat on the edge of the bed, my feet tucked underneath me as I tried to calm my racing heart. I could still feel the otherworldly chill lingering in the air, a reminder of the terrifying dream.

"Yes. I think he wanted me to see it."

"Did he say anything?"

"No, but I think he wanted to," I confessed. "He was sad, Eidolon. Something upset him." I looked down at my hands, itching to write, and the key lying against my chest started to warm. "I think he wanted me to help."

"We need to tell the rest of the team," he said, getting up from his seat and walking to the door. I felt a wave of emotion hit me as he walked away. Tears formed in my eyes. The past few days had been difficult, and it was starting to take its toll on me. He swung around. "Hey now, there's no crying in baseball." He hurried towards me, wrapping me in his arms.

"I don't know how to play baseball," I hiccupped. Eidolon laughed into my hair.

"I'll teach you," he said. We sat there for a moment before he pulled away to look down at me. I wiped the tears away with my sweatshirt sleeves and sniffed.

"I can't throw," I admitted, pushing my glasses up on my nose.

"We'll find something else to do then," he chuckled. "How about I head downstairs and get us some coffee." He gently grabbed my chin to look at him. "You stay here and write everything down. That way, I can help you carry some of the burden."

I nodded in agreement and smiled. He leaned in and kissed me on the forehead, and some of my stress drained away. It wasn't romantic, nothing that a spicy romance novel would be proud of, but it was gentle and sweet. Just what I needed.

"Give me a second." Eidolon stepped out of the room, and the chill in the air returned once he left. Why did I always feel that way whenever he left? I shook off the thought and focused on the task at hand. I needed to document everything, and thankfully, Eidolon was there to help me shoulder the weight.

But what about the story I had no intention of documenting? Who would share the burden of knowing where his parents were and what steps needed to be taken to keep him safe? What about *that* skeleton in the closet?

As my hand wrapped around the key against my chest, I felt a gentle vibration and flicker, almost as if the key acknowledged my secrets. It may have been odd to talk to an inanimate object, but I whispered all the stories that I couldn't share with anyone else. With each word, the heaviness in my chest lessened.

The key had taken my secrets for me and locked them away.

Eidolon strolled back into the room, a silver tray balanced delicately in his hands. The rich, intoxicating aroma of freshly brewed coffee wafted toward me, tempting me with its warmth. Instinctively, I tucked the key under my shirt as I made my way over to make myself a cup.

"Ready to tell your story," Eidolon asked as he held out a pen and my copy of the Book of the Veiled.

With a huge smile, I took it from him and walked to the desk, pausing to peek out the window at the scenery. I stood there until the last rays of sunlight filtered across the landscape, filling the sky with delightful reds and gold as the sun sank lower and lower into the horizon.

Then I sat down and wrote until the moon appeared high in the sky and the stars twinkled.

Chapter 34

'Everyone Has A Part To Play.' -Book of the Veiled Instructions.

Over the next three days, Eidolon and I researched, argued, discussed, and breathed every possible roadblock we could encounter while contacting Arawn. I'd hoped he would return in a dream, but he never appeared.

Aelle and Max spent most of their days locked away in Max's family's library. They even took an overnight bag with them, so they didn't need to travel back and forth. According to Max, it would be more efficient to keep their minds on their task. However, I couldn't help but think he just wanted some privacy with Aelle.

She did not put up much of a fight for whatever reason, except when she insisted on everyone carrying pens and notebooks everywhere they went. As the self-proclaimed leader of the research team, she pressed on us that no matter how trivial any information we discovered seemed, it had to be documented.

A group chat was even created, and bodily harm was threatened to those who failed to share vital information on time. By the look on her face, she meant it.

A tiny part of me wasn't comfortable with Aelle having Eidolon's phone number, but it was a matter of jealousy more than anything else. Although I was irritated whenever I heard his phone chime with another message from her, I had to remind myself I had no real ties to him. But neither did she.

And I was sure she was doing it to get under my skin.

In true adult fashion, I bit my tongue and told myself to be grateful she was willing to tackle the mind-numbing task of sorting through dusty old books. But it didn't ease the desire to throw Eidolon's phone whenever she texted him.

Esme and Sydney, accompanied by the curious and silent Victor, embarked on a journey to visit all the clan homes scattered throughout the land. Their goal was to speak with the elders, hoping to uncover any oral tales that may have been passed down through generations but never recorded in written form.

Isabelle and Watson made their way to her coven, eager to consult the family grimoire on contacting lost gods. It was also a perfect opportunity for Isabelle to gather any necessary supplies for potential spell-casting or potion-making.

Even though she reminded us all that potions were not magick. Simply family recipes, as she liked to call them.

Emma and Crichton stayed at the hotel with Moll, Eidolon, and me, giving Moll time to rest and recover. Traveling to Scotland took more out of her than she wanted to admit, and most of her day was spent researching at the hotel library.

Moll's main focus was to unravel the mysteries and contradictions surrounding the God of the Otherworld, one of the most perplexing characters in history. She was determined to uncover any common themes or patterns that may shed light on his true nature - whether he was benevolent, malevolent, or a deity with questionable dietary habits like devouring souls.

The one thing I knew would remain consistent throughout history was that for a mortal to enter the sacred realm of the gods, they must first traverse a river, pass through an unyielding door, and present a humble offering as tribute.

After years of studying death, I was well-versed in the solemn ritual passed down from one generation to the next. It was a test of worthiness and a way to show respect for the divine beings who resided beyond the threshold.

That sounded easy enough, but unfortunately, there were no records of what people offered in the past.

What did we need to do to attract Arawn's attention?

And where was the entrance?

Chapter 35

'The Anwers To The Most Important Questions Are Usually Painful.' -Book of the Veiled Instructions

I approached Eidolon and Moll with an idea as we sat by the fire. It'd been another long day of discovering nothing useful. As I doodled in my notebook, I realized that the physical and the mystical were interconnected, which meant that the reality here might also be reality elsewhere.

The landscape in my dream bore a striking resemblance to the Scottish countryside. Could they be the same? What if Taliesin's tree was the entrance we've been searching for? I remembered seeing a glowing tree in my dream, but I didn't think much of it then.

So what was to say that the dream tree wasn't the same as the Taliesin tree? A portal to another world.

My theory was purely conjecture, lacking concrete evidence. Still, I couldn't shake the feeling that it was worth exploring. Perhaps if we were closer to the entrance of the Otherworld, we would be granted access. Or we might stumble upon a hidden button that would activate an elevator heading downward.

After telling them about my theory, Eidolon was not inclined to allow me to wander alone and appointed himself as my protector and caretaker. A brief fight ensued between the two of us. Despite my insistence that

Eidolon couldn't be near Taliesin's tree, he reminded me that he was a big boy capable of making rational decisions.

"Did you forget about the fog that had no respect for personal space? Vivian or Lilith will know you are there if you go back," I reasoned through clenched teeth. "We barely got you out last time, and only because of Sydney's massive paws dragging you away."

"Yes, I happen to remember," Eidolon looked down his nose at me in frustration. "I also know I am carrying around the rest of the Book of the Veiled, so unless you want to conduct your experiments here in the hotel's safety, you need me to come with you."

"Fine, we will stay here." I plopped down on the couch and crossed my arms in irritation. Eidolon was not going back to that tree. I waved my land at my laptop, sitting on the coffee table. "I'm sure google.com has the answers we're looking for."

Eidolon barked a laugh and narrowed his eyes at me. "I didn't take you for a woman willing to let a little fear back her into a corner. Here, I was under the impression you were a fighter."

Ouch! Low blow, I grimaced.

I was a fighter who knew when to stay in the ring and when to throw in the towel. I narrowed my eyes at him as his words danced around. What *was* the real reason why I didn't want him to go to the tree? Was it because I thought he couldn't protect himself? No. Was it because I thought there was another way? Because there wasn't.

The real reason was that I feared losing someone else I cared for in my life. I would rather take all the chances and walk into the blackest fog than see someone hurt or even killed. But the look in Eidolon's eyes told me this was not the time to pretend I was Wonder Woman.

"Fine. Whatever," I grumbled as I stood up and marched towards the fireplace, snatching the poker from its stand. I vented my frustration on the burning logs. Turning to face him, I brandished the poker in his direction. "But if you are dragged into the black mist of horror, don't expect me to run after you this time."

Amusement sparkled in his eyes. "I have no doubt you wouldn't let it get that close," he grinned.

Rolling my eyes, I headed for my room. "And you have to carry everything yourself," I called over my shoulder as I walked up the stairs.

The following day, Eidolon met me at the base of the staircase with a backpack full of food, a thermos filled with coffee, and Aelle's mandated notebooks. I still wasn't convinced this was a wise decision, but I had to admit it was better than going alone.

Despite my eagerness to reach the tree, Eidolon kept slowing down as we followed the Merlin path, his eyes fixated on his arms. He ran his fingers over the intricate patterns etched into his skin, examining them with a curious intensity.

I stood at the forest's edge, tapping my foot impatiently as I watched Eidolon struggle with the backpack's weight. His muscles bulged under his rolled-up sleeves as he finally threw down the bag and wiped the sweat from his brow. "I told you I could carry some of the stuff," I reminded him, feeling a twinge of guilt for not helping out earlier.

"No, smart-ass. The books feel like they are trying to escape," he groaned, rolling his arms in front of him.

Irritated, I headed back, attempting to suppress the comment that books couldn't escape.

But the fact was, they could, and that's why we were trudging through Scotland in search of them. He held out his arms for me to see, and my jaw dropped.

His arms overflowed with words, glittering and changing as if characters were jostling for position. It was captivating, and I suddenly understood what he meant when he said the books were inside him. His body had become a living library. The scent of fresh paper, aged leather, dry ink, and the warmth of a brand-new book wafted around me.

Heaven.

The way Eidolon clenched his jaw made it clear that he did not share the same sentiment. "It's like being tattooed in the same spot repeatedly," he mumbled.

"Do you think they are trying to tell us something?" I reached out to touch the words. Their movements were like a perfectly choreographed ballet, fluid and graceful. The look on Eidolon's face told me it felt more like a children's tap recital.

He muttered between gasps of air, "Whatever they're doing is definitely not enjoyable."

My eyes widened as a sentence started to form.

Ask us a question.

"Eidolon, look!" I cried. "That *is* what they're doing. They're answering our questions."

"Great!" He winced as they moved again, sweat forming along his forehead. "For the love of the gods, ask for something useful."

It took a while for me to understand how to shape the questions; simplicity was the preferred method. They had to be specific and direct, and the books preferred to give simple answers like *yes* or *no*. Complex answers were too painful for Eidolon to endure.

But they also liked to play.

If you have me, you want to share me. If you share me, you won't have me. What am I?

"A secret," Eidolon chuckled as I stared down at the question in confusion.

What do I have in my eye if I am holding a bee?

My lips curved into a smile as I waited for Eidolon's reaction. "It's a clever play on words," I giggled while he glared at his arm in frustration. "The riddle is based on the saying, 'Beauty is in the eye of the beholder.' So, if I hold a bee, I have beauty in my eye."

Eidolon's usually serious face was suddenly transformed by a carefree smile directed at me, and I couldn't help but be struck by his attractiveness. For a moment, I wanted to reach out and tuck the hair that had fallen into his eyes back behind his ear, but I resisted the urge.

It was almost Samhain, and we were no closer to figuring out what gift we needed to bring Arawn.

"I think I have to ask the questions." I pulled my copy of the Book of the Veiled from my backpack. "You have the answers, but I am the one that needs to write them down."

Eidolon gave a slight nod; his mouth turned down at the corners in a slight frown. "Might as well try. What's the worst that can happen?"

Hours later, I was as frustrated as a FedEx driver at Christmas. Each question required careful consideration and had to be meticulously written in my Book of the Veiled copy. Then, I had to navigate through hundreds of books scattered throughout Eidolon to find the answers.

Each misstep of questioning was painful to Eidolon and exhausting to me. By the end of the day, we barely crawled through the hotel door, panting with effort and exhaustion. Crichton was the first to find us, called for Moll, and ran to fetch us something to eat and drink.

As soon as Moll arrived, I explained what we had discovered and asked if she had ever experienced this happening with another Writer and Librarian. Unfortunately, she had not, and when she tried to ask the books a question- the words stayed hidden.

Two days later, I was in the middle of a royal hissy fit, pacing around Taliesin's tree. "I don't know what the hell to ask!" I complained on my third lap. "We've asked everything!"

After a morning of invisible tattooing, Eidolon lay on the forest floor, trying to regain his strength. "We haven't asked the right question, then." He struggled to sit up and look at me. "Come sit beside me," he demanded, patting the ground.

"I feel like I am failing you and Moll." I plopped down beside him, drawing my knees up to my chest. "What if things go wrong?"

"What are you talking about?" Eidolon turned to look at me. "This is not a failure, just a plot twist."

I turned to look at him, falling into the darkness of his eyes. Traces of indigo and silver drew me in as our breaths began to sync. Eidolon turned to look back at the sky, but he took my hand, his thumb drawing small circles against my palm.

"You, Chloe, are not a failure," he whispered. I glanced at him and was surprised when he leaned over to kiss me.

As our lips touched, I felt no explosive sparks or intense heat. Instead, it was like being covered by a soft blanket of feathers. I melted into the kiss, and he pulled me closer with his hands gently entangled in my hair.

A smile spread across my face as his teeth grazed my bottom lip. As I deepened the kiss and our tongues intertwined, he groaned in pleasure. The alluring scent of smoke and cedar surrounded us as I explored his arms with my hands, feeling the strength and power of his muscles beneath my touch.

In an instant, a spark of connection ignited between us, and it grew into an unbreakable bond. I was the first to break the kiss, turning my head with a smile on my lips.

"What are you thinking?"

The words slipped from my mouth before I could even process them. "You belong to me," I blurted out.

A smile spread across his face, and his eyes glimmered with amusement as he responded. "I suppose that's doable," he stated confidently. Then, a sudden gasp escaped from him, and he jumped up in pain, clutching his arm. "Shit," he cursed through gritted teeth as the intensity of the pain increased and drained the color from his face.

I quickly got my feet to help him. As he turned to face me, he extended his arm, and I took a step back in shock.

The son of Taliesin and the daughter of Morrigan,
To walk the Otherworld, this you will need
The Words of the Old and the Blood of the New
The Key to Demise and the Key to Breath
Then, you will see the God of Death.

"I think you asked the right question," Eidolon chuckled. My eyes shot up, and a wave of fear washed over me.

With a raised eyebrow, he read the passage over again. "I still don't get it. Who's the offspring of Taliesin and Morrigan?" He glanced up, his eyes searching mine.

I hesitated, knowing my following words would hurt him.

And there we have it, ladies and gentlemen, the shortest relationship in history!

"We are," I sighed. "Eidolon, I have to tell you something."

Chapter 36

'Monsters Hide Behind The Doors Of Reality.' -Book of the Veiled Instructions

"Where's the fun in that?" a voice echoed from the dark abyss. It was a youthful and enthusiastic sound laced with touches of madness. Eidolon quickly stepped in front of me, ready to face whatever was approaching us.

"Don't move any closer." He took a few steps back, gently pushing us towards the trail. Eidolon gripped his arm tightly, and I could see the strain in his expression as the words angrily crawled up his forearm.

A powerful gust of air slammed into us, pinning us in place. Eidolon's arms wrapped around me protectively, his solid frame shielding me from the ferocity of the force. The pressure was suffocating, making it difficult to breathe. Just as I thought I couldn't take it anymore, the wind suddenly stopped, leaving a strange silence that stretched on for miles.

I raised my gaze to Eidolon, noticing the same terror etched on his face that I felt inside.

This was not good.

"Or what, Eidolon? What do you think you're going to do?" The tone was oddly familiar, but I couldn't place where I had heard it before. I tried to peer around Eidolon's muscular frame, but my view was obstructed. I took a small step to the side.

"Chloe, my dear! I've been eager to meet you in person!" she gushed, gliding towards me with excitement sparkling in her eyes.

Her beauty overwhelmed me. She had a face like an angel and an unnatural walk that seemed like she was floating above the ground. The wind teased her long wheat-colored hair, highlighting strands of gold and red shimmering like a sunset.

Her eyes were mesmerizing. They were a vibrant shade of green, like a fresh spring leaf, speckled with hints of gold and radiating an otherworldly aura. I couldn't look away as I plunged into their captivating depths, consumed by thoughts of desire, indulgence, and longing. When she noticed my gaze, she smiled, her eyes dancing with delight.

"When we last met, I wasn't fully myself," she laughed and spun around, her arms extended. "But now, I am complete."

My mouth dropped. It couldn't be. Could it? I narrowed my eyes, trying to piece the puzzle together.

"What do you want?" Eidolon barked, his body trembling with rage.

She stepped into the light. "Oh, dear Eidolon. You'll find out soon enough." The unmistakable odor of electricity permeated the air, and Eidolon's apprehension diminished as his eyes glazed over and he visibly relaxed. "It's not just nightmares that come true, you see," she purred.

Eidolon's thoughts were elsewhere, and no matter how hard I tried to connect with him through our bond, I couldn't break through.

"Don't fret, dear Chloe. He's content at the moment. I've always found it unfair his visions are constantly of death instead of something more alluring," she said with a slight frown, gazing at him with a quirked eyebrow. "Such a good-looking man. So willing to do anything for his mate." Her eyes darted at me. "I can see why you're so infatuated with him."

Her delicate fingers hovered, poised as if about to caress him. I sneered at the movement. Her gaze flickered back towards me, and a wicked smile tugged at the corners of her lips as she slowly dropped her arm, an unspoken challenge in her eyes. The tension between us crackled like electricity.

"It was the essence of him that brought me here. You must be doing something right for me to hear from the Otherworld. If I had arrived any later, I might have encountered something quite inappropriate," she chuckled.

"Stop," I growled, my voice guttural and fierce, as my fingers curled tightly into fists. My nails dug into the tender flesh of my palms, drawing tiny droplets of blood.

"What was that, Chloe?" She tilted her head. "Cat caught your tongue?"

My eyes narrowed as I glared at her. The grip of terror that held me in its grasp was replaced by a pulsing rage surging through my body. Behind me, Eidolon groaned, his voice laced with desire or pain - I couldn't tell which and didn't want to think about it.

"I said stop," I sneered as I stepped around Eidolon, the key at my chest warming in a warning. "I know who you are, Lilith." My voice dripped with disdain as I spat out her name. "I know what you are planning, and it will not work," I declared, raising my eyebrows defiantly.

Curious, she asked, "What do you think you know? You haven't truly seen who I am."

"I know enough." I bristled at her condescending tone, and my gaze turned wary as Lilith floated closer to me. Her ethereal feet grazed the invisible circle on the damp forest floor before she halted abruptly, a mischievous glint in her eyes.

She couldn't cross over. She must have known what I was thinking because she looked down and frowned.

"No, I can't," she affirmed. "But it doesn't mean I won't be able to one day. And when the time comes, what will your books have to say then?" she challenged. "Will they simply repeat what you already know- that fate cannot be altered?"

Lilith's question struck a nerve. For days, I had been asking myself the same thing. "What do you want?"

"To say hi." A vague smile danced across her face. "And to meet the girl the Fates speak so highly of. It's not every day I get to meet the person who will right the wrongs done against my children. You are a hero, and I wanted to be the first to welcome you home."

Hero? Welcome me home? Right the wrongs? "What are you talking about?" I asked angrily.

She paused. "Did Moll not teach you anything? Or did she leave you helpless like the others?" she questioned, looking at me with pity. "Oh, she didn't tell you... hmm. But no matter, it's a story for another day."

She looked over at Eidolon, who was still locked in whatever fantasy she had played in his mind. A slow smile formed, chilling me to my bones.

"I came to send you a message, lil' Writer." She peeled her eyes away from him and back towards me. "You can call Arawn; I invite you to. But be careful what you wish for. I am not the only one fighting to be released from the prison created for us."

I couldn't help myself and took a step closer, intrigued by what she was saying. My logical side warned me against it, but my curiosity won out. "What do you mean?"

"The truth will reveal itself to you soon," she said with a dismissive wave. "I'm sure the other members of the Raven Society have already stumbled across the information. It may offer insight into why Taliesin and Diana are in their current positions and who is responsible for putting them there."

"You did," I accused. "You locked them in their prison. Tore them away from their son! The son you are currently tormenting!" I hissed.

Laughter filled the forest, bouncing off the trees and vibrating the forest floor. "I promise he is not being tortured. I merely gave him what he secretly desired." She glanced at Eidolon again. "He is quite happy in his vision." She turned back to face me. "Is *that* what Taliesin and Diana told you? That I was the one who locked them away?" she tsked. "So many half-truths, so many secrets...."

"They wouldn't lie," I hesitated.

"Wouldn't they, though? Why, I wonder, did they send for you- Daughter of Morrigan and not their dear and beloved son? Why would Taliesin not want his son in the Otherworld? Why confine him to the mortal world?" she asked. "When he was meant for so much more."

"So you can't use him to annihilate the world!"

Her laughter echoed throughout the area again, shaking the ground. "I never wanted to destroy this world. Why would I? With all its pleasures and curiosities, I was quite content to wait for mortals to shatter it themselves. They have been doing such an excellent job of it on their own," she admitted, tilting her head to the side as if deep in thought.

"Power? Yes, I wanted power! Power to save me, and others like me, from those who would cut off our heads and burn our bodies to ashes. Dear Taliesin, he was never one to see the big picture. But his story fits the narrative well, doesn't it?" She stared into the woods momentarily, considering the tree behind her.

"There were more like you, you know? Not with the same power you have, but with enough to entice Taliesin and his merry band of mischief-makers. Powers that could change the course of history with the swipe of a pen. But then you were chosen. Why, I wonder," she asked, still looking at the tree in wonder. "Did you know there were other Writers before you? But none of them could withstand the visions. They all faltered. Most driven insane by their visions.

"But you, lil' Writer, have not," she turned to look at me in awe. "You are the one we have been waiting for. The one who will help bring us back to our former glory."

"You got it all wrong," I laughed. "I'm a nobody. To tell you the truth, I think you all are out of your minds." I shrugged. "Stolen books, time traveling, witches, vampires, shapeshifters, and glowing trees...this is a Twilight episode gone horribly wrong."

"You have Morrigan's spunk," Lilith chuckled. "I warned Arawn you would be different."

"You know Arawn?" I asked in surprise, not expecting this new tidbit of information.

Lilith shrugged her shoulders, dismissing my question. "I must be leaving. I have been here too long, as it is. But my warning still stands, Chloe," she said with a reluctant smile this time. "Be careful when you call Arawn; you can never be certain what monsters are behind locked doors."

"Wait!" I called out as she turned to leave, gliding back to the tree line. "Why are you telling me this?"

"Because lil' Writer, Moll was right about one thing. You were chosen for a reason. With your help, my children can lift themselves off the brink of unreality and reclaim their spot in this world. They deserve to be remembered as they once were."

She reached out to touch Taliesin's tree, gazing up at the branches in sadness before drawing her hand away. "You're the Writer now, Daughter of Morrigan. Let's finish what she started, and maybe you'll have the happy-ever-after you've wished for."

Chapter 37

'Precipitation Is A Mind Set. Not A Reality.' -Book of the Veiled Instructions

I watched Lilith retreat until she was a tiny dot of light disappearing into the thick forest. Rubbing the back of my neck, I tried to ease the growing tension as I considered her words. Maybe there was a chance she was telling me the truth. But with so many conflicting versions of the same story, it was hard to tell what was real and a lie.

My mind was wandering when her voice carried to me in the wind.

If you want to speak to Arawn, you and Eidolon must ask. Together.

Pivoting on my heel, I scanned the area for any sign of the witch, my senses on high alert. But she wasn't there. Frustrated, I rubbed my tired eyes, wondering if exhaustion was playing tricks on me. Her voice sang out again, reaching out from beyond the shadows.

I look forward to seeing you again, lil' Writer. We have a lot to do.

Before I could question what she meant, Lilith's powerful enchantment over Eidolon dissipated in a dazzling burst of energy. The air around us crackled and hissed as the intricate web of words she had woven into his skin slowly faded. With a heavy thud, Eidolon collapsed to the floor, gasping for breath and fighting to regain control. Every muscle in his body battled against her magic as he tried to break free.

I hurried to his side, my heart pounding in my chest. His body trembled with barely contained fury, and I could see the faint red marks where Lilith's words had seared into his skin. He struggled to sit up, his skin a sickly shade of gray and beads of sweat glistening on his forehead.

"She's gone," I assured him, rubbing his back.

He let out a frustrated sigh and leaned back, resting his weight on his ass as he ran a hand through his tousled hair. The setting sun cast a warm glow on his face, highlighting the lines of worry and confusion, his eyes searching the tree line. "Where did she go?" He glanced over, his eyes searching mine. "What did she want?"

"I don't know. She just disappeared." I hesitated for a moment, unsure of how much to reveal. The conversation with Lilith had left a permanent mark on my mind, making me question everything I'd been told. Despite the red flags, there was a grain of truth in what Lilith told me. "Are you okay?"

"I... I don't know." His words stumbled out, unsure and hesitant. "It felt so real." He shut his eyes tightly and inhaled deeply.

"What exactly did she do to you?" I wasn't sure if I wanted to know, but my curiosity got the better of me.

"I didn't see her, if that's what you're asking," he answered, his eyes meeting mine. My breath caught as his eyes transformed from a vivid color to a deep black, with flickers of silver lightning dancing within them. "I saw you. The day you threw a coffee mug at me. We were in your dining room, and you were crying. When I looked down, you were wearing nothing but a robe," he confessed shyly.

My cheeks flushed with embarrassment as the memory of the afternoon we spent together flooded my mind and all the inappropriate thoughts that I'd had. He heard every single one of them. I wanted to crawl under a rock and hide.

"Then the robe fell off." I had no chance to defend myself before Eidolon was on top of me. My hands wrapped around his neck as I reveled in the sound of his groans while he pulled me closer.

"Chloe," he breathed as his lips trailed to my neck.

My mind was a whirlwind, barely able to hold onto any one thought as his fingers expertly danced across my skin. Every nerve in my body sparked and tingled with pleasure, begging for more of his touch. I moved in sync with him, my body yearning for release until we teetered on the edge of bliss. And then he stopped, pulling back to look at me.

What the hell? I closed my eyes in mortification.

Eidolon delicately traced the outline of my chin with his finger. "Open your eyes, Chloe," he demanded softly. I didn't want to, worried about what I would see. I shook my head, shitting my eyes tighter.

He chuckled. "You're cute when you're embarrassed." He flicked my nose. I peeked through one eye and found him smiling at me. "Perfectly imperfect," he said appreciatively as he pushed a lock of my hair behind my ear. "And all mine."

Both eyes shot open, and I stared at him. No one had ever said that to me before. And I believed him.

"We'll continue this later," he said with a mischievous grin, plucking a twig from my hair. "When we're not on display for everyone to see." His hungry eyes roamed over my body with a raw and primal desire.

I *really* didn't want to wait. I shifted under his weight.

"So impatient," he laughed. "Don't worry, Chloe; it will be worth the wait." He lifted me effortlessly in his arms as the first rain droplets fell. The gentle pitter-patter rhythm echoed through the forest, slowly coating the leaves and branches with a glossy sheen.

I stood, resecuring my hair into a messy bun and dusting the leaves off my sweatshirt. Eidolon quickly gathered our belongings, grabbing the

Book of the Veiled before it got wet and tucking it safely into my backpack. Our hands touched as he handed it to me, and a jolt of electricity shot through between us. A mixture of conflicting emotions surged - disappointment, hope, arousal, and dread of what we still had to face.

It was overwhelming. I let out a deep breath and adjusted my glasses. But for now, I decided to savor the moment.

Eidolon understood my inner conflict as he took my hand. We walked back to the hotel, both lost in our thoughts. I knew I had to tell him the truth. I may have bought myself a little time, but I sensed it wouldn't last long.

Chapter 38

'What Was Lost Will Be Found.' -Book of the Veiled Instructions

We were met with a furious voice as we entered the hotel lobby, both drenched and in dire need of something warm to drink. Max was pacing back and forth in front of the fireplace. Aelle glanced over from where she sat on the couch, surrounded by meticulously organized stacks of books and papers on the coffee table. "Where have you both been?" Her eyes fixed on me, and I took a small step back.

Why the hell did she dislike me so much?

"We ran into a small issue," Eidolon collapsed in one of the armchairs and stretched his legs out. "What did you find, Aelle?"

I plopped into one of the armchairs by the fire, hoping to hide my anger at Aelle's tone with a mask of indifference. She was the last person I wanted to deal with. All I wanted to do was take a bath and finish what Eidolon and I started in the forest.

Isabelle's feet dancing down the hallway snapped me out of my thoughts. I turned to see her and Watson entering the room. Moll, Crichton, and Emma followed behind them, making their way to the couch, uprooting Aelle. She gave a brief scowl before noticing Eidolon's hard gaze and quietly moved to stand beside Max.

"Where's Sydney and Victor?" I asked, looking around.

"Your knight in shining black wool has arrived, my dear lady," Sydney boomed from the staircase. "Have no fear, Sir Sydney and his faithful sidekick are here."

Victor grumbled under his breath as he crossed the room to sit on the arm of the couch. "If he's responsible for keeping us safe, we might not make it through the night."

Sydney feigned a hurt expression, placing his hand over his heart. "Your lack of faith in my abilities hurts me deeply."

"I don't doubt your abilities. I just question if you can stay undistracted long enough to protect us," Vincent shot back. "We had to stop four times today for something to eat," he explained to the group.

"It wasn't my fault," Sydney confessed, rubbing his stomach. "Esme's cousin made us lunch, and I didn't want to hurt her feelings."

"Yeah, that's definitely the only reason we kept going back." Victor winked. "The food!"

A flicker of embarrassment flashed across Sydney's face, and we all laughed.

I took a quick peek at Isabelle and Watson, noting their unusual silence. "How was your visit home?"

"Informative, to say the least," Isabelle murmured, picking at the hem of her shirt. "Family gatherings are always interesting. You never know what's going to happen next."

Watson's grip on her shoulders tightened as he forced a smile. "That's one way to put it," he replied with an insincere grin.

"Well, that's fantastic," Aelle interrupted with a wave of her hand. "If we're done gossiping, I have news. While you all were out on social calls, we found something about Arawn in Max's library." She glanced up, her eyes narrowing in concern. "But I warn you- nothing about it is pleasant."

Isabelle breathed a sigh of relief as the subject changed, and I made a mental note to ask her about it later. "What did you find?" She leaned forward, her muscles coiled and her hands producing small bursts of light.

I glanced over at Eidolon, taken aback. He shrugged and furrowed his brow, his gaze fixed on Isabelle's hands.

Aelle studied her intently before saying, "The poem is rather cryptic, but it appears that Arawn requires a sacrifice in order for us to make contact with him." She cited the words from the poem she and Max had discovered.

The blood from the old
The words from the new
Combined, they form the truth.
Travel by night
Enter by day
And lose not your way
Many have entered
None will leave.
Death will not rest until he has spoken his peace.

"Crypticptic," Victor commented, rubbing his chin in thought. "How does that help us figure out what we need to do? The blood from the old and the words from the new?"

"Chloe came back from her last trip smelling old." Sydney wrinkled his nose. "And Eidolon has all those words swirling around him like a modern-day Encyclopedia Britannica."

"Does it say anything about what kind of sacrifice we must make?" Watson asked.

Max shook his head in frustration. "Unless we resort to something completely absurd, like dancing naked under the moonlight with our enemies' blood and offerings from our harvest, I'm afraid our search has been in vain," he admitted with a defeated tone.

"I know what it wants," Emma said quietly. With a sad smile, she considered Isabelle and Watson, whose faces had turned gray when the poem was read. "The verse is about you two."

"Isabelle and Watson?" Eidolon's eyebrows raised in confusion.

"Yes, Isabelle and Watson," Emma confirmed. "Watson's ancestry carries the blood of the ancient ones. As the last living descendant, his blood is considered the oldest in existence. As for Isabelle, she has her own story to tell." Emma glanced at Isabelle, her eyes filled with pain and sympathy.

"Isabelle?" Eidolon turned to look at her.

Isabelle looked like she wanted to be anywhere but where she was, but she took a deep breath and told us what happened.

"My aunt was murdered," Isabelle started.

My mouth dropped in disbelief. "I'm so sorry."

She nodded in acknowledgment. "There's more," she said sadly. "My mother was the high priestess of our coven. My aunt reluctantly accepted the position after her death, offering to hold it until I was ready to take over. When Watson and I married, the council denied me the inheritance, claiming our union would disrupt the bloodline."

Watson tenderly brushed his lips against her temple and murmured softly in her ear. She smiled and gazed at him affectionately. Reaching for her drink, she intertwined her fingers with his as if he were her lifeline.

"On the drive, I felt a surge, and I knew that my aunt was gone. When we arrived, the council met us." Her tone was devoid of emotion as she tried to contain her anger. She glanced at Watson, silently imploring him to continue the story.

Watson squeezed her hand and looked at Eidolon. "Whoever was responsible for the crime left a note. A warning. The elders refused to open it until we arrived, fearing it had been enchanted."

Sydney sat up, his shoulders rolling as if preparing for a fight. "What did it say?" he growled in a low tone.

"It was an ultimatum: join their ranks or face the consequences. Signed with blood." Watson's words hung heavy in the air, a warning echoing through the room. The tension was palpable as his unwavering gaze remained fixed on Isabelle.

Eidolon stood up and lowered himself to his knees before Isabelle, tenderly grasping her hands. "I am deeply sorry for your loss, Isabelle. I promise we will not rest until the person responsible is found and held accountable for their actions," he vowed. Seeing him kneel before her, Eidolon resembled a chivalrous knight, offering his sword and shield, and my heart skipped a beat.

"You don't need to worry," Watson snarled. "I've already sent out word through my channels. No one attacks my family and lives."

Eidolon nodded his head in understanding. "I am at your service if you need me." He stepped back and turned to Emma. "Explain."

Emma peered at Moll, and she gave her a small nod. Squaring her shoulders, she looked back at Eidolon, her eyes hardening. "Moll asked me to retrieve something we had once thought lost." She paused. "Not so much lost as happily misplaced," she clarified. "It contains the history of the Otherworld. Isabelle and Watson are necessary for casting the spell, but you and Chloe are the ones that must travel to the Otherworld." She looked over at me with pity.

Her words sent my mind reeling. Eidolon in the Otherworld? The warning from Taliesin and Diana echoed in my thoughts. It was far too dangerous for him to go. "Do we have to go?" I asked shakily. "Can't we find a way to bring Arawn here?"

"Are you afraid, Chloe?" Aelle sneered. "I thought this would be a walk in the park with all your traveling."

I shifted my gaze to the imposing scholar standing by the fireplace. Our eyes locked in a fierce stare until she finally looked away, the tension between us palpable.

"How do you know?" I clenched my fists, fighting the urge to stand up.

She huffed. "Am I blind?" she asked incredulously. "It wasn't too difficult to see what was going on. Moll looks like a stiff wind could blow her down. Emma gets sent on a secret mission to 'find something' only she can track. And as hard as Eidolon tries, the words start crawling down his neck whenever he looks at you."

She glared at me with hatred. "And you? You're being protected like you're the only hope for humanity. The CIA would be impressed with how well you're guarded, which means you're Moll's successor," she scuffed. "It's easy to pick up on things when no one knows you're in the room."

She spoke with such bitterness and spite that I couldn't help but feel a shred of empathy for her. It must have been difficult for her to come to terms with the fact that no one liked her, evident by the tone of her voice.

"We know you're in the room," Isabelle said, using her powers to try to defuse the situation. "I am sorry if we made you feel...."

"Stop, Isabelle." Aelle held up a hand. "Don't even try. I don't need your pity. I'm merely stating a fact. How it's received is solely with the receiver. Not me." Her eyes narrowed. "Maybe if more people told the truth or refused to skirt around valuable information, we wouldn't be sitting here, wasting time. If anyone is holding up progress, it's you all," she finished, glaring at everyone.

I didn't want to admit it, but Aelle was right. For the past few days, we all had been keeping information from one another, creating more problems.

After a lengthy and uncomfortable silence, I spoke up. "Aelle's right. We've not been completely transparent with each other." Taking a deep breath, I revealed the details of my conversation with Lilith.

I played with the hem of my sweatshirt, not wanting to know Eidolon's reaction to my confession. "She wants us to call Arawn, but she warns us that if we do, we might not like what other monsters are released."

"You talked to Lilith?" Sydney asked, aghast. "*The* Lilith. Mother to all supernatural and mistress to the demons?"

"She reminded me more of Elphaba," I joked half-heartedly, looking up at him. "To be honest, I believed her. I don't think she's completely evil. Something happened to her. She mentioned her children dying, but she didn't go into any details."

I didn't mention what she had done to Eidolon, but he was thinking about it. A slight blush rose to his cheeks, and a shimmer of longing flowed down our connection. I restrained myself from crossing my legs as I felt a surge of desire. Eidolon wickedly smiled at me, and I turned to face Esme.

"What do we need to do?"

"It won't be easy. The book we have holds the true story of Arawn, a lost manuscript of death before it was rewritten. It tells the history of who he was and the reality of the Otherworld," Emma explained.

"If it's his story and he needs it, why hasn't he just taken it back?" Aelle interrupted, taking out her notebook.

Moll took control of the conversation, her cane spinning in her grasp. "The book was bound by a spell, making it impossible to open. When it mysteriously disappeared, I assumed it was safer to leave it be instead of drawing attention to it. After all, who knew how Arawn would react if he ever returned and discovered what humans had done? However, the book eventually reappeared, and a Writer sensed a change within its pages. It seemed that someone had added a new chapter to the story."

"Who was the Writer?" Victor asked.

Moll and Emma stared at each other, neither wanting to say anything. But I caught Crichton's eye, and I saw the look.

"You were the Writer," I whispered. "It's one of the books that your grandfather gave you. He asked you to hide it."

Chapter 39

'Without Faith The Gods Will Die.' -Book of the Veiled Instructions

"You must understand the 1600s were devastating for the supernatural. Thousands were hunted down like sheep and slaughtered. Their blood ran deep into the soil, rotting away at civilization's foundations and dripping into the Otherworld. Lilith was angry with the mortals for their lack of humanity and misguided belief that uneducated men were speaking for the gods," Moll explained.

"Lilith approached the Fates with a warning. She told them there would be an omen from the gods of their impending wrath. In December, the sign came in the form of a comet bright enough to be seen worldwide. The mortals believed it was proof from God that disaster was soon to come."

"The comet Isaac Newton saw," Max whispered.

"That's the one." Moll nodded. Her hand gripped her cane tightly as she continued the grim history lesson. "London experienced its coldest winter in history. Then the plague arrived. Not as many deaths as the Black Death, but enough to wipe out a good part of the population. After the Great Fire of London, hatred shifted from the supernatural to religion. Mortals were suddenly murdering their own in the name of the Christian God. Lilith was able to change the narrative."

Aelle paused in her notetaking to look up. "What does this have to do with Arawn?"

"Lilith's plan had the opposite result from what she wanted. Rather than reminding people of the old gods, it caused them to begin mistrusting all religions. It led to the Age of Enlightenment, where reason, science, and technology replaced faith. The loss of believers crippled Arawn, and his powers over the Otherworld were weakened."

"But Taliesin was still determined to contain Lilith there. Arawn cautioned him that no wards would hold her. Undead souls are not allowed in the Otherworld. But Taliesin was confident he'd created a binding charm she couldn't escape."

"Why was Taliesin so mad at Lilith?" Victor asked.

"No one knows for sure why," Chrichton answered for Moll. "What we do know is that all gods depend on people's faith to stay relevant. If no one believes in them, they will eventually be forgotten. Arawn was more or less jailed with Lilith."

"If Arawn gets back his book, does that mean he can change his story back?" Eidolon asked. "Can he become a god again?"

"He has always been a god, but yes, his full powers would be restored." Moll nodded.

"Doesn't seem like a terrible thing." Sydney shrugged. "Arawn just wants his truth to be remembered. And from what Max told us, he was one of the better gods. What's the issue?" His eyes danced between us all. "We give him the book, and he helps us keep Lilith contained. Win, win!"

"There's one thing I don't understand," Max interrupted, looking at me. "What does all this have to do with the Book of the Veiled?"

"You said Vivian initially imprisoned Taliesin. What if Lilith and Vivian stole the books to ensure he can't escape?" I guessed.

"But why imprison him in the first place? And why was Lilith banished to the Otherworld?" Eidolon ran a hand over his face in frustration. "There's more to this story than what we know. Something in those books is obviously more important than just imprisoning someone. So, what is it?"

"What would she gain by stealing them?" Watson wondered aloud. "And why did she wait until now?"

"Lilith said she wanted the power to protect her children." I glanced at Moll. "What if she found out how? She may need something from the Book of the Veiled to help her."

"A soul for a soul," Aelle said, all eyes turning to her. She squared her shoulders and took a deep breath. "In all my research, there has always been a common theme. You can't do magick without sacrifice, and you can't change the course of fate. But...you can replace."

"Explain, Aelle," Eidolon demanded.

"It's said that people have given up their souls to save someone else. I believe Taliesin intends to use Lilith and Vivian's souls in exchange for his sisters. Or Lilith could be planning on swapping humans for the supernatural. Either way, it doesn't look good for us."

We sat in stunned silence. We knew that Vivian and Lilith imprisoned Taliesin and Diana in a tree, but we also knew they were trapped with Arawn in the Otherworld. We hoped that Arawn had the power to help us find the Book of the Veiled, but there was a catch: communicating with Arawn needed a sacrifice. And none of us knew what kind of sacrifice he needed.

I rubbed my eyes, a headache pounding in my temples as I tried to put the story together. Beginning, middle, end...three parts to every story. That is what I needed to figure out. My fingers started twitching, eager to hold a pen and my book. I needed to write.

"I brought you something to drink," Crichton whispered in my ear as he placed a warm mug in my hands. "It'll help with the headache."

"Thank you." I looked up at him gratefully. Like a fairy godfather wearing an elegant three-piece suit, Crichton had always looked out for my well-being. I allowed the warmth of the mug to seep into my hands and focused on releasing the tight muscles in my neck, one by one.

Eidolon sat quietly in his chair, lost in deep thought, as he worked through all his questions. The line between us was humming with excitement and dread. After sending a slight tap down the bond to get his attention, he glanced at me.

Are you okay? I asked.

I'm fine. I was looking through the books. I can feel them shifting around as if they know what we are about to do, he responded, his eyes hesitant at his next thought. *I don't want you in the Otherworld. It's not safe. You should stay here. I will meet Arawn and hear what he has to say.*

Over my dead body, you will. You go with me, or you don't go at all.

Chloe - it's not safe. What if you get stuck? What if something happens and I can't get to you?

I will be with you one way or another. There's a reason the Fates brought us together! Remember what the book said? It needs both of us. I could have kicked myself for letting the thought out. I had been avoiding our interaction with the books like the plague, and I just reminded Eidolon.

Damn it!

"Who's the Son of Taliesin and the Daughter of Morrigan?" Eidolon eyes shot to Moll.

She swallowed. "Crichton, be a gentleman and bring the book, would you?" Moll asked, her eyes never leaving his.

"Of course, Moll." He headed down the hall to retrieve it. We all waited in quiet anticipation as I tried to distract myself with my cup of tea, sipping it in a bid to relax.

Crichton returned and, on Molls' silent command, handed the book to Eidolon, who held it like a newborn. The key under my shirt began to warm, warning me that something was about to happen.

Something or someone was coming.

I grabbed the key and pulled it out to see it glowing. I glanced at Eidolon, and something crashed through the front door before I could say anything.

"I love a proper family reunion," a voice boomed as a massive hand lay on my shoulder. "It's been ages since I was invited to one!"

Arawn had arrived.

"Delighted to see you again, Chloe." His hand squeezed my shoulder.

I froze in place, fear trickling through my body as I tried to calm my racing heart. The key began to hum, a reassuring sound that promised me I was safe. I lightly shook off his touch and forced my shoulders to relax.

"And you, Arawn. Were you just in the neighborhood and decided to drop by?"

"I'm just answering your summons." He dropped into the seat next to me. I glanced around, surprised that the rest of the group was frozen.

"Don't worry." He smiled, looking at everyone. "They're fine. I thought you and I should talk before everybody gets their panties in a twist." He turned his unnerving gaze at me. "Why did you call me Daughter of Morrigan?"

"I didn't technically call you Arawn. I don't have your phone number." The expression on his face deterred me from making another sarcastic comment. Darkness, amusement, and death filled his gaze, and I was mesmerized by his power.

"Ah, but you did." He waved his sizable arms around the room. Without the heavy gray cloak I had first seen him in, I realized he was the most attractive man - or rather, god - I had ever seen.

His dark, wild hair cascaded over one of his dazzling silver eyes. His clothing—black trousers and soft gray sweater—highlighted his sun-kissed skin, athletic body, and formidable stature. The sweet aroma of white heather filled the room, and I breathed in deeply.

His eyes danced merrily as he eyed the room, and a wolfish smile tugged at his full lips. Lips that ached for someone to touch them. I quickly placed my hands under my legs, fighting the need to tuck his hair behind his ear and run my hands over his chest. I glanced at Eidolon's frozen body and pulled at the line between us.

Still connected. Thank the gods.

Arawn eyed me with amusement as I exhaled an exasperated breath.

"I thought there needed to be some type of sacrifice before a god showed up for a summons," I said impatiently. I was tired of being pulled into these visions whenever they suited someone else's fancy. As soon as I had time, I wanted to learn how to put a wall up to keep unwanted visitors out.

"What? A blood sacrifice?" Arawn asked. I nodded my head, feeling foolish suddenly. He shook his head in amusement. "Too messy. You mortals and your desire for blood. It never made sense to me."

"Then how are you here?"

"You had everything you needed." He glanced over at his book, now lying on the coffee table. "It just needed to be in the same room with you for me to detect it."

"So, you know I need your help?" I arched an eyebrow at him.

"Did you call me here for assistance?" He peered at me in surprise. "It was all your bickering that gained my attention. It was disturbing my poor hounds," Arawn grumbled, looking around again. "It's been eons since I've been in this realm. Do they still have those savory pastries filled with meat?"

"Scotch pie?" I asked, surprised at the sudden change in our conversation.

"Yes! Scotch Pies!" He sat up. "Do they still make those?" he asked as he examined the side table of food. The disappointment on his face when he didn't find one nearly made me laugh. For being the god of death, he didn't look formidable but almost cute in his boyish excitement.

Of course, he wanted food.

Chapter 40

'Once The Key Opens A Door, There's No Going Back.' -Book of the Veiled Instructions

"I will take you to get one if you answer my question," I promised, taking a deep breath. "How do we find the Book of the Veiled? We need to stop Lilith and fix the mess that she created."

"And what mess do you think she created, Daughter of Morrigan?" he asked in all seriousness, his eyebrows raised in anticipation.

I struggled to form coherent sentences as my thoughts raced in my mind. It took a few moments for me to gather my words before I answered. "She and Vivian stole the Book of the Veiled and want to eliminate all mortals," I stumbled, unsure if I was conveying the message accurately.

"Lilith and Vivian?" Arawn chuckled in surprise. "Interesting. I was not aware."

"How could you not be? You and Taliesin locked them in the Otherworld as punishment."

Arawn laughed. "I think that's a broad overview of the situation, and punishment is a powerful word, lil' Writer." He leaned forward. "They are not in the Otherworld to protect the world from them. They are there because they are protecting something from the world."

"What?" I asked in disbelief.

Arawn sighed loudly, rolling his eyes and crossing his arms across his broad chest. "Long story short? The gods walked on this world in the beginning. Over time, it became dull with just seven of us, so we created others in our image.

"Our original plan was to work together, dividing the responsibilities equally between the two species. However, as mortals multiplied and began spreading out across the world, it became clear that we gods would need assistance in managing everything.

"So, we created the deities. Versions of the original gods separated into different regions: Rome, Greece, Mesopotamia, Persia, China, etc... each had their own god with a dedicated deity to oversee daily life."

"The seven original gods," I breathed, naming them off in my head.

"Actually, there are eight," he corrected. "Each represented by a gate surrounding the Tree of Life in the Otherworld. It was my duty to oversee them all. At the time, I had a strict policy of not turning away any soul; the good was rewarded, while the wicked received the appropriate reprimand.

"Unlike your version of hell, my punishments were not eternal but matched the severity of one's sins. I've always believed that every person has a chance at redemption." A proud smile formed on his face before fading away.

"Dividing my power among so many souls was draining, so I created Taliesin and Morrigan - the twins. Each had their own divine abilities, but a unique bond also connected them. They helped me shepherd the souls. Mortals turned out to be unpredictable and unstable, so the gods created Lilith. She was our secret weapon." He grinned.

"Taliesin and Lilith despised each other from the start. Something happened between them, but I don't know what," he said with a tinge of sadness. "All I know is that it had to do with Morrigan." Arawn's eyes drifted towards the warm glow of the fireplace. "Before the battle,

I knew Taliesin had gone to consult with the Fates. I also knew that they can be tricky, and one must choose their words wisely striking a bargain. Unfortunately, Taliesin wasn't careful enough."

"Why didn't you stop him from going to see them?" I asked.

"The gods do not interfere with what the deities do," he said gruffly. "They were created as humans were, with free will."

"Oh..."

He turned to look at me. The sadness in his eyes was overwhelming. "I was helpless as I watched Morrigan die."

"I'm so sorry." My heart ached for the deity. I could empathize with the pain of losing someone that you loved.

"Me too," he said, walking over to the teapot and pouring himself a cup. As he took a sip, he turned to me. "But Morrigan had been forewarned by the Fates of what was to come. And for reasons still unclear to me, she struck her own bargain. She would sacrifice her own life in exchange for Lilith's safety. Her power for Taliesin's life."

"She sacrificed everything for them," I whispered. "Why would she do that?"

"It was a gamble. Morrigan had the gift to predict the future and knew what would become of the supernatural. I think she hoped her sacrifice would keep everyone safe."

"Why would Lilith steal the Book of the Veiled now? After Morrigan made her sacrifice, I mean?"

"Your guess is as good as mine, maybe from stopping her story from being erased. But you're not asking the right questions, lil' Writer. Whose story are you missing?" He eyed me with amusement.

What other story did I need to know? I looked down at my mug, trying to work it out. Lilith. Arawn. Taliesin. Morrigan. And...

"Vivian!" I cried. "What does Vivian have to do with all of this? Other than she brought back Lilith?"

"Finally," Arawn rolled his eyes. "You're beginning to sound like a real writer. Vivian is protecting her daughter."

"Daughter? She had a daughter?" I asked, even more confused than I was before.

"You've met her." Arawn walked back to the armchair with an amused smile.

"I have?"

He glanced over at the fireplace. "She's standing right in front of you." He pointed to Aelle.

"You've got to be shitting me...." I groaned.

"Nope. I'm not sure what version of the story you've heard, but Aelle is the result of a short-lived affair between Taliesin and Vivian. If only things ended differently; perhaps if Vivian hadn't kept secrets and Taliesin wasn't consumed with seeking revenge for Morrigan's death, none of this would have happened. But when Taliesin found out about Vivian's pregnancy, she was forced to go into hiding. I suspect deep down, she always hoped they could reconcile."

"Why didn't they?" I glanced at the god and back at Aelle, my head reeling with all the plot twists.

Arawn shrugged and explained, "He met Eidolon's mother, and that was it. Vivian had no chance of getting between them. Devastated, she sought revenge. She waited for the perfect moment when Taliesin would be at his weakest and do to him what he once did to her, tearing him away from the one thing most precious to him: his child.

"And now, Chloe, you are caught in the middle of a never-ending battle with no winner." He concluded with a sigh before glancing at me with a smile. "Now, when can I expect that pie you mentioned?"

"One last question, then we can get whatever you want," I said as I leaned forward. Everything was beginning to fall into place except for one critical piece. "What about your book? Why do you need it?"

"That, Daughter of Morrigan, is not a story for now. But I promise the reason will make sense in time." Arawn looked over at Eidolon and smiled.

"The first time I saw him in the Otherworld, I was shocked. He was so much like his father. So curious. He hounded me for hours, asking questions about life and death and how to make the transition easier. I hope he survives. I hope you all survive because we are family," he laughed softly. "One big happy, dysfunctional family."

I sat back in my seat and gave Arawn a half-ass smile. Dysfunctional was right. The Addams Family had fewer skeletons in their closet than this one.

"Does this mean Eidolon and I are related?" I asked before I lost my nerve.

"Heavens, no!" he barked. "Taliesin and Morrigan might be twins, but they were not conceived in the same way as mortals. I assume you are referring to the bond you have with Eidolon?" I nodded, and Arawn glanced between the two of us.

"I see the link between you two. Interesting," he said as he pushed back his hair out of his eyes. "I've only ever seen it once before. Many lifetimes ago. Just as strong between them as between you and Eidolon. Their story was made for books. It had everything. Angry parents, war, love, children, and a not-so-happy ever after."

I started to ask him what he was talking about, but he waved me off.

"It's not my story to share. But soon enough, you'll understand. It's remarkable how similar your connection is to theirs. It's as if..." he briefly looked at me with a question in his eyes that vanished right away. "But no. You have nothing to worry about if that is what you are implying," he concluded with a wink.

Relief flooded my mind. I would have been sick if I discovered I'd made out with a cousin. I still had a lot of questions about family lines, but I decided to figure that out after we addressed the first hurdle.

"You never told me what we needed to do to stop this so-called civil war."

"Oh, that! Yes, I guess if you want to get into the middle of it...."

"I do," I interrupted.

"Then, Daughter of Morrigan, I suggest you visit the Fates yourself. See if there's a bargain they are willing to make."

"How do I find them?" I asked hesitantly, not convinced I wanted to find them. It hadn't worked out for Morrigan.

"Your key that you're hiding," he said, pointing to the lump under my shirt. It'd been humming the whole time, absorbing all the information he was sharing and storing it away for me. "It will open the door to where the Fates reside. But be careful, Chloe. Once you open the passage, there will be no turning back."

"And where do I find the door?"

Arawn looked over at his book. "Right there." He nodded at it. "Words written have many variations of reality, but the truth lies in the inconsistencies- and that's where you will find the Fates."

He got up to walk out, but before he could leave, I called out, "Thank you."

He turned to face me, his eyes narrowing with worry. "I hope you find what you're searching for, lil' Writer. The path you're on is not an easy one," he warned before disappearing into the moonlit night. I continued watching him until he faded into a mere memory, but I could still hear his voice calling out to me from afar.

"Don't die. You still owe me a Scotch Pie."

Chapter 41

'The Truth Is Never Forthcoming.' -Book of the Veiled Instructions

"Where did he go?" Moll's eyes darted around the room, searching for any sign of Arawn. How she knew he had been there was beyond me, but I was too tired to ask.

"He left." I was disappointed myself. Despite his elusive nature, the god had been helpful, and I wished he'd stayed longer to provide more details.

Moll let out a deep sigh, her frustration evident. "I hoped he would stay for a while," she said, absentmindedly fiddling with her cane. "I had some questions for him."

"What did he say to you?" Eidolon asked. "Did he tell you how to get to the Otherworld?"

"He said everything we need is in this room. And that my key would open the door." He waited for me to say more, but I wasn't ready to reveal anything. Arawn's words still muddled in my mind, and I needed time to sort through them.

"Are you alright," Sydney asked, concerned. "He didn't hurt you or anything, did he?"

"No," I assured him, sending him a grateful smile. "I think Arawn is more comfortable just talking to one person. But he says hi." Of course, it was also possible he didn't want to discuss the matter in front of Aelle and Eidolon, as they would undoubtedly have questions.

"That explains the odd fragrance in the room," Isabelle sniffed as she glanced around the room. "A blend of white heather, vanilla, and raspberry - a common choice."

Puzzled, I lifted my cup from earlier and inhaled the faint reminiscence of raspberries and vanilla—Crichton's favorite drink to serve me. Carefully, I lower it onto the coffee table and use my finger to nudge it away. "Explain," I demanded.

She grimaced, her eyes falling on the offensive mug, guilt written over her face. "Magick has a distinct scent, depending on its intended purpose. A sweet aroma typically indicates someone is trying to block its use."

I suddenly realized that they had been drugging me. Diana had also offered me the same tea, which now made sense in light of what I'd just discovered. My heart sank in disappointment. I glanced at Crichton, but he avoided eye contact. Removing my glasses, I massaged the bridge of my nose.

Why?

Not noticing my inner conflict, Eidolon asked, "Did he say anything else?"

I stared at him for a moment, weighing my options. I'd just expressed the need for transparency and sharing of information. However, it was clear they were all keeping secrets from me.

I shrugged. "Nothing much. Just that we need to talk to the Fates, and they will tell us what to do next." He wore a peculiar look, but I glanced down at my sweatshirt, wiping away an imaginary crumb.

Sydney's voice dripped with sarcasm, "Oh, is that all? Goody." I glanced up and saw his glare directed at me. "Just one question," he continued, his eyebrows furrowed in frustration. "How the hell do you find the Fates?"

"I think I might be able to help," Max volunteered, playing with a knick-knack on the mantel. He sat it down and faced us. "We found an entry about my grandfather's journey to the Fates. It was a strange tale." Max ran a hand through his hair, pieces of it sticking up. "Apparently, he traveled to the Otherworld. He claimed he went on a series of quests trying to gain an audience with the Fates."

Victor let out a dry chuckle, his tone tinged with sarcasm. "Did he happen to leave a detailed map for this 'quest'? Maybe one with a large 'X' marked for the starting point?" He raised an eyebrow, a smirk playing on his lips.

"No." Aelle rolled her eyes. "But he did mention a book containing details of the paths to the Otherworld. According to him, there was an island that he had to find. That's the starting point."

Max's head bobbed up and down in agreement, clearly getting more enthusiastic about what they uncovered. "In addition, the journal notes the Tree of Life was located at the center, its branches dividing into two - one symbolizing birth and the other representing death.

"Freyja and her thirteen Valkyries are the guardians of the tree," he explained excitedly. "Those seeking an audience with the Fates would have to prove their worth to Freyja first, and only then would she protect them on their journey to where the Fates dwelled.

"And your grandfather was proven worthy?" Watson asked, surprised.

Max's face flushed with embarrassment. "No," he confessed. "But that's not why he did it. He wanted to prove the supernatural existed." Max raised an eyebrow, clearly proud of the fact. "He firmly believed in coexisting peacefully with the supernatural world."

Aelle listened intently as he spoke, her gaze fixed on him. After he finished, she reached out and gently touched his shoulder. He glanced at her in surprise. She responded with a small smile before turning to glare at Watson.

"Max's grandfather's book inspired future novels like *Letters on Natural Magick*, *Dracula*, *Lectures on Witchcraft*, and *The Lancashire Witches*. Of course, these future books are famous for keeping the supernatural a myth, but it was Max's grandfather who first tried to bring them to life."

"So, in other words, he found a way to make supernatural the inconsistencies in history." Eidolon's brows furrowed in deep concentration as he tried to process the information. "Not really dead, but not alive either." Max nodded.

"But he never met the Fates?" I pressed.

"No," he shook his head. "He never went into details about why, but I think it was because he felt he accomplished all his goals." He shrugged. "I guess he didn't need to ask them for anything else."

"So, how do we access the gate?" Watson asked Moll.

Moll's lips curved into a half-smile as she spoke, "You should ask Chloe." I turned to face her, still wary of anything she said. She leaned in closer and whispered, "You know what needs to be done," her eyes filled with sorrow.

My fingers trembled as I retrieved the key under my shirt, its metal surface cool against my skin. As I gazed at it, a strange force pulled my eyes towards Arawn's book. Moll's words echoed in my mind, reminding me that I knew what I needed to do next. But despite this knowledge, fear and self-doubt crept in, clouding my thoughts like a thick mist descending over a dark forest.

If I chose to continue this journey, I would need to accept that everyone I encountered – Taliesin, Diana, Lilith, Vivian, Arawn, and even

Moll – had their own motives. No one was going to be completely honest with me, and I shouldn't expect them to be anytime soon.

Was I willing to live with that?

I shifted my gaze to Eidolon, who was eagerly awaiting my response. I could feel his unwavering confidence and faith in me through our connection. Could I trust him? I wasn't sure yet. But the quest might give me some answers.

Taking a deep breath, I started. "Isabelle, you are now the official high priestess. I assume that came with instructions. Maybe something that explains how to open a bound book?"

She gave me a slight nod, and I shifted my gaze to Watson. "And I'm guessing your blood can strengthen her spells?" Watson nodded, and I let out the breath I'd been holding.

I was *finally* on the right path.

Excited, I turned my attention to Sydney, "And your tracking skills rival those of Emma's, correct?"

"Sir Sydney, at your service. As long as I have my trusty sidekick, I can find anything," he declared, his head bobbing up and down in excitement and glancing at the man beside him. Victor gave him a cold glare and rolled his eyes before reluctantly nodding.

"Max and I will stay here," Aelle announced. "We have access to Max's library and the skills to find the answers you will need on your journey."

Aelle glanced over at Max, who looked euphoric. I couldn't stop myself from wondering if he understood the potential repercussions of his choice, but that wasn't my responsibility. He would have to face the consequences on his own. I just hoped Aelle wouldn't end up hurting him in the end.

Moll's voice was soft and gentle as she spoke, her fingers tracing the intricate design of the raven on her cane. "It goes without saying you and Eidolon will also journey to the Otherworld?"

Eidolon approached Moll and knelt before her, gently grasping her hands in his. "Moll, you know I have to go," he spoke softly. "We've always known this day would come." Moll nodded with tears in her eyes, and Eidolon reached up to wipe one away. "I will find the Book of the Veiled. And with any luck, my parents, too," he said with hope.

She reached out and lightly tapped his cheek. She peered over her shoulder at her friends, declaring, "We'll stay here and keep them grounded." Crichton, Emma, and Esme all gathered around her in silent agreement. Her gaze shifted to Eidolons, "Stay safe, okay? I need you to be more like Sherlock Holmes and less like James Bond."

"I swear," he said solemnly.

"Alright, let's hit the hypothetical road!" Sydney exclaimed as he stood up and headed towards the kitchen. "I'll grab some essentials, just in case. I highly doubt we'll find a McDonald's along the way."

Victor rose from his seat with a hint of exhaustion and trailed after him. "I'll make sure he leaves something for the anchor crew. Let's regroup at midnight," he proposed, and we all nodded in unison.

Isabelle and Watson retired to their room to pack and rest while Aelle and Max returned to Max's library to search for additional information on the Valkyrie and the Fates.

Esme, Emma, and Crichton ventured into town to partake in the holiday festivities, leaving Moll, Eidolon, and me behind to bask in the warmth of the crackling fire. The tranquil atmosphere enveloped us as we retreated into our contemplative thoughts.

Chapter 42

'The Future Is Fluid.' -Book of the Veiled Instructions

After a long moment of silence, Eidolon finally spoke up. "So, how exactly are Aelle and Victor involved in all of this?"

I'd hoped that he wouldn't bring Aelle up, but apparently, my silent prayers would go unanswered. I waited for Moll to say something, but she just stared at her grandson.

I replied, relieved to have one less secret to keep buried. "Aelle is Vivian's daughter. I don't think she knows yet."

Eidolon's mouth dropped as his eyes darted between me and Moll. "Shouldn't someone tell her?"

Moll shook her head, "Not yet. She's not prepared. Aelle has an insatiable desire for knowledge and a remarkable knack for remembering everything she learns. She's always been aware of her uniqueness, but I'm not sure how she'll react once she discovers it wasn't solely due to her abilities but partly because of magick."

I began to worry as the plot thickened. "Can Vivian turn Aelle against us?"

"I cannot say for certain. Aelle and Victor's future has always been a mystery to me. I attempted to look years ago, but the constantly changing pictures gave me a headache. They are the only ones whose future is not already written. It shifts depending on their decisions."

I glanced at her in surprise. "Can you see my future?"

"One writer cannot predict the future of another," she reassured me, placing her hand on mine. I withdrew my hand with a scowl. Eidolon observed our interaction with confusion but remained silent.

I couldn't explain why it gave me a sense of relief. Realizing that my fate was still a mystery made me feel like I held some power over my life.

Eidolon's dark eyebrows lifted in surprise as he questioned, "Why were you looking into Victor's future?" His voice was curious and laced with suspicion, his sharp eyes searching for answers.

"Victor will be your secret weapon. His skills and abilities will prove invaluable on your journey." I waited for her to say more, but she remained silent.

"What are his talents exactly?"

"Your guess is as good as mine," Moll shrugged. "In my visions, I saw him as a shadow that danced on the periphery. But something was afraid of him; something knew his capabilities and was terrified."

"Sounds promising," I grumbled. Victor didn't seem frightening, but one never knew what kind of demons someone else might be hiding."

"This will not be an easy journey," Moll warned. "You will need all the help you can get. I am afraid you're entering a world that has not existed in reality for a long time. The rules will be different. The creatures do not trust outsiders. Their hatred of what was done to them has had time to fester and grow. They may not want you there. Many of them support the idea of a world without mortals."

The situation was far from reassuring, and I let out a groan. "Any ideas on how we can earn their trust?"

"Let's break this down into smaller, more manageable parts," Eidolon advised. "Let's focus on reaching the Otherworld and locating Freyja first. Once we have the books, we can then consult with the Fates to figure out how to undo this mess we're in."

Moll and I nodded in agreement to his seemingly straightforward plan, although we didn't have much other information to consider when making our decision.

So that would be Plan A.

Plan B?

No idea.

With a yawn and a stretch, Moll rose from her chair and made her way to her room. The weight of the impending task hung heavy on her shoulders, evident in the slight slump of her posture. She disappeared behind the doors, leaving us to watch her retreating figure.

Eidolon's hand found mine, leading me towards my room. I could feel the tension in his muscles as he silently mulled over our upcoming adventure. Even in the quiet moments, the air was charged with anticipation and worry.

"Do you want to come in?" I asked shyly as we stood in front of my door.

His eyes darkened as I extended the invitation, and I laughed nervously. It had been a while since I had invited a man into my room, and I couldn't recall the proper protocol.

What happens if he says yes? Did I offer him something to drink? Did I throw him on the bed?

"I want to say yes, Chloe, but you need some sleep," he said with a hint of regret. I must have looked disappointed because he traced his finger along my jawline and leaned in for a soft kiss. "If we go in now, we might not meet the others on time," he whispered as he pulled away. My eyes widened at the thought, and a silly grin spread across my face.

"It will give us something to look forward to once we return," he promised. I nodded and allowed him to open my door for me. "Get some rest, and I will meet you in a few hours."

I giggled as I flopped on my bed, wondering how long it would take to make good on his promise.

Chapter 43

'The Space Between Here And There Is In The Details.' -Book of the Veiled Instructions

After Eidolon dropped me off in my room, I must have been more exhausted than I realized because I slept deeply until 11:00. Which left little time to take one last hot shower, braid my hair, and hastily put on my go-to outfit - jeans, a sweatshirt, and boots.

Figuring out what to pack for the trip to the Otherworld was another issue entirely. I had no idea what I should take or if there were any rules regarding clothing. And what about necessities like running water and coffee - would they even be available where we were going? My mind raced with questions as I tried to predict every possible scenario and prepare accordingly.

Thirty minutes later, I was exhausted and rethinking my life choices. Before zipping up my bag, I encased the Book of the Veiled in a waterproof cover and gently set it inside next to my favorite sweatshirt.

Five minutes to midnight, I headed down the stairs in search of coffee and eager to hit the mythical road to the Otherworld. I tugged at the connection and found Eidolon already downstairs waiting for me.

"Sleep well?" he asked, handing me a mug. I took a sip and smiled. Three creams and one sugar- the perfect cup of coffee.

"Yea. And you?"

He leaned in to whisper, "As much as one man can when a beautiful woman is lying in the room beside him alone." I playfully punched him in the arm and walked away.

"You could have woken me up," I called over my shoulder. He groaned as he turned to follow after me. Laughing, I slipped into the main lobby, where everyone was gathering.

Watson and Isabelle were dressed like they were going on a safari, complete with off-white hats and boots. Sydney and Victor, however, looked prepared for battle with knives strapped to their thighs and military-grade rucksacks.

"You can never be too careful," Sydney said happily as I eyed all his gear.

"Don't worry." Victor pulled at one of the straps to tighten it. Tying it off, he stood up and winked. "Most of it is food."

Eidolon moved past me, his shoulder brushing mine, to stand in front of the fireplace, instantly drawing all attention towards him. I had almost forgotten how powerful and commanding he could be. Another reminder of why we had unanimously decided he should be the leader of our little group.

He looked at us all, arching an eyebrow at Watson and Isabelle's outfit before shaking his head.

"Aelle and Max reached out to me earlier. They're researching the Valkyrie for us. We agreed that we would take advantage of the connection between Moll and Chloe to communicate with each other." His dark eyes darted at me, sizing me up appreciatively, and I blushed.

Watson cleared his throat, and Eidolon redirected his focus to the group. "Right. Isabelle and Watson have already caught me up on how they will transport us all, and I will use my link to the Otherworld as a guide. According to the journal Max gave me, once we arrive in the Otherworld, we need to locate the Tree of Life, which is where Freyja should be."

"How will we find the Death Gates?" Sydney asked, raising a hand.

Eidolon rolled his eyes. "One- they're not Death Gates. Two- because I have already been there. I'll retrace my steps," Eidolon assured him. "Moll will serve as our anchor in this world should we need to withdraw for any reason."

"Where *is* Moll?" I asked, noticing her absence. "Shouldn't she be here?"

"She was worried her presence might make it harder for Isabelle to focus. The journey is already difficult enough without dealing with extra people in the room." I nodded. It made sense, but I was a little hurt that she hadn't come to see me off. Or give me pointers about what I should be doing in the Otherworld.

"Isabelle, are you ready?" Eidolon asked.

"As prepared as I'll ever be," she chuckled, readjusting her hat. "Do you have Arawn's book?" He nodded and retrieved it from his bag, handing it over. She took a moment to hold it, closing her eyes and inhaling deeply. "Excellent. Now, Chloe, we'll need your key," she said, turning to me. I walked over, pulling it from around my neck.

"No, luv." She held up a hand to stop me. "Only you can use it. When I tell you to, close your eyes and envision the book in front of you. See the worn leather cover. Breathe in and imagine the scent of old parchment mixed with ink. Then picture Arawn. Sitting alone in his room, his fingers tracing over the words as he reads them aloud. What kind of tale is he telling? I want you to see the world he describes. Let your imagination run wild as you become fully immersed in the story."

"Okay," I hesitated. She made it sound so easy. But I wasn't sure that I could do what she was asking.

"Eidolon." Isabelle's words rolled off her tongue like a spell. "You are tethered to Arawn and the Otherworld. I want you to close your eyes and remember the first time you were called to its gates. Can you recall the scent of magic in the air? The anticipation coursing through your veins as you stand before the threshold of a new realm. And when you finally stepped inside, what did it feel like to stand under the grandeur of the Tree of Life, its branches stretching up to the heavens? Now, imagine yourself as an arrow, guided by my hand as the bow, soaring towards your destiny."

The spell weaved around him, and Eidolon nodded as his eyes lit up. At that moment, I realized this might feel like a homecoming to him. He was destined to journey between realms. My heart sank at the thought of him deciding to stay there forever.

What would I do then? I didn't know, but this wasn't the time to think about it.

All eyes turned to me as Isabelle handed over Arawn's book. A familiar melody echoed through the room as if a long-lost song were being played. As I grasped the key, its deep tone harmonized with the music. Isabelle stood behind me, placing her hands on my shoulders and directing Watson, Sydney, Victor, and Eidolon to hold a corner of the book.

"Okay, Chloe," she said as her eyes shut. "Think about what I told you, envision it in detail, and put the key on the book when ready."

I looked at Eidolon one last time. His eyes closed as if he was already painting the picture and directing us. From his head to his neck, the words flowed down and into the book... recounting the story of the Otherworld.

As the words crashed into the binding, my senses took over, and my mind began to visualize what was written. The aroma of the leather binding filled the room: woody, smoky, earthy, all the smells of Eidolon.

My hands grasped the weighty pages made from ancient trees that towered three stories tall in my mind's eye. I could almost hear the rustle of the wind through their branches and see children playing beneath them. The words danced in my mind as I envisioned Arawn putting them on paper, penning the letters as small as possible to make the most of every sheet.

The longer I held Arawn's book, the more vivid the tale became. He was desperate to complete his work and get it down on parchment before something else happened. The hand gripping the pen trembled as if holding it was a matter of life or death.

I leaned forward in curiosity, keenly aware of the tugging at my core demanding I go to the Otherworld. It was up to me to save his story. I took a deep breath and pushed through the space between us and into the vision.

Chapter 44

'Not Everything That Exists Can Be Seen.' -Book of the Veiled Instructions

"Welcome home, Chloe," a voice boomed behind me, and I opened my eyes to discover Arawn standing over me, chuckling. "Took you long enough. I was beginning to get worried."

I let out a heavy sigh and tried to massage away the throbbing headache that had formed. "Hi, Arawn," I said flatly, attempting to keep the annoyance out of my voice as I motioned behind me. "I brought my friends."

"I noticed." He swept a curious gaze at the rest of the group, still clutching his book, sleeping off the effects of the journey. "I see you have decided to continue your mystifying adventure." His eyes darted to me in amusement.

"You know I'm trying to help you too," I snapped, my voice sharp and edged with frustration. I pressed my hands against my temples, trying to calm the spinning chaos surrounding me.

"Yes. And that is the only reason I am not expelling you and your companions from my kingdom." He gave me a piercing stare. "While your motives may be noble, they are also reckless and unwise."

"You don't think we can change things?" I stood up on shaky legs, trying to keep my balance. *This is what it must feel like to skydive*, I thought as my stomach protested the movement—*checking that off the bucket list!*

"You're facing more than just a battle of wits between Lilith, Vivian, and Taliesin." He frowned. "You're attempting to rewrite the laws governing humanity and the supernatural. Even if you somehow manage to outsmart them, do you honestly believe you will be able to find a safe place for all lost souls?"

"Oh ye of little faith," I muttered, jutting my chin out and straightening my posture. "You were a god! The Otherworld was a place of beauty and peace. Look at it now," I swung my hands around. "*50 Shades of Grey* had more color than this."

"We will see, Daughter of Morrigan," he conceded as Sydney started to stir. "Your comrades are regaining consciousness—best wishes on your first assignment. Freyja is not to be underestimated," he cautioned before walking away.

He paused at Victor's slumbering figure, his gaze quickly flicking up to meet mine before returning to Victor. "Fascinating," he muttered before disappearing without another word.

I lingered as the group slept, mulling over what Arawn had told me. More importantly, what he hadn't said. Arawn had lost his faith.

"Gods, I have a headache from hell," Sydney moaned before chuckling. "Get it, hell?"

"Yes, Sydney. We all get it," Victor replied, opening one eye before shutting it quickly with a wince. "Who would have thought the Otherworld would be so bright."

Watson grabbed Isabelle's hand and pulled her up from the ground. Her face was gray, but I could tell she was pleased that we all made it. He dusted his pants off, looking over to our leader. "Okay, Prince of Darkness; we are in your world now. Where to next?"

Eidolon's gaze swept across the landscape, his expression a mix of confusion and frustration. The rest of us waited patiently for him to gather his bearings. "I'm not entirely certain," he said, fiddling with his bracelet. "It doesn't look familiar."

The sight of defeat on his face was heart-wrenching, and I immediately wanted to console him until I remembered what Diana had shared about what she and Taliesin had done.

"Eidolon?" I called softly.

He spun around to face me, his expression turning into a scowl. I instinctively stepped back, the shadows growing darker and enveloping him. "What?"

I walked towards him and instructed, "Take off your bracelet."

"My bracelet?" He looked down. "Why?"

"I think it interferes with your abilities." I took another step forward cautiously. I didn't want to explain why I knew what to do.

Eidolon glanced at me in puzzlement but removed the bracelet from his wrist. As soon as it was off, I saw a newfound expression in his eyes. He turned, taking in his surroundings with a blend of despair and optimism. "So many souls..." he whispered.

"What did he say?" Victor asked, turning to look at me, eyes wide. "What does he mean 'souls'?"

"I think Eidolon can see the souls bound here," Isabelle explained. "I can feel them, but I can't see them."

Sydney took a deep breath and scrunched up his nose in disgust. "They're everywhere," he confirmed, his eyes swinging back and forth at the invisible intruders.

I couldn't see or smell them, but I could hear them. The sounds of distant voices and movements overwhelmed me. A woman's panicked cries for her missing child echoed while a man's desperate pleas for help pierced the air. In the distance, I could hear a soldier's rhythmic footsteps, accompanied by the clatter of their weapon against their equipment.

The stories tumbled out, one after the other, leaving no space for silence. Tears trickled down my face, and I covered my ears to block them out.

"I understand." Eidolon swept me up in a hug, and I leaned into him.

"Is this what you saw as a child?" I questioned.

"Yes."

I couldn't imagine what it was like to have his ability. It must have been so emotionally draining. Just listening to the stories made me want to go back to the hotel's safety and dive beneath my covers.

"They're coming closer," he whispered. A few seconds later, Sydney and Victor pulled out their knives and stood ready to defend us against invisible threats.

I winced as the voices got louder, pulling my sweatshirt hood over my head to muffle the sound. Isabelle's body tensed up as sparks flew from her fingertips, and Watson moved to stand in front of her protectively.

"Wait." Eidolon put a hand up. We all paused, afraid to breathe. "I need to talk to them." He released my hand and took a few steps forward, his arms outstretched in a powerful gesture.

My heart raced in anticipation as I scanned the area for potential threats. Tension filled the air as he stood still, his head tilted in concentration. After what felt like an eternity, he slowly lowered his arms, and a small smile played on his lips. Clearly, he was communicating with the souls, and I couldn't help but marvel at the power and mystery of it all.

The voices were finally silent. I let out a breath of relief.

"He is talking to them, isn't he?" Sydney asked in awe. I nodded, afraid to utter a sound.

Eidolon was in his element, and fear gripped me.

Chapter 45

'Punishments Should Fit The Crime.' -Book of the Veiled Instructions

We stood watching Eidolon for what seemed like minutes that stretched into hours. Bored and tired, we made our way to an old, forgotten tree and sat underneath its lifeless branches.

As the rest of the team began to strategize, I watched Eidolon. It was the first time since we met that he was comfortable in his skin. Relaxed. He sat for hours, listening to one soul after another share their thoughts and make themselves known.

Is this where we end up when we die, and people forget about us? I asked myself, not really wanting to know the answer. Because if it was, it was a depressing possibility.

As the sun faded into darkness, Sydney and Victor made a fire and cooked a simple meal while Isabelle and Watson prepared places to sleep. However, I stayed on guard duty, watching Eidolon in case he vanished into darkness.

The warning that Diana and Taliesin gave me still lingered in the back of my mind. I wasn't sure why they didn't want him to meet Arawn, but it seemed like Arawn didn't want to meet him either.

Lilith was a different story. I wasn't willing to take any chances in case she showed up.

It was nearing midnight when Eidolon headed back. His steps were heavy, and his shoulders slumped with exhaustion, but there was a glint of excitement in his eyes.

"How did it go?" I asked.

"As well as is to be expected for as long as it has been since I last came," he said with a slight frown as he looked into the distance.

I turned my head to see what had caught his attention, mesmerized by the sight of a city nestled in the mountains, lit up like a beautiful starry night. The aroma of burning wood wafted towards me, and as I focused my senses, I could hear the distant sound of laughter. Despite living in the Otherworld, they were still very much alive.

"Do you need anything?" I asked, looking back at him.

"No, I just need some rest. It's been a long day," he gently kissed my cheek. "Goodnight, Chloe."

As he settled into his sleeping bag, I said good night. I waited until his breathing slowed, and he fell asleep before getting up. I needed some time to clear my head. The riverbed where I first arrived wasn't too far from our current site, so I quietly slipped away in search of peace and quiet.

The stars twinkled brightly, providing a path for me to find my way. I slipped off my shoes and dipped my toes in, surprised to discover the water lukewarm- like the world around me. Lost in my thoughts, I didn't pay attention when another person sat beside me, their bare feet slipping into the water beside mine.

"Hello, Chloe," she said with a sideways grin. "I've been waiting for you."

I had been expecting her arrival. I didn't know who was coming, but I knew someone would—someone I was supposed to meet.

"Do you remember me?" she asked when I said nothing.

I slowly turned to face her, narrowing my eyes to study her. Her features were unremarkable and easily forgettable, the kind of face you would walk past without a second glance at the grocery store. She appeared like any other exhausted woman in her forties who could use a good night's sleep.

"You're the woman from the Book Store Book Club," I gasped. "Aelle's friend."

She smiled and nodded, pleased that I had quickly put the pieces together. "Yup," she answered, kicking her legs playfully in the water. "Although I wouldn't exactly call us 'friends,' more like acquaintances."

"I didn't know souls from the Otherworld could join book clubs." I shrugged, returning my attention to the river. "Something to look forward to, I guess."

"Freyja sent me."

I raised my eyebrows in astonishment, "Freyja? She sent you to spy on me?" Did Freyja know that I was going to join the Raven Society? Did the Fates tell her that I would be coming to the Otherworld?

"Not you," she said dismissively. "Aelle."

I stared at her in bewilderment. Why would Freyja, the leader of the Valkyrie and guardian of the Tree of Life, assign someone to protect Aelle? And who was this mysterious individual sitting next to me?

As if she understood my unspoken question, she explained. "I'm Brynhildr. But you can call me Bree; it's a lot easier to pronounce."

I let out a small sigh as I leaned back, the soft blades of grass tickling my arms as I rested them behind me. "So," I asked with curiosity, turning my head to glance at her. "What's your story?"

Bree chuckled. "Well, it's a pretty long story. But let me give you the abbreviated version for now." She took a deep breath. "I made the mistake of angering Odin and am now paying the price for it."

I raised an eyebrow, skeptical of the information. "Your punishment was guarding Aelle?" I asked. "You must've done something pretty horrible to get that sentence."

Her expression twisted into a grimace. "I may have unintentionally caused the death of a king." She shuddered at the memory. "And then retaliated by killing another who wronged me."

I couldn't help but laugh. "As they say, 'Hell hath no fury like a woman scorned.' So let me guess, Odin and Freyja punished you with a lifetime of babysitting duty?"

She grinned as she threw a rock. "That was the plan," she replied with a hint of sarcasm. "Until they felt I had paid my debt and regained my honor."

"How's that working out for you?"

She turned to face me, crossing her legs underneath her. "Interesting, to say the least," she commented, her voice dripping with amusement.

I plucked a blade of grass and spun it between my fingers. "Why Aelle? I mean, what makes her so special that she needs you to guard her?"

She looked at me, surprised. "You don't know?" I shook my head. "Aelle was the Writer."

My mouth dropped open, and I stared at Bree. "What?"

"Aelle was Moll's replacement." Her words came out slowly, with narrowed eyes as if she couldn't believe I didn't know. "Until a couple of weeks ago."

With a sharp intake of breath, I sat up and turned my body to face her fully. "I wasn't supposed to be the Writer?" Every inch of my body tensed as I awaited her response.

"Nope."

I waited, shocked and speechless, for her to continue. But she remained silent. Frustrated, I pushed my glasses further up my nose and asked, "Then how am I one now?"

She shrugged and replied, "Nobody knows. Even Freyja was taken aback by the sudden change. But who knows what mischief the Fates are up to? One minute, Aelle was the Writer, and the next, she wasn't." She laughed lightly. "I can't complain. I got to come home. Debt paid in full," she said proudly.

The chaos of the past few weeks swirled through my thoughts. Moll had told me she couldn't see Aelle's future. Was it because I had taken it from her? I shook my head. That didn't quite add up either. Diana and Taliesin mentioned waiting for me as if they knew I was coming.

Did they have something to do with this?

Aelle's sharp, cutting remarks about my writing echoed in my mind, her disapproving stares burning into me with each word. And the way she would look at Eidolon, with a mixture of sadness and longing. Everyone could feel the tension in the room whenever the three of us were together, like an unspoken battle waiting to erupt.

She knew.

"She was supposed to be bonded to Eidolon," I whispered. No wonder she hated me.

"She used to be, but not anymore." I must have looked concerned because Bree quickly tried to ease my worries. "But don't worry, it's not like the bond you and Eidolon share; that was never meant to be her fate," she clarified. "The connection between you two is rare. I've only seen it once before."

I shrugged, still doubtful. Aelle was supposed to be the Writer. What caused the Fates to reconsider their decision? "So now what?" I questioned, unable to hide the skepticism in my voice. My mind raced with questions, unsure how to move forward from this unexpected turn of events.

"Good question," she admitted. "Apart from Morrigan and Vivian, you're the only one who has dared to approach the Fates. We need to find out why you were chosen as the Writer. The Fates must have had a compelling reason for changing their mind. And not tell anyone," she added.

"Arawn, Taliesin, Diana, Moll...no one mentioned anything to me. But they all must have known about Aelle, right?" My heart sank again as I added another lie to the growing list. Could no one tell the truth anymore?

Her eyes filled with understanding as if she could sense the turmoil in my mind. "I'm not sure. It's possible," she shrugged, studying me closely. "We could try asking Claire. She might have known." I could see the excitement in her eyes as she mentioned Claire's name.

"Who's she?"

"She's one of the goddesses of dreams, prophecy, and sleep. And she might be the only deity who could tell us why a prophecy would've changed."

"Do you think she'll tell the truth?" Bree nodded. I took a deep breath, knowing I would regret my next words. "How do we find her?"

"You're in luck!" Bree exclaimed, a smile spreading across her face. "Today is Samhain, and I bet she's at Loch Bél Dracon. She makes a point of visiting every year during the three-day festival."

A glimmer of hope sparked as I asked, "Is that close by?" This meant changing our plans a little. But I needed answers and wouldn't stop until I had all the puzzle pieces. It was time to take my destiny into my own hands.

"Not far. A few hours, tops. We can leave when your friends wake up." There was a glimmer of excitement in her eyes like she'd been waiting for this moment.

"You're coming with us?" I asked, relieved to have a guide.

"Sure, why not? It sounds like a fun adventure, plus Freyja said I needed to keep an eye on you now. She warned me that you have a knack for finding yourself in sticky situations." Her eyes sparkled with mischief. "But I'm always up for a challenge."

"Freyja knows that we are here?" The thought of meeting the Valkyrie caused my stomach to drop. If I was honest with myself, it was more because I was intimidated by her reputation as a complete badass.

"Of course she does," Bree scoffed, her tone filled with exasperation. "No one enters the Otherworld without her knowing."

"Oh..." I nodded.

She sighed and explained, "Freyja is a deity like Morrigan, Lilith, and Taliesin. If you wish to gain the favor of the Fates, it is Freyja who you must impress. But be warned, it won't be an easy task." She gestured towards the tree where my friends were slowly waking up. "I'll see you soon, Daughter of Morrigan," she said with a knowing smile. "I have a feeling we have quite a journey ahead of us."

I blinked once, and she was gone. I felt a pull as Eidolon searched our bond to find me.

Are you all right? I woke up, and you were gone.

I'm good, I reassured him, my gaze still fixed on where Bree had just been. I squared my shoulders and added, *There's a slight change to plans.*

How did I guess? he laughed.

Chapter 46

'Every Story Has A Plot Twist.' -Book of the Veiled Instructions

While Sydney made breakfast, I explained what I had learned from Bree to the group.

It was uncomfortable to tell Aelle's story, but I needed to justify the change in mission. I watched carefully as Eidolon's eyes darkened at the idea of Aelle being destined to be the Writer. But he quickly shook it off and squeezed my hand in reassurance, and a small part of me was relieved.

Isabelle intently followed my story, her beautiful face in deep concentration. When I finished, I sat patiently as she worked through whatever was whirling in her mind. Eventually, she nodded at Watson and turned to me.

"I believe Bree's story, but I still don't know what we're doing," she confessed. "If the Book of the Veiled was meant to hide the supernatural, why are so many souls abandoned in the Otherworld? Who are these people?"

"I think I can answer that question for you." Appearing out of thin air, Bree appeared from behind the tree with a pack slung over her shoulders. She strode confidently towards us and gracefully settled beside me, her backpack thudding softly against the ground.

"When Arawn built the Otherworld, it was a place for supernatural and mortals—created to give each culture its own region where they could find peace in the afterlife. But as religion progressed, the concept of the Otherworld changed so much that it was not recognizable anymore. Then, as belief in the re-imagined concept of hell continued to take root, the Otherworld realms began to fade.

"As a result, only the souls of those without anyone to remember them, primarily the supernatural, live here. As their stories were retold, their essence blurred. Neither who they were nor what they became. No one remembered their names. As a result, they are trapped in this limbo."

"That explains why our species are dying out," Watson mused. "And why are our abilities deteriorating."

"Yup. The gods were able to keep some of their powers, enabling them to keep the supernatural safe. However, as belief in them declines, so does their power to keep us safe."

"How were they able to keep some of their abilities?" Sydney asked, eyeing the Valkyrie with interest. His muscular arms were on full display as he crossed them in front of his chest. The sun's rays hit his face, highlighting his handsome, tanned complexion. He ran a hand through his hair and smiled at Bree. It was the first time I had seen Sydney try to look sexy, and he was doing an excellent job.

I glanced at Isabelle, who was watching in fascination. Watson was trying to hide his amusement with a sip of coffee, and Eidolon's light laugh made it clear he, too, had noticed what was going on.

Bree looked over, approval in her eyes as she studied him. "Because they were extensions of the original. It doesn't matter how often religion is reinvented; the original god remains a constant in a world of inconsistencies. Thankfully, the thread of the original's power has never been severed."

"But the Writers should have been able to see this happen, right?" I asked hesitantly, pulling the group's attention away from the smokey stares between Bree and Sydney. "Someone must have predicted the supernatural would lose their powers. Why didn't they do anything about it?"

I felt a jolt of understanding and excitement rush down Eidolon's and my bond, and I glanced at him with surprise.

"Those are the books that are missing," he declared. "They are the books where the Writer mentions they saw this coming. It had to have been intermixed with Morrigan and Taliesin's story. Because they are the ones who started the chain of events." His wide eyes glazed over me blankly as if he were reading a book in his mind.

For a moment, all of us were silent as we tried to make sense of the information. At least we now knew what was written in the books. But we didn't know who the books belonged to.

"What would happen if we didn't find the books?" Sydney asked. "What if this is what was supposed to happen? Lilith and Vivian taking the books and supernatural getting their powers back. We've had the raw end of the deal for a long time, so what if we came into some good luck"?

"That is not going to happen," I said, shaking my head. "Don't get me wrong, the supernatural should regain their powers. No one should be forced to spend eternity in this bleak world. However, handing over control of the world to Lilith just because they've had a tough break is not the solution. We need to find a way for both species to coexist harmoniously."

"It's an idea," Bree said slowly. "But how do you rewrite history to make it happen?"

"We ask Claire. If she can predict the future, she might be able to see if it's even possible. No need to bug the Fates yet if we are not sure what we are doing." I suggested.

"Awesome! We have a plan. Let's go," Sydney jumped up and started packing his bag, whistling the *Whistle While You Work* song as he moved. I couldn't help but grin at his unbridled enthusiasm for our adventure.

Granted, it was a hazy plan at best, but while the fate of the supernatural was hanging in the balance, at least Sydney would provide comic relief along the way.

I was too focused on getting prepared that I didn't notice Eidolon standing nearby, gazing out at the City in the Mountain. Curious, I joined him and took in the view of the landscape stretching before us.

The charcoal-colored sky hovered above the mountains' harsh peaks and rugged ridges, giving a hostile look in broad daylight. The lights and aromas from the previous evening had vanished with the rising sun, leaving a dismal ambiance as bleak as a mid-winter gale. Gazing out, all I saw was gray – innumerable shades that made me question if there might be any chance of reviving its vibrancy.

"What's on your mind?" I inquired, edging closer to Eidolon, tucking my arm into his for warmth.

"I am thinking about the people who live out there," he said, pointing to the city. "You should have heard them last night. So many souls couldn't find peace, not able to enter the town because they had become anonymous. The fortunate ones, who still had fragments of their stories remembered, could find some semblance of a home." He glanced down at me. "They need someone to help them."

I could hear what he was trying to say but didn't want to put it into words. He was torn between his obligation to the Raven Society and his need to help the lost souls. And I didn't know what to do to support him.

He glanced at the City in the Mountain once more before forcing a grin. "We should pack. Big day ahead of us."

"Eidolon," I said before he could walk away, and I lost my nerve. "What if you stayed here?"

"What?" his eyes narrowed on me in confusion.

I tucked a piece of his hair behind his ear and smiled. "I don't think the missing books are the only reason we are here. I think they're just a piece of the story."

"What are you trying to say, Chloe?"

"What I'm trying to say is that a good story often has an unexpected plot twist. It's like taking a different path when you reach a fork in the road." I chuckled as I gestured towards the visible trailhead. One path led left towards the City in the Mountain, while the other veered right towards a massive lake. "I think you are meant to stay here. I will head to Claire and ask her the questions we need answers to."

"No!" he said firmly. "We are not splitting up. We are in this together; you said so yourself."

"Yeah, I did." I arched an eyebrow. "I said we would travel to the Otherworld together. And we did Eidolon. We are here." I wrapped my arms around his waist and glanced up at him, praying he would see the certainty in my eyes. "But you and I know the Librarian and the Writer are not always at the same place at the same time. If they were, no story would ever be completed. They have two distinct roles."

"So, you want me to stay here? And you head out and face whatever danger is there alone?"

"No," I laughed. "Sydney, Victor, and Bree will come with me. Isabelle and Watson can stay here with you. Isabelle's gifts might come in handy." I shrugged. "Sydney is a tracker, and Moll implied Victor has some magickal talent he hasn't shared with us yet. It might be helpful along the way."

I didn't know Victor's hidden talent; something inside me told me I would need it. And soon.

"Besides, have you seen Isabelle and Watson's costumes? They wouldn't make it two days without real food, running water, or somewhere to take a shower."

Eidolon looked at me intently, considering his next move. He pulled me in for a strong embrace, and I knew I had emerged victorious in our small battle.

"As soon as you find your answers, you come straight back. Do you understand?"

"Of course. And you are not to do anything that draws attention to yourself," I countered with a smile.

"I don't know if you know this, but I can talk to the dead. I think people will notice the ability," he joked.

"So, who gets to tell Isabelle the fabulous news?"

"I will give you the honor," he said, lowering his lips to mine. "As long as you promise to hide some of the food in your bag so Sydney doesn't eat it all before you find Claire."

"I promise," I replied and leaned up to kiss him. It was a slow kiss, full of promises of more.

Chapter 47

"Even Santa Claus Exists.' -Book of the Veiled Instructions

Isabelle and Watson were thrilled to stay with Eidolon, promising me they would watch over him like a kid waiting for Santa Claus.

I couldn't contain my laughter when Bree innocently asked who Santa Claus was. After Victor explained, Sydney was heartbroken when she revealed she'd never participated in a Christmas celebration.

This led to an hour-long explanation of his favorite Christmas traditions and the story of Santa Claus in detail. His mouth fell open in surprise when she mentioned encountering someone who looked like Saint Nicholas during one of her Valkyrie missions.

With excitement bubbling, he asked, "Are you sure?" She nodded, walking away. Undeterred, he trailed behind and bombarded her with endless questions about Jolly Kris Kringle until she threatened to stuff him up a chimney and light a fire beneath him.

In retaliation, he whistled the tune of Here Comes Santa Claus for an entire hour. I had to step in when Bree started to clench her fists, and it looked like she was about to start a fight. Mostly because I didn't think Sydney could handle her, but I wasn't dumb enough to tell him that.

After tidying up our temporary camp, it was time for us to part ways. As the moment drew nearer, I tried my best to maintain a cheerful demeanor, cracking jokes and suppressing the dread in my stomach.

Although I had suggested this plan, it still weighed heavily on my mind. I didn't want to leave Eidolon behind. I wanted to embark on a grand adventure with him and the others. United in our mission to save the world.

But I also refused to be overbearing and protective. Eidolon was needed in the City in the Mountain, and I was determined to support him even if it clawed at my heart.

Eidolon stayed quiet, observing me closely. Sydney noticed and gestured for the others to follow him. He slyly winked at me before they departed - his way of granting us privacy without needing to say it directly, and I appreciated his consideration.

"So, I guess this is 'see you soon,'" I said as we walked towards the tree together. Eidolon responded by pulling me closer, wrapping his arms around my waist, and resting his chin on the top of my head.

"You know, you are quite short for someone with so much personality," he chuckled.

"That's how you intend to say goodbye, Eidolon? With short jokes?" I forced a small laugh, wanting to enjoy the moment for as long as possible.

"It seems proper that I remind you that you are not a giant and should probably avoid looking for trouble. I would appreciate it if you returned like you left."

"Same here, buddy. No falling for any lost damsels in distress while I am gone."

He kissed me on my forehead and whispered, "I won't have time for anyone else in my mind except for you."

"Good," I replied softly.

"Don't fall for any handsome supernatural who can create flower gardens or massive libraries with a wave of his hand," he warned, looking down at me in mock horror.

"I highly doubt Sydney or Victor will allow any male within ten feet of me," I laughed. "Or Bree, for that matter."

His hand gently pushed my chin to face him. "Good. I am unsure how my walking library powers will match up to real magick."

"Don't worry, Eidolon," I rolled my eyes at him. "We will be back before Isabelle finds the beauty shop." His chuckle warmed my heart as I watched his laughter reach his eyes.

"So, you will be back by sunset?" We laughed and fell silent as I rested my ear against his heart.

"We should get moving," he said softly as the rest of the group walked up. "Just promise me you will stay safe, Chloe."

I looked up, memorizing his face. "I promise."

He flicked my nose. "I am determined to hold you to that. We have a date planned when this is all over," Eidolon reminded me with a mischievous grin.

"Yes, we do," I leaned up, kissed him quickly, and turned to leave. "And there better be coffee wherever you are taking me. I tasted whatever Sydney claimed to be coffee this morning, and I almost had a heart attack. I will have heartburn for weeks." I said over my shoulder as I picked up my bag and placed it firmly on my back.

The others had already loaded their gear, and Sydney, Victor, and Bree patiently waited for me at the trailhead. I took one last look at Eidolon before glancing at Isabelle and Watson, smiling sadly.

"Don't worry, luv, I will protect him as if he was my own," Isabelle promised, and I could only nod my thanks. It was difficult for me to say goodbye, so I waved in their general direction and hurried to meet my companions.

I felt Eidolon's eyes on me as I walked away, but I didn't turn around. Second glances were always bad luck. I learned that the hard way long ago and was reluctant to make that mistake again.

I wanted a happy ever after.

Chapter 48

'Reanimation Is A Dangerous Gift.' -Book of the Veiled Instructions

After two hours, I was rethinking my commitment to getting to Loch Bél Dracon and finding Claire. The hike through the rolling gray foothills to the massive silver lake proved more challenging than I initially thought. Navigating the rugged path was a treacherous task of lose rocks, pesky tree roots, and prickly thorns from the bushes whose unforgiving grasp tore at our clothes and left angry red scratches on our bodies.

Not my idea of a fun time.

As soon as we left the other, Sydney and Bree began debating who would win in hand-to-hand combat: a shapeshifter or a Valkyrie. What had started as lighthearted teasing quickly turned into an intense argument. Victor and I exchanged knowing looks, silently deciding not to interfere with their passionate debate.

I had my money on the 5'2 Valkyrie, who somehow towered over the 6'3 shapeshifter.

"This is the first time we've had a chance to talk. Just the two of us." Victor commented, watching Bree stomp away from Sydney, her face flushed and her hands balled into fists, ready to escalate the fight.

A knot of worry tightened in my stomach as I watched Sydney follow her. I considered going after them but quickly dismissed the idea. They were two grown adults, and I refused to become entangled in their drama, determined to stay on the sidelines and let them work it out on their own.

"I was just thinking the same thing," I admitted, turning to face him. His dark eyes locked onto mine, and I couldn't help but feel a twinge of curiosity. "So, tell me. How did you come to be a member of the Raven Society?"

"Not sure," he replied with a nonchalant shrug. "A string of lucky breaks, I suppose. I was surprised when I got the invitation. I don't quite fit the mold of who they usually pick."

"What do you say that?" I asked, confused.

He smiled shyly and confessed, "I wouldn't call myself a writer. I'm more of a scientist who has a talent for storytelling."

"Really?" *I knew it! He looked like a scientist, more comfortable in a lab coat than a tweed jacket.*

He nodded, his hand reaching down to deftly unclip a canteen hanging from his belt. The silver metal gleamed in the sunlight as he took a long sip before offering it to me. I gratefully accepted, my throat parched and dry after the grueling ascent up a steep hill.

"Yeah, really," he grinned. "My team and I were researching how to isolate the specific genes responsible for Huntington's Disease. Our ultimate goal was to develop a cure."

"Did you?"

"Hell no," he laughed. "We were able to find ways to lessen symptoms, but we couldn't change the course of nature. No matter how hard we tried. But it opened doors for a new way of thinking."

"What do you mean?" I asked, intrigued.

"Well, it got me thinking: if something as small as a cell changing its structure could affect a life span, what's to say there wasn't a possibility to tweak our DNA to alter our abilities? If scientists could manipulate cells in a controlled environment, why couldn't we do the same outside of it?

"Like witches?" I'd never tried to find a rational explanation for magick, but Victor's statement seemed logical.

He reached into his back pocket and pulled out a granola bar, breaking it in half before offering me a piece. "Exactly. I wanted to prove that there were individuals in the world who could manipulate their bodies into becoming something else."

"Like the Hulk?" I asked around a mouthful.

Victor rolled his eyes. "A little extreme, but yes, like the Hulk. I was thinking more like Sydney's ability to shapeshift or Isabelle's ability to alter moods." He paused briefly. "Or the ability to reanimate things."

My mouth dropped, and I stopped. "What are you talking about?"

He stepped closer to me, glancing at where Sydney and Bree stood deep in another argument and lowered his voice. "If it's not too far-fetched to believe Sydney and Isabelle's ability to manipulate their surroundings and bodies, what's to say someone can't rebuild themselves? Wouldn't you agree?" He eyed me, and I had the suspicious feeling the conversation was taking a dark turn.

I paused before responding. "I suppose not?" I shook my head in uncertainty.

"Would it scare you?" He pressed.

Would it scare me? "I don't think so," I admitted. "But if someone did possess such a power, I would be concerned for their well-being and would want to protect them from being taken advantage of."

A grin spread across his face, and I could see the tension melt away as if he had been holding his breath. "That's a relief," Victor said with a nod. "Because that's my ability."

I was not expecting that.

My eyes widened as I stared at him. Reanimation was something I had only read about in books or seen in movies. I never thought it could happen. But this did clear up some low-hanging questions I had.

Moll had mentioned that Victor possessed a unique ability that would terrify others, and she couldn't predict his future. This was likely because he could manipulate his DNA, making it impossible to track anything consistent about him.

Curiosity tugged at me as I glanced over at Victor as we made our way up the path. "What's it like?" I finally asked, my voice betraying my eagerness to know more.

Victor's eyes lifted before he spoke, searching for the right words in the sky. "It's like free falling from a plane without a parachute and somehow landing on your feet," he explained with a shake of his head.

"I was in a car wreck a few years back. A drunk driver, too busy texting to pay attention, ran a red light and plowed into my car." He paused, taking a deep breath before continuing. "I don't remember anything about the accident; just waking up and feeling like I'd been put through a meat grinder. Blood was everywhere."

"The paramedics called it an unsurvivable accident." Victor paused his body tense with emotion. He reached down, picked up a small rock, and hurled it into the distance. "It was like a firecracker was exploding inside me. I felt my bones healing, my cuts and scrapes mending, and my blood replenished. Magick—raw and beautiful magick—was coursing through me."

A soft chuckle escaped from him as he threw another rock. "The paramedics couldn't believe it," he said, recalling the moment. "They murmured something about divine intervention as I walked away." His lips curved into a wry smile. "I didn't quite buy into the theory until I was sitting in the back of the ambulance and a stranger approached. He looked like any other man off the streets, but then he said something that still sends shivers down my spine."

"What?" I whispered.

Victor's head snapped around to face me, his eyes narrowing with wariness as he readjusted the weight of his rucksack on his shoulder. "He said he'd been waiting for me. Waiting for me to reveal my true self. And then, just like that," he snapped his fingers, "disappeared into thin air."

"Who was it?"

"Honestly, Chloe, I'm not entirely sure," he said, raising an eyebrow. "But my best guess is Taliesin. He came to see what I was capable of. Over the next few years, I studied everything about him, from his background to the myths of Merlin and the powers of the supernatural. My curiosity eventually led me to the Raven Society. I was convinced Taliesin had some connection to it. So, I wrote a book about a modern-day Dr. Frankenstein. And then I received my invitation."

He stopped suddenly, gently placing his hand on my arm. However, the intensity in his eyes blazed like a fire as he locked his gaze with mine. "The ability to sense connections between things is one of my gifts. As is the ability to detect subtle similarities between individuals. When I first met Eidolon, I knew." He looked expectantly at me.

"What did you know?" I whispered. *Please, please, please... don't say what you are about to say.*

"Eidolon is Taliesin's son, isn't he?"

There you have it, folks. Finally, the cat is officially out of the bag. I nodded, feeling like I had betrayed Eidolon somehow.

Victor nodded. "I won't breathe a word of this to anyone," he promised. "But I must admit, it does add an extra layer of complication to our situation."

I couldn't help but laugh. Complication was the theme of our entire situation. "So, what do we do now?"

He shrugged nonchalantly. "Nothing we can do now except keep this to ourselves and see how things unfold." He glanced over to Bree and Sydney, then back to me. "We should hurry and catch up." He nodded in their direction. "Before we have another complication."

As we closed in on our friends, I couldn't shake the curiosity nagging at me. "Victor," I whispered, unable to contain my question any longer. "Why do you think Taliesin was interested in what you can do?"

"I don't know, Chloe. That's one of the mysteries I want answers to. But I'm not sure he had good intentions if you ask me."

I was afraid of that.

Chapter 49

'Size Matters On The Battlefield.' -Book of the Veiled Intructions

When we finally caught up to Sydney and Bree, they were both perched on large boulders facing each other, their eyes locked in a fierce stare, daring the other to make a move.

"What's going on? Are you guys okay?" I asked, eyeing them with interest.

"We're good," Sydney mumbled, taking a bite of an apple and looking out towards the lake. "Nothing to see here."

"Nothing, my ass," Bree retorted, pointing a finger at him and glaring. "This four-legged sorry excuse for a man dared to sneak attack me from behind with his oversized horns."

"Well, you shouldn't insult people. It's rude," Sydney shot back, refusing to turn and face her.

"You don't attack people just because your feelings got hurt," Bree jumped down from her perch and stormed across to stand in front of him. "And let's be real, if anyone was being insulting, it was definitely you, you oversized goat."

"For the last time, I am a Black Ram. NOT A GOAT!" Sydney bellowed, jumping down to face her.

She cocked her head. "You could've fooled me," she smiled sweetly. "I swear I'm looking at a fainting goat."

"Look here, you pint-sized pixie," he growled.

"I am NOT A PIXIE!"

Max jumped into the middle of them as I stood to the side, trying to hold back my laughter.

"Everyone to their corners of the boxing ring," Victor instructed as he pushed them away from each other. "Go cool off, and then we'll come back and discuss this like adults."

"Fine," Sydney huffed, walking back to his boulder.

"Fine with me, too. But don't expect much civil conversation from the wool factory," Bree mumbled as she walked towards me.

Sydney sprang from his seat, his movements quick and agile. Victor reacted instantly, stepping in front of him and holding him back with outstretched arms as I grabbed Bree's arm and pulled her out of harm's way.

"What is going on?" I asked once we were out of hearing range. "What started the fight?"

Bree stood with her arms folded, eyeing Sydney as if calculating the space between them before making her next move. I positioned myself in front of her and waited.

It took a few minutes for Bree's breathing to calm down. Her gaze fixed on me.

"Nothing," she finally said.

"It didn't sound like nothing." I arched an eyebrow.

She dismissed me with a wave of her hand. "Sydney overreacted when I giggled at his announcement of being a Black Ram," she explained. "But it wasn't because I was making fun of him. I had just assumed he would be a lion or a wolf. It was an innocent mistake."

She shot a quick glance back at Sydney, her expression turning into a frown. "The Black Rams are known for their honor as warriors, and I made sure to explain that to him," she said, her eyes filled with anger, "but then he had the audacity to call me a Tinker Bell."

How did the Otherworld know about Tinker Bell?

Bree saw my confusion and scoffed. "We have libraries, in case you didn't know. We're not barbarians."

"I'm sorry, I didn't know," I said quickly, instinctively stepping back as her eyes filled with anger.

Bree sighed deeply and ran her hands over her face, dismissing my apology with a wave. "No, I'm sorry," she said, clearly frustrated. "I just hate when people judge me because of my size."

"I'm sure Sydney feels the same way," I retorted, my reply sharp, dripping with irony. "It's frustrating when someone is judged on appearance and not performance. Like when someone calls them a goat?" I suggested.

Bree opened her mouth, ready to argue, but shut it quickly. She cast her gaze downwards towards her shoes. "I suppose," she murmured.

"Maybe you could talk to him and clear the air before we see Claire?" I mentioned, hopeful that we could get this cleared up before we went to see the goddess.

"Of course. It's the right thing to do," she said, smiling at me enthusiastically.

Her quick agreement made me uneasy, and I let out a long exhale, knowing this would not end well.

As Bree approached him, Sydney's glare never faltered. She was aware of his disapproving look, but instead of letting it affect her, she flashed a mischievous grin before calling out to me. "It's always easier to take the high road when your opponent has to revert to their human form just to meet your gaze."

Sydney responded to Bree's suggestion with a wicked smile and a snarky comment. "Looks like you forgot your fairy dust, Bree. We can wait here while you retrieve it; I wouldn't want you to be without your secret weapon." He wiggled his eyebrows.

"Don't you start, you miniature horse on steroids..."

Ignoring the insults that flew past me like arrows, I strode over to my bag and rummaged around until I found an apple. I sat beside Victor against an old, weathered log, our backs propped against the rough bark.

"It's going to be a long journey," he said as he pulled out another granola bar.

"Do you think we can leave them here?" I asked, grinning, watching them stand inches apart, trading insults.

"Sydney's got the coffee in his pack."

"That sucks. Guess we're stuck here until they sort themselves out."

"We might as well start a fire," Victor suggested as their voices got louder. "This might take a while."

Chapter 50

Luckily, Bree and Sydney's argument ran out of energy after only an hour, and Victor stepped in to make them reconcile. He had to threaten them with a hug before they finally settled on shaking hands. From the looks on their faces, it looked like it pained them both.

I sighed in relief when Sydney extended a piece of his beef turkey to Bree, and eventually, an unsteady peace was established between them.

We may make it to our destination in one piece, after all.

After two more hours of grueling hiking, we reached the shores of Loch Bél Dracon. As far as the eye could see, a sea of watery gray glass formed a semi-circle around the beachfront. Three islands floated in the lake's center, looking like a sea serpent gliding across the surface.

"Those are the islands where the last dragons lived," Bree explained, walking toward a run-down rowboat. "The one on the left is Ollipheist, the one on the right is Ellen Trechend, and the one in the middle is the Muirdris."

Sydney's eyes widened with excitement as he exclaimed, "Dragons? Are you telling me dragons are still around? My grandmother used to say they were extinct, but I never believed her." His enthusiasm was contagious, and I couldn't help but smile.

"Don't dragons eat people?" Victor asked, his eyes traveling over the rowboat with disdain. "And are we getting into that to get over there?" he asked, pointing between the boat and the islands.

"Do you have a better idea?" Bree scoffed, shaking her head as she found the two paddles and handed them to Sydney. She stood tall with a challenging look, silently daring him to object, but Sydney took them with a mischievous grin on his face.

"The boat has more holes than a block of Swiss cheese. Can it even make it to the island safely?" Victor asked.

"We are about to learn, aren't we?" she answered, shrugging.

I also doubted the boat's steadiness, but we had no choice as it was our only way to the islands. To save weight, Sydney suggested hiding our bags in a makeshift shelter made of marram grass stalks and a heap of sand.

I was worried about the safety of my copy of the Book of the Veiled, but Bree soothed my fears by explaining that nobody came to the area because of the dragon's preference for fresh meat. Victor blanched at the thought but said nothing as he climbed into the boat warily.

After pushing us off the shore, Sydney jumped in and started paddling us to our destination while Bree guided us from up front.

At least it isn't filling with water, I thought as I peered over the edge, trying to find the bottom of the loch. The lake was shrouded in darkness, its depths an impenetrable black void.

"You aren't likely to find much down there," Bree said over her shoulder. "And I would be careful how far you lean over; these parts are known for the occasional lost Kelpie looking for its next meal."

"What are Kelpies?" I asked as I shifted back to my seat.

"Water shifters. On land, they look like you or me. But when they're in water, they morph into a black horse, capable of staying underwater for days as they hunt."

Sydney leaned over the edge, his eyes fixed on the murky depths. "What do they eat?"

"Black rams," she replied dryly. Sydney sat back up, glaring at her.

"Wonder how they feel about a miniature leprechaun," he mumbled.

"They wouldn't," she replied. "They like things full of piss and vinegar."

Sydney opened his mouth to respond, but Bree continued her story before he could say anything.

"Before the narrative changed? Fish. Occasionally an unexpecting bird. But now? They have been reduced to feeding on whatever washes up on shore. Carcasses, trash, the occasional small child."

"That's horrible," I exclaimed.

"That's why so few Kelpies live in their natural environment anymore," she shrugged. "Most were so disgusted with what they had become they ended up heading further inland. It's been years since they reverted to their original forms. I don't think they could, even if they wanted to."

"But some of them still choose to live in the Loch?" Victor asked, pointing to the water where a small dark shadow skimmed across the top.

"Occasionally, someone will be pushed to the brink of insanity by their craving for open water, and they'll return. Most of the time, they never come back." Bree gazed off into the distance with a sorrowful expression. "I believe they would rather be alone than confront what they've become."

"That is so sad," I commented.

I couldn't bear the idea of someone becoming disconnected from their true self because of a manipulated narrative. My hands tingled with excitement as I considered how I could rewrite their tale and guide them back to their authentic state. My eyes drifted toward the approaching island, and the weight of my new role as the Writer settled upon me.

I was going to need a much bigger desk when I got home.

An hour later, we finally reached the shore of Muirdris. A thick, impenetrable mist surrounded the island, adding to my growing unease. The last time I encountered such dense fog, Lilith found me. An encounter I had no desire to repeat.

And there was no telling what other monsters could be lurking in the darkness.

The warmth of Bree's hand enveloped mine as she helped me step out of the boat and onto the soft, damp sand. Sydney gracefully followed suit, his movements fluid and confident as he quickly pulled the vessel further up the shore. Victor's eyes widened in wonder as he scanned the area.

"Saddle up, boys; I highly recommend that you do NOT let go of the hand of the person in front of you. I warn you; if you let go for any reason, you will get lost." She pointed to the fog, and my heart dropped.

Sydney's strong fingers intertwined with mine, and he reached out with his other hand to grab Bree's. A flicker of emotion crossed Bree's face, something I couldn't quite decipher before disappearing as quickly as the mist surrounding us. She cast a determined look towards the darkness, her eyes filled with determination and a hint of fear.

"Okay, here we go." With a deep breath, she stepped forward, her feet sinking into the soft earth with each step. "And remember," she reminded us, "don't let go."

The mist shimmered and sparkled with flecks of silver, beckoning us to enter. The air was thick with warmth and the heavy scent of decay, an overwhelming combination that sent shivers down my spine. As we stepped forward, I could feel a sense of disorientation and confusion washing over me, like I had entered a different dimension entirely. It was a feeling unlike any other, being utterly adrift in a place where time seemed to stand still, and reality blurred at the edges.

The fog closed in around me, squeezing tight like a vise. My breaths came in short, panicked gasps as I struggled to breathe.

Bree gave my hand a reassuring squeeze, and I bit back my cry.

Finally, the mist began to lift and reveal the world beyond. As if emerging from a dream, we were suddenly surrounded by an explosion of vibrant colors that seemed almost surreal in their beauty. The greens of the trees were more vivid, the blues of the sky more intense, and the reds and yellows of the flowers seemed to glow in the sunlight. It was a breathtaking sight that left us momentarily stunned and breathless.

"I don't think we're in Kansas anymore, Toto," Sydney whispered.

I nodded in silent agreement. This was not the dull, dreary Otherworld we had just left - this was what I'd always imagined heaven to be like.

Surrounding us were mountains that would rival the beauty of the Alaskan range in spring. Snow cascaded down brilliant green mountainsides, and pink, yellow, and red patches danced along the ridges, promising vivid bouquets. Tiny black moving figures dotted along the inversion line as herds of animals wandered down to the river below.

I drew my eyes away from the mountains and focused on the town tucked into the valley. It was an explosion of colors and smells, stretching as far as the eyes could see. Swans swam lazily around a large lake in the middle of town, surrounded by pagodas painted in brilliant reds and striking whites. White cherry blossom trees encased a dirt road, and quaint fountains darted along large green meadows. Strings of colored ribbon wrapped large poles, each with small tabletops and chairs beneath them.

To the left was an English city street in 17 Cherry Tree Lane style, complete with a small ship mast on top of one of the homes. A marketplace was seated next to it, sizable enough to hold at least a hundred vendors, all marked with wooden signs painted in bold colors and pictures. Fruit stands, crafts, baked goods, fresh bread, vegetables, and pottery combine to form a lively place on a warm summer afternoon.

With its fifteenth-century towers, narrow passageways, cobblestone streets, and ornate churches, I could have sworn the town to the right was a replica of Sighisoara. Church bells rang, announcing the time, and a flock of sheep strolled by the city center fountain. A three-story medieval building stood behind the fountain, with carvings of knights, gargoyles, and saints watching from its steeples.

There was more beyond, further out than what I could see. But I knew that each world region was represented in this utopia. I couldn't help but wonder how. How did this exist when on the other side of the fog lay a world that was living but not alive?

"What the hell is this?" Victor asked with a hint of awe in his voice.

"This?" Bree asked. "Well, *this* what the Otherworld used to be like."

"I didn't know," I said breathlessly, looking around in amazement. "It's perfect." I turned to look at Bree. "Does Arawn know this still exists?"

Bree shrugged but didn't answer.

"So, where's Claire?" Sydney asked eagerly.

"Wait!" Sydney interrupted. "I thought we were here to see Claire. Is she down there?"

"She should be down there." Bree pointed to the lake. "Once a year, at Samhain, Claire returns to the spot where she first met her soulmate.

It's an annual event that the whole village celebrates with three days of parties."

"Let's go find her then," I announced, determination fueling my steps as I descended the steep hill toward the town center.

"She can usually be found in the lake in her original form," Bree answered, trying to catch up with me.

"What is her original form?" I asked over my shoulder.

"A swan."

"Great, she should be easy to find."

Bree caught up with me, her hand gripping my arm to bring me to a sudden stop. "No, Chloe, she won't be. That's part of the test," Bree explained, a dangerous glint in her eyes. "You must select her out of fifty other swans. Just like her soulmate had to."

"Okay, so let's go pick her out," I said as I started walking back down the hill, feeling frustration bubbling under my skin. This was becoming a bigger challenge than what I expected.

"Chloe, STOP!" Bree's commanding voice had me tripping over my own feet. "Think before you go and screw everything up. You pick wrong, and we don't get a second chance."

I paused, taking a deep breath, and inhaling the crisp, cool air. Bree was right. I couldn't just go charging in without a plan.

"Anyone got any suggestions?"

Chapter 51

"We find ourselves a swan!" Sydney declared, his eyes alight with determination. He turned to me. "Shapeshifters can't hide their true form from others."

"Try not to get too carried away, woolly mammoth. We don't want you falling into the lake accidentally." Bree rolled her eyes. "I'd rather not have to jump in to rescue you."

"First of all," Sydney started, walking closer to her. "I think you secretly want me to fall into the lake so you can see me with my shirt off." He held up a hand before she could protest. "And secondly, just ask, and I'll happily oblige," he said with a charming smile before turning away with a jaunty whistle and a slight sway in his step that made me chuckle.

I grinned at Bree as she stared after his retreating form, unable to come up with a witty retort fast enough.

Putting my arm through hers, I guided her down the hill. "Come on, Bree, you can think of something to say on our way to meet Claire."

The eerie stillness enveloped us as we descended the narrow bridge towards the town's lake. The once lively party had suddenly been abandoned, leaving the city desolate and devoid of any signs of life. Strands of lifeless ribbons hung from tree branches, swaying gently in the wind.

Fairy lights suspended between tall poles remained unlit. And on the massive platform, the band instruments sat untouched and forgotten.

A semi-circle of round tables decorated with autumn colors of red, orange, and brown sat unused. Despite the enticing aromas of roasted meats, fresh vegetables, and delectable desserts filling the air, no plate had been touched.

It was a haunting sight. Like a ghost town frozen in time.

Sydney's eyes swept over the scene before him, a deep frown creasing his brow. "Thought you said this was a party."

"It was," a delicate voice said from behind us. We all turned on our heels to face a woman standing before us dressed in a magnificent red, gold, and silver robe. Her sleeves were embroidered with tiny black ravens that hovered so perfectly that they seemed to fly when she walked toward us. Snow white hair cascaded down her back in soft waves, while small bells nestled inside tiny braids chimed with every step as if to warn people of her movements.

As we gawked at her beauty, we were greeted with a smile that didn't reach her brilliant silver-rimmed eyes.

"It was. Until it wasn't." The words fell from her lips sorrowfully, accompanied by a melancholy shrug as she scanned her surroundings.

Bree stepped forward, her eyes wide with confusion. She reached out to clasp the hands of the goddess, tiny sparks of energy crackling between them as they made contact. "Where is everyone, Claire?" she asked, her voice barely above a whisper.

"They're in hiding," Claire answered, showing no emotion.

"Why?" Bree looked at her in surprise.

"I warned them that it was time." Claire's words sliced through the silence like a sharp knife, sending a shiver down my spine. She turned to face me, her eyes locked onto mine with an intense and unflinching gaze.

They were deep pools of darkness, rimmed by silver lining. I couldn't look away.

"Time for what?" Bree asked, rubbing a hand across the back of her neck.

Claire turned her head, her gaze piercing through the air and locking onto Bree's face with an intensity that could rival the fiercest warrior. "Lilith was here."

The energy between the two was painful. "Why don't we sit down, and you tell us what happened?" Sydney suggested taking a small step toward Bree to protect her.

Claire's eyes flew to him, watching his movement with interest. She nodded once, her hair swaying with the motion and her eyes scanning the surroundings.

I breathed a sigh of relief, wishing that Isabelle, Watson, and Eidolon were with us. Isabelle's calming powers could have diffused the tension in the air, while Eidolon's natural leadership would have taken charge of the situation.

Maybe splitting up was not a brilliant idea after all.

"No, it was the right decision," Claire said suddenly, her eyes sparkling with an otherworldly intensity as she turned to face me. "This is your journey, not his."

Great, she could hear my thoughts too.

Claire nodded once. "You should get something to eat. You've been traveling long and still have a long journey ahead." Claire gestured towards the plates and made her way to the closest table.

Traveling a long time?

I turned to face Victor, who mirrored my confused expression. He shrugged and headed towards the food. Sydney was already loading his plate with food like he hadn't eaten in days. My nerves were on high alert, so I settled for a cup of coffee instead.

"Claire," Bree started as soon as she sat down. "I would like to introduce you to..."

Claire held up her hand, her eyes turning to me. "I know who you are and why you are here."

I swallowed. At least I didn't have to try to explain. I didn't even know if I wanted to. At least not coherently. "Can you help?" I asked, toying with my coffee mug.

She nodded once. "The path that had been decided by the Fates years ago faded into nothingness. In its place lay three roads, each distinctly different in color and territory. Black symbolizes mystery and death and follows the path to the Lost City of the Unspoken. Blue represents truth and sadness and leads across a vast body of water to a city built on top of another. Green, representing nature, wisdom, and envy, follows the path through a dark forest to reach a city that claims to hold the Gates of Secrets."

"Each road leads to a book, hidden in the shadows that will open with a key forged at the same time as it was written. Each one is a different possibility of what could be. Every road is obscured by darkness, threatening to overpower the magick of the books. Travel all three roads successfully, and you will reach where the Tree of Life and the Gates of the Otherworld are abandoned and dying. Then, with the blood of the last, you can reopen the path for all."

A long pause followed as we all stared at the goddess in disbelief.

"Well, I am delighted this wasn't another vague suggestion of what to do next," Sydney murmured, taking a bite of a massive turkey leg.

Claire glanced at him, a tight smile appearing on her lips. "You are correct, my wooly cousin; predictions are never clear. I offer you a glimpse of what is possible. Not a guarantee."

"What about Lilith? You said you warned the souls to leave. Why would you need to?" I asked.

Once again, her unsettling gaze locked onto me, and I shrunk back into my chair. "Lilith," she said, drawing out each syllable for emphasis. "Neither a deity nor a human. But a being born from terror. She has the ability to overthrow even the gods themselves."

"Cryptic," Victor huffed. "What is this place?" Victor asked, his hand gesturing around us.

Claire glanced at him, tilting her head to the side. Her eyes stayed fixated, but I could tell she was evaluating him with interest. After a moment, she spoke, "Avalon, Son of Odin."

Victor's coffee cup crashed as all eyes turned toward him in awe.

Son of Odin?

"Were you not aware?" Her nose wrinkled. "His blood runs through your veins."

"No," Victor shook his head. "I would have remembered that branch on the family tree."

Claire leaned forward to rest on her elbows, looking at him intently. "Odin, too, was able to resurrect himself."

Victor sank into his seat, his face pale. "Good to know."

Sydney observed the interaction with curiosity, savoring a bite of chocolate cake before commenting, "That's a useful skill. Its practicality in the Otherworld is yet to be decided," he waved his fork around, "but it certainly makes for an impressive party trick."

Victor rolled his eyes, and Bree frowned at him.

"What?" Sydney asked innocently, glancing back and forth between the two. "I'm simply pointing out that living conditions in the Otherworld are not ideal. Having someone with the power to resurrect may not be a wise addition. Before we know it, everyone will be trying to go back to the mortal world. It would be chaos."

"He's got a point," Bree agreed, shrugging her shoulders.

"What about Lilith?" I asked again, trying to steer the conversation back on track. "Does she know we are here? Is she coming after us?"

Claire closed her eyes. "Only the person with the key has access to the missing books. It doesn't matter where you start or how far you go; it always leads back to the beginning."

"And where is the beginning?" I asked, trying to control my frustration. Talking to Claire was like speaking to a toddler; the words were there, but the translation lost meaning.

Bree fiddled with her cup, refusing to look at us. "I think I know." She glanced at Claire, who nodded.

"Great! Where?" Sydney said, leaning forward.

A look of agony washed over Bree's features as she gazed at Sydney. "The City of the Unspoken houses the abandoned library of the Otherworld. The Library of the Unread. No soul has been permitted entry since Arawn sealed its doors centuries ago." She looked down, playing with her fork. "I don't know if I can bring you there."

My key started to warm, and I realized she was hiding something from us. But before I could ask, Sydney interrupted.

"Can you call Moll and ask how to get there?" Sydney asked, looking at me as he dug into a piece of pie. Victor stared at him and the empty plates surrounding him with raised eyebrows. He shrugged. "What? I'm hungry."

"The veil prevents anyone from calling out," Claire stated matter-of-factly, never breaking her gaze from Bree. "You will return to the City in the Mountains and navigate to the City of the Unspoken." Bree's face drained of color as she nodded once at the command.

I saw the interaction but dismissed it. We had a plan. And we were heading back to Eidolon. I stood up, anxious to be on our way.

"Before you leave, Chloe," Claire said as she stood up. "This is not going to be an easy journey. The Fates are never clear. Look at the whole story before choosing your path."

"I promise," I assured her. "Thank you for your assistance." Claire held my gaze momentarily, and I sensed she was trying to warn me. But I brushed it off. Eidolon was waiting.

"My pleasure, Daughter of Morrigan. Try not to die; it would be very inconvenient."

It was the second time someone had mentioned not dying to me. How dangerous WAS this journey?

Chapter 52

'Time Is Relative.' -Book of the Veiled Instructions

Only the sound of Bree and Sydney paddling through the dark waters broke the silence on our way back across the Loch. I was anxious to get back to Eidolon and share what we'd learned.

We had to find the City of the Unspoken—the first of three mysterious roads.

After what felt like an eternity, we finally stepped onto the shore and made our way towards our gear. We still had a long journey ahead of us to get home. Victor proposed that we stay overnight on the beach and leave at dawn, but Bree interjected, reminding us of the nearby dragons and urging us to brave a late-night hike instead of risking becoming their next meal.

Seeing as we were on a time crunch, I wasn't comfortable asking the group if we could take a break to allow me to write a chapter or two. Instead, I confided in my key, still hanging around my neck, hidden under my hoodie. Throughout the journey into Avalon, it had hummed against my chest, a quiet reminder that I had someone rooting for me.

Besides, I was anxious to see Eidolon again.

The trail was more exhausting than it had been earlier. We moved slowly, one behind another with Sydney as our guide, through the darkness punctuated by glimpses of the moon and stars. Black Rams had remarkable sight in the dark, and Sydney was in his element as he ushered us forward.

Bree brought up the rear of the group; the sword slung across her back now held loosely in her left hand at the ready. As we stumbled through the darkness, she pointed out every obstacle in our way - every rock and tree root that tripped us up. Her frustrated voice pierced through the silence. Sydney finally asked if she would like to take the lead and clear the path, but she had no answer for that offer.

"That's what I thought." A sly grin accompanied his words, and I could hear the smug satisfaction in his voice. Sydney was clearly enjoying himself. The Valkyrie was not. And to him, that just made it even more enjoyable.

A little past midnight, I could start seeing the distant light of the city in the mountains. My heart raced. We were close. I reached out through the bond to see if Eidolon was awake.

Not hearing anything, I assumed he was sleeping and tried to reach out to Watson and Isabelle.

Nothing again.

Strange. Maybe the bond doesn't work long distance?

Rather than saying anything, I asked Sydney if we could move faster because I needed a restroom that wasn't a tree or a hole in the ground. He happily obliged, and within an hour, we were standing under the tree we originally came from a few days before.

The gray grass looked fuller since our departure, and the tree had bluish-gray leaves covering its gnarly branches. I glanced at it curiously. We hadn't been gone that long. Maybe trees bloom differently in the Otherworld?

Although we were only a mile from the city, we needed a break. While Bree and Sydney went to fill our canteens at the river, Victor and I found refuge against a nearby tree, keeping an eye on our gear.

"It feels like we have been traveling for weeks instead of days," he remarked while changing socks. "Even the air smells different."

It hadn't registered with me before, but as soon as he mentioned it, I couldn't deny that he was right. The air had a distinct smell of bonfires, warm fireplaces, and comforting meals. When we first left, it felt like fall was around the corner, but now it seemed like winter had arrived.

Something was not right.

I stood up and took a few steps towards the city when I heard heavy footsteps behind the tree. Victor jumped and stood before me.

Victor cautiously glanced around, his hand inching towards the knife strapped to his boot. "Who's there?" he called out, ready for any potential threat.

The sound of footsteps grew increasingly closer and heavier, with the added vibration of a large animal approaching. Except it wasn't just one animal - there were multiple of them!

My heart started racing as I thought of all the ways that we could die. Monsters lurked in the shadows, and we had been lucky not to run into any of them so far. But it looked like our luck had finally run out.

I peered around for a fallen branch to protect myself when a faint whistle floated through the air. It sounded like the theme song for the Addams Family.

Seriously?

"Arawn," I called out, scanning the area for any sign of him. My eyes darted back and forth, searching for the elusive god.

"Is he coming here?" Victor whispered, and I nodded.

A tall, ominous figure appeared from behind the tree, gazing at us with an intimidating stare. He was draped in a long black cloak and had a heavy hood pulled over his head. As he stepped forward, four snow-white hellhounds with piercing red eyes appeared beside him. It was clear why people were afraid of the god. My stomach churned, and I knew who he was.

"Daughter of Morrigan, how kind of you to finally return. How was your journey?"

"Amazing, Arawn. We actually talked about you a little," I stepped around Victor and headed for the tree. "I was telling my friends about your obsession with meat pies."

"Did you bring some with you?" He cast a curious glance at my bag. "I'm starving!"

"I wasn't sure how well they would travel. But as soon as we get home, I will send some to you. Just send me your address, and I will FedEx them to you overnight." I rolled my eyes.

His laughter filled the space, wrapping us in a blanket of warmth. Thank goodness the God of Death had a sense of humor.

"Speaking of home, you could help us with something. Can you point us in the right direction to the City of the Unspoken from here?" I looked at him hopefully.

"I can." He nodded. I waited for him to tell us, but he stayed silent.

"Do you want to tell us?" I asked slowly.

"I will, but let's wait for the rest of your friends to arrive. That way, I won't have to repeat myself." He turned to sit, leaning against the tree as his hellhounds settled around him. They watched Victor and me cautiously, but their tails wagged as if waiting for us to come over and pet them. I moved forward to oblige when Victor stopped me, fear clear on his face.

"What?"

"What do you think you are doing?" he asked, aghast.

"I am about to pet the puppies," I pulled my arm back, rubbing where his fingertips had dug in.

"I don't think you realize those *puppies* are the size of a pick-up truck." I turned to the hellhounds again and greeted them with a smile.

"More like rhinos if you ask me. But they like to be scratched behind the ears. Don't lose your nerve now, Victor. Besides, if one of them eats you, you can stitch yourself back up."

"Not if I'm in one of their stomachs," he muttered, moving away from the hellhound that was scooting forward on its stomach toward him.

"Chloe, what on earth are you doing?" a voice shouted as I was shoved aside.

"What the hell?" I yelled as I got up to dust myself off and find out who had the nerve to take me out like that. If I was bruised, I was going to ...before I took a step, a muscular arm wrapped around me and enclosed me in his body. The aroma of cedar and smoke filled my senses.

Eidolon!

"What did I tell you before? We don't touch magickal things we don't know anything about," he muttered into my hair.

"But I do. They are hellhounds," I laughed, wrapping my arms around him.

Home, Eidolon felt like home. When I lifted my head, I realized he had started growing a beard, and his hair looked like it needed a trim.

"Wow, you have changed in seventy-two hours." He looked completely different from the person I last saw seventy-two hours ago.

Eidolon's narrowed gaze and slight frown conveyed his confusion. "What are you talking about, Chloe? It hasn't been seventy-two hours."

"What are *you* talking about, Eidolon? Of course, it has." I pushed out of his arms and glanced at Victor, who was shrugging his shoulders as if he didn't understand either.

"That is what I want to talk to you about now that your friends have joined us," Arawn called from the tree. "If you could be so kind as to dislodge yourself from Eidolon, that would be wonderful!" He paused and stared at Eidolon, who had moved to wrap his arms around me again.

"Back off, old man. She can hear you just fine from here," Eidolon shot back with a touch of venom in his voice.

"You know each other now?" I asked, looking between the two of them. When did they have time to meet?

"Well, luv, you were gone for a little longer than we had anticipated, so we called in reinforcements," Isabelle said as she walked up with Watson, a giant smile on her face. "And a lot of things happened while you were away."

"What happened?" Sydney asked as he walked up with Bree. Isabelle studied the Valkyrie warrior with interest as Bree met her gaze with a frown. Sydney put his arm around Bree, and Isabelle's smile grew even broader.

And so did Sydney's.

Arawn stood up and walked closer to us, pushing his hood away from his face and running a hand through his hair. "Your friends here caused quite a commotion, rattling the fabric of what holds the Otherworld together. But unfortunately, their actions caught the attention of the two people they were supposed to avoid." His eyes narrowed on Isabelle and Watson, who were looking guilty.

"In our defense, luv, we were merely trying to find our friends. How could we know the town was filled with busy buddies and gossip?" Isabelle shrugged lightly. "I will admit it has caused some negative outcomes, but we are willing to move forward if you are."

"What negative outcomes?" Victor asked.

"Now, before you get all worked up, we have a plan," Watson said casually.

"Why do we need a plan? What happened?" Victor asked again, taking a step closer to Watson.

"I think the better question is, how long have you been gone." Arawn frowned.

"How long have we been gone?" Victor swung around to ask him.

Eidolon slowly released me from his arms and pulled me to his side instead, "Three months."

Chapter 53

'Secrets Have A Way Of Revealing Themselves When Least Expected.' -Book of the Veiled Instructions

Three months? There was no way we were gone for three months. It was impossible.

"I don't understand." Sydney furrowed his brow in confusion as he and Bree approached. "A day there, a day on the island, and a day coming back. That's it."

Isabelle's powers enveloped us, protecting us from the imminent news. "No, luv," she spoke softly, facing me. "It's been three months." She paused, her gaze searching mine. "At first, we weren't concerned. Eidolon could still sense your bond with him. But as time dragged on and days turned into weeks, we started to worry.

"Then the bond broke. He couldn't sense you anymore." She glanced at Eidolon with a sad smile. "He almost lost his mind." As Eidolon ran his hand through his hair, I could see the pain and torment in his expression.

Bree pieced it together in her mind. "That must have been when we passed through the fog," she explained. "Claire mentioned that Chloe couldn't reach Eidolon through the veil."

Isabelle gave a confirming nod. "We combed every inch of the area, questioning anyone who might have crossed paths with you guys. We even made the journey to the Loch, but we couldn't find any evidence that you made it that far."

"We hid our gear in the grass," I explained. "So no one would steal it."

"You did an excellent job. We searched everywhere. When I couldn't contact you, things got chaotic," Eidolon said through gritted teeth. "That's when Arawn showed up. He didn't appreciate us disturbing his hellhounds' and threatened to turn us into meat pies if I didn't calm down."

My gaze bore into Arawn, but he seemed unfazed as he nonchalantly shrugged his shoulders in response.

Ass!

"We needed Aelle and Max's help, but without Chloe and Moll's connection, we had to resort to the traditional methods," Watson interjected before I could say something foolish.

Sydney frowned, scratching his head. "What's the old-fashioned way of sending a message from the Otherworld? Smoke signals? Pigeon carrier?"

"No." Eidolon straightened his posture. "We figured out how to send a message through the root system of the trees."

It made sense. It was how Taliesin was able to communicate in the mortal world. What was to say that it couldn't work in the Otherworld? It was ingenious, really.

So what's the issue?" I inquired, looking at the tree with curiosity. How did it work? Did it have a mailbox or something? Did someone collect the messages and send them up?

Eidolons' shift in demeanor caught my eye, and I pivoted to meet his gaze. My body flinched involuntarily upon seeing the rage etched on his features.

"Because *someone* didn't warn me that people were looking for me. As soon as I sent the message, they knew my location and what I'd done."

His fists clenched as he stared at me. I took a step back when his eyes darkened.

Arawn positioned himself between us, his gaze condescending as if to say, 'I told you so.' "Which means they found a way to leave the Otherworld," he stated bluntly, arching an eyebrow. "A distraught mother was reportedly seen leaving, searching for her missing daughter."

Damn you, Moll. I knew we should've told them the truth. A lump formed in my throat, and I couldn't bring myself to meet their accusing eyes. I stared down at my worn shoes with a heavy feeling of shame and regret. "Did she find her?" I whispered.

"Yes, she did. Along with Max and Moll." Watson glared at me.

"Where are they now?" Bree asked. "Where did they take Aelle?" Fear snaked across her face as Sydney tightened his arm around her.

"To the City of the Unspoken," Arawn explained. "Lilith is using them to try to find the Book of the Veiled."

"But she needs our keys," I protested. "Claire said she couldn't open the books without them."

"Don't underestimate her, Arawn warned, his eyes sparking. "She has an ace up her sleeve."

"What ace?" I asked quietly.

"The City of the Unspoken resides in Valhalla, one of the twelve realms of Asgard. And do you know who else lives in Valhalla?"

"Odin," Victor whispered.

"Exactly. Lilith and Odin go way back. Combine their powers with Moll and Aelle's abilities, and they may not need the key."

"This is not good," Sydney commented. "On a scale of one to ten, this is a fifteen on the oh-shit scale."

"It gets worse," Eidolon said, looking down at me.

"What could possibly make this worse?" I asked, meeting his gaze, crossing my fingers that he wasn't about to say what I thought he would say.

"Lilith knows where my parents are," Eidolon said through gritted teeth. "Did you forget to tell me something else, lil' Writer?"

He knows! My eyes widened as I watched him walk away, Watson following.

Arawn leaned towards me and whispered. "I tried to warn you."

"What do I do now?" I asked, meeting his gaze.

He shrugged. "I don't know lil' Writer. Some mistakes are unforgivable." He turned and walked away, his hellhounds following.

I stood frozen, watching Eidolon walk away, and my heart broke.

How was I going to rewrite this story?

About the Author

Raise to believe in the power of the untold story, Rose had the pleasure of spending 20+ years serving in the U.S. Army where she was able to visit places that were only a small dot on a world map.

After hanging up her boots and spending an adventurous five years living in interior Alaska, she finally settled down in Washington State with her family.

She is a reader, blogger, connoisseur of all things coffee, and a self-proclaimed Beat Saber expert.

Acknowledgements

A story begins with a thought...

To my mother, who was the one who instilled in me a love of history, books, good music, and homemade macaroni and cheese. She taught me the extraordinary gift of being comfortable eating alone and confidently walking into new adventures.

And more importantly, she taught me that even the dead had stories that needed to be heard. Thank you, Mom, for remembering the stories with me.

To my husband, who let me buy two computers, a laptop, 17 notebooks, and countless books just because I had a dream that couldn't be put into words. Thank you for understanding that I needed to do this on my own, even with all the headaches and heartburn.

To Kekoa, who has pushed me to become a better writer, mother, and role model for years. Every coffee trip, lunch break, and grocery shopping adventure, he pushed me not to write what I thought others wanted to hear but what I wanted to say. For being so young, you are wise.

To my two oldest sons, who have forged their own paths in this world. I hope I taught you one thing- your life is what you want it to be. No one person dedicates who you should become. So, dance in the rain, make mistakes, do daring things, travel, laugh, drink (responsibility), but more importantly... I will always have a light on for you.

To my family, by blood and by choice, who supported me when I finally started telling people what I was doing.

To my dad and sister, who didn't fully understand but never rolled their eyes at me.

To Rita, who had to listen to me for hours while traveling around Alaska talking about my imaginary friends.

To my friends who supported me- thank you!

To those who didn't- thank you more.

Most importantly, to the four that I will not name. I remember you. Everyday. Your stories will not be forgotten.

Also By R. L. Geer-Robbins

In 537 A.D., a fierce struggle took place that would decide the world's future. The victor wields the ability to alter the future of humanity.

Rising from the ashes, The Raven Society was formed to guard and maintain the purity of history. Their mission? To find the inconsistencies in history and protect the ones whose stories have been forgotten.

Rising from the ruins, three women, whose lives have spanned the ages, are united by an invisible thread woven by the Fates. Their mission? To safeguard a weapon feared by the gods themselves.

In order to find the missing Books of the Veiled, they will have to build new bonds, confront their demons, and unearth a new reality.

Failure is not an option. Their lives depend on it.

Also By R.L. Geer-Robbins

Does a person truly exist if no one remembers their name?
Long ago, when someone died, their fate was sealed. Their stories would become a memory that faded with every generation until nothing was left but whispers in the wind before they were forgotten forever.
Unless you could find the one who had the ability to move between life and death
The Raven Society has uncovered the first missing Book of the Veiled, but it came at a great cost. Now, they must regroup as they navigate the turbulent history of fanatic religious leaders, mad Kings, and crypt prophecies.
Time is not on their side as they uncover the dark secrets that lurked during a long-forgotten era when displaying even the slightest hint of magic could send a person to death.
Two women, one prophecy.

History doomed to repeat itself.

Made in the USA
Middletown, DE
03 March 2024

50179618R00209